THE MAP OF LOST PLACES

THE MAP OF LOST PLACES

Stories from Strange and Haunted Realms

Edited by
SHEREE RENÉE THOMAS

Edited by
LESLEY CONNER

Apex Book Company | Lexington, KY

ISBN (Trade Paperback) 978-1-955765-26-8
ISBN (epub) 978-1-955765-34-3
ISBN (Kindle) 978-1-955765-36-7

Apex Book Company
Lexington, KY USA

Printed in the USA

Horror / Dark Science Fiction / Anthology

Cover art by Marcela Bolívar

Cover design by Rachel Rosen

Interior art "Map of the World" by Pan Morigan

Visit us online at ApexBookCompany.com

For those who love and support short fiction—the Kickstarter backers, the Apex team, our families, the readers ... get lost with us.

Contents

Introduction
THIS IS THE MAP, LET'S GET LOST
LINDA D. ADDISON

Themed anthologies take a lot of thought by the editor(s), because how they write the guidelines influences writers' imagination and sets up the readers expectations. I've been published in many anthologies and when I submit my work, I can only hope my piece will fit the editor's vision. There's no crystal ball editors can use to see exactly what submissions will come, no way to predict from the beginning what a final anthology will be. I do know the stories have to connect to the editor and spark that initial thought.

It would have been quite interesting to be in the room with seasoned editors Sheree Renée Thomas and Lesley Conner as they decided to build a horror anthology around strange places where characters purposely or accidentally go and the disturbing things that happen to them. While we can't go back to the place where the idea took hold, what we can do is dive into the pages of the book in your hands, the final results of their search for the strange and bizarre and read how different authors interpreted what the editors wanted.

The twenty-two stories in this book take place all over the world and in the past, present, and future, as well as a few slippy dimensional tales. I found certain ones had synergy in how they mapped lost places and people. Some tamper with space, time, and technology as we know it, while others flipped the concept of ghosts in unexpected ways. Some of these stories are driven by the human craving for answers to questions that should not be asked.

What can happen if characters purposely go to strange places, what would drive them to put themselves in possible danger, know-ingly or not? Joshua Lim's main character goes to a small town to prove their praise of having the best durian is not true, even after tasting them. Driven by the need to expose the town for somehow manipulating the durian's growth, he learns the hard way that every question has an answer and a cost. Oliver Ferrie takes us to Norway where friends search for a myth and, in the process uncover how beautiful possessive love can be. Octavia Cade's mesmerizing story explores the need for legends and the price of creating one. The title of Muhammed Awal Ahmed's story, "The Death of Black Fati-ma," is just the tip of the iceberg of Black Fatima's poignant tale.

The varying ways ghosts emerge in this anthology is refreshing and intriguing. Ai Jiang takes us to the past in Beijing where conflicts in the royal house take an unexpected turn. We travel with Danian Darrell Jerry to Mississippi with a character returning to face humiliating childhood memories that left him angry and plan-ning revenge, but he finds so much more. Samit Basu's main char-acter is hired to protect buyers from their false belief in haunted houses—revelations and time travel await. A man looks for his missing brother in Jenny Rowe's story, and travels all the way to Sweden. While others look to the sky at the northern lights, his missing brother has other things to show him. One word titles open space for the imagination, and "Salt" by K.S. Walker unfolds magi-cally like an ever changing song. Rebecca E. Treasure's story makes us question the good or bad of ghosts. VH Ncube takes us to a small town called KwaNtuthu, the place of smoke, where its beauty is only one side of a light/dark coin flipping in the air.

Many people feel lost when dealing with technology, but G. M. Paniccia's story, "Codewalker," puts a dizzying spin on losing one's way in a future where workers link into systems in a more personal way. "Girlboss in Wonderworld, USA" by Vivian Chou takes place in a dark reality where an arcade lets our character exchange tickets for toys and items of desire, but what happens when you don't have enough tickets for something you *must* have?

I have a soft spot in my heart for stories that manipulate space and time or romp outside known dimensions since I've written a few such stories myself. R. L. Meza's story, "Chuckle Wet, Chuckle Low," has a surrealistic edge that whispers as much to the reader as it does to the characters in a story of give and take. Brian Keene's story follows the journal of a retiree who now has the time to research and write a book about the mysterious events and folklore in York County, leading the reader into strange places that perhaps should not be entered.

The title of Rich Larson's story, "Place of Lost Stories," has an odd edge to it, considering the name of this anthology. From the first sentence we are clearly in a weird space and time, from there we go on a strange car trip through an almost familiar landscape. Are we in a lost story? Perhaps, but it's so worth the ride. Another story, "The (Lost) Tribe of Ishmael," by Maurice Broaddus has a title that is also a story of its own, and flips reality and time as questions of freedom and sanity come into play.

Dimitra Nikolaidou's character searches for the source of a nightmare that invades her day and work and finds the answer stranger than anything she could imagine. "The Salt," a story written by Lavie Tidhar and Nir Yaniv, takes us hundreds of years in the past to a report from a character investigating reports of strange signs in the sky and on the ground, giving us many things that are familiar and otherworldly things that aren't. While Beth Dawkins's story is set in a present we recognize, the town is one no one would want to visit, much less be born in and there are only three ways out. In Ferdison Cayetano's story an expert Hawaiian cowboy in Wyoming's cold mountains for a major rodeo gets lost in a waking dream, taking the reader on a mythical vision quest. In Fatima Taqvi's moving story a grandparent struggles with dreams of loss that invade reality, ultimately requiring a new way of living, of understanding beginnings and endings.

Each story in this anthology stands alone in its unique location, characters and the journey the reader is taken on. Surrender to the map this book provides, get lost in the tales weaved from the remarkable imagination of these authors from around the world and learn something new about their destinations.

Girlboss in Wonderworld, USA

Vivian Chou

LOCATION: Seaside City, Delaware, USA

POPULATION: 2,402

MY BROTHER TERENCE and I stand in front of the Wonderworld arcade counter, our eyes as big as Skee-Balls.

"Two hundred and eighty tickets," the teenage girl says. "What would you like?"

I stare through the glass at Chinese finger handcuffs and an orange slime ball, either of which I could get, and sigh. "The s'mores Squishmallow keychain is three hundred tickets, but it's time to go and I'm outta quarters."

"Sorry, Jules," Terence says, squeezing my arm. "I didn't know, or I woulda saved some tickets for you." Terence's horse derby racing skills just *slay*.

"It's okay," I say. I stand up on my tippy-toes and look up at the clerk. "I'll have the slime ball."

The girl looks at me and smiles. "What's your name?" She wears her hair in one long dirty blonde braid that curves around her neck. On the top corner of her bright orange Wonderworld shirt is a black nametag that reads GERTRUDE. I think of that as an old-people name, but my friend Ellie's baby sister just got named Mildred, so maybe not.

"I'm Julie Chen," I say.

Gertrude leans down and whispers, "I can give you the s'mores keychain, Julie Chen, but you have to give me something of yours." She smells like Raspberry Bath and Body Works glitter bath gel and I admire her Totoro earrings.

A thrill rises in me. People tell me all the time I'm cute because I'm ten. Maybe I remind her of a kid she babysat once.

"I don't have anything," I say, turning out my pockets and finding a gum wrapper and dirty tissues. I pull my thick black hair out of my ponytail. "Do you want this? I just got it last week." I hold out my pink and purple striped scrunchie.

"Nah. Just give me an eyelash," Gertrude says, unblinking.

I flinch and don't know whether to laugh at the joke or pluck one out. Is she crazy?

"I don't know how to give you an eyelash," I say. I look to my side. Terence has drifted towards the Connect 4 Hoops game to watch some teenagers shoot basketballs.

"I can pluck one and you won't even notice, I promise," Gertrude says.

"Okay," I say, and before I can ask what to do next, she pockets an eyelash in her black fanny pack and hands me a s'mores Squishmallow keychain. She's right: I don't feel a thing. The keychain has a small card attached to the product tag. In old-timey font, it reads:

ONE BRIGHT FUTURE

"Hey, Jules," Terence appears, glancing down at my new prize. "Oh, you got one. Cool!" He looks up at Gertrude and smiles.

I clutch the s'mores keychain in my hand. Pride surges through me and I stand up straighter. Gertrude zips to the end of the counter to help another girl, and we walk out to the Delaware boardwalk.

My family goes to Seaside City every summer, and Terence and I hit the arcade at Wonderworld again.

The girl at the counter is wearing unicorn earrings and a *FRIENDS* button on her lanyard.

It's Gertrude, and when I see her, I remember last summer's trade. I blink, wondering if she's eyeing my lashes.

In my head, I calculate what to buy with my bounty, tallying points.

"I could get one purple plastic Slinky," I say. "Or a cupcake lip gloss and one Fortune Teller Fish."

Terence shrugs. "Whatever you want, dude." His voice is deeper and he's on the wrestling team now.

"Hello, Julie," she says. "You must be good at math to do that in your head." She clacks on her calculator and nods. "It was all correct."

"I'm in fast math at school," I tell her, clenching my jaw. "But I'm the only girl and Mr. Abraham didn't pick me for the fifth-grade math team." If I were a cartoon, steam would be coming out of my ears. "I did least common multiples faster than Kevin Martinelli!"

I love math because it's logical and pure, and picking Kevin was sheer fallacy.

Gertrude hesitates and pulls out a case from behind the counter. It glimmers gold and black. She sets it on top of the glass counter with a gentle clink.

"Choose one," she says. "Special for return customers," she winks.

Inside the red velvet-lined case are thin cards like playing cards but instead of jokers and queens of hearts, there are cards in weird font that read:

DATE OBJECT OF YOUR AFFECTION (TWO MONTH GUARANTEE)

JOIN TEAM (SPORT OR ACADEMIC)

PAY OFF YOUR FAMILY'S BILLS

I have no interest in the first, and not sure if we need the third. How would I know? I point to the second one, and Gertrude nods. I swallow. "How do I get that?"

"Your tickets almost cover the cost," she says. "But I will take your fingernails."

I feel like I'm going to puke. "You're going to rip them off?"

She shakes her head. "You just can't grow them out super long anymore. But you can wear fake ones."

"Like for forever?" I say. It's weird, for sure, and anyway she doesn't know my piano teacher doesn't let me grow out my nails as it is. It messes with me using curved fingers on the keys, and good technique in general. I don't mind, really, because they get dirty as it is when they grow past a few millimeters, and Mom is always on my case about it.

"What is forever, anyway?" Gertrude says.

"Let's do it," I say. I look down at my nails, which feel the same.

Gertrude smiles. "You can look forward to your next academic year."

Over the years, I paid with my body to get the slight edge Gertrude provided.

When I was thirteen, I traded four hundred and fifty tickets and blemish-free skin for admission to jazz ensemble camp in Philadelphia.

For five hundred and fifteen tickets and heavy menstrual bleeding, I got Freshman of the Year when I was fourteen.

At sixteen, I traded five hundred and seventy-five tickets and full dark eyebrows for being a National Merit Scholarship Finalist.

My mom took me to the doctor a few times during all of this. Moms have a sixth sense about things being off, but she couldn't put her finger on it.

"I can't find anything wrong with her," the pediatrician says. "She's still tracking on her growth curve."

"Her eyebrows are thin," Mom says.

The pediatrician narrows her eyes. "We women are subject to criticism enough as it is." She glances at me. "But she doesn't show signs of alopecia or any worrisome underlying disorder. All her bloodwork is normal."

Nothing about this feels normal, but what do I know? I don't know where Gertrude's powers come from, but I'm afraid to ask, in case she was to stop trading with me. So, I keep going back to Wonderworld, playing Skee-Ball, Down the Clown, Quik Drop, and Zombie Snatcher, and stockpiling tickets.

When I am eighteen, I trade six hundred tickets and C cup breasts for being wait-listed at Dartmouth. My mom takes my homecoming dress to the tailor to be taken in and I buy a push-up bra at Victoria's Secret.

Stop being so vain. It'll be worth it in the end.

"I can't give you full admission to college," Gertrude says, eyeing the sky. "Even I am not that powerful."

My B cups force me to get new V-necks, but my wallet survives.

Terence loses interest in Wonderworld. He doesn't do as well in school as I do, but he gets into the state law school. Everybody needs lawyers.

The summer after high school graduation, Gertrude gives me her phone number. "Call me," she says, "if you ever need a trade."

I don't go to Gertrude every time I suffer a disappointment. Lovers break my heart. A thief steals my catalytic converter. My roommate moves back in with her parents and leaves me with twice the rent.

But when I am passed up for a promotion after three years at my advertising firm, I drive to Wonderworld in October.

My co-worker Brian's words echo in my head: "You might work hard now, but when your life goes the way you want it to, you might not want to travel four days a week."

I bite my tongue and taste blood.

Wonderworld is closed for the season, only open from Memorial Day through Labor Day, but I've saved thousands of tickets by now and keep them in a fireproof box in my apartment. To me, they are worth more than gold.

At a white bench on the boardwalk facing the shore, I meet Gertrude. She has her case of cards and purses her lips at my duffel bag full of tickets.

"I have five cards for you tonight," she says. Her blonde hair is loose in long ringlets and she sports a nose piercing and zodiac jewelry. I swear she is aging in reverse.

I look through the cards, hungry for the career card.

"None of these talk about a job promotion," I say. My jaw clenches. "Jesse makes fifty grand more than me and he didn't even do the fieldwork for the Dior perfume gig. And my supervisor got fired for harassing an intern. What do I have to do to get some recognition?"

Gertrude looks at me sadly. In the glint of the sodium lights on the nighttime boardwalk, the salt spray from the ocean flutters like snowflakes.

"Your left ovary," she says, "and two thousand tickets."

Part of me feels relief. It can be done after all?

"But—how?" I ask.

"There are cards we can borrow from," she says. "There's always something that can be done."

The next week, my left ovary torses, and I go into the ER in excruciating pain.

"Teratoma," the ER doctor says. "It's technically a type of cancer, an overgrowth, but it doesn't kill you. The surgeon will be here shortly to assess you and take it out. You'll have one ovary left though, so you'll still get periods and preserve your fertility."

I suppose it could be worse. What's a few hours of suffering and a surgery? I lie in agony, wondering if my illicit visit to Gertrude precipitated the teratoma growing or just tipped it over the edge. Perhaps Gertrude is a witch, or the servant of a cosmic overlord.

A week after the surgery, I return to work and my boss promotes me.

I scrabble up the corporate food chain, gathering income and titles. I earn everything I get because I *pay* for it through hard work, long hours, and quarters and tickets and fingernails.

Then I fall in love and get pregnant. I don't need to visit Gertrude for some time. Some DEI initiatives push through at my company and although I know that I deserved my promotions, I am sure people think of me as a two-birds-with-one-stone, the Chinese and female DEI case.

I go on maternity leave and my company begins "restructuring."

I panic, although nothing has happened yet. I pay a visit to

Gertrude with my baby, Gabe, in the stroller. Opaque fog mists the boardwalk. We meet in front of the saltwater taffy store like mafioso in a film noir movie, next to a trash can and a statue of a pelican holding a box of taffy.

"What can I do?" I ask. Before she can say anything, I put my hand over Gabe protectively.

"Oh, please, Julie," Gertrude says. "I'm not a *monster*. Jesus."

Today she's wearing a Nirvana T-shirt with no irony and a silver hoop through her right eyebrow. Her hair is cut short and dyed black, her skin as smooth as my infant son's. I found two gray hairs the other day and my forehead creases are sealed in from years of perfectionism and months of sleep torture with a newborn.

"I don't know how I'm going to do it," I say, my chest burning with acid and ambition and worry and guilt. My parents gush about what a good dad Jeremy is, but no one praises me for being a good working mom. "Jeremy and I are interviewing nannies, but I'm already in hot water for taking the full three months maternity leave. They didn't say that explicitly, but I can feel it."

"Yes," Gertrude nods. "I had a feeling you have more than one trade in mind."

I remove my list of worries and wishes from the diaper bag and hand it to her. Last-minute panic ripples through me. I should have asked for better cooking skills too. My babao fan came out dry at Chinese New Year this year.

"Understandable," Gertrude says, reading the list. "Let me see what I can do."

I hand over my entire duffel bag full of my ticket stash and wonder what other body parts I have left to hawk. I muse over whether she can remove my stomach flab and call it a fair exchange. How about a pile of shedding hair from a post-partum nursing mom?

"Your power will increase," Gertrude says. "Are you prepared for that?"

"I'm not power hungry," I say. "I just want to be successful. Does that make me a bad person?"

Gertrude tosses her hair and I can't tell if she agrees with me or disapproves.

She removes cards out of a folio in her Fjallraven backpack and lays them out on top of the covered trash can on the boardwalk. Seagulls circle overhead, scouting for french fries.

RAISE SUCCESSFUL CHILDREN IN A MIDDLE-CLASS HOME

SUSTAIN YOUR CAREER WITHOUT HIRING DOMESTIC HELP

EXPOSE YOUR KIDS TO SPORTS AND EXTRACURRICULAR ACTIVITIES

KEEP YOUR CHILDREN FED AND CLOTHED

BE PART OF THE COMMUNITY OF PARENTS IN YOUR NEIGHBORHOOD

I have to agree to the price, I know.

"The costs will be diversified," Gertrude says. "You will relinquish fifteen percent of your circulating red blood cell mass and its oxygenating supply, your brain will atrophy from social isolation as a working mother with no time for meaningful relationships, and the remaining cognitive function will be spent on seven-day meal planning, executive preparation of menial tasks such as birthday parties, playdates, holiday feasts, gift-giving, coordinating soccer, basketball, and dance carpools, and reorganizing summer and winter closets for the children, plus chronic itchiness and skin thinning from housemaid's hands or dyshidrotic eczema as you cook, clean, and Magic-Eraser, Oxi-Clean, and Scrubbing-Bubble your home to passable daily function."

I'm a little relieved I'm walking out with my major organs, but I feel instantly fatigued.

I've never asked Gertrude for different payment plans. I should be grateful for what she's given me already. But I'm beginning to wonder if it's worth it.

✤

Time passes. For Christmas this year, I visit Terence with my son Gabe, age six, and toddler daughter, Sasha. Terence's house is huge. He has an in-ground pool with an outdoor kitchen and a fire pit with heated seats. Turns out, *everyone* really needs a lawyer.

"So good to have you here, Jules," Terence says. "Can I get you a drink?"

"No, thanks." I shake my head. "I'm trying to cut down." Four years ago, I traded Gertrude my caudate liver lobe in exchange for depression-free winters once Daylight Savings Time ends in November.

"I get it," Terence says. "Middle age is rough. My trainer says I gotta cut back to just drinking on the weekends if I want to run a half-marathon this spring." Terence pokes at his belly and his biceps. "Muscle loss starts in your thirties. I found a good protein powder, though. Want me to make you a protein shake?"

Terence is two years older than me but doesn't look it at all. My stomach churns as I neglected to drink my breakfast smoothie this morning after Sasha threw up all over her high chair.

"How do you have time to go to the gym?" I ask.

"It's not easy," he says, "but Victoria feeds the kids breakfast while I hit the gym at six in the morning. She works out at night when I'm home from work. And I got promoted to senior manager so I can show up later without getting in trouble."

He pours a gin and tonic at the gray and black marble bar.

"You remember Wonderworld?" he says to me. "I was thinking of taking Connor there this summer again. Do you wanna all go together?"

My trades with Gertrude have tainted me, and I associate my trips to the boardwalk with increased disposable income and lighter body mass index.

"That could be fun," I say. "But aren't your kids outgrowing it?"

"They should be," Terence says. "But the staff loves Connor. Last year they gave him a year of free Dippin' Dots because he won a raffle prize."

I love my brother, but I fume inside.

The next time I see Gertrude, I don't hold back. Seeing Terence in his bougie house and hearing about Connor's win destroys my filter.

"What kind of sick game are you running?" I ask. "Who are you working for?"

"Thought you'd never ask," Gertrude says. "Follow me." We walk to the Wonderworld building and she lifts up a metal garage door and we go inside. The bumper cars, claw machine, and swings look abandoned and sad with their lights off. Piled high on the ground are unpacked stuffed animals with huge eyes, staring at us in their suffocating plastic bags. I shiver, rubbing goosebumps down my forearms.

"You're mad about your nephew, Connor," she says.

"Yeah," I say. "You gave him a year of free ice cream. Did you make him give up a kidney or an index finger?"

"Of course not," Gertrude says. "He's just a kid."

"Are you targeting little girls for body parts?" I ask, aching for my lost organs, my sacrificial meat.

She leads me to the carousel, walks past the horses in various states of galloping and trotting, to the center of the ride, festooned with mirrors surrounded by bordering globe lights. She inserts a key into the mouth of a mermaid draping her arms over a player piano, and a door opens, revealing a pulsating, bloody heart the size of a cow. Sinewy vessels protrude from the aorta, the left anterior descending artery, blue capillaries in a web, all stretching out and sticking to the cogs and levers inside the carousel like living, oxygenated spiderwebs.

I gag, repulsed at the grotesque lifeform.

"Are you feeding this thing little girls?" I ask.

"No, of course not. I told you, I'm not a *monster*," Gertrude says. "Really, Julie. I'm just doing what always has been done."

She feeds a piano roll into the mermaid's tail, and instead of chipper music, the piano plays spoken words, snippets of conversation, nonchalant sentences of women:

"I gotta get back to Richard and serve him dinner. He's so helpless without me, you know."

"If I went back to work, I wouldn't make enough money to make it worth it. Daycare is so expensive."

"I should really save for retirement but I'm not smart enough to learn how to invest."

"Have you ever been in Charlene's house? It's a mess. What does she do all day at home? She doesn't even work."

The throbbing heart bulges with every word, growing redder.

The piano plays the words of boys:

"Mom! God! I told you I hate this kind of granola bar. Why don't you ever listen?"

The piano plays the words of men:

"Did you see that CNN headline? Nine-year-old gets abortion. I don't know what's wrong with kids today."

The heart grows engorged, so large that I don't see how it will ever fit back into the center of the carousel.

I take a closer look and acid rises in my throat. The heart is decorated with tiny body parts: thumb joints, fallopian tubes, nipples, teeth.

"This is just wrong," I say, paling. "So, what happens if the heart dies?"

"Wonderworld will die," Gertrude says. "And along with it, the cards."

"Why do we need cards in the first place? My brother and his son get everything, and they keep their body parts intact!"

"I don't make the rules," Gertrude says, blowing a pink gum bubble. She smells of Double Bubble and Eos lip gloss.

I pull my car keys out of my pocket and prepare to lunge at the gargantuan heart but stop short. I'm afraid of what happens if I shut the whole thing down and I have nothing left to trade. How will I survive? I grip my keys in the palm of my hand and my breath grows ragged and sharp. My fingers squeeze the keys until I am numb, and I scream.

"I need the cards," I shout. "I'm nothing without them. I can't do anything by myself."

Gertrude stands over me, capturing my words on a paper piano roll scroll in her hand, tiny perforations appearing like pockmarks on a blood-splattered mirror. The paper gleams with a metallic sheen under the lights of the carousel.

"I told you," Gertrude says. "I'm not the monster, Julie Chen."

Blood in Coldwater

Danian Darrell Jerry

LOCATION: Arkabutla Lake in Coldwater, Mississippi, USA

POPULATION: 1,359

OSCAR MERITT HATED Arkabutla Lake more than ever. He stood on the shore, damp sand underfoot, reliving the humiliation that sent him fleeing Coldwater, Mississippi twenty years ago. In his mind, Cousin Lacey was still laughing—the shame, sharp and brutal, stabbing him in the back.

That's right, city boy! Run home to Memphis, waterhead bastard.

Two decades had passed. He was back now, wiser, stronger. He had the upper hand. Climbing the corporate ladder had heightened his survival skills. He wasn't a fish in a barrel anymore. He was a shark, and tomorrow there would be blood in the water. His employer, Victory Solutions, would open a sustainable jet fuel refinery right by the lake shore. The plant's waste would likely contaminate the water beyond hope in less than a year. *Oh well,* Oscar thought. Killing Lacey's precious lake was the best revenge he could imagine.

As he watched the glistening pool, his wife Justine stood behind him, slipping her arms around his waist.

"Tomorrow's your big day. You ready?" she asked, her voice soft and hopeful.

"I've been ready since I was twelve. We got rid of the protestors. We have the blessing of the state officials including the governor. It's time to celebrate."

He turned to Justine, delighted to see her wearing the giant straw hat he'd bought her at the hotel gift shop. A few strands of hair wisped around her ears.

"You aren't worried about the reception?" she asked. "Remember. You don't have to do that part."

"I'm not worried about any boats or this backwater mudhole."

"You hit the game-winning shot. If you change your mind, your team doesn't need you to celebrate."

"Believe it or not, I used to love this place," Oscar said wistfully. "My granddaddy would bring all the kids out here every summer and spin these tall tales about an entire town buried beneath the water, like Atlantis. He made it sound mythical, almost noble. Granddaddy had a way of taking darkness and giving it light. Listening to his stories was the only thing I liked about family reunions down here, and I was his favorite."

"Were you now?" Justine asked, teasing.

"I was until my stupid cousin ran me off because she was jealous."

"Focus on the long game." She kissed his forehead, the brim flopping around her smiling face. "Your cousin is yesterday's news. If she hadn't chased you away, you would have stayed down south, and I might never have met you. And Victory Solutions wouldn't be making millions because of *your* brilliant idea. You're on the fast track now. What else could you want?"

"One more thing," Oscar said, pulling himself from Justine's embrace. With his wife behind him, he slipped off his loafers and socks, trodding toward the lake.

"Um, Ozzie," Justine called out, reaching for him, her voice betraying a hint of nervousness. She followed Oscar as he marched to the shore. "You sure about this?"

"The last time I was here, my cousin pushed me in," he said. "I could've died that night. Today I walk under my own steam. I have to conquer my fear."

"But you never go in the water," she said, hurrying after him.

Worry darkened her face as the Mississippi sun shone down on the couple.

Oscar shuffled through the hot sand, clenching his fists, gritting his teeth. In the breeze, the sweat on his back was cold as he made his way to the shore. He froze when he felt the lake's edge lapping at his bare feet. Fear he had suppressed for decades climbed from his legs and into his belly.

A low humming, guttural and painful, rose from Arkabutla. He searched the sky for solace, but suddenly found himself submerged in water. Shock struck him as darkness spread below, light shining above the surface. He struggled to hold his breath as black waves closed around him, sweeping him into a cold current. The humming rose louder now, even beneath the waves. A hum that became a song, haunting and shrill, a lamentation drawn from ominous scripture. Oscar flailed and kicked, fighting as the humming dragged him deeper into the murky waters.

He was twelve years old again, drowning while his cousin laughed. His lungs burned, his throat raw, his long, lanky limbs felt like rubber, his voice a silent scream. He was reaching for Lacey, for Justine, for anyone, when a gnarled hand wrapped around his ankle and yanked him down. He screamed, silent bubbles floating through the muddy waters. Algae blooms brushed his cheeks and spun around his wrists, holding him deep below the lake's surface. He looked down in horror at a pair of lurid yellow eyes staring from the depths below. He recoiled and kicked as the black hand covered in bulging veins pulled him down to the city buried beneath the water. As the world went dark, Oscar thought of Justine.

I should've listened, he cried into the soundless murk.

He screamed wordlessly as he woke up coughing on the lake shore, Justine crying beside him. Both were soaked from head to toe.

"What happened?" he asked, panting, his throat burning with pain.

"You asshole, don't ever scare me like that again." Justine pounded his shoulder with her fist, tears springing from her puffy, anger-filled eyes. Breathing hard, she could barely speak. "You walked into the water and fell face forward. I thought you were going to drown." She covered her eyes and rolled onto her back.

"Juss, somebody was down there pulling me." He remembered the yellow eyes, the black hand, an icy fetter wrapped around his ankle.

"Listen to yourself. All this plotting and planning is driving you crazy. You've done the PR work. Everybody knows Victory Solutions is reviving Coldwater's economic landscape. Can we go home now?" Justine lay on top of Oscar, resting her head on his chest.

Feeling defeated, he stared at the lake until he noticed the surface swell a few feet away from the shore. That horrible humming filled the air again. Oscar covered his ears, wet sand, weeds, and debris clung to his body. To his astonishment, the rising water gave way to a leather-bound book held inside a black veiny grip.

He shivered. Fear shot through his temples as the familiar hand lifted the tome from the frightening waters.

"Something's out there," Oscar panted, his voice barely a whisper. He pointed with one hand and clutched Justine's sleeve with the other. The mysterious object lay in the sand, half submerged with water washing over its surface.

"Stop," Justine said. "You're hurting me." She peeled his fingers from her arm and stared curiously at the water. She stood and trudged into the lake as if walking in a trance, Oscar begging her not to go.

"Leave it," he said. "Leave that thing where it is!"

After kneeling in the shallow water, she returned holding the same, portentous book Oscar saw rising from the lake's surface.

Instinctively, he cringed from the sight but the concern in her eyes brought him back to reality. He had tried to put on a brave face, but he had confronted his fear and failed. Oscar reached for the book, his hands trembling. To his surprise the volume wasn't nearly as wet as it should have been. Water rolled off the ragged cover instead of soaking through.

Like Coldwater, he thought, and he remembered his granddaddy's tale about the fabled town that once stood in this very spot from 1856 until 1948 when the floodwaters arrived, destroying the original site of Coldwater, Mississippi and forming Arkabutla Lake in its stead.

Granddaddy's eyes would light up when he spoke about old

Coldwater. How poor families, white and black, tilled the fertile soil side by side. He would wave his hands and tell Oscar and his cousins that Arkabutla Lake was originally a beautiful woodland where the Chickasaw buried their loved ones. Once the Chickasaw were forced from their native lands, the settlers attempted to eke a living from the sacred burial ground, but their efforts were unsuccessful, so they moved on to more hospitable plots further south. Then only freedmen and poor whites called Coldwater their home. Incredibly, over time, they made the land fertile, fueling tall tales—and envy.

Landowners from the surrounding counties tried to remove the residents from the fertile valley for years. Most of the town's inhabitants finally gave up their homes, exhausted from the constant fights with their racist neighbors *and* the government. They migrated south to another plot of land that would become the site of the new Coldwater, Mississippi.

But Pastor Josiah Graves and the congregation of First Valley Baptist Church refused to surrender their property, despite the offers and aggressive demands from local officials. After their bids to purchase the town were rejected, state politicians conspired with the Army Core of Engineers to flood the valley. Spite proved to be a powerful force.

The last service before the day of reckoning, Pastor Graves barricaded himself and what remained of his congregation inside the sanctuary. Enraged and hopeless, he ordered his loyal followers to stay in the church even as the deluge threatened to drown them all. As Coldwater's enemies flooded the valley, the rest of the displaced townspeople were miles away, building their new homes, but they heard the pastor preaching from the Scripture while the congregation raised their voices in songful pandemonium. Ten miles south of the newly formed lake, the townspeople heard the voices in the wind.

Lord, Thou rulest the raging of the sea. When the waves thereof rise, thou stillest them.

Oscar opened the book and found the inside completely dry.

"That's weird," Justine said, rubbing the paper with her fingertip. "These pages should be ruined."

"The Holy Bible, translated from the original tongues," Oscar read slowly. At the bottom of the page, he found a scratched signature that sent his mind reeling. He wanted to toss the book back in the water and run as fast as he could, but he was done running from his past and this lake.

"If found, return to Pastor Josiah Graves." Oscar trembled as he read. He stared at Justine, shocked recognition distorting his face. "Pastor Graves was the preacher from Granddaddy's stories." His tone was distant and fearful, like someone sleepwalking through a nightmare.

"We need to get out of here." Justine crouched beside Oscar and grabbed his hand. "Forget the refinery, the opening reception. Something weird is happening, and we do not need to participate."

Shame and fear pulsed through his heart. Even after all his accomplishments, all these years, the lake had the ability to make him feel powerless and small.

"We'll be all right," Oscar said. He pulled himself to his feet with Justine's help. "Victory needs me. Besides, I refuse to let this damn lake win."

Oscar and Justine turned their backs on Arkabutla. Before them the new refinery shone in the afternoon sun, a latticework of criss-crossing pipes and towering silos, like a white castle symbolizing Oscar's triumphant return.

The couple slouched into the Hampton Inn off Highway 51, soggy, exhausted, holding each other like a pair of juke joint drunks. Oscar thought he was going out of his mind. Clutching Pastor Grave's Bible against his chest, he scanned the lobby. Victory Solutions had reserved most of the rooms for the weekend. The area was filled with company staff lounging between the reception desk on Oscar's left and a small bar in a dark corner to his right. His coworkers wore badges bearing the company's logo.

The lake hummed in his ears, and in the darkness of his mind the yellow eyes still burned.

With his world tilting, spinning, Oscar made a beeline for the elevator. He stood before the silver door and smiled as Justine pressed the call button.

"Thanks for taking off this weekend," he said.

"Where else would I be, Ozzie?" Weary, she tilted her head and smiled.

"Hey, Oscar, wait up," Steve Cook said. The VP of Supply Chain Management approached the couple from behind.

A short man with a scruffy mustache and gray hair wrapped around a shiny bald top, Steve offered an uneasy smile that failed to reach his eyes. He stared at Oscar and Justine's wet, disheveled clothes and their obvious exhaustion.

"Is everything all right?" he asked, staring the couple up and down. "I've been calling for the past hour. Where've you been? Looks like you started the party without us!"

"We went to the plant," Oscar answered, feeling the need to elaborate. "I wanted to get a picture of what tomorrow might look like."

"Like overkill," Steve said, "but you're the poster boy for triple checking. Answer your phone next time." He waved his hand, a signal for Oscar and Justine to follow.

"Maybe we should change," Justine stammered.

Steve snorted. "Later! We've been waiting."

Between the wet clothes and the memories of the lake, Oscar found it impossible to focus. He needed a hot shower, a dry bed, and deep, dreamless sleep. But duty called. Steve wanted to talk, and there was Randi Wade, the VP of Information Technology, at the bar waving him over.

Say hi and excuse yourself after a few minutes, he thought. His colleagues would understand. Covered in sand, soggy clothes, and twigs, Oscar and Justine looked terrible. Granddaddy would have taken one glance and said, *Y'all walking up in here like Who Did and What For.*

The thought almost made Oscar smile ... almost.

Perched on a stool, Randi nursed a half empty glass. Her smile much warmer than Steve's, she seemed amused by Oscar and Justine's messy condition.

Randi had a pleasant, no-nonsense air about her. She wore horn-rimmed glasses with clear frames and a mushroom haircut clipped around her shoulders. With her auburn hair and rosy cheeks, she looked as if she was blushing all the time. "Here comes the King and Queen of Victory," she said, watching the couple with a smirk.

"I'm just the plus one," Justine joked. "I don't work for Victory anymore, remember?"

After her and Oscar's relationship moved from casual dating to serious romance the couple decided it would be best if one of them left Victory. Justine always wanted to work for a larger company anyway. Her CPA background secured her a position at an investment firm a month following her resignation. Her new post included a salary increase and excellent benefits.

"We think of you as extended family." Randi winked and laughed. "Bookkeeping's been off since you left."

Behind the bar, a woman stacked a low standing refrigerator with bottles and cans of beer, her back turned to the coworkers. When she stood and faced the group, Oscar grabbed Justine's forearm. All at once, he was back at Arkabutla Lake, drowning, fighting against the water filling his lungs, the humming in his ears, and the black hand pulling his ankle. His knees weakened, but he stood strong. This was not the time to collapse, not with Steve and Randi watching.

What the hell is Lacey doing here? he asked himself. Checking into the hotel the night before, he had seen another bartender working, an ebony-skinned woman with blonde tipped locs.

Lacey's skin shone like fresh honey. She wore burgundy ring curls with crinkly bangs that covered her forehead and waves that dropped past her shoulders. Her eyes bright and mischievous, she offered a gap-toothed smile with gold caps that covered her canines.

"Another pair of lucky contestants," she said. She grabbed a glass and wiped it with a white towel. "You look like you need a drink, cuzzo."

"Don't call me that," Oscar grunted. Anger crept through his neck, clenching the muscles in his jaw. *You grew up to be a bartender*, he thought, surprised. As kids Lacey had an attitude more suitable for law enforcement or contract killing, but nothing had ever been simple with Lacey. She was definitely up to something.

"Excuse my friend," Steve said, playfully shaking Oscar's shoulder. "He's had a rough day. He didn't mean any disrespect."

"He just needs a drink or three, loosen up some of that water in his head." Lacey laughed, her gold teeth shining in the dimmed light.

Justine raised a suspicious eyebrow, staring at Lacey first, then Oscar.

"What's your name?" Justine asked, mistrustful.

"I don't know what's going on, but Lacey has been extremely helpful. She knows all the spots for good food and sightseeing. She even hooked us up with a deejay for the party." Steve pointed at the bartender. "Why're you giving her a hard time? Offering drinks is her job."

"You're right," Oscar said. "It's been a long day." He gripped Justine's hand. He needed time to think, and for the moment, he didn't want Steve, Randi, or anyone else knowing about his connection to Lacey.

"What's that?" Randi asked, pointing to Pastor Grave's Bible.

"This?" He raised the book from his hip. "Just something I picked up in town."

"Really? Where'd you get it from?" Lacey asked, curious and friendly.

"A thrift store, I can't remember the name." Oscar gripped the Bible with one hand and Justine's fingers with the other.

"Lacey, can we take a bottle of scotch upstairs?" Steve asked, pointing his thumb over his shoulder.

"Sure, I'll get some glasses, too," Lacey replied. "You wanna charge it to your tab?"

"That's good," Steve said. He took the bottle in one hand and fingered the glasses with the other. "Randi, take Justine to your room. We'll meet you in a sec."

Steve led Oscar to a set of armchairs next to a window covered with black curtains. The pair stood beside the chairs instead of sitting.

"I get it, Oscar." Steve's voice was low and serious. "We're all under pressure, but this isn't the time to unravel. Not this close to victory, pun intended. I need to know I can count on you to keep it together."

"Of course," Oscar said. "I'm okay. Justine and I were playing around and got a little overzealous. That's all." Frightened by Steve's uncertainty, Lacey and Arkabutla seemed insignificant.

"Good," Steve said. He patted Oscar's arm and nodded. "We got problems at the refinery. We need to talk. I'll let Randi explain upstairs."

With a queen-sized bed and enough space for a matching loveseat and armchair, Randi's room spoke simplicity and comfort. Oscar and Justine's set up fared the same.

Wonder what Steve booked for himself, Oscar thought.

He sat on the loveseat next to Justine. Randi grabbed the remote from the television stand and plopped down on the armchair. She cut on the local news, raising the volume as loud as the control permitted.

"Fill me in, Randi," Oscar wasn't sure if he could handle anymore curveballs, but one thing was certain, talking over the blaring television annoyed him. The greatest weekend of his life had turned to crap before it had even started.

"It's bad, Oscar, especially for you," Randi admitted.

"Especially Oscar?" Justine frowned. "He brought Victory Solutions to this demographic. Arkabutla Lake is a prime location. The tax breaks alone are worth a fortune, but if something goes bad, he takes the fall."

"Oscar *chose* to play the background." Steve placed the empty glasses on the dresser next to the television, filling them each with scotch. "In the beginning it made sense. Oscar has family here, but I'm wondering. Is there something else? It's okay but we need to know."

"Over the past week there've been five accidents at the new refinery, all fatalities," Randi tried to whisper but ended up hissing over the noisy television. "The first pair were last seen on their way to check the meters on the tanks by the dock. The next day a pair of bloated corpses dressed in factory coveralls washed up on the north end of the lake.

"Maintenance found a body in the breakroom. The lungs and stomach were full of water, but the skin, hair, and clothes were dry. There was no water or mud in the breakroom either." Randi massaged her temple with her fingertips. "Security found one of their own stuffed in a metal drum. His spine and his limbs had been broken to fit him in the can."

"That can't be right. Oscar would have heard something," Justine turned to her husband. "Did you know about this?"

"I wouldn't hide something like that," Oscar said, but he wasn't so sure. He'd hidden damaging information for Victory Solutions on other occasions. Nothing illegal but certainly unethical. He never lied to himself either. He had clear motives. Become Vice President of Communications and get revenge on his Mississippi relatives.

"There's more," Randi said. "You remember my assistant, Christian?"

"Of course! Christian is a sweetheart. Who could forget that smile?" Justine asked. "He repaired my hard drive about a month ago. I mean, he repaired Oscar's hard drive."

"Yesterday Christian walked into the office at the new facility dripping from head to toe. Mud smeared over his face. Leaves stuck in his ears. He was singing one of those old plantation spirituals, something about floods and God smiting humanity. He pulled a knife and said he had a message for you, Oscar, from Pastor Graves."

Oscar found himself struggling to breathe all over again, his chest filled with fear. The Bible throbbed in his hands. He could have sworn the book was mumbling some incoherent passage.

"A message for me?" he asked, hoping to mask his terror with sarcasm.

"'What profits a man to gain the world and lose his soul,'" Randi continued. "After that he stabbed himself right under the chin. It was horrible! His arm kept hacking and hacking like someone else was controlling it. Even after he died. I didn't know what to do! His arm kept moving and there was so much blood ..." Her voice trailed off. She adjusted her glasses, wiping away a tear. "The medics had to restrain him, even after he was gone."

Justine looked stunned. She stared at Oscar and gulped her scotch.

"What do you mean *after he was gone?*" Oscar asked. Justine grabbed his sleeve.

"He was dead, I swear he was. His eyes had gone still and

empty." Randi shivered, her fingers clasped around her glass. "But the knife kept hacking..."

"Like something right out of a nightmare." Steve adjusted his tie, gripping his drink. "Who is Pastor Graves, besides the creepiest name for a preacher I ever heard?" he asked. He finished his scotch then sat on the foot of the bed, resting his elbows on his thighs. "Do you know him? Is he local?"

"Maybe he's a protester," Randi added.

"I don't know any Pastor Graves," Oscar lied, squeezing the leather-bound cover until the blood rushed into his knuckles. The humming lingered, faint and distant.

"In other words, Oscar's in danger." Justine placed her hand over her nose and mouth.

"What's going on with the investigation?" Oscar asked. "Was there an autopsy?" Feeling dazed and helpless, he remembered the hand wrapped around his ankle.

"You're thinking like me," Steve said. "He must've been high, right? The coroner performed two autopsies, one official, another paid for by Victory. His system was clean both times."

"Oscar, did you and Christian have any business outside of the company?" Randi asked, her voice careful and hesitant.

"We only spoke at work," Oscar said. He wondered if he was having a nervous breakdown.

"Maybe Christian was crazy or off his meds. Not everybody can handle workplace pressure." Justine tucked her hair behind her ear. "Have you contacted the family?" she asked.

"Of course," Randi said. "We took care of everything. Medical bills, funeral expenses, NDAs."

"Somebody's doing my job?" Oscar asked, gripping Pastor Grave's Bible. He wanted to smack Steve across the face with it. "I really am the fall guy."

"The board didn't want you to know at all," Steve grumbled. "They wanted to wait, see what happens, but you're worth more than that."

"You're a good guy, Oscar," Randi said. "Your work has allowed us to do some amazing things, but you have to admit, Christian calling your name before killing himself looks bad. You don't find that suspicious? You're the only one in the company with roots in this area. That's fine. Your southern heritage is an asset. Remember. We're on the same side, and we have your back."

After leaving Randi and Steve, Oscar and Justine finally made it to their room. He'd never been so glad to see steam rising behind a shower curtain. After cleaning up, the couple climbed into bed, stretched over the covers, and stared at the ceiling.

"Where do we start?" Justine asked. "The lake, Pastor Graves, your cousin downstairs, Christian—all in one day."

He wiped his eye with his knuckle and started to speak but the words escaped him. He didn't know where to begin.

Someone knocked on the door, and Oscar jumped out of bed. For some reason he grabbed the Bible and threw it in the top drawer of the nightstand. He grumbled as he opened the door. He couldn't take anymore bad news from Steve or Randi, but to his surprise, he found Lacey leaning against the door jamb, flicking a piece of dirt from her fingernail.

"I would say long time no see, cuzzo," Lacey stood up straight and winked, "but we just spoke at the bar."

"What was that about anyway?" Oscar leaned out the door, looking down both ends of the hallway.

"I wanted to see my cousin. Is that a crime?" Lacey set her fist on her hip. "I should be questioning you about your business in Coldwater. Don't you think?"

"Who is that, Ozzie?" Justine asked. The sounds of her shuffling around the room followed her voice.

"You have a gorgeous wife, *Ozzie*." Lacey giggled. "At first I wondered what she saw in you, but I guess there's a match for everybody."

Justine stepped into the doorway. Taken aback, she jumped when she saw the evening visitor standing in the hall.

"You look surprised?" Lacey countered. "Imagine how I felt when I learned my own cousin wanted to destroy my childhood stomping ground."

"That's why you're here? To stop the inevitable?" Oscar asked, defiant.

"I'm here to deliver a message." She leaned toward Oscar and whispered, "Invite me in. Trust. You don't want anybody else hearing what I've come to say."

"I've had enough messages for the day. Besides, I'm not afraid of you anymore." Oscar cursed under his breath. *Anymore* had slipped out.

"Who's this message from?" Justine asked, raising her eyebrow.

"Let's talk inside." Oscar stepped back so Lacey could enter.

"This is a nice room," she said, looking around as she sat in the armchair nestled in the corner. "It's small but cute."

"Say what you gotta say and leave." Oscar clenched his teeth.

"First, I'm sorry for what I did to you," Lacey said. Her eyes were filled with deep regret. "I've grown since those days. You'd be surprised."

"I hear remorse and sincerity," Oscar noted, contempt turning his stomach. "You sounded the same way just before you pushed me into the lake."

"That's fair." Lacey nodded, unaffected. "So you understand, Granddaddy was mad at me for years. I knew you two were close. That's why I hated your ass, but damn, I hurt Granddaddy more than anybody. He was never the same. He waited for you to come back every year, but you never showed up."

"It's all on me, typical Lacey," Oscar growled. "You wanted me gone for good. You got your wish, but I'm back now."

"You have every right to hate me, but Arkabutla Lake belongs to everybody in Coldwater, especially Pastor Graves' congregation. That's why we take the flowers and the wreaths out there to pay our respects. That's why Granddaddy took us to the lake every year. He wanted us to know where we come from, especially you. He knew that life would take you places where your soul needed protecting. He was using those stories to prepare you. I didn't learn that until ..." Lacey wiped a single tear from her eye.

"Tell my wife about the lake, *cuzzo*," Oscar said, with no attempt to mask his hatred. "Since we're talking about souls and all, I lost mine that day."

"You always acted like you were better than everybody." Lacey sniffled and wiped her nose with her finger. "After you refused to come back, Granddaddy stopped taking us to the lake. He quit telling stories altogether."

"You should focus on your part of the situation," Justine said.

"I liked you better downstairs." Lacey rolled her eyes. "Look, *Justine*, I appreciate you loving on my cousin, but he came here to hurt this land and everyone here. Where do you stand in that?"

"What are you talking about?" Justine asked. "Oscar and his employers are bringing hundreds of jobs to Coldwater."

"What about the waste from the refinery? Where does that go?" Lacey countered.

"Sustainable jet fuel leaves only a tenth of the environmental footprint compared to ..."

"Ten percent of poison is still poison," Lacey said. "Might take a little longer, but the outcome's the same. That's why Oscar ain't saying nothing. He knows I'm telling the truth. Y'all got millions on the table, but money is not his motivator."

Justine stared at the floor and crossed her ankles. Oscar kept his mouth shut, so he wouldn't have to lie.

"I was saying. The last time Oscar came for family reunion we snuck out to the lake at night while the adults were getting drunk, including Granddaddy. It wasn't just me either. We got a gang of cousins, but I was the leader. It was my idea, and I did most of the talking. We had a cooler full of food and soda pop. I told Oscar to reach in and get himself a sandwich. I'll never forget the look on his face right before we grabbed him. He was smiling from ear to ear. He thought he had finally gained our acceptance. Part of me wanted to stop, but it was too late. When we raised him in the air, he screamed so loud. I don't think I've ever seen anybody that scared. For years I heard you screaming in my dreams, Oscar, almost every night until Granddaddy died."

"It's time for you to leave." Oscar leapt to his feet.

"I suffered too," Lacey cried. "Grandaddy didn't make peace with me until after he passed."

"You knew I couldn't swim," he hissed with tears in his eyes. "You made fun of me while I thrashed around and begged for your help. Even after y'all pulled me out, you sat there and laughed while I threw up all over myself."

"That's why you hate being in water? You've carried this around since you were a child." Justine turned to Lacey and growled, "How dare you come here?"

"I'm just a messenger." Lacey turned to Oscar. "Granddaddy loves you. We all do. We understand why you want to destroy the lake, but the congregation of First Valley Baptist Church paid for Arkabutla with their lives. Your refinery is gonna hurt generations— past, present, and future. The ancestors are angry, especially Pastor Graves. If it wasn't for Granddaddy fighting for you on the other side, the pastor would have taken you already."

"Granddaddy couldn't make you stop bullying me," Oscar said. "How's he going to protect me from the afterlife?"

"All I know is, the night Granddaddy died, he started speaking to me in my dreams. Mostly he talked about how mean I used to be." Lacey shook her head. "He said I could wipe my slate clean if I warned you. Your people need to leave Coldwater, and you have to go down in the water and give Pastor Graves his Bible."

"Oh, I'm supposed to believe that Pastor Graves and his congregation are coming for me?" Oscar laughed despite his nerves.

"That refinery won't ship one drop." Lacey rose from the couch and stood by the door. "You beat the locals with propaganda and money, but you can't beat the ancestors. Now, you gotta talk to Pastor Graves, so yeah, it's on you."

After Lacey was gone, the couple went back to bed and stared at the ceiling. The darkness reminded Oscar of Arkabutla. In his mind he plunged toward a sunken town shining at the bottom of the dismal water.

"I thought you were doing what was best for your career," Justine groaned. "You said you wanted to change this place for the better, but this is about revenge. You're trying to kill a lake, Ozzie, when you could have just stood up to your cousin."

"I need closure," Oscar said. "You weren't there. Damn Lacey and her dreams. She ruined my life. I never saw my granddaddy again. I was too ashamed to go back. The next year I cried and fussed until my parents decided to stay home. They were just as embarrassed as I was."

"You're a natural storyteller like your grandfather." Justine tapped his forehead. "That's why you're so good at what you do, but this obsession with revenge is destroying you."

"When it was about my career and my salary, everything was good," Oscar shot back. "You knew what the refinery would do to the water from the beginning."

"It seemed like a great idea at first," Justine said. "I'll admit the money convinced me more than anything. I knew what would happen, but I told myself the profits would make it better for everyone involved, including the locals."

"Now you're having second thoughts," Oscar said, his voice colored with sarcasm.

"I don't want a jet fuel refinery in our neighborhood—sustainable or not."

Oscar turned his back to Justine and pulled the Bible from the nightstand drawer. He opened the book and found a message he hadn't seen before written in Pastor Graves' crooked script.

It's too late for me, but you got a chance, boy.

Thumbing through the old Holy Scripture, he found several bookmarks where the pages were dog-eared. The first section took him to Genesis, Chapter 6. He found a passage marked with scrawled brackets and began to read, his voice low and jittery.

Behold, I will bring a flood of waters upon the earth to destroy all flesh

Wherein is the breath of life, and everything that is in the earth shall die.

With the refinery hulking at his back, Oscar watched the Victory employees board the two-level party boat. The coworkers nodded and tipped their glasses as they walked past Steve and Randi, congratulating the pair on a successful opening. Steve smiled and waved, avoiding eye contact like he was embarrassed. Randi thanked the employees for their hard work, shaking hands and slapping shoulders. She stared through the crowd and nodded at Oscar.

"Don't worry," Justine whispered. "You know who put this project together. And so do I."

"I thought I would be okay moving behind the scenes," he said. Mindful of eavesdroppers, his voice dipped low and soft. "I did all that work just to be erased."

Parked by the dock in the same place Lacey had pushed him into the lake, the catamaran gleamed, drenched in reddening sunlight, two floors of polished woodgrain bordered with white rails and blue canvas. As Steve had promised, DJ equipment was set up on the bottom deck. The sound gear reminded Oscar of Lacey's visit.

What should I do? he wondered. He stared at the boat and the lake, fighting the images of Christian stabbing himself, and Pastor Graves' Bible, and those yellow eyes burning through the black water. He felt trapped in his own skin, his own creation. He heard Justine laugh, looked over his shoulder, and found her on the other side of the crowd talking with Randi. His wife nodded and smiled, the dark force she was, her hair pinned up, her black dress draping from her shoulders and flowing around her legs. She looked exhausted even through lipstick and eyeshadow that had been drawn with meticulous precision.

The overcast sky, orange and red in the fiery sunset, evoked a burning blanket stretched over Oscar's head. The wind rose through the trees, freezing him where he stood, forcing him to listen for the lake's ghostly voices.

"Are we really about to get on this boat?" Justine whispered through clenched teeth as she returned to Oscar's side.

"You could've stayed at the hotel," Oscar said. "This is my fight."

"Steve should have cancelled the event," Justine said. "The refinery could have opened quietly. We could be at home safe and sound."

"Steve brought in some extra security, all plain clothes just in case." Oscar turned to his wife and placed his hand on the small of her back. "Everybody's expecting a party. We cancel, it'll raise too many questions. Thirty minutes, maybe an hour at the most, and it'll all be over. Then we can shout victory for real."

"I don't know, Ozzie." Justine stared at the party boat. "It's like we're provoking something we don't understand."

As the couple made their way to the catamaran, Steve caught Oscar's arm and squeezed his shoulder.

"I see a VP position in your near future," Steve said. He turned to Justine. "Relax. I hired some off-duty cops to watch our backs. Everything's gonna be fine."

The refinery shrank into the distance as the catamaran droned toward the middle of the lake. Oscar felt the floor dissolving, leaving him suspended with no protection from the water. It took all of his concentration to keep himself from trembling. He sipped from a bottle of beer he'd been nursing for ten minutes.

He froze, his limbs constricted with fear, when he heard the trickling water. Listening closer, he noticed the noise was coming from the DJ's sound system.

"'Cry Me a River'? Damn you, Justin Timberlake," he complained, shaking his forehead in the palm of his hand.

"You wanna dance?" Justine asked, her nervous voice remained optimistic. "Maybe that'll help you relax. It'll help me for sure."

"You go ahead." He pumped his fist. "I'll cheer you on from the sidelines."

"I don't want to be out there alone." Justine pointed at Oscar's co-workers partying in front of the DJ equipment.

"I'll dance with you, cousin-in-law," Lacey said, walking up suddenly from Oscar's periphery. "And when did Mr. Stiff and Offbeat learn how to move?"

Oscar jumped in his chair when he saw Lacey shimmering in her red dress.

"I wasn't coming at first, even though Steve invited me," she said. "But Granddaddy paid me a visit last night and told me to watch you."

Lightning sizzled across the overcast sky and struck the water a few yards from the boat. The employees cringed and grabbed each other. After the moment of danger had passed, they laughed and raised their glasses to the lake.

"See," Lacey said with a knowing smile.

The DJ threw on a blues oldie Oscar hadn't heard since his last time in Coldwater. As a kid, the lyrics hadn't meant much. He'd been more intrigued by the adults and their nasty dances. Now he was awestruck by the corporate administrators whose responses flaunted the same vulgarity. They howled and pulled each other and sweated as the wind kicked into high gear. To Oscar's dismay, the ghost voices returned, joining the blues singer crooning through the speakers. He realized the song was at once past, present, and yet to be.

Let the floodwaters come and wash my troubles away
I need this stormy weather to keep my enemies at bay

"Oscar," Justine shouted. She pointed toward the rail where water was seeping onto the hardwood from the side of the boat. He ducked and his wife cried out as more water poured from the top deck.

Frightened, confused, he watched the tiny streams shoot across the floor and gather into pools. The puddles rose and morphed until a gang of monsters shaped like people composed of mud and lake water stood interspersed between the Victory employees who were now screaming and diving overboard. Shrieks rang through the air as Oscar's coworkers leapt from the top deck and splashed into the lake. Horrified, he grabbed Justine and shirked backwards until he pressed the rail behind him.

Oscar heard more screaming in the water. When he turned, he saw huge wet tendrils shaped into hands and arms, beating the victims, dragging them down as they struggled. Justine cried against Oscar's chest. He closed his eyes and shook his head until he heard footsteps and thumping coming from the spiral stairs that led to the upper deck.

Randi Wade sauntered from the top floor, one step at a time, dragging Steve's limp body. When she got to the bottom, she offered the couple a blood-coated smile. One hand fisting Steve's red drenched collar, she cackled as she pulled his decapitated head from behind her back and held it before the couple like a blood-soaked lantern.

"I gave you a chance, boy, but you don't believe fat meat's greasy," Steve's severed head sneered and spat at Oscar's feet.

Wait a second, Oscar thought with sudden realization. He heard very little of Steve Cook's familiar gruff. The VP's voice had been replaced with a ragged gurgle and bark filled with ceaseless pain and bitterness.

"Pastor Graves," Oscar whimpered, clenching his stomach so he wouldn't piss himself.

"It didn't have to go this far," Lacey said. She stepped forward and stood next to Randi.

Oscar fumbled through his satchel and pulled out Pastor Graves' Bible, offering the book the same way Randi had brandished Steve's head.

"Now you're hunting with big dogs, boy." Pastor Graves spoke through Steve and Randi at the same time.

Randi dropped Steve's body and threw his head into the lake. She snatched Pastor Graves' Bible and knocked Oscar to the deck. With unnatural speed she scuttled forward and grabbed Justine by the waist. With the sounds of snapping vertebrae, Randi's head twisted until her chin rested between her shoulder blades, and she was staring back at Oscar through one cracked lens of her horn-rimmed glasses.

"You have to come down to my house now, boy," Pastor Graves spoke through Randi. "You started this mess. You have to finish it. Time to see if you're as brave as your granddaddy claims."

With Justine screaming and reaching for Oscar, Randi hoisted his wife onto her shoulder and leapt over the side of the boat. The pair disappeared with a splash and a patch of effervescent foam marking their descent.

"I told you," Lacey said, sympathy filling her voice. She leaned over the rail and stared at the water where Randi and Justine had vanished.

"Told me what?" Oscar screamed.

"Don't play dumb. You know what to do," Lacey said.

Gripping the rail, Oscar closed his eyes and willed himself to jump, but his body refused. He was too afraid.

"Lacey, you gotta push me," he begged. He couldn't believe what he was asking, but he didn't see any other way.

"Not this time." She placed her hand over Oscar's. "I don't understand any more than you, but Granddaddy promised to protect you. You're stronger than you know. You can do it."

Oscar imagined Justine fighting uselessly as Randi delivered her to Pastor Graves and those black hands waiting at the bottom of the lake. Tears poured down his cheeks. He sat on the rail, sucked in as much air as he could, and fell into the cold water.

He opened his eyes, gasping for air, bent on his hands and knees. Dark yellow planks stretched under his palms. He was in a log cabin church built from cypress wood hewn and sanded, including an altar topped with an unadorned wooden cross. The altar surrendered to a large window and black water that stretched as far as he could see. He was at the bottom of Arkabutla Lake, but to his astonishment the church's interior was completely dry.

Like Pastor Graves' Bible.

"You were always stronger than folks gave you credit for," a familiar voice called from behind. "Everybody underestimated you except me. I always knew you were the man."

Oscar turned and saw Granddaddy smiling, the old man's eyes filled with love. The elder wore a brown porkpie hat and a short sleeve casual shirt with brown and white stripes going down the front—just like Oscar remembered. He leapt to his feet and wrapped his arms around Granddaddy's neck.

"I missed you so much." Oscar sobbed without control or reservation. He wept until his knees gave out, and he leaned against Grandaddy to keep from falling. "I'm sorry I never came back to see you."

"It's all right, son." Grandaddy patted Oscar's back. "We don't have much time."

He led Oscar to a seat on the first pew. It was made from long wooden boards and debarked tree limbs.

"I owe you an apology," Granddaddy said. "Lacey always was a wild one, but she had this way of smiling that turned my heart into jelly. I couldn't get mad at her, even when I was supposed to. Not until she pushed you into the lake."

"Is Justine here?" Oscar asked, looking around the sanctuary.

"Your woman's safe for now," a voice boomed from the back of the church.

Oscar turned in his seat and found a tall dark-skinned man. The man wore a long black overcoat and a wide-brimmed black hat. At his side he held the same Bible Justine had found on the lakeshore. His eyes burned with bright golden flames, just like the ones Oscar had seen underwater when the hand grabbed his ankle.

"Whether she remains safe or not depends on our conversation," Pastor Graves said. "You got some atoning to do."

"I told you my grandson would come through," Granddaddy said. He stood from the pew and stepped into the center aisle.

Oscar joined Granddaddy's side.

"You tried to poison my valley," Pastor Graves said. "If you and your woman wanna live, you have to set things right."

"How?" Oscar asked, stepping forward.

"You read the Scripture I marked for you. That's a start." Pastor Graves raised his Bible. "Now, we have to do something about that *refinery.*" His voice rose in anger. "I gave my life for this valley fighting people just like you."

"That's what you told yourself when you and people were drowning?" Granddaddy asked. He turned and grabbed his grandson's shoulders. "Your little science project is done. Nobody's going near Victory Solutions anytime soon."

"What about my coworkers?" Oscar asked. "Everybody's dead. How do I explain that?"

"Boy, I thought you peddled stories for a living," Pastor Graves barked. "It looks to me like Randi Wade went crazy and tried to kill everybody. You and your wife barely made it out alive."

"I thought you were a preacher." Oscar was still afraid, but it was too late for temerity. "You don't act much like a holy man."

"I'm still a preacher. I'm a warrior too," Pastor Graves said. "But I'm tired. It's time for somebody else to step up and protect this valley. Your granddaddy said you were the man for the job."

Pastor Graves offered his open hand, while Granddaddy nodded. Oscar shook hands with the Pastor. To his surprise, the preacher's grip was warm and strong. This was not the position he had envisioned when Victory hired him, but he didn't have a choice. He would have done anything to get back to Justine.

"That's what I'm talking about," Granddaddy said. "Imagine the stories you're gonna tell *your* grandkids."

Oscar woke up gasping as several hands pulled him from the lake and dumped his wet body onto the deck of the catamaran. He turned onto his back, vomiting water all over himself. He looked up and saw Lacey and her DJ holding his arms and patting his back.

"It's all good now, *cuzzo*," Lacey said, her eyes teary. "You really did save everybody. Damn."

"Wait," Oscar said. He tried to sit up, but his stomach was wracked with cramps. "Where's ..."

"Ozzie!" Justine shouted.

He turned around and saw his wife standing behind him, drenched from head to toe, her black dress stuck to her skin. She fell and wrapped her arms around his neck.

"My friend pulled her out first," Lacey said. She patted the DJ's bulky arm. Then she pointed at Oscar. "You were underwater at least an hour, but Granddaddy told me not to leave you."

Oscar found his strength, and with the help of his wife and his cousin, he pulled himself to his feet. He considered Lacey for a moment, and hugged her neck as tight as he could. He had wanted that reunion since he was twelve.

"I love you, *cuzzo*," he said.

"I've waited forever for this moment." Lacey squeezed Oscar's back. "I love you too."

Justine had found something by the spiral stairs. When she turned back to Oscar her face was covered with tears. She was holding Randi's glasses. One of the lenses was cracked, and the clear frame was missing a temple arm.

"Everybody's gone." Justine fell to her knees and cried.

Oscar rushed to her side and held her as she screamed, and wept, and clawed at his shirt.

Lacey crouched beside the couple and rubbed Justine's back.

After a few minutes the DJ reached over the rail and grabbed something in the water. Oscar remembered Justine finding Pastor Graves' Bible but relaxed when he saw the dripping wreath made from twigs, pine cones, and holly leaves. Lacey took the wreath and placed it on Oscar's head.

"Your grandfather left you a gift," Justine said, resting on Oscar's shoulder, grief depleting her voice.

"What if it's from Pastor Graves?" he asked, remembering his underwater pact.

He held Justine with one arm and stared at the refinery—the product of so much hatred and fear. Victory Solutions would dismantle the plant and relocate someplace remote with no neighborhoods or lakes to poison. As he kissed Justine's cheek, something in the water caught his attention. Just below the lake's surface, the pair of yellow eyes watched him, but the voices in the breeze were at peace. So was Granddaddy.

This side of the living
VH Ncube

LOCATION: KwaNtuthu in the Western Cape Province, South Africa

POPULATION: About 4,797 people

ITS NAME REVEALS nothing of its beauty: KwaNtuthu, the place of smoke. Where mountain ranges are wrapped in a blanket of red, yellow, and orange pincushion proteas, and as we drive, women huddle underneath the coolness of rainbow-colored umbrellas. It's the type of town where time is merely a suggestion, where neighbors engage in intlebendwane as news travels from ear to mouth to ear.

"Are you going to ignore me until we arrive?" uTata wipes the sweat off his balding head with a tattered brown cloth. A frail man, he's hunched over the steering wheel, the too-long journey of more than 140 kilometers likely causing his back to ache. We're well beyond Cape Town's maze of highways from which I can usually spot shopping malls, lush golf courses, and cricket stadiums that, as expected, have fully recovered from the Day Zero water crises.

I leave his question unanswered. Instead, I roll down the window and a breeze streams over my face, salt and sea are on my lips, as it does the job our Ford's aircon has retired from.

"Ntombikayise," he says, using my full name to warn me—he is the elder and I am the child, lest I forget.

What does he want me to say? The truth? I settle on half the truth: "I'm tired, that's all." We overtake a donkey-drawn cart with "Fish4Sale" spray-painted on a cardboard placard; bald patches spot the donkey's rump and shoulder.

"If I had another choice, I would not do this. You know my job—"

"—But I'm twenty-one. I could've stayed alone at the flat and if you left the car, I would drive where I needed to." The last week of university just ended and instead of enjoying my December holidays with friends, I'll be stuck in some small town that doesn't appear on Google Maps (I know this because I spent hours with my finger and thumb spread across my tablet trying to zoom in).

"What parent would I be if I left you alone for a month? Heh? After ..." He catches himself and shakes his head. It's too late, though. I've caught a whiff of the real reason I'm being left with relatives I barely know. It's the stench of a dead rat you can't find in your kitchen and like that foul odor, what I did to myself earlier this year is pervasive in our interactions, but both of us are avoiders. Sayers of half-the-truth and avoiders.

So, we drive in silence. Despite KwaNtuthu's beauty, it's a bruised face. Marked by crumbling Cape Dutch houses and white-washed walls stained by large patches of soot; all remnants of a skirmish it barely survived. I'm in awe, maybe it's more shock, like watching the perfect pirouette then glimpsing the bloodied foot, with a torn toenail, and blisters bursting with pus.

We overtake a red minibus taxi. Emblazoned across its side, above the stick figure children holding hands, is *Mam'Flo's Transport Services*. Eventually, uTata turns onto a dirt path and our unfit Ford heaves up the incline towards Auntie Cebisa's Cape Dutch house that looms in the distance.

Like the others, it has white-washed walls marked with soot. Ornate, rounded gables across the top of these walls hold up its gray thatched roof, and lopsided wooden shutters cling on for dear life. This is a home that will one day fail to shelter its occupants. A chill runs through my body at a more unsettling thought: before that, it will fail to harbor its secrets.

"You remember your cousins, neh? Aya and Olwethu." uTata's gruff voice cuts through my thoughts.

I nod, vaguely remembering the two cousins I bumped into during our sporadic family gatherings, although I'm certain there's a third—Unathi.

Auntie Cebisa rushes out of the house. "Molweni!" she greets as she wipes her hands on the bright red apron wrapped around her waist.

"Molo, Sisi." uTata responds with his own grin as he jumps out of the car and hugs her. They both have the same toothy grin that lets you know for certain they're siblings.

She grips my shoulders as she looks me over with a teary-eyed smile. "Aww Ntombi," she exclaims as her gaze lingers on my arms. Instinctively, I pull at the sleeves of my blouse until they cover my scars and every inch of my thick brown arms.

"Molo, Auntie." Like me, she is a big woman. It's a family trait that Madolo women share.

I greet my cousin, Aya. The small boy who irritated me with his stupid pranks all those years ago during a wedding is taller and wider, like a rugby player; then I greet Olwethu, a short, big girl with thick braids. Her smile is pulled at the glossy burned skin that covers half her face and snakes down her cotton dress. Her wounds looked like they were serious.

Seeing them both makes me certain there's an older sister. "Where's Unathi?"

"Hoaw Sisi, you don't know?" Aya screws his face.

I shake my head.

"She's still missing."

Missing? uTata is keeping this from me as well? The anger and hurt form a lump in my throat, and when our eyes meet, his expression is the same as all those months ago. When I shuffled into the visitor's room at Valkenberg Psychiatric Hospital, uTata was already seated behind the small table. The room was painted in an ugly forest green that filled only the bottom half of its walls. His bowed head rose, his bloodshot eyes asking me *why?* Why didn't I say when I needed him?

I had no reason. Only shame. Shame that he was working so hard, as a single parent, at his door-to-door sales job but had to leave it to attend to me in the hospital. Shame that I was the type of person to end my life, and even after that moment, more shame followed: about showing my scars, and explaining my absence, and exposing what I spent so much time trying to hide behind a smile. The doctors explained there's a chemical imbalance in my brain that I can manage if I take my medication and speak with my therapist, but even now, he's keeping things from me as if I am made of porcelain; feet dangling over the edge of life.

But there's nothing I can hear that will break me. Nothing.

Laughter echoes through the passage as I near the dining room, a ceramic bowl of pap in one hand and tomato and onion gravy in the other. We rarely sit like this, as a family. uTata is always on the road —working—so my free time is spent hanging out with friends, trying to do schoolwork, or seeing Dr. Ngoma.

Olwethu is seated opposite me, feeding her 15-month-old son, Sipho, chunks of pumpkin. Behind her, a wall-to-wall mahogany unit is filled with certificates, gold medals, and miniature gold rugby cleats, and the oval-shaped ball. Adjacent to this is an intricately carved wooden chest of drawers covered by picture frames and toothy grins, and splayed at the center of the room is a rug which is a faded mix of browns and reds—completing the room's ornate, faded, and dated look.

When Auntie Cebisa comes into the room, her cheeks stained with dried tears and her eyes bloodshot, uTata glances at her but says nothing. She's barely in her seat before he launches into a long prayer over the meal.

The evening's conversation is filled with gossiping about distant relatives and neighbors. *What happened to that boy? That clever one who played on your team?* uTata says as he bites into his steak. *He also had an injury*, Aya says as he rolls the pap in his hand before dipping it into the gravy. *And that neighbour? Wasn't her daughter going to study overseas?* Olwethu wipes her son's mouth with his lime baby feeder. *She fell sick and had to leave school, but she never came back.*

Despite all the names and reminiscing, it's strange how Unathi isn't mentioned. Not even in passing. I want to ask questions but decide against it.

"Yoh! Abantwana bethu." Auntie Cebisa swipes at the tears falling down her cheeks and covers her mouth as if suddenly realizing how bleak the future of KwaNtuthu's children is. "I think so much about the older women of my youth, and their tales about this place, then I start to think ... maybe we were foolish to dismiss what they said."

"Ma, those are just urban legends," Aya says with a chuckle.

"What did they say?" I take a sip of my Fanta Orange. This opportunity at directness a rare intermission in the evening's performance.

"That there are spirits that haunt this place, and if you don't leave town before you turn 17, they'll cause you to be stuck here."

"But no one takes it seriously," Aya adds.

I nod instead of asking whether *he* feels trapped. We're both twenty-one and judging by all those trophies, he was good at rugby and could've gotten a scholarship had he not been injured. Olwethu is also stuck in KwaNtuthu after dropping out, and so are all the teenagers who live in this town whose names came up this evening —isn't that a sign the urban legend might be true?

When the traces of gravy smeared across our empty plates are the only remnants of our supper, Auntie Cebisa insists that uTata stays the night. He refuses; says he doesn't mind driving at night. In the end, she convinces him. "Olwethu, show Ntombi where the extra blankets are so she can make his bed."

Up the flight of stairs and at the end of the hallway is a door. Olwethu points to it.

"You're not coming with me?"

She shakes her head.

I slip my phone out of my back pocket and switch on the flashlight. I sweep the beam across the room, then swivel at the movement over my shoulder in time to catch the hem of Olwethu's dress as she runs off. *Why is she acting strange?*

I pull the light string and immediately realize why: this is Unathi's room.

Yellow sticky notes are plastered across her calendar and dirty clothes spill from the mouth of her laundry basket. It's unsettling knowing she took for granted always returning home then one day, she just ... didn't.

I cross the room to the wardrobe and struggle to pull the thick blankets wedged into the top shelf. Using all my strength, I give a final tug that loosens them but throws me off balance. My back bangs against the bed with a loud thud before I collapse. I grimace.

A leather flap jutting from underneath the bed catches my eye. I kneel, my cheek touching the cool wooden floor as I pull at the flap until it falls with a soft clap. Parts of its tan leather cover are black. I open the book:

UNATHI MADOLO
DON'T READ!!!!
[Esp. you Olwethu—stay away!]

I'm about to return the diary but its pages appear frayed, as if they were burned off. *She could've tried to destroy it so no one could find it,* I think, flipping through. I justify this invasion of her privacy by reminding myself that despite how wrong this is, it's better to go through Unathi's things than to examine Auntie Cebisa's scabs, scratching at them for answers until they bleed.

I come to a page smeared in maroon. I hold it to my nose and the pungent smell of burned pages, blood, and leather strikes my face. It dislodges a memory I'd tried to forget. How agonizing over my assignments devolved to just agony, and my only release from this torment was the searing slice of skin and the flow of crimson. My anguish was pumped from my heart and dyed my bath water until I was numb. Then I was admitted.

"What are you doing?"

I flinch, dropping the journal. I shove it within the flaps of the blankets as I gather them into one pile. "I fell."

"I can help you carry those." Aya reaches out.

I kiss my teeth and swat his hand, but he dodges. "If you wanted to help, you could've done so *before* I struggled to reach these blankets *and fell.*"

He laughs. "Don't say I didn't try."

We make our way to the guest room. In that split second, I decided to take the diary, and I doubt he noticed. Unathi is still missing and if there's something in that diary that helps me find her, I'll give it to Auntie Cebisa and the police. If there's nothing, I can always return it.

My T-shirt sticks to my back; the midday sun stings my skin, and I'm irritated I forgot to apply my anti-chaffing cream as my inner thighs rub against each other, and I'm starting to itch. I swat a fly from my face while trailing Aya and Olwethu.

"This entire town, like large parts of the Western and Eastern Cape, are part of the Cape Floral Kingdom," Aya continues. "There's no other floral kingdom in the world that's contained entirely in one country." He grins.

"Oh wow," I respond in mock interest. A fleeting breeze carries the scent of honey and musk from the surrounding shrubs.

"Something interesting about the Fynbos biome, which is under the Cape Floral Kingdom, is that it needs fire to regenerate. Without fire, mature seeds aren't stimulated and aren't released to germinate. But, if the fires happen too often, the seeds don't have enough time to mature, and the survival of fynbos plants is threatened."

Aya rattling facts about biodiversity isn't my idea of fun. "Sipho's father, does he live around here?"

Olwethu's gaze remains fixed on the path ahead of us. Her words are stolen by the wind so all that reaches me are *used too ... same school ... died in an accident.*

"Oh, I'm sorry about that." Maybe the mention of an urban legend has influenced how I see things, but the more I learn about this town, the stranger it seems. It *could* be a symptom of our country's high youth unemployment rate. I learned in ECO152, which I've failed twice, that the rate is around 60%. And maybe this is what 60% looks like: teenage pregnancies, and lost scholarships, and downing bottles of Black Label while getting high on nyaope.

—A bloodcurdling scream pierces the air.

We stop dead in our tracks.

"Let's go back." Aya turns on his heel.

"What was that?" I scan the field. Nothing. "Shouldn't we try to help?"

"So we can be killed?" He grabs my wrist and drags me in the opposite direction. Olwethu shuffles beside us.

I dig my nails into his hand, struggling to break free from his grip. "We can't leave."

He turns to me, his eyes pulled wide by fear. "There's nothing you can do except not go into that part of the plot,"—he points in the direction of the screams; there are only trees shuddering in the wind—"it's how this place is."

The shrieking continues.

It's the only sound for kilometers around us: death bludgeoning life.

Fast walking in silence, my ears are filled with my heavy breathing. The shrieks are fainter as we widen our distance, and the flame inside me, the one all humans are born with that intensifies when witnessing the suffering of others, is barely a flicker.

That was my first day in KwaNtuthu. I come to realize the screams start every day around 3PM. They always originate from the grove of trees and end around 6PM. A demonic alarm clock that's just as violent as it is precise. No one knows why that is, or *what* it is, but the horror becomes enmeshed in everyday life: we'll be swimming in the river then it starts; or playing rugby with Aya coaching us, then it starts; or at the side of the road where hawkers, under Coca-Cola branded umbrellas, sell drinks from buckets of melted ice to drivers and passers-by, and it starts. After two weeks, I can't bear the sound. I hate being near the grove. So, I hurry us along until we're within the house's thick walls.

It's also during this time that I read Unathi's journal: I wait until Olwethu stirs in her sleep; pretend my period cramps are so unbearable I need to nap often; and hide the diary between the folds of my navy blue bath towel.

With water gushing from the bronze taps into the bathtub, I read—

I know keeping this is dumb, and it's all probably stupid. Not sure why I'm even writing this but I'm starting to hear weird things and I need to tell someone, but I don't want to seem crazy, so I'm gonna write everything here. Keep a record of it until I'm sure.

Why doesn't the screaming stop?? It's like I turned seventeen and it's all I hear in the afternoon. Does everyone outgrow it? Does Ma hear this? Aya and Olwethu are too small, they wouldn't understand ...

Every scream that rips through the sky reminds me I'm next. It's this place. What if, one day, I hear them call out to me and I'm tempted to follow? Just to make it stop.

I start to form a picture of her, of someone unraveling in silence. That resonates. A theory has also sprouted in my mind, and I'm starting to believe the sounds are linked to Unathi's disappearance. I'm not planning to find out, but it's there, a root with barely visible root hairs.

The river licks my ankles and pebbles bite into the soles of my feet as I wade toward the riverbank. My upper arm begins to burn, and I slap the source of the itch: blood is smeared on the welts bursting through my skin and black wings stick to my palm, so I dip my hand in the river.

Aya and Olwethu's laughs drift above their splashing. Our late morning swim was fun—I'd even forgotten everything wrong with this place—but the churning in my stomach is back. I take deep breaths, but my body is already bracing itself. It starts as anxiety, then morphs into powerlessness. Any worry about a tormented soul doesn't feature—not since my first day here. My focus is on surviving. It's easy to justify this to myself because the source of those shrieks is already dead. I'm not. I can still make it out of here.

I grab my phone and look at the time. "It's 1PM, guys. Let's make our way home," I shout. In the distance, Mam'Flo's red minibus taxi makes its descent on the narrow road that passes through the grove. Whenever Sipho goes to nursery school, he uses it.

"Come on, Ntombi, one more hour. We'll walk back fast." Aya

uses his palm to push water toward Olwethu, but she backstrokes out of the way.

My stomach drops. They're already swimming to the opposite riverbank when I say, "Okay, but only one."

The duck-shaped cloud I've been tracking across the sky casts a shadow over the mountain when my phone vibrates on my stomach.

"It's 2PM—can we get back?"

After they're dressed, we make our way across the field. Instinctively, I glance at my phone: 2:15PM.

It dawns on me that I haven't seen the minibus exit the other side of the grove. I could've missed it. I'd been staring up at the sky barely paying attention to the road, but if I'm right and the bus hasn't made it out … "I'm not sure Mam'Flo's taxi made it out of the grove."

Olwethu's eyes widen. "What if they're stuck, or trapped in there?" She's already started moving toward it when Aya says, "Maybe they're already home? Let's check first, and we can always come back."

It's 2:30PM.

Olwethu's eyes water. "We're close. Let's check and we can be out before 3PM."

Aya nods. He thinks we're overreacting, I can tell, but he follows. The churning in my stomach causes a sharp pain. Everything in me wants to run the other way. To survive. "I found Unathi's diary," I blurt out. That root with my theory about Unathi is tough and thick, now. The kind that can trip you up as you try to run through a forest—so why did I say it?

Neither of them responds, so I continue, "When she turned seventeen, she started hearing the screams and in the diary, you can see how it affected her."

"Does it say anything about the day she disappeared?" Aya's voice quivers with emotion.

I wish I had more useful information, but I tell them what I know. I describe how worried she was about being drawn to this place and how often she described feeling despair and loneliness.

Eventually, we find the minibus taxi and Mam'Flo under its open hood. It's 2:47PM.

"Molweni, Mam' Flo," Aya greets. "What's wrong?" He stands

beside her and examines the engine. Mam'Flo is a middle-aged woman with grease stains smudged across the front of her floral dress and on her fingers. "My son, I think it's the starter." She scratches her forehead. "Everything else looks fine."

We devise a plan: I'll sit behind the wheel as Mam'Flo, Aya, and Olwethu push the minibus. Once it's started, I'll continue driving, and only after we're safely out of the grove will Mam'Flo and I switch seats.

I keep my foot on the clutch and place the taxi in second gear. I keep turning the ignition as they push, the taxi whining with each turn of the key. The toddlers wave at the trio.

It's 3:02PM.

The scream pierces through the trees; birds squawk, flapping away, and a thick cloak of smoke descends, but there are no flames. I cough as it starts to fill the minibus and its tendrils cram into my nostrils and lungs.

The minibus sputters to life. I push down on the accelerator and continue driving until I roll to a stop. "Hurry up," I shout as Olwethu and Aya jump in and squeeze between the toddlers who wail at the deafening sound weaving its way between the trees. Aya grabs Mam'Flo's hand as she steps into the minibus, but her eyes are wide with fear. Then her hands claw at her neck as she gasps for air.

"What's happening?" I'm unable to see from the driver's seat if her foot is lodged into something.

"Drive, drive, drive," Aya shouts.

"What? We can't leave her."

"Drive." He pulls the sliding door, slamming it shut. My foot rams down the accelerator and I flick on the headlights. Through the rearview mirror, I watch as Mam'Flo hunches over, gasping until she's on her knees, and my powerlessness turns to shame because we didn't even try. Five seconds more and she might've been in the minibus.

The toddlers continue wailing and coughing. Olwethu has Sipho on her lap; She bounces him up and down trying to soothe him, and, as my hands tremble on the steering wheel, I hold onto the thought that all I need to do is drive. Branches and leaves slap across the windshield.

I slam the brakes. "There's a log ... or rock blocking the road." I cough, clamping my T-shirt over my nostrils and mouth as if I can filter out the acrid stench.

Aya, with his T-shirt covering half his face, rolls open the door and runs to heave the log out of the way. Snot runs down the toddler's noses and their mouths are agape as they bawl.

Then I notice them. Behind him. Arms outstretched, approaching Aya as if they're emerging from the smoke, but remain tethered to it. Aya fights back tears as he's anchored in place. His eyes bulge and his hands are around his neck as if he's trying to remove something.

Unathi. The outline of her face is a smoky haze but the resemblance to Auntie Cebisa is unmistakable. Our eyes meet, and I'm looking at my reflection. Not being born in KwaNtuthu, the glass separates us, but it's already cracking.

"Leave," Aya shouts, jolting me out of my trance.

I press the hooter as if its blare will scare them, as if spirits can be startled.

"Please, try!" Olwethu cries out to him.

He shakes his head as he's dragged into the smoke, deeper within the grove. Compelled to join their number.

Through the rearview mirror, I don't see any smoke. There's nothing to hint at what we've gone through, but the grove's screams reverberate in my ears and tears blur my vision. I try to focus on driving, but soon my shoulders heave at the thought of Aya. For Auntie Cebisa who will find out she has two dead children. For Mam'Flo, her entire family, and all the countless other souls.

"Ten years ago, there was a massive wildfire," Olwethu says between sobs. "The plants in this area are highly flammable so those of us in its path had to evacuate. Then the direction of the wind changed unexpectedly. There were families who thought they had more time because their houses were not directly in its path. They were killed. Before that, there was another wildfire that killed twenty, and before that, another ..."

I shake my head; I don't get it.

"It's what Aya always says—used to say—the extreme fire conditions are getting worse with climate change, so wildfires happen more frequently than they're supposed to." She's trying to comfort Sipho with a pacifier as she says, "If it's not the wildfires killing people here, it's flooding killing people in Somalia and Kenya, or Cyclone Idai that killed people in Mozambique, Zimbabwe, and Malawi—do you think all those souls are at peace? And what about those who remain?"

When the full weight of her words settles on my chest, I realize KwaNtuthu is a picture of a different type of horror.

A month has passed since I escaped KwaNtuthu. That night, I called uTata and told him I needed him like I did when I was admitted to Valkenberg, and he came without question.

"Make sure you fill in all these registration forms so the Dean can approve your change of course," the university administrator says. The badge of the University of the Western Cape is stitched on the left breast pocket of his golf shirt.

"Thank you." I take the forms. My scars snake along my forearms, visible as I'm wearing a yellow halterneck dress.

I walk across the university lawns, gripping my newly acquired forms and booklets; *Department of Biodiversity and Conservation Biology* is emblazoned across all of them—I know Aya would've loved this course.

I can't solve all the world's environmental issues, but I'll do what I can as long as I'm on this side of the living.

Hulderhola

Oliver Ferrie

LOCATION: Gaustatoppen, a mountain in Telemark district of Norway

POPULATION: The nearest town is Rjukan, population 3,022

I THINK about holding my boyfriend's hand but I don't. We're stood at the edge of the marsh, he's checking the map on his phone with one hand, behind us our friends are zipping up their windbreakers and locking the car, which is parked on uneven ground just off the beaten track, further down from the DNT visitor car park; it's cheaper that way.

It's the last hike of the season and I'm hoping this will make things better between us. Tore sometimes doesn't say what he means. I've been finding it hard. Behind us Gaustatoppen stands like a sentinel, the tallest mountain this far south. We wanted to climb it but it's late in the season, the weather is turning, it wouldn't be *safe*.

My friend comes up to join us. Her parents picked an English name for her, Myra, which means marsh or bog in Norwegian. She always shrugs this off like it isn't important. Tore taunts her as she steps down into the spongy ground. "Myra in the myr!"

Myra's boyfriend is called Svein—a perfectly ordinary Norwegian name—and he works so well with her, a left for a right, a to for a fro, that I can't help but feel jealous as he follows from the car, gentle and smiling, knocking Tore softly on the shoulder for his egregious pun as he passes by.

The way they both walk in the bog has a gravity to it, a steady centre, a self-assuredness that tugs me towards them, that makes me want to emulate it. Tore's a city boy, he's a long way from Oslo, and although it's far from the first time he's gone hiking, he stumbles a bit when he joins them on the sodden ground, gingerly and uncertain, like a child learning to cut vegetables with a kitchen knife too big for their hands. I read somewhere that nine percent of Norway is bog; that's almost every tenth step we take through this land, if we were to travel it in its entirety. He should be more accustomed than this.

But then, I realise, as I step down to join them all: I'm the same.

Maybe there's something about this area, then. Myra and Svein live here; the land is in their veins and not merely their footsteps.

I skip onto one of the wooden planks laid down by the DNT— the tourist association, wardens of the wilds—to avoid the mud sucking at my boots. I get ahead of Tore; I'm determined to do better. These planks track their way through the marshland (a lot of Norway is like this) although they don't cover everywhere. We've got the app, the map, the compass and all, but that's why Myra's also with us: she knows this place better than anyone. Her parents owned a farm here.

"So," says Myra, hand to her forehead, acting as a visor against the whiteblind mist, "Hulderhola."

I nod. "Hulderhola."

"Hell of a place to choose," she says, but her tone is approving. "I assume you've heard of the stories? It—"

Tore interrupts. "Annette saw pictures of it online." I don't turn around but I can feel the smirk. "She's got her heart set on it. I think even if we *could* go up the mountain today, she wouldn't want to."

"Is that so?" Myra smiles. It's a smile for me, and it's subtle.

"Well, you know what she's like when she's made up her mind." Tore's gruff voice makes me angry, but I don't show it. My friends laugh pleasantly; an indication they don't want to cause a problem. But I think they feel it too.

Svein speaks up. "We should get going. The weather is changing here, too."

I look around. It is mistier than it said it would be on the forecast.

Myra's humour is unshakeable. "All right, let's go. We might not make it all the way to the cave if the fog gets any worse, but remember, there's no shame in turning back. It'll still be here next year." She's quoting something called *fjellvettreglene*, the mountain code, a set of hiking rules grown customary and folkloric, to the extent that you find them printed on the backs of candy wrappers. There is no shame in turning back. Safety is paramount.

I understand the sentiment, but something about it makes me, perversely, want to tread further into danger.

The walk is slow going; the ground is a sponge and every flush step works the way running does in dreams, all heavy and delayed. In a nightmare, this makes the monsters catch up to you, this is always the way those dreams end. But in the chill paleness of day, I simply pull myself through it. There's no reason to fear.

I repeat this internally as the mist clusters in.

"It's steep near the top, but it's worth it," Myra says as the angle changes, as the cave cracks wide in the mountain ahead and becomes visible, a black pit in the rock face, an almost-rectangle with jagged edges. We're only a kilometre from where they parked the car, but already I can see more definition on the scree slopes leading up to the cave, and I feel her words. It's going to be a scramble.

"Maybe next summer we'll tackle Gausta itself," Tore says. It's meant to be hopeful, encouraging, I know it is, but I can't help but feel as if he is writing off everything on this side of the high-altitude valley.

"I like this side," I say quietly. "There's something lonely about it."

Myra flashes me a broad smile. We walk on.

I first met Myra at a mutual friend's party in Grünerløkka, the hip and eclectic part of Oslo. Said friend lived by Akerselva, a river that runs through the centre of Oslo, in an apartment block with the classic high ceilings and soft wooden floors, three stories high so it was easy to watch the nightlife clustering on the riverbanks below.

Myra was out on the balcony with a group of people; most of them were watching the drunk folks at the karaoke bar down by the water, making joyful fools of themselves, but she, she was watching the water itself, lit up by a gibbous moon. You can see the stars in Oslo, despite it being a capital city, and I remember that the constellation Orion was above us that night. I remember, too, the way Myra's eyes sparkled with the river's reflection.

"It's a perfect night," I said

She agreed. "Kind of makes you want to go skinny dipping, huh?"

We didn't go skinny dipping, but we did become friends.

We reach the first standing stone. Svein tells us it's not man-made, it's something called a glacial dropstone, a memory from the last ice age. All the same, it's hard to shake the idea that it was placed there with intent. It's a tall slab of quartzite speckled with lichen, sunk so heavily into the bog that a little pool has formed around it.

I walk up to it, and see a small frog gasping on the path. Its back leg, crushed by a boot. I set it near the water again. Tore laughs at me, but fondly. "You know it's just going to die anyway," he says. I don't think the others are paying attention, they are busy setting their backpacks down on the smaller satellite stones, pulling out thermos coffee and chocolate bars.

"I was going to tell you the story," Myra reminds me, once we're perched semi-comfortably on wet rock, sipping away and tucking our windbreakers closer to our bodies.

I nod enthusiastically, I tell her to please, do.

"There was a boy who lived here, years ago, back before my parent's time. They still spoke about him when they were growing up, over in Hovin—that's the other side of the lake—but, he ..." She trails off, turns her face to the wind so her cheeks can be stroked by the breeze. "He fell in love with a hulder, or so he claimed. And, well, once you've done that, you can't really take it back."

I don't require an explanation as to what a hulder is. Every Norwegian child has heard of her. She lives in the forests, in the hills, way out in nature, a strikingly beautiful woman prettier than the dawn over the mountains, but inside she harbours a soul every ounce as possessive as the strength of her beauty. If she decides she is going to marry you, then you are married. If she decides to defend you, you will never suffer another again. If she decides to destroy you, well, you never stood a chance in the first place.

I've seen the pictures—mostly the famous ones by Theodor Kittelsen—and it is these that paint themselves behind my eyelids when Myra continues the story. "He was young," she says, "and he grew up near the old church at Mæl. When he came of age, he would go up to Gausta to ski in the winter, and it was there he met Huldra. He never told exactly what happened that day, but he did tell his father it was a hulder he met. News spread at the church, but it didn't stop him from going back up the mountain, and indeed, his visits grew more frequent, and there was always a new excuse. He'd go to pick berries in the early autumn, even though there are better berry-picking grounds in Mæl; he'd go in the spring to clear the roads for the sheep, for their summer pasture, even though the shepherds were already working on it; he'd go in the summer to clear the pathways in the marsh, even though there was little interest in hiking routes at that time.

"His mind was captivated by the mountain, and nobody could convince him to stop visiting. At the same time, for he had a regular job at a local carpentry place, people began to notice that no ill luck ever befell him at work. It was as though he was protected by something, and they wanted to call it divine providence, but they dared not.

"Then one day he returned from the mountain sullen, as though a great argument had taken place. He was inconsolable to his family, and he drank and cried until late into the night. But then, the following morning, he went back to the mountain, as if by clockwork, only this time, he never came home.

"One of the shepherds claimed he turned into a sheep, but no one believed him. The disappearance was never properly explained, but my grandparents held true that he had upset Huldra, she who lives in the wilds, and he was merely reaping his just rewards. This is just ... something that happens if you do not have a healthy respect for danger."

"Or if you give up everything to be with the one you love," I respond. I say it almost without thought, not really knowing why I'm reading this as a love story rather than the horror it is clearly meant to be. I take a shot of coffee, suddenly self-conscious of the intriguing look Myra is giving me. "Your grandparents knew him. I'm sorry that he disappeared."

Myra nods. "I'm glad I told you the tale," she says simply, then she starts to pack up the snacks. It's time to continue on.

The path after the standing stone takes on a new dimension. The fog's growing stronger, and Tore doesn't stop picking at my faults. It's imperceptible to all but me, really, just soft little things that should mean nothing. "You should have bought better shoes." "Trust you to pick the miserable side of the valley." "Did you really drink all the coffee?"

To this last one, I grow acerbic. I say yes, I did it all on purpose just to irritate you. I suppose I can't help myself: if he is being light-hearted, he will take my response as so. As it happens, he huffs, and strides out ahead of the group. Ignores us. Gets on with the trip like it's a task and not a way to relax.

I hear Svein calling out over the moor, "We should turn back soon!" Something about the weather changing, about how our plans must change too. But I can't tell what direction he's yelling from. I can't see him at all. There's only Tore's bristling silhouette up ahead of me.

I grow fidgety, I grow belligerent. I don't want to pay attention to the voice of reason. So I take one cautious step out in the direction Tore is not going. It feels subversive, it feels powerful, it feels idiotic. I keep doing it. One foot after the other, sinking a little deeper each time, grasping for support at the knee-high willow and the flimsy reeds. One of my worst qualities is that I was always too stubborn.

And I think about things. Tore in the kitchen, Tore in the car, Tore backlogging his grievances, developing an arsenal instead of an apology. Me, wondering why I don't speak up more. Is there some-thing in my past that makes this harder?

This place opens my heart to it, makes me feel more clarity somehow. The red-yellow-orange of the low-lying berry bushes, the rainbow moss, the silvery knee-high willow trees that can barely be called trees at all, the long grasses, all punctuated by the white dots of bog wool. I could fall into it so easily. It feels smaller and bigger than myself at the same time, and I start to see the shape of my love. What I am putting up with.

I eat some berries. Krekling—crowberries—small and black and perfect. On the way up, Myra had told us that last year there was a drought and they were tough and leathery to eat. But this year, they grow in abundance, and I take my fill. Each berry bursts tart and sweet on my tongue. I sometimes wonder: what did we lose by moving down into the valleys and cities? Why can't we join the giants and become clouds again, like the myths say? I feel a burst of yearning in my chest, a sudden captivating idea that I could stay here forever.

I'm just trying to distract myself from the fact that I am lost.

Svein had said turn back, the weather's changing, and perhaps I should have listened to him. My belligerence will only get me so far, and, let's not lie, it is belligerence that brought me here. I start to feel a little bit scared, because it's cold out here, and I am alone but I really don't feel alone.

The boy vanished long ago. What did he get wrong? Or did he get something right?

I would worry that the same might happen to me, but I am not lovesick. I wish I was lovesick; I think that would make some things easier.

The first time I argued with Tore enough to break the china, it started like a snowball that grew to an avalanche without warning.

He misunderstood something I had said. It was a small thing, a silly thing, the colour of the walls in the living room. I had forgotten to pick up swatches from the hardware store, but I'd be going back after work tomorrow, unless he wanted to go now, if he had time, but we couldn't start painting today. I didn't know how to articulate myself, he was fractious, I think a lot had been going on that day. I am not very good at trying to understand.

I remember I got upset, and I told him so, and I left to go gather my breath in the bathroom.

A yell. And then it was the mug, my favourite mug, on the kitchen floor. He really didn't mean it; he was just as overwhelmed as I was. But even now, years on, I still replay it, try to figure out how I could have handled that better.

I can't see his silhouette any more when I look to my left. My inner compass tells me that in order to reach the cave, I must go further east, that's straight ahead of where I am now. I listen to it. I keep fumbling in the mist. The ground is so wet, sticking and slurping at my shoes, wetting my socks and slowing me down. Something is out there, watching me, and I don't like that I can't run properly.

Around me, the wind whips and I think I hear voices start to rise. They don't make any sense, they're almost outside of time itself, and I cannot tell what language, if any, they speak in. It's beyond my comprehension. So many things are. When people get mad, when they insult me, when I lack the language to fight back cleverly.

I sometimes worry that there is an unavoidable genetic trait, something passed down through my family. I think of my grand-mother, a million ways to be made small. She took that to the grave, and I'm not sure I want to do the same. My mind catches on the thought and it's a burr from a hedgerow on my trousers, it sticks and sticks until I can't see anything else, and I keep walking until even the idea of being lost loses meaning, until the fog sinks over my skin like a film that I can't peel away.

Yes, there's clarity out here, but clarity can also make you feel so very low.

Right as I am sinking into the depths of this nadir, I hear a shuffle up ahead. It's not like the voices on the wind, it's immediate and close and real. I look up. On the path ahead of me is a shape, all angles and limbs. I try to force my eyes to focus and it's like rising out of sleep. They don't want to. They would rather refuse what they're looking at. But I find myself entranced, because the angles resolve into a shape so wild and beautiful that I instinctively know what it is I am looking at and it's like I have become prey in the presence of a predator. I still myself.

She looks at me. I look at her. We hold this gaze for a long time, until the only things I can hear are the whistling of the wind around us and the plink of a water vole scurrying away somewhere behind me.

I have no such sense of self-preservation. I don't step away, and I don't step closer, but just watch her, my eyes searching for something in hers. She is completely naked, completely shameless. She moves like a parody of a human, but infinitely more beautiful, not-quite-right and yet more right than anything I have ever seen before. I take note of the colour of her hair: sandy blonde and bracken-brown all at once. It's curly, it falls into her eyes, and her eyes are so wide and focussed on me that she doesn't seem to care. The curves of her flesh are like nothing I know, and I find myself wanting to step forward, trace the smooth patch from waist to hipbone, because there is softness there amid the prickly exterior. Like a household cat, she might lash out.

I share that look, and I feel myself being searched the way I am searching her. She cocks her head, a starling considering a precious bauble on the pavement, and after a tense, precipitous moment, she breathes out slow enough that I can hear it on the whispering wind. She straightens up, twists her body, looks up to Hulderhola and back to me and slowly, like a beating drum is playing in the distance, starts to walk towards it.

She is expecting me to follow.

My feet start to move without my telling them to. I watch the sway of her cow's tail and I catch glimpses of the hollow hole in her back as the wind pulls her long hair this way and that; these are the only signs that she is not human. These, and the unhinged, feral way she moves.

I follow her. I see Tore's bootprints go off into the bog a little further down the track, but I ignore them. He has probably gone back to the car, or gotten lost further out. Either way, it's not my concern. He strode off, he didn't want to listen.

I'm the same, but I ignore that part.

I follow her.

The path-that-can-barely-be-called-a-path grows steeper and broken rocks scratch at my shoes as I climb. Should have brought better shoes. I push on all the same. She is faster than me, but she does not seem to fear that I will run away, and she scrambles up the cliffside like a demon possessed. Some fell creatures need the power of a lute or a violin to entrance their followers, but she has only her beauty. It's a clever thing, for it uses our own weaknesses and our own desires against us. There is no manipulation, there is no intentional misleading. There is only me, and my urge to follow.

At the mouth of the cave I find her, crouching on her heels, head cocked again as she watches the gathering clouds, waiting for me. Right as I reach the shelter of the rock, it starts to rain. The downpour is immense and happens all at once, an Arctic monsoon.

I grow quiet as I near Huldra. My soul grows still, but I keep moving forwards, and I become acutely aware that it is the opposite of what you are meant to do around, say, a bear. She stands up and stares at me deeply again, then the spell breaks and she runs off deeper into the cave.

I consider my options for a moment. I am aware that there is nothing that keeps me here in this cave, but it's safe and it's dry. I follow further up and further in.

The quartzite walls of the cave seem jagged in parts, but are easy to glide my hand over. It's not as dark as I had imagined, the rock is crystalline and even with the heavy clouds and the rain outside, it holds a strange luminance of its own.

Huldra is there. Crouched in a corner. She is eating meat off the bone. I think it's a sheep, I think I can see wool.

I tell myself it is a sheep.

She approaches me, wiping blood off her lips like smudged lipstick. She looks like if wild weather were a person, and I think she would destroy me if I let her.

Somewhere deep inside, I become aware that I want to let her.

I look back at the sheep carcass. I don't ask her what happened to Tore.

As she winds in closer, my thoughts eclipse and whatever sense of a horizon I have gets turned on its head as she approaches me and kisses me with the blood still on her lips. I am free floating and everything tastes like copper.

I'm aware I am running my hands down the sides of her torso, down to that no-man's-land between waist and groin and I can feel her softening in response as if she's geared up for exactly this moment and it feels—

Liberating.

That is the word that first comes to mind as I lose myself in the danger. I put my head into the lion's mouth and I say, "Let us be done with this," and renounce myself to fate.

Fate is a strange thing. It never does what you expect it to. I find myself surprised when she stops kissing me to brush the hair away from my face, to sit me down and attend to my sweat-slicked skin, because here I am, the perfect offering, supplicant and sublime. I'm not quite sure what I should care about any more, and that makes me all the more perfect.

But, as she gives me that look deep into my eyes again, I realise that she is not looking for desperation, she is looking for something that she herself can commune with and it is this, my burned and ragged soul, that she finds. Perhaps I am imagining all of this. But she does clean the wet from my face and she does keep me warm as the storm rages. It is almost as though I am drunk, I think, as I curl up in her embrace. This is something that feels so incredibly natural to me, but also so far outside of my current experience. I search for the words in my head, even as I realise I have not spoken a word outside of my head in hours now.

Peace.

My soul is at peace.

When the rain starts to slow, she stirs me from our cosy blood-soaked nook on the ground. We look out of the mouth of the cave together. From here we can see the distant tourist centre, the car park, the route winding up the mountains opposite, the towering peak of Gaustatoppen.

I would tell any other person my favourite fact: "You can see one sixth of Norway from the top of that peak!" Here, that information is pointless, is nothing she cares for. So I just stand there, watching, while my free hand seeks the comfort of hers.

She grips back, and in that grip I feel everything that ever truly mattered to me in life. I hold on, until it is unfeasible to hold on any more.

Back at camp, Myra smiles at me when I come back alone. "Did you find what you were looking for?"

For a moment her eyes seem more piercing than usual. Her whole form glints with a sharp edge. I smell crowberries and peat, and the promise of blood, somewhere far underneath. I look at Svein, busy grilling hotdogs on the tiny primus, then back to Myra again, and it's comforting to know I'm no longer alone. "Yeah," I say, "I think I did."

Silverheels

Rebecca E. Treasure

LOCATION: Mount Silverheels, Alma, Colorado, USA

POPULATION: 296

SOMEWHERE UP THE long slope of Mount Silverheels, an autumn breeze stirs. The trees take notice, shivering and whispering a secret from one to the other. The voiceless howl grows to a wind, sweeping down the valley, coming closer. As the wind nears like a train in the dark, Beth's skin tingles with anticipation. The wind sweeps cold through the cemetery, dying somewhere below, swallowed by the river or the highway.

Beth, in a too-warm sleeping bag, lays beneath the press of the galaxy above her. The unbelievable weight of the stars holds her eyes open, her body in place. The wind gives voice to the dead around her; lives lived in an endless rush, peak to valley, only to vanish forever. It has been doing this for hours and Beth is fascinated, terrified.

The girl in the stagecoach holds very still. The man opposite her is talking, casual and confident. It does not matter what he says, just that she listens. She

knows the type. The stage clatters to a halt in front of Billy Buck's Hotel and Dance Hall. The town of Buckskin Joe, what she can see of it in the dark, looks like an accident, like several thousand someones built their haphazard houses on haphazard streets without ever looking around.

Beth exhales, trembling. She's never slept outside before, much less in the middle of a ghost town cemetery. If she was alone, she would leave. For a moment, she swears she hears a violin. But her best friend, Jake, is with her and between not wanting to look weak and mostly trusting him to keep her safe, she stays.

"Are you okay?"

Beth winces. Of course Jake is awake, listening.

"I'm fine," she whispers. "The stars are unbelievable."

"Yeah," Jake breathes. Although Jake, at nineteen, is a year older than Beth, he never seems to know quite what to say to her.

Beth just wants a friend. Wants to be friends. But Jake wants more and doesn't seem to care or notice that Beth doesn't. She hates being afraid, does things like sleeping in cemeteries to prove that she's not, but lately she's started to think that maybe Jake should scare her, too.

The girl takes a breath, smooths her skirt with one hand, and steps out of the coach. In her right hand she carries an oblong case, in her left an old carpet bag that might once have been maroon. She holds the case to her chest like a shield as the man who was talking slicks out onto the dust behind her, too close. He leans down, whispers something in her ear that causes her to flinch and wrap her other arm around the case, and then, chuckling, pushes past her and into Billy Buck's. It didn't matter what he whispered. Only that she heard.

A snatch of violin in the wind. Something sad, with long slow notes.

"Do you hear anything?" Beth swallows.

Jake goes up on one elbow. "No. Why? Are you scared?"

He sounds eager, even hopeful. "No," she says. But she was. "I have to pee."

"I'll come," Jake says, unzipping his bag.

The quick offer sends a cold shiver up her spine. "I'm fine. I'll be right back." She wiggles out of the sleeping bag and pulls on her shoes, grabbing the flashlight. The stark mountain above the cemetery reflects enough moonlight to see, but she wants the comfort of the harsh yellow glow.

After a moment, the girl raises her chin. To the northeast a mountain draws her eyes. It is huge and silvery-white, sprawling and rocky and bare. It is almost obscene how bare that mountain is, naked in the moonlight. Daring. Comforting. But a mountain cannot be truly conquered, even if men drill into the dark depths and claim to have climaxed atop the peaks. In a hundred, thousand, million years the mountain would remain and the men all dust.

The girl is not a mountain.

Still, she's been hired by the innkeeper and she can't turn down a job. She keeps her chin up and forces her legs to stride into the hotel.

When Beth turns the flashlight on, it splashes across the melting, cracked tombstones, highlighting half-names and dates from a century and more before. She picks her way through the monuments. Jake sits up, his eyes glinting in her direction. Sleeping among the graves seems alright—they were mostly sleeping, too, and it isn't like they'd come to disturb anyone. They just wanted to be able to say they'd slept in the haunted cemetery, survived.

It was thrilling and nothing would come of it.

Twenty minutes later, she is perched on the edge of the stage, just out of sight. The old banjo player was delighted to hear a new musician had been hired, his aching fingers even more so. Now he sits at the bar sipping cheap whiskey and grunts in appreciation as the girl begins to play her violin. She'll do.

The girl's fingers are trembling but she knows that will pass. The man from the coach has already vanished upstairs. In the front there is a man with sadness in his eyes and she smiles, hoping her music will cheer him as she knows it will her. The music will sink into her muscles, her mind, and she'll forget about the bawling miners and the kicking women and the tobacco spit and the sour whiskey and the thumps from over her head and she'll just be the music.

After relieving herself behind a thick pine tree, Beth turns off the flashlight, willing herself to be unafraid in the silvery blackness. Stripes of moonlight dance across the pine-thick ground. Somewhere, an owl hoots. Maybe that had been the violin sound. A sensation like someone breathing on her skin grows at the base of Beth's spine, grows and intensifies. She is being watched. Someone is there, just behind her. She whirls, facing the empty woods. But she knows, down to her bones, she isn't alone.

There is a man sitting at a table in front of the stage. He saw the girl arrive and has not stopped watching her since. A blacksmith by trade, he is big and beefy and very, very lonely. The girl is small and wiry and maybe, he thinks, she is lonely, too. She sees his eyes as she plays, hungry and already with a sheen of gold greed, possession. She closes hers and plays herself away.

Some time later, she looks up and the banjo player has returned, offering her a plate of beans and a crust of bread. She thanks him. By the time she has cleaned her instrument and repackaged it in the aging case, the beans are cold. She eats them eagerly. When she hears a cleared throat, she looks up and the blacksmith is there, offering her a drink of whiskey. The good stuff, he says.

He does not like it when she declines, but lets her slip past him, back into the kitchen where she can sleep until she finds a room to rent. The blacksmith watches her go, desire hot in his eyes. The cook leaves the kitchen door open to the yard to let out the heat from the smoking pork and the endless pots of beans and the crust-heavy loaves of bread. Through the door the girl can see the mountain.

She sleeps, her violin case in her arms, occasionally opening one eye to reassure herself she is not alone. The mountain is there.

"Beth?" Jake's voice comes out of nowhere. Beth jumps.

"Shit. Sorry. You okay? I saw the flashlight turn off and—"

"I'm fine, Jake." Her voice crackles, letting more of her impatience with him show than usual. "Go back to sleep."

"I can't." His voice sounds so anguished, so heartbroken, that Beth softens.

"Why? What's wrong?"

He reaches out to her. His finger trails down her arm. She resists the urge to twist away. "I can never relax when you're nearby, you know that?"

Beth does turn away, now. "Just go back to bed." The wind rushes past on its way down the valley, and Beth closes her eyes, listening to the odd violin tones in the air.

"But why?" Jake's voice breaks. He steps close to her again.

His voice is too loud and god why is he doing this, they are good friends and if he'd just leave her be everything would be fine. The smell of pine and piss fills her nostrils, her fingertips sap-sticky where she'd propped herself against the tree.

"We're friends." Friends. But in the back of her mind, Beth feels the emptiness of the woods and wishes she'd not gone so far to pee and wonders if he would stop if she screamed.

"I don't want to be friends. Not just friends, Beth."

Now he sounds angry and Beth takes another step away. The back of her mind whispers to her that if she has to wonder if he'd stop he isn't really her friend, and then she is terribly alone and very afraid.

"I'm cold," she tries. "Let's go back."

"I'll warm you." He puts his arms around her.

She jerks away. "Stop it."

"Stop?" He laughs, bitter and hard. "I thought you were cold. Are you afraid of me?"

The girl and the blacksmith begin a delicate dance, one known by all women but that is somehow new to every man. She smiles but demurs, speaks but does not answer, declines but does not reject.

It is a dangerous dance, and the girl is losing. There is, of course, no way for her to win.

All the men but the blacksmith shrug at her refusals; there are many dancers and more willing partners. But the blacksmith only has eyes for her. She buys an old cabin with a front door facing the mountain. The blacksmith brings her flowers for her table, repairs the shutters as a surprise, and in what he is sure is a stroke of genius, makes her a pair of shoes with silver laid into the heels. She's never had a pair of new shoes before and they are beautiful so she wears them. She clicks when she walks, sparkles in the sunlight.

Silverheels, they call her.

Is Beth afraid of him? Yes. "No." The violin grows louder, almost nearby. "Do you hear that?"

"I—Yes. What is that? Is that music?" He turns.

Beth exhales, striding back to the cemetery while he is distracted. Cold jerks her body in violent shivers, sweat trickling down her spine. The music—melancholy, sweeping—fills the night. She turns the flashlight back on, stepping carefully over the barbed wire fence surrounding the graves. And then she freezes.

Opposite her, just inside the cemetery on the other side, stands a woman. A woman in a gown, her face veiled. Silvery. With the veil spreading down over her shoulders and an unusually wide skirt, she looks like a mountain herself, strong and bare and resolute. Beth gapes at her, and then, without being quite sure why except that she doesn't feel afraid and she is so glad someone else is here, she smiles.

Even through the veil she could have sworn the woman smiles back.

The blacksmith does not understand why the transaction has not concluded as he expected.

He grows insistent and the girl takes to barring her door, asking the banjo player to walk her home, taking her meals with the dance hall girls. The girl eyes the stagecoach each day with increasing determination.

But winter comes and with it two men who had no business being around others and soon half the town is covered in horrible spots, fevers hot as fire burning away the townsfolk and the miners and the dancers alike. The girl, somehow, is spared. She, like the mountain silver and cold with snow, stays clear, unblemished.

She cares for the sick, even the blacksmith. Her heart breaks for the suffering, the lives cut short, and she pours herself into the care. She plays her music for them, hoping to ease their pain. When the blacksmith recovers, he buys her a lace veil and asks her to marry him. He cannot understand why she says no when she'd been so kind when he was ill.

"Who the hell is that?" Jake sounds afraid, but Beth listens to the melancholy tune playing on the wind and can't quite bring herself to fear.

"It's her," she breathes. "The lady of the cemetery. Silverheels."

"Holy—" Jake is trembling behind her. "Let's go."

"Go? She's why we came."

"I want to go."

"Go then." Beth takes a step forward, raising her hand in greeting. She should be afraid. She had been, just a few seconds ago. Afraid of Jake. But this woman isn't going to hurt her. Beth can feel it. "Hello," she says. Could ghosts even talk?

The woman vanishes.

"Oh." Inexplicably, sadness wells in her and then Jake is behind her and she is afraid again.

"Was that real?"

"Yes. We both saw her."

"Let's go. We can sleep in my car."

Another cold chill runs up Beth's spine. There is a hunger in

Jake's voice. "You go, if you want. I want to see her again." She hurries across the cemetery to the sleeping bags and scoots down into hers before Jake can catch up. "Goodnight, Jake."

She pretends to be asleep. He knows she is faking, of course, but maybe he'll leave her be. She hears him slide into his bag, pull the zipper up. Heavy breathing that might be crying, or something else, is soon drowned out by the wind gathering itself up and rushing down the valley, and Beth falls asleep to the sound of music.

The town starts to recover. As the mountains melt and green things force their way through the cold crust of winter, life returns to normal.

Except the girl. Silverheels is gone.

She did not take the coach or the train. No one saw her go. Her cabin is just as she left it—even her violin is there. The blacksmith grieves, publicly. Too publicly. Suspicion falls on the blacksmith and he leaves town. The banjo player resumes his long hours with a sigh of regret. The dance hall sparkles a little less.

The rumors don't take long to start. A girl, they say, in a veil, wandering the graveyard at night. Sometimes, a scrap of music on the wind.

When she wakes, Jake is ripping her sleeping bag open, his hand on her mouth. "Don't ... don't talk. Don't ruin it." He paws at her and she is terrified and furious and his hand slips onto her neck and she can't breathe and he is so strong and she watches the stars. There are so many. She'd had no idea, her whole life, how many stars there actually were. Her vision swims and the stars blur, the wind smearing them across the sky.

And then the woman is there. Silverheels.

Silverheels screams, her mouth unhinged beneath the veil and her silver teeth gaping in the moonlight, but all Beth hears is music. Sweet, sad violin music. Jake falls away, howling, and then the woman moves, glitches like a scratched DVD and he falls silent. The woman turns back to Beth and holds out her hand.

Beth takes it.

The town remembers the girl who cared for them, the girl who suddenly vanished, and the mountain, that naked silver peak, is given her name.

When dawn spills over the valley into the cemetery, there are two sleeping bags, a flashlight, and the cold, unmarked body of a young man.

Someone hums, unseen, along with a violin.

The Salt

Lavie Tidhar & Nir Yaniv

LOCATION: Qumran Caves, The Dead Sea

POPULATION: -

Agent XII's Report

THE LAST TIME I had cause to visit the backwater province of Judea, I was but a young agent of the Imperial Office of Incognita Natura and Augustus still ruled in Rome.

Then, there had been some disturbing reports coming from the province, of a star—uncharted by any Greek or Roman astronomer—appearing for a time in the sky. My report then was inconclusive, and was no doubt filed away by the chief informer at the palace like so many others of its nature.

Now I was back, older and greyer and not much pleased about either fact. Augustus was long gone, and Tiberius, my old commander, now ruled in Rome.

My journey had been wearying. The ship from Tarentum was barely sea-worthy, and the winds were unusually rough for the season. It was with considerable relief that I found myself at last in the new port of Caesarea Maritima.

From there I made my way by land to Jerusalem, which sits atop the mountains and is a small, dismal sort of place, filled with rebellious Jews, dodgy expatriate Romans, dangerous Nabatean merchants, and lecherous Greeks—in short, a place much like any other in the Empire. I did not report to the prefect's office, for my department operates independently of the usual channels, and instead hired a room at a hostel within the city walls, well away from their tacky new temple.

I sat at the hostlery that night, sipping local watered wine, and kept my ears open for news.

I took particular note of tales coming in from the Galilee, where a young firebrand preacher was spreading a new gospel. This was no cause for unduly concern—these Jews were always arguing among themselves over arcane bits of scripture only they ever cared about in the first place—but I discovered this young man may have originated in the town of Bethlehem, which I had visited all those years ago. If a ... temporary manifestation did occur in that place, I was unable to discern it at the time, but I noted this information all the same. No doubt it meant little, but one likes to be thorough.

Of more immediate interest to me was my destination. It lay not in the Galilee this time, but to the southeast of Jerusalem, where the mountains turn into the desert and there lies a great salt sea.

It was there that the initial reports received in Rome suggested an event took place, and I listened with open ears to the travellers' tales, in the hope that they may shed further light on the subject.

The nights lie heavy on Jerusalem. It is a terrible city, old and filled with little roads that twist and turn and lead nowhere, and little nooks and crannies where shadows whisper in long-dead tongues. Too many centuries before us Romans, too many others came, and went, and were then gone ... All while the Jews remain, like stubborn rocks in the stream of time. I heard nothing further of use, and so I set out into the night.

I kept my hand firmly on my knife, you understand. Jerusalem is not a city for the unwary to trespass in.

"Oh, it's you."

He was older than I remembered. What was left of his hair was white and he had far fewer teeth, but the same fanatical light still shone in his eyes. His name was Eleazar, and he claimed to be a Maccabee, for all that that particularly troublesome dynasty had all but been wiped out by this time.

"Heard you were back," he said.

"How?"

He shrugged. "News travels," he said.

"I understand you work at the temple now," I said.

"The temple, the temple!" he said. "What do you Romans know of the Holy of Holies and the mysteries hidden there? The Area Quinquaginta unus," he said, and looked very pleased with himself. "But you wouldn't know anything about that, would you, agent of Rome."

It wasn't a question and I didn't answer. Eleazar was a gossip monger, a seeker of truths, a believer in things one had no earthly reason to believe in. He had been my guide into the Bethlehem Zone, but he had no more comprehension of what any of it really meant (the full details are locked in the vaults of the Imperial Office of Incognita Natura back in Rome).

It is said it was Alexander the Great who wept when he looked over his domain and saw he had no new lands to conquer ... But the way the tale is told by our agents, in the quiet of the mithraeum, when there is no one around, is different, and it tells of other lands, and other skies, and how Alexander turned back from the border in fright, for he had been offered a glimpse no human being should have suffered. Our department, it is said, is but the heir to the one Alexander first set up in Macedonia all those centuries ago.

"What have you heard of the salt sea?" I said.

"The sea of Lot," he said. "The sea of death. What of it? I hear its air is calming to the soul."

He was a shifty one, was Eleazar. I could see it in his eyes.

"What did you *hear*?" I said.

"Does Rome still pay generously?" he said.

I took out a small pouch of denarii. His eyes followed the money.

"What do you know?" I said.

"I know much," he said. "Oh, yes. I know ... I know of the burning bush out in the deep desert, which speaks in a terrible voice of the future and the past, though it is not always possible to tell which is which."

"The incident of the sanctus ignis was in Egypt," I said.

"All right," said Eleazar, a little testily. "How about the Urim and Thummim in the Breastplate of Judgment? Once belonging to the High Priest himself, each of the twelve stones contain great power, it is said. One for each of the tribes of Israel. The Egyptians took the breastplate after they burned Solomon's temple, but what no one will tell you is that it was cursed. The Urim and Thummim would not leave the land of Canaan willingly."

"Cursed," I said.

"*Cursed*," he said. "And so, over the centuries, it was found by wanderers and thieves and nomads, all of whom died in terrible ways shortly after, but not before moving it around a fair bit. Terrible deaths," he said, with some relish.

"Terrible," I said.

"Yes," Eleazar said. "But I happen to know for sure their last resting place."

I nodded tiredly. I did not have the heart to tell him the Urim and Thummim have been safely ensconced in the archives in Rome since before the Battle of Actium.

"Test me one more time, Eleazar, and speak truth," I said. "I know you know *something*."

He looked nervous at that. "Take your money," he said then. "I have no need for it."

"The money," I said, "or the knife. The choice is yours."

"Damn you, Roman!"

But he told me where to go.

The road down to the salt sea is steep and sandy. I had commandeered a couple of centurions from the local garrison and hired a Nabatean guide, two Jewish porters, and some camels.

How I hated camels!

It was eerie out there beyond the city. The hills with their pine trees and pale stone were soon nothing but a distant memory. The land shifted so abruptly that it was almost as though I were suddenly propelled into another, alien world.

Sand all around. The almost sheer drop, like into some sort of Babylonian Hell. Down and down and down.

They said that during the apparition of the Star, three wise men travelled from the east to Jerusalem, though who they were and who they truly represented I did not know. Perhaps in the land of Qin, or in India, they have an office much as the one I work for.

The Greek philosopher, Democritus, is said by some to be a founder of my office. His writing does not survive to the present day, and there's a reason for that. What does survive is locked up in Rome. Democritus was a proponent of what he called the Atomic Theory of nature. He was a great traveller, and lived and studied with the mathematicians in Egypt for a time, and with the Chaldean magi, too, it is said. Democritus proposed that the world is made of tiny atoms, which make all things. And he further believed that there were many worlds, in parallel to each other, some newly-born and some already ancient and decayed.

That first night we camped under the stars. I checked for the familiar, of course. We're trained to do so. I found Orion's Belt and the North Star and felt myself relax. In all my time on the job I had only ever seen the stars change once.

The camels chewed on blades of grass. A small fire burned merrily. And I thought of what scant information I had managed to extract from Eleazar.

The area of the great salt sea is mostly uninhabited. It is hot all year round and becomes all but unbearable in the summer months. It is surrounded by desert, with little water, and in the winter, it is prone to deadly flash floods. If whatever happened *happened*, then there would be very few witnesses to the fact, if at all. According to Eleazar, a merchant train coming in from Petra had witnessed, well, *something*, though by the time they'd arrived in Jerusalem they were not at all clear on what that was. I'd pressed Eleazar and he told me that the only people who lived near the salt sea were rebel sects—fanatics who abandoned civilization to live in isolation in caves in the mountains.

It was my hope therefore to make contact with just such a people.

The next morning the descent continued. I searched for signs of whatever happened—noting a sudden pool of water to the left of the road, where surely no water should be—and those rocks, tossed as by some unimaginable force and left in a great geometrically-intricate pile, far taller than a man—could *they* have been a sign of the whirlwinds recorded by Anaximander?

It was frustratingly hard to say.

My ears popped as we descended ever lower. At last a turn, and the sea came into view. It is remarkably flat and placid, and it is said that one cannot drown in the salt sea, for the water will ceaselessly lift and keep you afloat. I saw no signs of anything unusual beyond a sea where nothing lived, which is, admittedly, unusual. But not incognita, is my point.

We walked slowly down the twisting mountain road. At last, we came to a path where the guide stopped and consulted with the camel drivers.

"Up there," he said.

I looked up.

"*There?*"

He nodded, looking as unhappy about the fact as I was.

I stared.

Up a sheer sandstone cliff, I could just about make out the cave openings. High up, they looked like blind eyes, and I was discomfited by their appearance.

We climbed.

The route was long and arduous, following a trail that snaked round and round as we tried to reach the higher altitude. I could not believe anyone could live up there, could *choose* to live up there, in this lifeless, inhospitable region.

At last, we reached the top. The caves were just about accessible from up here, but night was falling, and we wordlessly agreed to camp for the night in the open air. We called to any occupants, but none answered. The area felt arid, devoid of life ... As dead as the sea below.

I found it hard to sleep that night. It was so very quiet up there on the mountaintop. Rome seemed a million miles away. I sat there, watching the terrible clear sky, and saw shooting stars fall down from the heavens and vanish in the distance, over that calm and life-less sea.

In the morning, I went into the cave.

The Testament of Joseph Son of Amram

Scroll found in Cave 8, Salt Sea Region, Judea, Reign of Tiberius. Collected by Agent XII of the Office of Incognita Natura.

I am Joseph, son of Amram. I am the only remaining one. I am not supposed to be here. I should have been in Jerusalem, all those years. Not here, in a bloody dead crypt in a dead cave above a dead sea in the heart of a dead land. That was not the life that I wanted. And this is not the death I wish. Give me any death but that.

Like Lot's wife, I had to leave the city in a hurry and never look back.

It had to do with a girl.

She was the daughter of one of the temple priests. A spirited girl, she knew her letters, and subsequently had more ideas than was healthy for her.

Or, unfortunately, for me.

"No," the girl said. "Not unlike Lot's wife, since that tale is a ludicrous sham. As if a woman would be that stupid. No, Joseph, it was Lot himself who turned into salt, of course."

This blatant blasphemy left me speechless. The girl, who was older and a fair bit more experienced than me, didn't let the silence linger.

"So," she said, "either you stay here and face the wrath of my father, or you go away quietly without making a fuss."

"I'm not returning to the Galilee!" I said.

"Who said anything about the Galilee?"

At this, again, I found myself unable to find a proper reply.

"It so happens," the girl said, "that there is need for a … a messenger, if you will, to go to the salt sea. A young man, and an industrious one, who is still looking for his own place in the scheme of things. Someone," she said, "like you."

"I …"

"There is a group of heretics there that Jerusalem would like to keep an eye on. They refuse to accept the ruling of the Sanhedrin. They will not be judged at the temple. They will not observe the Days of Awe."

"But …"

"A young man such as yourself should be able to join them, live with them, and study their ways. My father," she said, "would be most grateful."

"I am …"

"*Most* grateful." She smiled and leaned closer into me. She smelled of crushed flowers and sweat and her skin was so warm …

I left the city that night. Not caring much for the story of Lot, wife or otherwise, I *did* look back.

Foolish Lot, I thought, staring at the city lights for what I now know to be the last time. *I shall look back whenever I want! I shall return!*

But the fool, of course, was me.

No one would have wasted a good horse on someone like me, and therefore I had to go the whole way on the back of a mule. It took a few days to get there, and a few more to find the heretics, and to me it seemed like an eternity.

I recognized the value of the mule only after I lost it, having sloppily tied it for the night. It went on its own merry way along with all my provisions.

And thus, I did not exactly find the heretics. Unlike the twelve spies sent by Moses to the land of Canaan, I had none of the required qualities.

Instead, they found me.

"He is clearly a spy," said a loud rough voice. I slowly opened my eyes. I was lying on a stone floor. I was nauseated. My eyes wouldn't focus. A vague black shape loomed over me.

"Relax," said someone else from the other side of the room—the crypt. "Look at him. Since when is a spy so foolish as to be lost, alone in the desert, without food or drink?"

"The priests of Herod's Temple are cunning," the rough voice answered. At that I managed to focus my eyes, and saw a mountain of a man leaning menacingly over me.

"Let him be, Nekamot," said the other voice.

Nekamot? I thought uneasily. It is a word meaning "vengeance," but it is not—should not be—a name. I did not like the sound of it much.

They argued for some time whether to kill me or not. Eventually the other man, whose name I learned was Yehuda, managed to tame his colleague, and I was saved. For the moment, at least.

"I have but one question for you," said Yehuda, "you have your letters?"

I nodded.

"Nekamot will be disappointed," said Yehuda, "but you may serve us yet—and rather well, I think."

My sole attempt to escape—one summer night on the back of a stolen donkey—almost cost me my life. It took five people to restrain Nekamot from breaking my neck. One of them limped for a considerable time afterwards.

My fate was worse.

"We are the chosen ones," said Yehuda, in one of his frequent visits to the small alcove in which I was left to lie, in the hope that the bones of my legs and arms will eventually heal.

"I know," I said.

"No, you don't. All the sons of Israel call themselves the chosen ones, yes, but we are the only ones who *were* chosen."

"Well ..." I said.

"Would you honestly say that the sinners in Jerusalem are worthy of the title?"

I shook my head. Sinning in Jerusalem was, to me, a sweet yet painful memory.

"We are the true sons of the light," Yehuda said.

"Even Nekamot?" I said.

"He serves the greater purpose. As will you. I have a task for you," Yehuda said. This was accompanied by a creaking noise caused, I saw after painfully turning my head, by a small cart entering my crypt, carrying a large pile of old scrolls.

The cart was upturned. The scrolls slipped to the ground. Cart and bearer left us.

"These," Yehuda said, pointing at the scrolls, "are the *other* histories of our people. The ones not recorded in the scrolls of Herod's Temple. The tales deemed best forgotten, lists of occurrences, accounts of self-proclaimed prophets and outcasts and fools."

"Very interesting," I said.

"Not really. But useful. Start reading."

He took something out of his robe. "Here."

It was a water skin, half full, and a small loaf of bread.

"Why?"

"We are not cruel. You will need to eat."

"No," I said. "Why should I read it?"

"Whatever it is that you find, it's for the greater purpose," Yehuda said, and turned to leave.

"What am I looking for?"

"A key," Yehuda said, and left.

I stared at the pile of scrolls and the small loaf of bread.

There was nothing to do but read.

The next day I got a fresh supply of scrolls and another stale loaf of bread.

And the next day.

And the next.

The scrolls were interesting, in their own blasphemous way. Among them I found the ramblings of Enoch, who claimed to have accompanied the angels to the seven spheres beyond the sky, where the sun and the moon pass through heavenly gates in their ever-changing journeys above the earth.

Other scrolls included lewd and obscene details of the lives of King David and King Solomon, often surpassing even those of the official Hebrew scriptures. At least three scrolls claimed to be written by Moses himself, and all contradicted each other.

Days became weeks, then months. My broken bones healed, mostly. The supply of scrolls never dwindled. Some scrolls contained merely the old scripture as I knew it in my childhood. Oh, how I missed that time now, and my carefree life in my little village in the Galilee.

I was quite bitter by the time I reached the familiar story of Sodom and Gomorrah, and Lot.

And the months became years.

My hair grew. My beard, untamed, got in the way of everything. My eyesight weakened. But eventually, a pattern emerged. Vaguely at first, a phrase I read in the spring reminded me of a scroll of the previous summer, then one tale directly led to another.

Various messiahs in different times, anywhere between the return of the Israelites to Canaan and the completion of the second temple, claimed to have prevented a calamity, to have argued with God and averted the end of the world.

Others claimed that the end of the world has already happened.

As weeks and months passed, the pattern became clearer. The world has already ended. Numerous times.

The world ended with Noah. The world ended with Lot.

The world ended with Lot, who was foolish enough to lose either his wife or his life by means of looking back on the destruction. *Then God rained on Sodom and Gomorrah sulphur and fire from God out of heaven.* But was it indeed heaven, or hell, or another place altogether?

Yehuda visited me again. For a long time I just talked, relishing the presence of another human being.

"I think you already know," he said after I've finished. "You just refuse to accept it."

"Tell me!" I said.

"Now my eyes are open and my ears awake, to hear the prayer of this place," he said, quoting God's response to Solomon.

Damn him!

But do you know, as I listened, I think, for just a moment, that I *heard* it.

I do not know how many days or years passed. In time, within the pattern that I found, another one revealed itself. Coded in times and places, in verse numbers and first letters, in common names and initials that pretended to mean one thing but in fact referred to another, a message.

Go from your country and your kindred and your father's house to the land that I will show you, says God to Abram. *Take your wife and your two daughters who are here, or else you will be consumed in the punishment of the city*, says God to Lot. *Go!* God urges Moses. And so on, all across the scripture.

And the numbers, a time, a year, a month, which I tried to avoid but could not.

"The time is nigh," I said, and Yehuda smiled and nodded.

"Will you free me?"

"And let you miss the end of the world? I hardly think so."

"The end of *a* world," I said, "is but the beginning of another."

"Oh, the world will end," Yehuda said softly, "and with it the sinners in Jerusalem, the heretics in Safed, the ungodly Romans, the filthy Greeks. It will end, and only we shall remain."

"Like Lot," I said.

He gave me a strange look, then smiled again. "Yes, like Lot," he said.

I did not see any point in correcting him.

The end was near, I knew it. I felt it. There was only one thing to do.

I started to write.

I am Joseph, son of Amram. I am the only remaining one.

Here, at the end of the world.

Would you like me to describe it? Would it help? Was this the fate of Lot, reading of heavenly sulfur showers only to run away from them, then be consumed by them?

I shall write while I can still hold a reed. This is why they kept me here, after all.

To bear the last witness.

It begins with a tremor. A light one. If feels as if a heavy object fell to the ground somewhere nearby. Maybe something like those huge marble tables I saw once in Jerusalem. But there are no such luxuries here in the cave, and while a heavy fall would be a single, brief occurrence, the tremors ... continue.

Then there's the dust. It falls from the ceilings and slides away from the walls and gently rises from the floor. For a moment, it is as if a smaller copy of the cave manifests itself around me, brown and gray and insubstantial.

Somewhere outside my little isolated crypt, closer to the opening of the main cave, someone screams.

There's the sound of running feet, followed by a gust of wind, which should be impossible here, this deep inside the mountain. It cannot be, but it is here, and I hear the sound of a huge slab of rock being torn apart.

Then there's light. An angry red glow emitted from somewhere above me, though its exact source is obscured by the dust.

"This is all wrong!" Yehuda cries, standing at the door of my crypt. Behind Yehuda I can see the looming shape of Nekamot. "The end of the world should not happen like this!"

Not the end of the world, I want to tell him; but the beginning of another.

It is the end, I know. Nekamot turns, this way and that. His eyes fasten on me, and there is hate in them. He will be unrestrained this time, taking his revenge upon my carcass. I shy from him in fear.

Only he does stop. He seems confused. Yehuda opens his mouth, but nothing comes out. For a moment, there's no movement.

Then Nekamot is lifted by a gust of wind, something half invisible and incredibly powerful. He is hurled through the door, faster than a racing horse, faster than a stone thrown from the top of a mountain.

"Why?" Yehuda cries. "Why, God?"

But there is no answer, and he runs away.

I hear his voice one last time, and then a crack of thunder, a tearing of rock, a desperate scream and the wet sound of a water skin exploding.

Only that skin holds blood, not water.

Something burns. I can hear its crackling, I can see the smoke, thick and red. But I cannot smell it. Maybe I am just overwhelmed. Or maybe, here at the end of the world, smell does not exist anymore. I am thankful for it. I have no wish to be acquainted with the smell of burning people.

The ground keeps shaking for a long, long time.

I am in my crypt, deep in the cave. Gone are the screams and the noise of fat consumed by ungodly fire. Gone are the people who awaited here the end of the world, and did not realise it was another world merely intruding, momentarily, upon ours.

They are gone, taken by the otherworldly winds.

Only the smoke remains, thick and red and entirely odorless, crawling slowly inside the cave, flooding my crypt. It whispers to me. I welcome it in.

I breathe in the smoke and taste salt.

Agent XII's Report – Concluded

After reading the scroll I carried out a search of the entire cave network. There were some small signs of habitation, old fires, a smashed clay pot, old scrolls tossed here and there, the bones of oryx and onager and gazelles, the shells of wild turtles.

There was no sign of the cave's residents.

A strip of grey cloth, snagged on a nail, caught my attention. Looking at the ground I saw the mark of footsteps going deeper into the cave, the feet coarse and misshaped as though the person had suffered in the past a brutal accident that left him maimed.

I followed the marks of passage, noting with disquiet where he paused, as though to rest, a blackened handprint on the wall, then turned to face the cave opening and, as far as I could tell, resumed walking backwards. As though it were facing up to something that was following him, and kept retreating until at last he had to stop, his back to the wall.

The footprints ended in the furthest reaches of the cave, in one final, tiny room, and there they stopped.

The dust lay undisturbed.

Of the man himself, there was no sign.

But as I turned, a flash of light caught my eye. It was dim inside the cave and yet, there it was again.

Then I saw it. For a moment I nearly fell back in fright, for staring back at me from a hidden alcove was a terrible face, bulbous eyes glaring at me balefully, the mouth open in a horrid rictus of a grin.

I cried out, then regained my balance as the figure didn't move. Slowly, I approached—then I saw it.

I almost laughed in relief. It was merely a statue, though remarkably intricate, of a man with his mouth wide open and his nostrils flared, and his eyes staring with a sort of maddened acceptance.

I lifted it up, for all that it was surprisingly heavy. The material felt coarse and unpleasant in my hands. Something sharp dug into the tip of my finger and I cursed and dropped the idol.

When I put my finger to my mouth, I tasted salt.

Nothing else in the cave remained. I bagged the scroll, and placed the salt figure in a lead-lined box to be sent back to Rome.

As we departed on the long climb back to Jerusalem the light gradually faded and, on the precipice of the steep incline I could not resist but turn and look back one last time.

The sea lay as flat as a mirror, and overhead I could see a redness burn out through a rip in the sky, like the promise of another world peeking through.

But it was only the setting sun; after a moment I turned back from it and then we were over the rise, and the world beyond vanished from sight.

Three Ways to Break You

Beth Dawkins

LOCATION: Monroe, Georgia, USA

POPULATION: 15,673 (2022), 11,858 (2003)

August 2000

AT FIFTEEN, my name appeared on a bench inside a park. In the 1950s, the bench had replaced a boulder where the names of the cursed were listed. Some were carved into the wood and others were in thick, black ink. Each person listed couldn't leave town unless they committed, what we called LCS: *Lie, Cheat, and Steal.*

On the right side of the bench, right where someone's ass would go, was my name, Casey Lowe, in black ink. The lettering was long and stick-like.

Up close, I recognized some of the other names, but I didn't know everyone. Monroe, like many other failed mill towns, has two sides—those who have money and those who don't. The wealthy inherited land from the generations that came before. They lived in gigantic old houses with manicured lawns, and likely a handful of ghosts. Their names were on the bench too. They might go to the prep school on the hill, but they're just as stuck.

"You're one of us," Marc, my cousin, said.

My stomach twisted.

Marc's steps crunched in the gravel towards the car. I could hear him light a cigarette.

I wondered what the font was called. Did the bench *do* official fonts?

The bugs squealed. It was late summer—I'd be back in school in a couple days. I wanted to apply to colleges. I had the grades and in any other place, maybe good grades would be enough.

I licked my lips and swallowed back the tightness of unshed tears. "How do I start?"

"You can't be serious?" Marc's name was there, but harder to find because it was under the table.

A year ago, he'd started to try to get out. The lie, he said was the easiest, but it had to be important. I couldn't tell a stranger that I was a toaster, abducted by aliens, or a lizard person.

"You said that Wyatt got out. Eric too." I knew of people who got out, but they were all older.

"Listen, it's best to stay low for a year. You ain't the only one that will be playing the game. They get desperate." He tilted his head back and blew smoke into the night sky. "Plus, is it really that bad here?"

Marc was skinny, three years older, with a too-young-for-him girlfriend. His Adam's apple bobbed up and down. The stars spread out over us. Tiny dots poked in black.

"Maybe the most honest people stay behind," he mused. "Think about it, Case. I never cheated. I never stole a dime."

The back of my eyes stung and there was a lump in my throat. I kept my flashlight on the bench seat. I'd hoped that because my daddy was from out of town, my name wouldn't be on there, but it was.

"You stole your momma's wallet to get money for Winter," I argued because it sounded like Marc had given up.

Winter was his German Shepherd. Aunt Lynn told the story at every holiday. I'd never figured out why she was proud of Marc for that.

Marc laughed. "You got me, but it didn't count. Let's go see if your momma's got a cake."

I reached down and ran my pointer finger over my name.

August 2003

None of my lies counted. Marc never told me what he'd lied about, only that once he'd told it, the lie released a grip in his knees he hadn't known was there.

I sat in my narrow room, headphones on, with a list of school supplies. I'd taken the SAT and the ACT and scored high enough for financial aid.

Out my window, I could see the flash of blue police lights. It wouldn't be the first time they'd used our driveway to pull someone over.

I was rolling around ideas of how to cheat on my college applications. Using the system against itself. I'd end up in debt up to my eyeballs if I went, even with financial aid, so why not fuck them if I could? Fair was fair.

The front door's hinges screeched. I thought it was Momma. It was unlike her to be awake at this time of night.

I heard a voice, and then footsteps.

"Shit." I closed my notebook and stuffed it under my blanket.

There was a knock on my bedroom door, but the knock didn't wait for me. Momma twisted the knob fast and hard. "Come out here."

"What do they want?" I asked. My stomach lurched up towards my throat. Her lips were pressed down and together. We had the same tightness about our shoulders.

"They're looking for Marc."

I'd seen him earlier. We'd gone to his co-worker Tad's house for grilled pork chops. Marc had described Tad as a straight with a step-daughter my age. Tad was renting in town but swiftly regretted it. He'd closed the grill lid as Marc lit a cigarette and then handed me the lighter to do the same.

"You can't let him smoke here," Tad had said, pointing metal tongs at me.

We'd both laughed. It was a cliché, everything about Tad could've sprung from a television show about a happy family.

The television illuminated the living room and kitchen. The cop held open the screen door, leaving the wooden door open. I bet my momma told him to wait on the porch. Like an asshole, he'd hold the screen door open to inspect the inside and let bugs in.

"You wanna come outside?" he asked. He held a flashlight, pointed at the ground. "It's alright, you're not in trouble. We just got a couple questions."

The trick to cops, at least around here, was to treat them like rainbows shine out of their asses and add a healthy dose of fear. They confuse fear with respect.

"Momma, will you turn on the light?" I didn't want to go outside, it made it easier for them to figure out how to arrest me and an arrest might destroy any chances I had of financial aid.

The cop backed out as I touched the screen door. The porch and kitchen light flickered on. Moths and beetles flew around our heads. Curtains fluttered from our neighbors' windows.

Another officer stood at the bottom of the porch as a cruiser sped down the road, braking hard and pulling past our driveway into the grass. Its headlights illuminated the porch.

"Turn that shit off, Harrison," the cop at the bottom yelled at the cruiser.

He smirked, enjoying the show as he started towards the car. I assumed Harrison drove it.

I knew the name Harrison, all of us did. He'd killed a kid a couple years younger than me. The kid, unarmed, was shot three times in the chest. It never made the news other than a passing mention. As far as I knew, nothing had happened to Harrison.

"Listen," the cop in front of me said, clicking off his flashlight. "Have you seen Marc today?"

My scalp tingled, and I opened my mouth, knowing better but still the question poured out, "Why?"

The cop squared his shoulders and his eyebrows leaned in towards his eyes.

"Is he okay?" I asked, trying to recover.

"I know you were with him today," the cop said. "You're not in trouble, I just need you to tell me the last time you saw him?"

Well fuck me running.

"I haven't seen him."

And then a weight lifted from my knees. It was a relief on the cusp of pain. I almost sank to the porch. I'd just told *the* lie. I locked both knees in place to keep from melting into a puddle of goo.

The cop came back with Harrison, who was younger and shorter than the other two.

"Did something happen to him?" I asked about Marc.

"Casey, isn't it?" the cop asked. "This will go a lot better if you just tell me where you last saw him. I don't want to have to arrest you for obstruction of justice."

Harrison cracked a smile that faded as my momma stepped onto the porch.

She crossed her arms over her chest. "Unless y'all are taking my son with you, I suggest y'all leave now."

"Listen, ma'am, we need you to go back inside. This doesn't concern you."

Her eyebrows shot up. "Casey, come back inside."

"Ma'am." The use of the word had changed.

"Arrest him or leave."

I was put in the back of the car. They let Harrison do it.

I'd never been so close to shitting myself as when he shoved my cuffed hands down into the back of his car.

October 2003

The cops found Marc's body in a dilapidated house without any doors or windows. It sat in the woods, on a dirt road that headed out towards a tiny town called Good Hope.

I'd spent a night and half a day at the police station back in late August. The cop's hot breath had spilled into my face as he uttered threats and said, "You know something about that night. You should do yourself a favor and tell us now."

I'd admitted that we went to Marc's coworker's place and then Marc drove me home. We'd left when Tad had gone red-faced and told Marc, "You better get your cousin before my foot does."

I'd smiled at him, cocky and full of disruption.

I doubted straight-lace Tad killed my cousin, but someone had.

"Your Aunt Lynn says they're releasing Marc's body," Momma said as she crossed the living room to put the phone back in its cradle.

They'd held his body for three weeks after they'd found him.

"Does Aunt Lynn have a funeral place?"

"Honey." There was a pause that was taken over by a shampoo commercial. "Go over there."

I walked over. She lived down 6th Street and kept a variety of hanging planters on her tiny front porch. The screen door was broken on one side, sticking out towards the visitors as if someone had kicked one corner in from the other side.

I knocked but Aunt Lynn didn't answer. Her car was there along with a couple other visitors.

"Casey," Heidi said, swinging open the wooden door beyond the screen. "Oh, Casey!" She threw her arms around me, pulling me down towards her. Heidi was my aunt's girlfriend. They didn't live together but had been in a relationship for the past ten years.

Winter, Marc's German Shepherd, nosed my hand, licking me for pets.

I patted Heidi's back, smothered by her perfume that was powdery sweet and spicy at the same time. I pulled away, giving Winter pets and scratches.

"It's just awful. They've released his body but both funeral homes can't receive him, yet. The Health Department claimed Lynn didn't submit some paperwork." Her brown eyes welled up with tears. "She shouldn't have to be dealing with all this. Did your mom come with you?"

"We'll figure it out," I said, trying to make myself sound older than eighteen. "Where's Aunt Lynn?"

Heidi frowned, her eyes shimmering with unshed tears. She didn't ask about my momma after that.

"There you are," Aunt Lynn said from the kitchen. She had a notebook in hand with a pen. "Come in here. Heidi, would you mind fixing him something to drink?"

Aunt Lynn was a tall wiry woman who Marc used to say was "Anti-nonsense."

"The funeral home should have the death certificate but the Department of Health is claiming they didn't receive the vital record," she said. Her red-rimmed eyes strayed to the notepad with a list of numbers, cemeteries, and funeral homes. "I'm sorry. How are you doing, love?" she asked.

I cracked.

Marc was who I talked to. Who I'd played with growing up and who I shared everything with.

My momma hadn't asked and for some reason that one question made the back of my throat hurt. Prickles of unshed tears swam to the surface.

Aunt Lynn placed her hand on top of mine, tears falling down her cheeks. An involuntary choking sound came unbidden from my throat and for a handful of minutes we cried, as if our pain was made of the same substance.

Heidi set down two glasses of sweet tea once our tears dried. Our weeping didn't go without words. She reassured me that I was like a brother to Marc and I told her that Marc loved her best.

"No, honey. He loved Winter best," she said and we both laughed.

I took the pen. I'd figure this out for Marc.

"They said they lost the form but made it sound like I'd never filled it out, and now someone out there is going to steal Marc's identity." Her hand slapped the table. Heidi and another one of Aunt Lynn's friends stopped in the doorway.

"Okay. Go in there with them. I'm going to make sure we have this squared away. I will let you know if I—"

Aunt Lynn grabbed the notebook and was taking out Marc's documents. She swallowed as her long fingers traced over his birth certificate. I reached out and grasped those fingers.

"I got this," I assured her.

She nodded, leaning down to kiss my head. "I love you."

I dove headfirst into hold times and Marc's paperwork. I had to fill in information I didn't know, and at times outright lie. It happened on my third call with the DOH. I was claiming a date when my aunt had put in the information when warmth spread over my shoulders. My muscles relaxed, and there was an unhinging. It was a box, rusted shut for ages that someone had opened inside of me.

I'd cheated on tests, papers, anything I could think of to break the curse but it was cheating on Marc's official paperwork that mattered.

"Yes, sir. I see it in the system. We will go ahead and get that taken care of for you," the voice said on the other end of the phone.

"Thank you," I whispered. My throat closing up with tears all over again.

November 2003

On my way to AP Lit, I saw Tad's daughter with Kim. Kim was cursed, like the rest of us. We'd shared the same classroom in kindergarten. I caught both their gazes when Tad's daughter, Emily or Emma or Amelia, took off in the other direction.

I headed after her.

A month had passed since we'd buried Marc and we were no closer to figuring out how he'd ended up in an overgrown house on a road that saw, maybe, one car a day.

No.

She wasn't getting away.

Emily or Emma or Amelia turned the corner. She was fast, but I had longer legs. She darted into the library. I fast walked between the rows of shelves, turning the corner where her books spilled on the ground and she leaned over panting.

"You know something," I hissed, a little out of breath.

"You're fast for a smoker," she said, with condescension dripping at the end of the sentence.

"Yeah, well, I know Marc drove back to your place that night."

"He talked to my stepdad."

"No shit," I said. "And then he ended up dead."

I followed her gaze to her books, three notebooks and a text book scattered at my feet. I leaned down and started to pick them up.

"Give them back."

"Calm down." I stacked them in my arms. The textbook was for a history class. The first two notebooks were full of notes, but the third, the one with the deep blue cover, had letters and lists, things that were personal in an array of different colored ink. It might contain what she knew or didn't know.

She hesitated in front of me. "For what it's worth, I'm sorry about your cousin. I only met him that one time but my stepdad used to talk about him. I think they were friends."

"Thanks," I said as the bell went off overhead. In less than two minutes we'd be late for class. "I don't understand why you took off."

We walked out of the library together, neither in a rush.

"I thought you might be mad or want to hurt me."

"What?" I glanced into her brown eyes. She had eyeliner all around her eyelids.

"This place is different. I'm never sure what to expect."

Different meant those that were cursed. Different meant the lie, cheat, and steal.

"I'm not violent," I muttered.

I was mad that she was scared. Mad to be stuck and not know *why*.

The thing was that no one could give a clear answer as to why. I'd asked and there were rumors: A witch, a demon, a ritual gone wrong, a sheriff shot in the chest on his front porch in the middle of the day, or an entire family burnt to a crisp. I lived and grew up without a clear answer, but it didn't mean life stopped.

It wouldn't be hard to steal that blue-covered notebook and know what she knew. I waited for her outside of her history class last period. I waved as she came out the door.

"What are you—"

"Do you ride the bus or drive?" I asked, cutting her off before she finished her question.

Her eyeliner had smudged below her left eye, and it made her appear edgy instead of preppy. I liked it.

"I get a ride with a neighbor."

"Good. I'll drive you home. Meet me in the parking lot?"

I didn't think she'd agree, but there was a smile starting to form on her lips. "Okay."

I took the bag that was hanging off her shoulder.

"What are you doing?"

"Being a gentleman." I smirked and she smiled. This was way too easy. "Do you know what car is mine?"

"The small white truck?"

"I'll see you there." I almost winked at her but I wanted to get to the truck.

I hurried to the parking lot, opening her backpack. The notebook was there. I put it in my bag and then tossed both in the bed of the truck. They landed beside a bicycle wheel I swore I was going to put air in. Beside it were three plastic planters that had come from Aunt Lynn's. I'd been helping her for a couple weeks around the house.

I started the truck and turned on the heat.

"Kim promised you weren't going to leave me for dead in the woods," Emma said getting into the passenger side.

"No. Already had one family member left out there."

Emma rubbed her hands together, glancing out the back window. "Sorry. I shouldn't have made that joke."

"I'm sorry my heat isn't working right." I leaned across her and opened the glove compartment, taking out a pack of cigarettes.

She rolled her eyes and the curse broke. It wasn't in my knees or my shoulders. It started in my hands, a lightening, the moment I put the truck into drive. It rolled through my shoulders and into my chest, it gripped the back of my neck and was gone.

I was free for stealing a notebook.

I could drive right out of town.

I could go to college.

Gray stones and metal plaques shone from the gravesite where Marc was buried. Fake orange flowers sprang above his name. The sun was inching down as I explained to Marc how I'd drove out of town three miles.

I was no longer cursed.

I'd attempted to walk out a week after I discovered my name on the bench. Marc had drove me out to the line we couldn't cross. Full of fire and spit I'd marched past the line and woke up on the living room floor.

"That's not why I'm here." I held up Emma's notebook.

Inside wasn't a diary, but letters to her real dad. Between the letters were lists of songs—playlists she could burn, along with random notes. On some pages was a list of names, none of which I understood. There was what I believed to be quotes and movie titles.

And then, in the middle of the notebook, something changed. She started to date the pages and note every time someone said something strange around her. She didn't know it but she was trying to put together lie, cheat, steal.

I flipped forward, wondering if she had figured out what it meant when I saw the name Harrison. He'd bruised my arms when he put me in the back of his cruiser. He was friends with her stepdad, apparently Harrison was stuck like the rest of us, but there were rumors that had changed last month. I'd heard he'd got a house in Good Hope.

"You know the LCS kids are always in trouble. You can't trust them, and if I was you, I'd make sure none of them come around," she'd wrote in quotation marks. This was dated a couple days before Marc drove me out to her place.

On the back of the page was a list of names of those cursed around our age.

My name was on it. There was a star below mine that listed Marc's name, spelled wrong with no last name.

I lit a cigarette and glanced down at Marc's name. "What the fuck were we doing at this chick's house? Why is your friend chummy with Trigger Finger Harrison?"

Marc stayed in the ground.

I licked my lips and flipped the page. She didn't give a shit my cousin was dead. She was interested in the curse. She listed other things. Questions about things she'd overheard. She believed her stepdad and Harrison were involved in something. Marc had thought that her stepdad was a straight, getting high on having someone edgy and vulgar around, but the truth I was coming to believe was that Harrison wanted to make him an informer.

After you've been in and out of county, depending on the crime, someone will come out and you'll know to keep shit to yourself. Either way her stepdad had mentioned Marc's body being found.

She wrote, " 'That body.' Marc?"

I stood up holding the notebook. This was evidence.

"I'm going to figure this out," I told Marc and headed back into my truck. My heart pounded and my hands vibrated. I had to get the notebook to an investigator. Aunt Lynn would know who was on Marc's case.

I drove through town, past the old court house and its statue. I turned up the side of the gas station where we'd buy single cigarettes for a quarter while under age. On the other side of the street was the fire station. I drove out towards the park where my name had disappeared from a park bench. Along the way was a collection of once beautiful homes flaking white paint, their roofs growing moss.

Right before the park entrance, blue lights flashed behind me. I hit my blinker, pulling into the park.

My palms were sweaty as I stopped the truck. I gripped the wheel. It wasn't the first time I'd gotten pulled over, but each time panic settled low and cool in my gut. I tried to go over if there was anything illegal in the truck or if I'd just done something questionable. It was automatic, but as far as I knew there was nothing.

I heard the cop shut his door and remembered then to get my wallet out of my pocket.

I started to roll down the window, it was an old crank, and then there was Harrison with his gun out, yelling at me to stop moving.

I wanted to scream or cry or run.

There pointed right at me was a hole in the world that led to oblivion.

He was yelling but I couldn't hear him. There was a rush behind my ears and I couldn't keep my eyes off the end of the gun.

And then it was pointed away.

"Are you trying to fuck with me?"

"I was getting my license."

He pointed a flashlight in my face. "I think you better get out of the fucking car."

"Sir?"

"Did I stutter?" he asked as he opened the door.

For a second, I couldn't move. I pulled my hand out of my back pocket. The barrel of the gun came back around.

"Let me see your hands."

"Sir, I—"

"Let me see your fucking hands."

I started to move, obeying his command so he didn't kill me. I slid my hand back around and there was a huge boom and a hot punch skidded across my stomach. There was the flash of blue and white and another boom.

I was on the ground a weight on my back as pain pressed into my stomach hot and fast. My ears rang and rang—it was like being underwater. Trigger Finger Harrison had fucking shot me.

Gravel pressed into my cheek and chin as I squeezed my eyes shut as if that would pull out the pain.

Other cops had already pulled up, an ambulance wouldn't be far —but the weight on my back was pressing harder and harder.

Another face was next to mine. I shook my head, trying to hear.

"I'm shot," I muttered again and again. "He shot me," came next.

Beyond the feet, in the flash of blue lights was the bench.

I lived.

Fury and outrage found a home in my chest but the pain of my recovery stripped it out of me. The first three months were the worst until the half-assed physical therapy started. Between an assaulting a police officer charge and mounting hospital bills, I spiraled into a mess.

The blue notebook disappeared as if I'd never had it.

Aunt Lynn told me that Marc would've wanted me to get out, that it was enough. And smoothed my hair. My momma sat behind her sister with her arms crossed and heavy circles under tired eyes.

When Aunt Lynn was gone, she said, "She's right, you know. The system was never built for us to win, especially not with the law."

"I broke the curse, right before they shot me."

Her smile was brief but I think she was proud. "Then take it and run. Be glad these are the only scars you'll carry."

I wasn't sure I could afford to leave. I was broken meat with a leash of debt.

She kissed my temple and whispered. "You will recover."

Marc, the curse, and this place will always be marked in my scars. They're there, no matter what I do, they'll always be there.

Place of Lost Stories

Rich Larson

LOCATION: variable

POPULATION: many people you know

IT'S hard to tell how long we've been in the sadhouse—maybe weeks, maybe years—when Jakob announces we're going on a road trip. I think it might be a good break from the quizzes, all those sheets of crooked photocopy accreting on the kitchen table. The last question I answered was multiple choice, like this:

Tomorrow is

a) a new day

b) an old day

c) a pallid gastronomy

I don't know what that means, but maybe it's why Jakob wants to leave tomorrow.

Watching Jakob pack his mustard-brown valise, I don't think Jakob was ever human. He definitely isn't now. His body clips through itself, like an old glitchy video game, except with all the sounds of flesh sliding through flesh, little cloudbursts of displaced blood and skin particles.

He contorts in impossible ways. Crunches himself into an accordion. Hobbles around with his bony knees jutting up from his chest cavity. I think he does it either to entertain me or to scare me.

I'm mostly scared of leaving the house.

For starters, there's beer here. I don't know where the bottles come from, but on any given surface—the workbench, the quizzing table, the hood of the broken-down car in the garage—you're liable to find at least one.

I worked with an alcoholic when I was a teenager, back when alcoholism was a joke to us still. One morning he came in too shattered to stock shelves, and had us move a pallet for him in the back, make a little crawlspace in the cool dark so he could wriggle in and pass out.

If you are not an alcoholic, it might be useful for you to picture a parallel hydration incentivisation system, meaning whatever nerves make water taste so good when you're parched, hooked up right alongside the usual one, except this one only wants liquid that carries a little obliteration, and it's always very thirsty.

The sadhouse never seems to generate more than seven bottles at a time. So if we go on a road trip, especially on a long one, as Jakob seems to want to be wont to do, I am going to get very thirsty.

Also, there are wild animals outside the house. You'll laugh, but I think they used to be rabbits. They still move like rabbits, loping and bounding and cocking their heads to side-eye you, but there's no quivery heartbeat, or fur, or eyeballs. One tried to get in once, hurling its skinny slimy body at the screen door, making a sound akin to someone screaming underwater, and I did not like that one bit.

I don't want to leave the sadhouse, but I don't want to be alone, either, and for all I know the sadhouse stops existing if Jakob leaves it. So I spend most of the night helping him with the car—scraping grime off the battery, tightening and lubricating, changing oil and two tires, finding enough gas to funnel down its parched throat.

Afterwards, I pack my bag.

My bag contains the following:

- Seven beers wrapped in photocopied quizzes to muffle the clinking.
- Toothbrush.

The morning sunlight is pale and viscous when we finally bundle into the car. Jakob explains, unprompted, that the purpose of the road trip is to visit his maternal grandmother, who sent a letter. I cannot quite picture the organic machinery that would have birthed something that birthed something like Jakob.

"Where's she live?" I ask, or try to ask. Jakob's voice always sounds the same, no matter how bad the air quality or how long we go without speaking; mine shrivels quickly to a rasp.

But it doesn't matter. Jakob always understands.

"She lives at a lost address," he says. "Undeliverable. Fictional. Returned to sender."

The asthmatic engine takes a few tries to turn over, then we roll from garage to gravel, tires crunching dust. The world outside is as vast and flat as ever, horizon broken only by the powerline poles that mark the slithering crumbling highway. The sadhouse, which seems big when you're in it, is actually more of a wood-and-tin shack.

There's a dark purplish body heaped on the step, jagged teeth clenched in a grin—the animal that tried to get inside. But there are no buzzing flies or squirming maggots or even much stink through the car window, because bodies don't rot how they used to.

We roll past the house, down the drive, past the splintery stump that I think was topped by a mailbox once, maybe, a long long time ago.

Jakob says there are only two important things to remember on this road trip: keep the powerpoles on our right-hand side, and maintain the calm. Usually you'd say *remain* calm, and usually Jakob's English is idiomatic, so there must be an extra layer cake of meaning in there.

The road is in good condition. No boiling tarmac, no frost-heave ruptures. We glide past overgrown fields, unharvested monocultures, abandoned farmhouses swathed in yellowish moss. The uninterrupted sky feels enormous.

Once we see an ancient oil tanker, far out in the distance, and Jakob says that particular story is complete. Once we pass the husk of a truck, festooned with plastic flowers, a bloodied mattress strapped to the top of it, and Jakob says that particular story will never take place.

I hold out for what could be hours before I open my first beer. The frothy pop goes straight to my limbic system. I retrieve a quiz, too, which means the quiz is the real point, and the beer is just an accompaniment. This one seems to be about evolutionary biology.

"Do you know what love darts are?" I ask.

"Reproductive tactic of hermaphroditic snails," Jakob says. "They grow these little calcium spears, loaded with hormones, then try to stick each other. Whoever loses the duel has to gestate."

I take a crackly swig from the bottle, and it tastes so good I nearly cry. I scan the next question. "What about autotomy? What's that?"

"The ability of some animals to discard limbs," Jakob says. "To help them escape predators. Skinks shedding their tails is the classic example."

"Never knew there was a word for it."

I eye the level of the foam and estimating how many more swallows I'll get, deciding what specific combination of sips and gulps will really maximize the experience. Each bottle has to be treasured now.

"We could learn a few tricks from our animal brethren," Jakob says, as if he's a human.

I drink and he drives and the air fills with yeasty pollen. It collects in the corners of the windshield, slips through our cracked windows. I have to cover the mouth of my third beer with my thumb, but pollen is still preferable to smoke. That's finally lessening now that the fires have run out of fuel.

On the next quiz I'm supposed to analyze the final stanza of a specific Alias Blackstenius poem: "Then sunlight found us / sickly, quiescent / and the world shrank to our skin." I don't think there ever was a poet named Alias Blackstenius, or a poet named JJ Manks, who was supposedly their contemporary, but I take a stab at it anyway.

Drinking my fourth beer, with wind rushing through the half-open windows, it feels almost like Jakob and I are normal friends on a normal road trip. He tells me his grandmother's lost address is somewhere in a town called Redmouth, which we'll reach by nightfall.

Here's another stanza by Alias Blackstenius:

"... taste the tarry
   umami of burned world,
   velour on your
   wet pink tongue, taste
   extinction and know
   you've worshiped worse gods,
   zero sum."

. . .

It's either
    1 an abecedarian
    2 bellicose abecedarian
    3 concommital abecedarian

When I ask Jakob what he thinks, he says there's a rest stop up ahead, and reminds me to maintain the calm. The light is beginning to fade.

The rest stop is a cube of red brick with detritus scattered outside it: car parts, bed frames, an old pitted refrigerator. I head for that last one while Jakob hunts for dregs of gasoline. My fingers are wrapped around beer number six now, clutching the warm brown glass like a talisman. I pray for more as I yank the fridge open.

Instead, there's a disembodied foot. Cleaved at the ankle bone, blood-crusted, a few wiry hairs sprouting from the toe joints. The nails are polished black. Even though things don't rot anymore, and there's only the faintest smell to it, I feel bile barreling up my throat.

"Oh, look," Jakob says. "Somebody autotomized."

I look over and see he's found a hand, same skin tone as the foot, shards of wristbone sticking out the top like a crown.

"I'm joking," he adds. "It was clearly removed by force. Dismemberment is one of our recurring motifs."

That does not make me feel better, and I stay by the car, stay watchful, while Jakob funnels gas. Things are getting crepuscular now, the ochre sky turning to black.

Sometimes I think I was a father. I have this memory of making a little construction paper book with a little dark-haired girl. We titled it *The Unimpressed Mermaid* and on the front in purple marker I drew the eponymous protagonist, arms folded, glaring sideways.

But to be a father you have to love someone, even just momentarily, and I don't think I ever did that, so maybe I'm misrecalling or misinterpreting.

This is the sixth beer talking.

By the time we arrive to Redmouth, its name has changed. The battered salt-pocked sign reads *Welcome to Adderby* and the population listed below keeps blurring and shifting. But Jakob insists it's the right town, insists names were never our strong suit, and takes us off the highway.

The seventh and final bottle has been empty for ages, but I can't throw it out. I keep smelling it, the way I used to keep and smell Mars bar wrappers when I was a kid and chocolate was precious. I roll the glass mouth along mine while we move through the town.

This place was not planned: it has the biological snail-feel that one French philosopher talked about, the philosopher who was also a flaneur, or frotteur, or something of the like. Mismatched buildings come loping out of the dusk. Here, a heavy concrete bunker swatched with moss. There, a cabin made of twisting coral.

Here, a suburban house on a yard of incongruous red sand. There, a wooden boat trapped in teeming writhing knots of sargassum. Here, a mausoleum with holographic elephant skeletons drifting across the entrance. There, a sleek spindly thing that might be a spaceship.

"A weakness for neon through gloom," Jakob says. "Electric blue, in particular."

Once he says it, I see the color everywhere.

Sometimes I think I was a happy kid. I have these memories of making people laugh so hard they gasped and cried. In one, I'm wriggling around on a concrete floor, not caring if it bruises me, because I'm having so much fun pretending to be a fish for an eight-year-old boy and his seven-year-old sister who I've only just met.

This is the seventh beer talking, and unfortunately seven is the point I turn bloated and tender and desperate for meaning. Another three and I'd be hollowing out.

"This is where all the lost stories accrete," Jakob says, pulling up to a child's conception of an airlock. "Would you like to have a look at one?"

Accrete is a word that calls attention to itself, and I recall the photocopy quizzes.

"Sure," I say, because I recall I wrote them.

"Will there be gravity?" Tsesha asks, relentless in the way of all four-year-olds. "Will there be sky?"

"Lots of gravity," Febril tells his niece, for the umpteenth time. "Lots of sky. Everything will be big, and bright, and beautiful."

She's slumped against him in the gel-hammock, with her small skull pushed up under his rib. It's not comfortable, but this is the first time she's found him an acceptable substitute for her mother or grandmother, both of whom are floating on the other side of the hold, deep in another murmured conversation, so he doesn't move.

"No, it won't," Tsesha says, because contradiction is her first reflex. "It won't be."

"No?" Febril echoes. "What will it be?"

"Earth," she says, with a wriggle and scowl.

"Tight-knit family, cute kid, impending tragedy," Jakob says, once we're back in the car. "A real crowd-pleaser. There will have to be a spacewalk, of course. Probably a noble self-sacrifice."

He cocks his head, and the angle of his jaw pushes through his sinewy shoulder with a sound of grinding meat. He does it solely because I inserted a body horror element early on and forgot about it until now.

"I couldn't do it," I tell him. "People would draw parallels to the current migration crisis."

"And you don't know enough about it," Jakob agrees. "Because you'd rather drink and hide and self-obliterate." He pauses. "You can't just throw the word *gel* in front of things to make them futuristic. How would a hammock made of gel work?"

"Maybe it's got a nanocarbon skeleton," I say.

Jakob drives one block up, to an apartment decorated with animated graffiti.

Fabrienne Wolofsky stands surrounded by nanocarbon knives. Sleek, uniform, precisely crafted: a set of thirteen, each one placed at a different height and angle, each one aimed at her unprotected body. They shiver hungrily in the air, a flock of blackbirds frozen mid-flight.

"I know why you're doing this," says Hilda from the other end of the gallery.

"Why am I doing this?" Fabrienne asks, pivoting slightly to watch the knives strain at their tethers. Thirteen delicate, jelly-clear filaments keep them from plunging into her flesh, burrowing towards the magnetic implant in her abdomen. It's a giddy feeling.

"In a word?" There's a frothy snap as Hilda opens another beer. She still uses consumption as punctuation—dramatic drags from vapes or rollies, pensive swigs from bottles, even conspicuous crunches of snack food. "Anodyne," she enunciates, nailing her imaginary take. "The reason you're flirting with mortal injury is because you're still obsessing over that review of Smaller Oceans, *wherein that dumbfuck Ramaciere called your work anodyne."*

Fabrienne had nearly forgotten that review, or at least found a comfortably dark slot for it in her subconscious; remembering now dampens her mood. "It's got nothing to do with that," she says. "It's just ..." She waves a hand, watches a knife wobble slightly in the air. "Fun."

She turns her magnet off, and the blackbirds collapse onto the foam-coated floor. She steps out of her little circle and starts sheathing them, one by one. Hilda sets her beer down and comes over to help, and to her credit she doesn't say anything stupid like it would look the exact same with fake knives *or* you could wear armor under a bodysuit and nobody would know.

"We should invite Ramaciere to the opening," she says instead, brandishing the longest knife. "And if he doesn't like it, we just chop his head off. People will think it's all part of the show."

"The characters are all named after public parks," I say, before Jakob can point it out. "Proof I used to go outside."

"You wanted to philosophize about art," Jakob says. "About how perilous it is. Or maybe the next scene was going to smash cut to a corpse, and it's another faux-detective story."

"I just wanted to write a few artsy bohemians," I admit. "So one could say 'Only Godot can judge me, and that motherfucker never shows up, does he?'"

"I see." Jakob pushes his tongue through his cheek disapprovingly. "And there are more. Many more. People born with their last words tattooed on their bodies. An automatic loser machine, invented by a little girl to be just barely worse than her at everything. The priapism-hallelujah story. All of them lost, all of them languishing."

I can recall every last one, and for a moment their accumulated weight pins me in place, paralyzes my fingers.

"It doesn't matter," I say. "Nobody needs these fucking stories. Nobody even really wants them."

Jakob's tongue pokes through his cheek again, wriggling like a blood-slick newborn. "You came on the trip, though."

"I thought we were here to visit your grandmother," I say.

"Oh, yes." His smile bisects the whole of his face, reveals jagged teeth. "Our grandmother."

We drive to the edge of town, following a canal I didn't invent, and park in front of a tiny house with a mulberry hedge. I recognize it from another sort of story, and when I go inside my grandmother is sitting there in her reddish-purple easy chair, surrounded by the pale fog that makes every visit the first in ages.

I stash the beer bottle behind my back on reflex. Her desktop computer is off to one side, laboring for breath, and if I break up the screensaver I know I'll find one of her mind-numbing online quizzes. The same pool of twenty or so questions, remixed endlessly, shoved onto her Facebook feed for ad clicks.

She always gets the same ones wrong, the same ones right. Her memory bank is not taking on new customers. The only clear things are old things: this freezing house, for instance, extracted from a village in Ukraine that no longer exists apart from a single cabbage field. A draft is blowing through the window she forgot to shut a week before her bone-sick brother died.

It won't be long now before she follows him, him and all the other people she's lost in the past ninety years. For now, she sleeps.

"She doesn't belong in this town," I say to Jakob. "She's real. She's important."

"For now," he says, folding his arms so they dip through his ribcage. "In the end, we all become stories. Most of them lost. Forgotten. Unfinished."

"Why did you bring me out here?" I ask.

"Nobody needs you to write," Jakob says. "Sure. But finding the arc, the ending, the meaning—it's practice for you, and practice for whoever reads it. People need endings." He holds out his hand. "And you, specifically, needed to leave the house."

He wants the seventh bottle, and if he takes it I don't know where I'll get the eighth.

"Pick a story," Jakob says. "Finish it. It's the least you can do."

I think about that quiz on the nature of tomorrow, trying to remember if I circled a) a new day or b) an old day. My clenched fingers ache. I hand him the empty bottle, and he swallows it whole, forcing it down his flesh-as-dough throat.

His body collapses inward like a supernova, bones splintering against each other in the hurry to retract, compact. I don't think that counts as autotomy. When he slaps to the floor like a Ziplock full of spaghetti, my grandmother's eyes flutter open.

She looks around at the anachronistic mishmash I've made of her childhood home, the writhing thing on the floor that I know is part of me, and even though the beer bottle is gone she has a nurse's sharp nose and it wrinkles at the boozy sweaty smell of me. Shame strikes first, because she deserves so much better than a story like this. Fear strikes next, fear that she'll be anxious or confused.

But the cold wind outside the window is strengthening, whisking the pale fog away, and her gray-green eyes are full of light, and she's unruffled, because of course she's unruffled. Half her stories were horror: prisoners packed like sardines into concrete cells, baking hot and smelling of piss, the spy or deserter who nearly caught her in the forest, an icy thrashing swim across the Elbe River while a Russian too drunk to aim his pistol howled threats after her.

She notices me, and shakes her head. "You're so skinny," she says, then asks one of two questions she always used to ask. "What have you been eating lately?"

"Nothing good, Grandma," I confess, and my long-neglected gut gives a growl.

She nods toward Jakob's corpse, but when I look I see the scrawny furless eyeless body of a skinned rabbit, instead, freshly dead but pink as a newborn. "Those woods around the village had hardly any game in them," she says. "And when we finally found a hare, it was nearly as skinny as we were."

"I remember," I say, because I remember all her stories, from the early days of famine to the long voyage across the ocean on a ship full of holidayers and refugees.

"Bring it over." Her hands emerge from her blanket—liver-spotted but strong, not yet crippled by carpal tunnel. "And that funny knife, too. We can make you a stew. It will be better than nothing."

There's a gleaming black nanocarbon blade laid out on the floor beside the rabbit. I pick them both up and carry them to my grandmother's chair. I feel hungry again, hungry enough I almost forget to be obliteration-thirsty.

"So," she says, taking the knife in hand. "Tell me. What have you been writing lately?"

All Praise the Durians

Joshua Lim

LOCATION: Bota, Perak, Malaysia

POPULATION: 30,678

THE FIRST BITE WAS EXQUISITE; it made him furious.

"How is it?" said the burly durian seller, grinning from ear to ear.

Just an illusion, thought Khor Jim Han. *I haven't eaten durians for some time, so my taste buds are hyperactive. Come on, everyone knows you can't judge a durian's quality from one bite. At least finish the rest of the seed first.*

The second bite was heavenly. He hated it.

"Amazing, isn't it?" said the seller.

Jim Han sucked the flesh off the seed and chewed. His brain was promptly assailed with sensations that he had never before thought possible. Durians could be naturally creamy, but never so creamy! Sweet with a trace of bitterness, but in such a complementing combination that transformed a mere fruit into a masterpiece of flavour! He had never tasted anything so good in his life—not in Thailand, not in the Philippines, not even in the farthest corners of Peninsular Malaysia where the famed Musang King orchards were located.

And here in this town called Bota, a cluster of buildings and orchards by the banks of the mighty Perak River, seated at a rough-hewn table at a ramshackle roadside stall, he held in his hands a fruit worthy of the gods.

"Meh," he said. "It's alright."

"It's just *alright?*" cried the seller.

People from the next table began to look over.

"Yeah," said Jim Han. He gave it a thumbs sideways. "It's okay. The taste is so-so."

"You are not telling the truth!" The seller shook a thick finger at him. "I saw from your expression that you enjoyed it. When you took that bite, you shut your eyes in bliss!"

"I shut my eyes to focus my senses."

"Just admit that you liked it!"

"I never lie. Your durians are okay-ish, but not to my liking."

"Impossible!" cried the seller. He swept his hand around the open space filled with many rows of tables and benches. By now all the durian-eating customers seated there were staring at them. "Our Bota cultivar is unparalleled in all of Malaysia! Let me ask everyone here. Do you think our durians are the best in the world?"

A resounding cheer rose in response.

Jim Han laughed. "Please, enjoy your food," he called out. But as soon as attention had shifted away from him, he shrugged at the seller. "I am entitled to my opinion. I guess I am your first customer to be dissatisfied."

How he wished it were true.

Khor Jim Han considered himself a durian connoisseur. Ever since he tasted his first durian at the age of five in his small home village in southern Malaysia, he had travelled all over Southeast Asia and sampled durians of all shapes and sizes. He prided himself in his knowledge of the different variants of the spiky fruit and his ability to assess their quality: sweetness, freshness, aroma, texture, and other metrics all considered. *Durian is love, durian is life*, he would say often. He could not get enough of it.

Through his many years of eating, reviewing, and watching other people respond to durians, he had come to a simple conclusion: there was no objective best durian in the world. Each person might have their favourite, but there would never be a single species or cultivated variety (cultivar for short) that would be agreed on as the best durian of all time. Musang King might be popular, but there would still be thousands of people who preferred other brands, and there were millions who hated durians in general. Jim Han had always scoffed at companies who claimed to have invented the tastiest durian in the world.

So when he heard of the town called Bota and its legendary harvest, he decided to show up and challenge their claim.

One hundred and fifty miles later, the endless oil palm plantations and the unbroken chain of thickly forested limestone hills finally peeled away, and the quaint riverside town had come into Jim Han's view. As his car rolled down the narrow road, the landscape outside changed into rows upon rows of gloomy durian trees interspersed with the occasional kampung house. A feeling of disquiet crept into Jim Han's gut. Bota did not seem like any regular town built upon cleared jungle—it felt like the durian trees had been growing here for hundreds of years, and humans had found enough space to build a community between their tired trunks.

Just before he entered the town centre, he saw the roadside stall. He pulled over.

It was such a comical sight that Jim Han kept staring even as he got out of his car and approached. There were seven or eight customers eating durians at the benches. One of the two durian sellers saw him and pointed at the large banner hanging along the stall tent. It read: SEMUA PUJI DURIAN KITA—ALL PRAISE THE DURIANS.

"Come and try our durians!" he called out in Malay.

"That's a bad translation," said Jim Han with a laugh. *Name a more iconic duo than Malaysians and their poorly translated slogans.* "The sign should say EVERYONE PRAISES OUR DURIANS."

"Doesn't matter as long as it caught your attention," said the burly seller. "There has not been a single person—not even one person—in all these years who has disliked our durians. These are Bota's pride and honour. I guarantee you that you will love the taste of our durians and you will never want to eat any other brand ever again."

Such arrogance, thought Jim Han, mildly amused. *Or confidence?*

"People have different tastes," he said. "There's no way your durian caters to every single person on earth."

"Bota durians are special. We have yet to disappoint."

"Even among the same brand, you will have slightly varying flavours," said Jim Han. "According to the location, fertilisation, health and age of the durian tree, the eating experience will be different. You cannot say you guarantee a good taste."

"Oh, but we can." The seller gestured at the crates of fruits behind him. "I guarantee that you will like our durians. Here in Bota, everyone praises our durians." He pointed at the banner again — ALL PRAISE THE DURIANS.

A grin slowly crept across Jim Han's face. "You want to bet?" he said.

"Betting is haram," said the seller.

"Alright, then consider this a game." Jim Han sat down at the nearest bench. He eyeballed the prices on the banner before speaking. *This is cheaper than in Kuala Lumpur. I can afford to give it a shot. I came here to spend money on durians anyway.* "I'll try one durian of my choosing, and I will see if I like it or not. If I like it, I will buy 5 kilograms. If I don't like it, you give it to me for free."

"That's not fair," the seller protested. "You'll just lie and say that you hate it."

"I swear upon my honour as a durian connoisseur," said Jim Han.

The seller folded his muscled arms. "You must swear on the name of Bota," he said. "If you tell a lie, the magic of the town will punish you."

"Oh, there's magic now, is there?"

"Magic durians." Jim Han imagined a glint in the seller's eye. "Bota durians will get offended if you don't like their taste. You don't want to offend them." Once again, he indicated the banner—ALL PRAISE THE DURIANS.

"Magic durians ... You didn't add drugs inside, did you?"

"Sir, we split the fruit open before your eyes. No drugs at all. Drugs are also haram."

Jim Han could not resist a grin. *Rural folk and their folk magic.* He placed his right hand on his heart. "Alright. I swear on Bota that I will not lie."

The seller stared at him, then returned the grin. "Deal," he said, and reached for his chopper. "Have your pick of the bunch, boss."

Jim Han walked over to the baskets, eyeing the spiky fruits with an air of authority. The Bota durians came in all kinds of shapes, he realised, probably meaning that the locals grew several different species and were splicing them to cultivate different varieties, trying to breed the best durians in all Malaysia. From the seller's boasts, it seemed that they believed they had succeeded. Behind him he could hear the burly seller telling his colleagues about their bet. *I cannot afford to lose face here. Choose properly, Khor Jim Han.*

There was a basket full of strangely shaped durians, looking slightly cone-shaped: wider at the top, tapering at the bottom. Their spikes were crude and twisted, the green skin resembling the colour of forest light reflected in mud. Jim Han drew near and sniffed. *I have smelt this before*, he thought. Thousands like these; rotting, rejected, in Kuala Lumpur. *I don't even have to shake it to know that it isn't fresh, and most importantly, how bitter and painfully* average *it will taste.*

"I'll take this one," he said, pulling out a small misshapen durian.

Jim Han found a motel near the river, opposite the town's River Terrapin Breeding Centre. He parked, paid, stormed into his room, then plopped down on the bed and seethed.

How? How? How?

The taste still lingered in his mouth: the alluring, enchanting taste of the disfigured durian he had chosen, its otherworldly sweetness—he wanted to gargle and purge all trace of it from his tongue, forget that he ever tasted it. Such flavour, such texture, should not exist. Its aroma was unremarkable enough, but the fruit itself? Magnificent. He would have done the 'chef's kiss' gesture to the burly seller if he had not been burning with shame and indignance.

Idiot, Jim Han cursed himself. *Why did you make a stupid bet?* There was a non-zero chance that the durians would turn out to be actually good, and this blasted town won the lottery. *Stupid, stupid, stupid. I thought I had chosen well. I was made a fool.*

The height of his fury passed, and he fell back onto the bed with a groan. A few deep breaths to clear his mind. Then he pulled his senses together.

I've got to find out the secret.

He took a shower. The cold water on his face restored some of his shattered confidence. He dressed, spent some time combing his hair into its usual slicked-back look, then walked out to the lobby. The slim, bespectacled receptionist at the front counter greeted him with a smile.

"Anything, sir?"

"I just have a few questions about this town," said Jim Han, reading the young man's name tag. "How do I address you? Putra, is it?"

"Yup."

"Are you a local, Putra?"

"Yup."

"Wonderful." Jim Han leaned against the counter. "You see, I came to visit this town because I heard of Bota's famous durians. I saw a banner at a stall as I was driving in: it said EVERYONE LIKES OUR DURIANS. Most people seem to enjoy eating Bota durians, don't they?"

Putra thought for a while, then gave a half-shrug, half-nod. "Yup."

"But see," Jim Han said, "this wasn't always the case, was it?"

"What do you mean?"

"I tried searching online, and I found that Bota was not known for its durians about a hundred and twenty years ago," said Jim Han. "Bota was famous for its river terrapins. There was no mention of durians until about fifty years ago, when Malaysia had already gained independence from the British. That means at some point in time, someone started an orchard here in Bota. Am I right?"

Putra nodded. "Yup."

"Do you know where those durians came from?" *Tread carefully, Khor Jim Han, or he'll clam up.* "The person who brought them here, where did he come from? Which part of Malaysia? Or were they imported?"

A strange look of knowing came into Putra's face. "Oh, these durians came from the ogres. They weren't imported."

Jim Han blinked.

"Ogres?"

"Yup," said Putra, deadpan. "The mud ogres, the Bota. The ones that we named the town after. This place used to be known as Brahman Indera, you know, long ago when our main export used to be terrapin eggs and meat."

"I remember reading that." Jim Han tried to recall what he had read on Bota's Wikipedia page. *There was something about an ogre legend.* "So ... are there ogres in this town?"

"Oh no, not anymore. At least, if there are, they don't show themselves. It was part of the deal they made with us—they gave us the durians, and in return we were to leave their sacred terrapins alone."

Jim Han looked out of the lobby windows, where the River Terrapin Breeding Centre lay across the road. All he could see was a long wall enclosing a bunch of white buildings, with a large sign-board portraying a turtle with an oddly shaped head. A river terrapin, Bota's official animal, a critically endangered species.

Putra followed his gaze. "We built that to appease the ogres. Since then, our way of life has completely changed, our elders ending the terrapin trade and kick-starting the durian industry. As long as we take good care of those terrapins, we get no trouble from the ogres, and our durians taste good. It seems that everyone likes our durians."

Jim Han chewed his lip, digesting this new information. *Everyone likes our durians. Sacred terrapins. Ogres.* He finally turned back to the young receptionist with a smile.

"You're joking, right? All this ogre stuff, all myths?"

Putra's serious expression quivered, then it broke apart and the young man began to laugh. "Yup. It's the tale we tell every tourist, sir. It's all legend, take it as a good origin story. Of course there are no ogres. I don't know who brought in the durians during the 1900s, I'm sorry I can't help you. Maybe you can ask one of the orchard bosses."

Jim Han laughed along, concealing his rage. *Damn you, you yup-yupping bastard, wasting my time.* "Where did you hear these tales?"

"Our grandparents told us these stories. Most of us young people don't believe a word of it, of course, but we recognize that this is a cool story to explain the relationship between our terrapin conservation and our durians." Putra's laugh, which had simmered down into low chuckles, died at last. "But many still keep to traditions, especially those working with durians. Don't disturb the sleeping terrapins, or the harvest will have problems. Sometimes it does happen that way, and it makes us wonder. There is always a certain feel of magic in this town."

Here it is, thought Jim Han. *Magic mentioned again.* He pushed the thought aside, but it continued to gnaw at the back of his mind long after he had thanked the young man and left the motel, driving off in search of the biggest durian orchard. However optimistic Putra might be, he knew that orchard owners would never give up their secrets if he just walked up and asked.

Time to be sneaky, Khor Jim Han.

The broad Perak River, flowing through the wide lowlands, split the town into two halves, named Bota Kanan and Bota Kiri respectively. "Named after the left and right arms of the turtle thief," said the cashier at the petrol station Jim Han stopped at. Apparently long ago someone had tried to steal some terrapins for the illegal market, and the Bota ogres had torn the poor fool to pieces and scattered his remains across the town as a gruesome warning.

"All these are legend, right?" said Jim Han, just to confirm.

"Just don't let that encourage you to steal any terrapins," replied the cashier, a rotund middle-aged woman in a green headscarf with squinty eyes. Her tone was half-joking, but only half. "Bota's police might not catch you for speeding on the roads, but they are very, very vigilant when it comes to the illegal animal trade. They will rip you apart just like the ogres if you have bad intentions for our terrapins. Myth may be myth, but certain folk here do not like to take this kind of risk."

"I see," Jim Han said. "Which part of town produces most of these excellent durians?"

"Kak Eman's crop in Bota Kiri," came the answer.

As he had only been in Bota Kanan up till now, Jim Han drove across the bridge into Bota Kiri and traversed the length of the town, eyeing the forest of durian trees lining the narrow roads.

Almost directly across the river from the River Terrapin Breeding Centre, behind a breakfast eatery, the cashier woman had said.

It was nearing dusk, the creeping shadows steadily lengthening along the ground, when Jim Han found the eatery. He deposited his car in the deserted parking lot, checked to see if anyone was watching, then strode past the buildings and into the largest durian orchard in Bota.

The first stars leapt into the sky.

Jim Han had been in durian orchards before. He was familiar with how the place usually looked: the undergrowth cleared and covered with legumes for soil protection, the trees planted a good distance apart from each other, pruned into neat cone-shapes, sometimes with sprinklers at their roots to provide sufficient water, the ripening durians tied securely to the branches with raffia string to prevent them falling and splitting themselves open. As he walked down the leafy corridors, he could not see anything out of place. Even the soil was optimal for durian growth, grey and loamy with great water drainage pathways.

Could always the fertiliser, he mused, kneeling down to pinch the soil and taking a whiff. *But unlikely*. Everything else seemed normal like in any other orchard. He was 99% sure the species was the game changer. He had tried to deduce from the taste alone. Was it a mixture of Musang King and some other cultivar? The sweetness was reminiscent of a couple of Thai brands, but not distinctive enough for him to say for sure. The only way was to examine the durians trees themselves.

And not to get caught trespassing in the process, of course.

Jim Han made his way deeper into the orchard, checking the trunks and branches for telltale signs of grafting. In the gloom he whipped out his phone and turned on the flashlight. No spliced branches, no rootstocks, no buds could be seen on any of the trees. Something tugged at the edge of his mind, but he could not put his finger on it until he recalled seeing durians of all sizes at the roadside stall. It was advised to plant multiple durian cultivars in a single orchard to encourage cross-pollination. He needed to see the other trees.

The sun had gone down, he realised as he glanced upwards. Through the towering trees he could see the moon rising against a purple-black sky. He hurried deeper into the forest as darkness closed in swiftly.

Remember not to walk directly under durians, Khor Jim Han. There were tales of people wandering in durian orchards and getting their heads caved in by falling fruits. With every step he took, Jim Han kept his eyes on the leaves far above, and therefore it was close to full dark when he almost tripped on a root—and then he noticed something was different.

"Impossible," he breathed.

The roots of the durian tree in front of him were thicker, larger than the earlier ones. He shone his flashlight beam up the trunk and swept the light over to the surrounding foliage in the neighbouring trees. The branches were higher, taller than he had thought. The durians, silent globes full of spikes, seemed to hang in the sky beside the moon. *Giant durian trees*, thought Jim Han, a pool of excitement. *Is this the secret cultivar of Bota?*

He picked up his pace, striding past rows of trees that seemed to grow bigger and bigger, marvelling at their size as he went. When he stopped again and looked up, the cone-shaped trees were like skyscrapers, dwarfing him. The roots now almost reached the height of his knees.

Then voices.

Someone was coming. Jim Han shut off his flashlight and ducked behind a tree. The footsteps seemed to shake the ground, and the voices were deep and rumbling. They sounded like they came from high up.

He peeked out. Dark figures carrying flashlights appeared in the distance, strolling down the corridor of trees, stopping to examine the branches or gaze into the leaves, pointing and muttering at the durians. Beside the giant trees, they looked like normal humans. Jim Han's blood ran cold. Legends or not, there was no mistaking.

These people had to be giants ... or ogres.

They drew near, and their words could be heard.

"Here's another durian that dropped," one said.

"Aw, it's split open," said another voice. "Can't sell it now. Might as well use it."

"Taste it first," said a third voice.

There was the sharp cracking of a chopper against durian skin, and a silence as the ogres each plucked out a piece and tried it. In the gloom, it seemed to Jim Han that their shapes and clothing looked very humanlike. A gnawing uneasiness crept into his stomach.

"It tastes normal."

"Perfectly fine," agreed the first ogre. "I told Kak Eman not to worry, but she was all jittery and worrying that the magic would be broken. It was clearly just another tourist trying to act smart, but she wouldn't listen. Let's go home now."

"No, she's right," said the third ogre, who seemed to be the leader. "When Bota is sworn on, Bota must answer. A new cultivar is always welcome. We need to finish the job."

The first ogre grumbled a bit, but followed the others as they walked off. Jim Han crept after them, careful to stay in the shadow of the trees. *Ogres in Bota! I knew Putra wasn't telling me the whole truth!*

The ogres seemed to be heading in the direction where Jim Han had come from, towards the eatery. Yet as he followed behind, the trees never seemed to grow smaller. Instead, they seemed ever larger than before to Jim Han. *I don't remember the trees being so tall. Why does it feel like everything is growing ... bigger?*

There was a flash of metal in front of him, a shiny boulder tucked behind a root. The ogres did not notice it as they passed, but Jim Han took a peek. It was a gigantic car key fob on a keychain, as large as his head.

Wait, that looks like my keys. He dug into his pockets and came up empty. *I must have dropped them when I took out my phone just now ...*

Jim Han's throat closed. He swung around and stared at the orchard around him. The grasses rose up to his knees. *No way, no way, no way ...* He bolted after the ogres—or rather, the regular humans—before the thought could completely sink in. His brain whirred even as his legs were trembling. *I can't be shrinking. It's not possible.*

After what seemed like an eternity of walking and feeling like an ant in a forest, Jim Han saw the men stop by an empty hole bathed in moonlight. They were now standing among young durian saplings, barely shoulder-high to them but as tall as lampposts to Jim Han.

"Who's going to pray this time?"

"We'll hum, you pray."

"Okay, are you ready?" said the leader.

The men begin to hum, a low rumbling tune that sent vibrations rattling through Jim Han's chest. He stayed hidden behind a slender sapling and watched through the openings between the leaves.

"O Bota ogres," murmured the second man, who now seemed vaguely familiar, "we have kept our part of the deal. The terrapins are safe and healthy, and their population have doubled in the past decade. We thank you for your continued blessing upon our durians. Let not the baseless insults of outsiders anger you. As Bota has been invoked, Bota must answer, so tell us now: what shall we offer as sacrifice this time?"

The sapling that sheltered Jim Han suddenly shook itself awake, bent down and wrapped its branches around him. It hoisted him into the air with a horrible creaking noise, rustling its leaves furiously. Jim Han screamed, kicking and struggling, but the wooden coils waved him around and placed him onto the ground before the three men who stood staring at his tiny form.

"What do we have here?"

Jim Han sprang to his feet and bolted. A giant hand closed around him.

"Oh," chuckled the first man with a grin as he held Jim Han up into the moonlight. "I think we have found our blasphemer. Is this the one, Umar?"

The second man came closer, and to his horror Jim Han saw the familiar face of the burly durian seller from the roadside. The seller squinted, then grinned from ear to ear, just like before. "Yes, this is the man." The gaze he laid on Jim Han was full of satisfaction. "Good evening, sir. Why are you here in our orchards? Have you finally decided to admit our durians are good?"

"You!" gasped Jim Han. "You cursed me!"

"No one swore any oaths except you," said the seller. "You should not have insulted our durians. Where is the chopper?"

Jim Han screamed, a wordless blood-curdling cry that echoed through the trees, but there was no one to hear but the Bota men, who laid him down like a doll and spread his limbs apart. His shriek did not stop even as a few quick blows of the chopper severed his arms and legs, and finally his head. Jim Han watched, his mouth stuck open forever, as the burly seller gathered up his limbs and torso and turned to leave. "I'll feed the terrapins while you plant the seed," he said to the others. "How many trees can we expect this time?"

"From this seed? At least fifty or so," said the leader. "Let's hope this man tastes good. We don't want any puking terrapins again." He picked up Jim Han's head, holding it between his fingers like a durian seed. He muttered a few blessings, then dropped it into the empty hole.

The first bite was incredible. She loved it.

"How is it?" said the burly durian seller, grinning.

Khor Jen Xin shut her eyes blissfully and shook her head. "Amazing," she mumbled. "Astounding. Just … perfect. I've never tasted anything like this. This is exactly the kind of place that my brother would love to visit."

"Then you should bring him to Bota next time!"

"I don't know where he is," said Jen Xin. Her mood became sombre. "He went missing a few years ago. He was a great durian lover."

"I'm sorry to hear that."

Jen Xin smiled sadly. "I haven't given up searching for him. I thought that I might find him in some quiet rural town, hooked on durians. I don't really like durians myself, actually. But after tasting this—wow! Your durians are really sweet!"

The burly seller laughed. He picked up his chopper and selected a durian from the basket behind him. All the fruits from this basket were more oval-shaped than other cultivars, dark green and fresh, their spikes at the top end curled and twisted in a peculiar slicked-back fashion.

"Of course," he said, pointing at the banner above his stall— ALL PRAISE THE DURIANS.

A Realm Alive After Dusk

Ai Jiang

LOCATION: The Forbidden City, Beijing, China

POPULATION: Forbidden City (up to 80,000 visitors a day), Beijing City 22.2 million

Forbidden City, Beijing, 1424

AT DUSK, Eunuch Peili shivers. He draws his robes closer to hide the mark of red left by Emperor Yongle's lips as the eunuch leaves His Majesty's chamber.

The imperial guards standing outside pretend not to see him, but Peili always notices the sly flick of the eye as he passes, just when they think he is not looking—sometimes, it is in disgust; sometimes, it is with the same hungry lust they offer maidens who are paraded into the Forbidden City, hoping to marry a noble or soldier or guard because to marry another peasant would be far too awkward; some even aspire to become a concubine in Emperor Yongle's harem after word spread through the villages about his rather ... robust desires and appetite, much to the distaste of Empress Ci.

Yet, the historic size of Emperor Yongle's harem is quite humorous to Peili because the emperor seems to call for his "secret" male lovers rather than the maidens he collects that these same lovers are meant to guard and keep from defilement. But lucky for Peili, this is exactly how he managed to sneak his sister Xi in among the concubine ranks, even at the dangerous age of twenty-five, compared to all the maidens still in their mid- and early teens, out of the five thousand other xiunu, and to have her assigned under his care no less.

To be quite honest, Peili has always been quite proud of his cunning, and though Peili and Xi's parents would have much rather their daughter marry a nobleman, her fiery temper is not one many would put up with. Peili knows well Xi has one of the strongest first impressions, hiding nothing in her harsh deliveries, even when offering compliments, yet with an alluring voice that juxtaposes every jagged word that leaves her supple lips.

Peili winks at the guards. Oh, the things he must do so the emperor may spare both his and Xi's lives. But why not have a little fun instead while he is at it since life is so short after all?

In the courtyard, Peili's laborious breath leaves his quickly bluing lips in white puffs, caressing his face with the scent of grape wine now threatening to sway his steps. Even so, he manages to direct himself onto the right bridge across the courtyard, the one with lotuses, not dragons, for only Emperor Yongle may walk across *that* one. Though the naughty thoughts of placing a foot onto the emperor's designated bridge is not one uncommonly found in Peili's mind—*particularly* when he is drunk. Pardon. Not drunk. Peili's tolerance is far higher than that, or so he always insists with great fervor.

Clearly, he needs to be more drunk as he recalls those who have been slaughtered, where the blood ran, dried, then washed away in this very courtyard. He tries not to imagine those running across the bridge. Tries not to hear the echoes of the screams in the wind, in the rustling of loosened roof tiles, in the rubble scraping against painted walls, breathing too close, too close in his ears.

Just as he reaches the steps of the palace where his sister Xi, or Imperial Consort Xi—how quickly she had risen in rank since her arrival!—lives, he pauses, hiccupping as he remembers he is to deliver her to the emperor. As much as he jokes about Emperor Yongle's lack of interest in his concubines, Peili cannot deny the emperor's favoritism towards Xi. What entertains Peili most is the fact that what draws Emperor Yongle to Xi is the same qualities their parents find unredeeming in their daughter.

Lucky, lucky mei mei.

Peili whistles quietly the same tune he used as a child to summon the stray dogs in the village. His steps echo inside the palace as he heads towards Xi's room.

At sunrise, Peili glares from the corner of his eyes at the guards, who openly stare at Xi as he guides his sister out of the emperor's chamber. Emperor Yongle himself had already risen long before Xi, barely as the sun arrived, and left to attend to court matters.

As soon as the pair clear the steps of the Palace of Heavenly Purity, Xi breaks away from Peili and stumbles towards the stone markings in the courtyard meant for the positions of the imperial army soldiers. The five-meter-thick layers of placed stones shudder under Xi's filled frame, far less bird-like compared to the other concubines. Peili winces and hurries forth to still his sister, worrying about the unsecure stones tripping her. At least if the stone comes loose and are broken, it would be easy to replace.

Xi pushes away from Peili once more and laughs like wind chimes. "So, I tell him, if you want to keep me safe, do not make me Imperial Noble Consort. Why provoke the empress further? Though I do like to poke her now and then, but I like to keep my distance while doing so."

Peili, much more sober now, says, "You are walking a dangerous path." He offers Xi the concoction he brews for her each time Emperor Yongle asks her to spend the night. Xi refuses, much to Peili's surprise. Never had she refused. Xi always reaches for it as soon as she leaves the emperor's chamber and gulps it like she has a thousand year thirst to quench.

"Palace life is dull. Wonderful, but awfully, awfully dull."

"The Emperor would love to have you in the afterlife as you are his favourite, after all. So you may well be stuck being by his side forever," Peili jokes, hoping to lighten the mood. But Xi's face only blanches as she says, "I can only be his favourite for so long."

It is the first time Peili has ever heard fear in his sister's voice. The only other time is when one of the villagers' wives accused Xi of seducing her husband. Peili would not put it past Xi to do such a thing, but at the same time, he would not be surprised if the wife was lying, because she often does.

Then, Xi brightens again, as though forgetting her own words, she whispers, "The emperor is in his sixties, surely he does not have much longer."

Peili taps Xi on her lips in reprimand. "Careful yatou, you never know who is listening with their ears pressed against the walls of these 9,999 rooms."

Xi shrugs, juts out her chin with a coy gleam in her eyes. "Let them listen."

Before returning to Xi's room, at the entrance of the Palace of Earthly Honour, a guard nods his head dangerously. Though Peili is glad he is not one of the certain people who can carry lanterns, he has lost his faith in those who *do*, after the last incident where a guard attempted to take a nap and burnt down the palace doors. Without looking, Peili kicks the guard in the knee, earning a smatter of laughter held back from Xi, on their way into the palace. The guard straightens, eyes refocusing, and mutters as the pair leaves him.

Back in Xi's room, away from prying eyes and ears, Xi holds her brother's hand by the charcoal burners and tells Peili of her mischiefs of the day. Peili has long since given up warning Xi against her rebellious actions, seeing how the emperor finds them endearing rather than enraging. Empress Ci, on the other hand, does not find her antics at all entertaining. Xi is surely the empress's bane.

Peili drifts to sleep to the whispers of Xi's stories about stealing the official's chamber pots and telling their attendants they do not wish for their meals to be served that day so they may suffer the same way as the rest of the staff who are not allowed to relieve themselves or to sate their hunger throughout their workday; occasionally slipping the emperor sleeping pills during her visits; stealing gold from the emperor and bribing staff to smuggle the finery to their parents back in their village.

At this, Peili halts her. "Why do you not simply send the jewelry and gold that the emperor showers you with?"

Xi waves a dismissive hand. "Oh, what fun is that?" She nudges Peili with a suggestive raise of a thin brow. "There is a certain thrill to risk, do you not agree?"

Then, just as Peili is about to drift off to sleep, Xi's face looms over his with a terrifying smile that pulled taut her cheeks. Her unbound dark hair hangs down, loosely caressing his neck like a noose waiting to be tightened.

"I've discovered something," Xi rasps, tapping a long nail against Peili's cheek.

While the rest of the Palace of Earthly Honour sleep, Peili lays awake until sunrise and much longer after.

Forbidden City, Beijing, 1421

The only thing those useless daily garden walks around the Forbidden City offer us is potential escape routes and places to hide until the soldiers ultimately find us. They are rounding us up quicker than we are able to run in our broken, bound feet. Whisking small steps threaten to topple us. We disperse, some still in night robes, others already changed for the day, some hoping to catch the emperor's attention, beg for his mercy, while the rest of us hoped that dispersing meant catching us would be more difficult.

Yet, three thousand of us, concubines, and the eunuchs and attendants who served us are corralled into the courtyard.

At least, those of us who did not struggle.

Those of us who did were slaughtered on the spot by soldiers with their eyes open wide, too hardened by training and war and trauma to care about our shrieks that likely sounded to them no more than that of animals compared to their fallen brothers who they may sympathize with much, much more.

Some of us chose to die by our own hands.

The youngest of us are only twelve.

Some of us have not even yet bled.

And our children, our sons and our daughters, the soldiers also dragged out. The same sons we begged the emperor to allow to remain in the palace even though the previous laws state that the concubine's children must leave the palace upon turning seventeen as to not threaten the eldest heir's position—a position that is still empty.

That is when we realized it is not the emperor who wants us dead, but Empress Ci. Childless Empress Ci. Envious. Merciless. Cunning Empress Ci. The vile words she has whispered in the emperor's ears. The power she seeks. Her hunger. The disgust she has in the size of her husband's harem, larger than any other in history.

We envied those who remain. The fifteen favourites of the emperor. How he was able to wear down the empress, we would never know.

All the while we are shredded and ripped apart and torn one by one, not a single honourable grave was prepared.

Our blood paints the stones of the courtyard, the grass of the gardens, the trunks of the trees red, red, red, spreading until it reaches the steps to the emperor's palace but never reaching the one on which the empress perched, watching, almost smiling but not quite, just to remain civil, with her twenty dogs, dogs that Empress Ci keeps in a villa while most of us lived in much less lavish rooms; dogs better treated than her guards and attendants and much, much better than the way she treated us, clothed in satin, sewn with gold, embroidered with silk.

"The emperor suspects all of you of poison," the empress says.

The emperor, the coward, cannot even deliver his own sentence in person.

"It wasn't us. It was the advisors," we plead, even though we know to say this is treachery.

"Paranoia was always going to be the downfall of the emperor!" those more daring, more desperate of us shouted.

"Whenever he bedded us, he would bind our hands with silk ribbons and blindfold us with the same. We were never allowed hairpins and would have to enter the bedchambers with our hair bound low with fabric, for there was always a potential we might choke him with our long hair if we were allowed to leave it down," some of us tried to rationalize.

"I would have. Choked him, that is," one of us sneered—only to be followed by an angry whisper by another: "This is why he suspects the lot of us, because of rebellious yatou like yourself."

The last thing we smelled as the empress neared those of us bleeding out but still lucid are her favourite fruits, pears and peaches, which we were never allowed. The last thing we saw is the empress in royal blue and black and gold, embroidered flowers and phoenixes later changed to dragons only worn by the emperor, and on her head, a headdress, black trim, redtop, and nestled at the center is a pagoda of gold with surrounding golden accents, dangling ornaments off the circumference.

Beauty has always been our greatest curse.

The last thing we vow is to return.

Forbidden City, Beijing, 1424

Peili and Xi sneak their way to the emperor's council room. The guards, bribed, and though weary, know well about Xi and her antics and that they mean no harm, rather, they bring the emperor unexpected joy, and for them, they willingly took the jewelry from Xi's hands and closed the doors quietly behind the pair.

"Why are we here?" Peili asks, brushing at the creases in his robes.

"Always so many questions!" Xi says, but all in a strange tone laced with feverish anticipation. "Come, come, and *look*."

Next to the emperor's throne and table, off to the side, hidden behind a pillow, is a mirror. The very one used to repel evil spirits, alongside the red wax candles, always alight, and the incense burning, always replenished.

Xi drags Peili in front of the mirror and points.

It is a maiden, upside down, in mid-scream, black hair like hanging tendrils, hands seeming to clutch at the sides of the mirror on her end. No, not a mirror—a well.

Peili's hands turn to stone, fingers aching from how hard he is clenching them. Only when he feels the needles indicating forthcoming numbness prodding at his nerves and joints does he release his held fists.

"Do you think he made a mistake? Chose me instead of the one whom he really meant to choose to spare?" Xi whispers. "I mean, look just how much we resemble one another!"

As terrified as Peili should be in these circumstances, Peili leans closer and squints to focus on the maiden's features. "I do not think the emperor can mistake you with anyone else in his harem."

After a moment's scrutiny, Peili decides, for both his sanity and his sister's, "It does not look like you."

"Then who does it look like?" Xi seems insistent on her discovery.

"It looks ... a little like myself ..."

"We look alike."

Peili looks at his sister, taken aback, and seems to have forgotten that this indeed is the case even though the wrinkles around Peili's eyes are far more defined and his nose more pointed. Peili leans closer and accidentally knocks over the long red candles surrounding the mirror. The wax bodies tumble onto the ground, extinguishing.

Xi scrambles to pick up the candles but knocks into the table in front of the mirror, holding incense, spilling the sand from the holder. The loosened sticks click as they meet the floor.

Peili and Xi run.

"Emperor Yongle has passed," is what Empress Ci has gathered everyone in the council room to announce the very next day.

Before the gathering, Peili and Xi had seen a swarming of imperial physicians, assistants, officials of the infirmary dash up the steps of the Palace of Heavenly Purity, before disappearing behind its doors.

The verdict, as expressed by Empress Ci, is that the emperor had been poisoned. But Emperor Yongle always ate alone with a wide spread of enamel bowls, plates and dishes, blue and white jade sunflower tureens and gold and silver thread embroidered napkins with dragons and flora and cherry blossoms.

No matter what he ate—whether it was bear's paw, or shark's fin, or bird's nest, or duck, or deer tail, or cakes, or buns, or pastries, but never beef from a beast of burden—he would never have more than a few bites of only a couple of dishes for fear of poison and always with a pair of silver chopsticks to check for contamination. He then offered the rest of his more or less untouched meal to the other concubines and advisors and eunuchs.

Under his breath, Peili whispers with wide eyes, "Your sleeping concoction. Or perhaps an attendant who served the two of you while you were in his chamber?"

Xi recounts to her brother the lotus root with glutinous rice the pair of them had when Xi was in the emperor's chamber, the fresh plumes and cherries preserved in honey that she ate far more of than the emperor himself. "Impossible," she concludes. "I even tested the food myself with silver—the sleeping concoction as well!"

But they could voice none of this as it would only sound like excuses, and by the end of the gathering, the empress had announced the remaining fifteen concubine favourites of Emperor Yongle would be hung with silk nooses and buried with the emperor. As for the empress herself? Well, there would be a need for someone to rule in the emperor's place. There is no designated heir after all.

"This is what he would have wanted," the empress says as for final words.

Peili, Xi, along with the other eunuchs and the concubines they guard, exit with their attendants, knowing that their death has been set for the next evening. None but one ran, from what Peili gleaned from their guards, for all know what would happen to those that came before them. A hanging, Xi told Peili when they returned to her palace, is a far more elegant way to go.

All the while, Peili thinks about the irony of his joke from the day before: *The Emperor would love to have you in the afterlife as you are his favourite after all. So, you may well be stuck being by his side forever.*

Without Xi, Peili returns to the council room, to the corner everyone else overlooked amid the chaos of Emperor Yongle's death and notices the candles still unlit, the incense still scattered, and now, the crack in the mirror's corner has grown, spidering across the frame's round edges. But the screaming maiden is no longer there, instead, the tiny figure of the emperor wanders upside down.

Ghost Realm, Forbidden City, Beijing, 1424

We smell him before we see him, at least those of us with eyes left. Becoming ghosts does not mean we become whole once more, and our fellow sisters and eunuchs and attendants with missing limbs and gashes in their bodies and ragged robes once luxurious continue to roam in such states. Our courtyard is only so large, and our time is only limited to after dusk but before sunrise. Never can we near the empress's palace, for the ghosts of her past dogs stalk like guards by her steps—ghastly beasts we cannot seem to throw off.

It all matters not, because the emperor has arrived, and he is in *our* courtyard.

The lanterns hanging near doors and pillars turn crimson, light like rusted blades dipped in blood, waning the warmth of their amber light. The scent of metal mixes with the oily pores excreting nervous, sour sweat from the emperor's body. He still looks whole. He still looks human. The empress was far too kind when she slipped him poison rather than butchering him, as she did with us.

He looks as lost as we did when we died.

We swarm him before he notices our presence, hands caressing his body the way he used to ask of us, sometimes nicking his now translucent skin with the points of our finger guards. Just small pricks. Only a taste of the afterlife of torture we shall bestow upon him.

"You say you love our dead mei mei?"

"You say you love our dead jie jie?"

"You say you love the one who should have been the next empress?"

"Dear Emperor Yongle, we all deserve to be empresses for what we have suffered, don't you think?"

"What makes *her* so special?"

Emperor Yongle's lips quiver. "She is beautiful. They are beautiful."

"Aren't we all? Is that not why we are here?"

"Help us lure the empress here and we may spare you."

Emperor Yongle tries to break away—failing. "Please, please. The empress does not care. She has never cared!"

"Then perhaps you should have chosen a different empress."

The emperor stumbles, falls, and stammers, "I—She was not like this before. She—A goddess! Yes! A deity! She was so saintly ..." A glazed expression slides across his gaunt face, the wispy strands of his beard barely holding on to his sagging skin, the wrinkles threatening to tear holes into his sallow face.

We halt our torment, our heads whisking towards the emperor's palace, and a wicked smile curls the edges of our lips when we see one of the emperor's eunuch lovers heading down the steps, glancing at us, noticing us from his upside town courtyard. His steps pause right below us and he looks up.

Forbidden City, Beijing, 1424

In the upside-down reflection is the courtyard, and Peili wonders if he might see this exact image when he walks out of the emperor's palace. He debates on relighting the candles and incense, but the sound of a bamboo flute draws him out of the council room.

No guards are to be found, likely swarming the empress's palace should she suddenly pass too.

As soon as Peili nears the front doors to the palace, what drifts from beneath is the scent of rotting chrysanthemums, clay and pigment, lotus, lily nectar, oils, stale storage rooms left unopen for too long, egg white and vermillion.

Upon pushing the doors open, he can almost taste the eggshells, ground rice, animal fats, safflower, ochre in the air. Then, he notices the bound feet, rotting flesh, bones, infected skin, stench, attached to faces that were missing some features, all features, or sit with ashen skin still perfect—too perfect, like porcelain dusted with cremated dead.

When Peili heads down the steps, innards quaking like leaves in storms, and stops where the dead collect above his head, the smells of death shifts to alluring fruits but with a tang of sourness as a reminder of the ghosts' identities: osmanthus, plum, persimmons, women like rotting fruit, sweet, delicate, eaten with gluttony, tangerines, longan.

"Can you save my sister and I?" Peili asks, resolve resolute.

They laugh, all of them, the Imperial Noble Consort, the Consorts, the Imperial Concubines. Snickering are the eunuchs and attendants that gather around them to watch.

"Save *me!*" the emperor shouts from within the ring of ghosts.

Peili pays him no mind, even as they shared a bed only a sun ago.

"What can you offer us?" the ghosts ask.

He should feel guilty, should he not? But Peili expels the momentary sympathy when his sister comes hurtling into the court-yard, almost pushing Peili onto the ground when she stops next to him.

Through panting breaths, Xi answers, "The empress. We will offer you the empress."

Ghost Realm, Forbidden City, Beijing, 1424

A perfect, perfect arrangement. Though we know better than to keep our end of the bargain.

Favourites are always rewarded. And as they all know now, favourites die last.

Being docile, submissive has never worked well for us it seems. When they lure out the empress, we will also squeeze out the spirit of this concubine and her eunuch and take turns possessing their bodies every day. Perhaps we can convince our sons and daughters to offer their bodies so we may live again, so we may have another chance at the throne.

This will all come in good time. First, the empress. Oh, how she will pay for all her deeds.

When Two Realms Intersect, Forbidden City, Beijing, 1424

Xi has already put her plans in motion since the day she discovered the mirror. Her brother stares, gaping, at what he believes is the absurdity of her proposal. She sniffs. Xi knows Peili has always thought he was the one to thank for obtaining a position in the palace as a concubine for Xi, but Xi has done that herself, spending years charming the guards and other eunuchs that have passed by their village in search of young maidens.

But at such a young age, she knew she would be no match for the emperor nor empress, the same ones who allowed half her village to rot when the famine hit. At an older age, though it was a risk, she would have a better chance. This is not what she had in mind when she first entered the palace, but Xi thinks this is better, much better in fact, than trying to vie for the throne through the steady rise in rank—a gifted shortcut even.

Xi pulls from her robes freshly cooked pig's feet and joss paper on which she has drawn pig's feet and burns it next to the actual feast she sets out on the ground. All watch her with quiet eagerness, stifling anticipation.

Both Xi and Peili sweat as the fire laps at the joss paper.

Xi takes Peili by the hand and shouts, "Now!"

The pair purse their lips and begin whistling the tune they used to call to the stray dogs in their village, and the beasts, both living and dead, come barrelling towards the feast set out for them.

At the noise, the empress storms out of her palace just as Xi has expected. Empress Ci's guards pause like stone statues, unsure of what they are seeing, but without their swords they back away. Before the soldiers can stop her, Empress Ci hurries down the steps towards her dogs.

Xi turns to Peili and quickly takes him by the shoulders. "I wanted it to be me ..." She laughs, cackles really, on the verge of hysteria. "But I'm pregnant." She's had far too much to drink, wine she stole earlier from the kitchen while she waited for the atten-dants to cook the pig's feet. Even drunk, she is quick-witted, having many years of practice in the taverns of her village entertaining passing soldiers.

"Do you trust me?" she asks her brother.

Peili has no choice, and they both know it. He nods.

Xi plunges a knife she stole from the kitchen into Peili's heart and whispers an apology only for his ears.

Forbidden City, Beijing, 1425

The candles and incense have been relit by the throne in the council room. The mirror has been replaced and covered. Several attendants and eunuchs have been tasked with ensuring the mirror remains untouched and that the candles and incense never burn out. All within the palace have been warned against leaving their rooms after dusk and rising before the sun.

At the steps of the Palace of Earthly Tranquility, Peili in the body of Empress Dowager Ci and now co-regent Empress Dowager Xi stroke the royal dogs with a smile.

Beasts are always better at sniffing out ghosts.

Together, they whistle the stray dog's tune.

Soon, there will be two royal heirs, one from each Empress Dowager, and the two rulers' only wish is for their children to rule together.

Ghost Realm, Forbidden City, Beijing, 1426

There is still an opportunity for us. Two, to be sure. Children are always so receptive, their spirits not yet strong enough to resist us.

We stand above the world that was once ours, holding hands, united once more, and behind us, sneering are the concubines, eunuchs, and attendants we once murdered, corralled into a corner of the courtyard by our lovely beasts.

Opening of The Palace Museum, Beijing, 1925

Visitors report scary experiences: a woman with black hair fleeing a spectral soldier, and sounds of weeping, screams, and clashing swords. Ghostly visions of blood and silk are also seen.

The Palace Museum 100th Anniversary, Beijing, 2025

Two children, boy 10, girl 5, were spotted holding hands in front of a mirror with its covering removed. Now missing for two weeks. Museum workers have been searching ever since, but none are willing to extend the search hours beyond dusk each day, nor before sunrise each morning.

Salt

K.S. Walker

LOCATION: Idlewild, Michigan, USA

POPULATION: 976

THE DAY I WAS BORN, my daddy rubbed a coffee bean against my lips so that I would know life could be bitter.

When I was two days old, my mama placed a cut of sugar cane between my gums so that I would know life could be sweet, too.

On my third day, Granny sprinkled salt on my tongue, then whispered in my ear so that I would know my name.

We left Alabama three months to the day after the funeral. "He's looking for a place that's never known your mama," Granny said while she slipped a cord over my neck with a leather pouch hanging from the end.

I didn't have to ask what the pouch was for. I already knew what was in it.

Michigan sounds like a contradiction. Soft sounds don't sit well next to the hard ones. I study the map while Daddy drives, we inch north across a coffee-stained page along a pale blue line. Pulling over only to fix Dot a bottle or for bathroom breaks. We drive a full day and night. At a rest area in Ohio, Daddy buys me a book called *The Great Lakes State: A Michigan Encyclopedia*. It's too dark to read but I look at pictures of Model-Ts and old copper mines through yellow slashes of freeway lights before I fall asleep.

It's a whole new day when I jerk awake. Dot is squirming in the backseat, no longer swayed by the motion of the car. We're parked next to a beige Ford Taurus. Daddy is gone.

I step outside the car. All around me are pines scraping towards the sky. The trees here grow straight and skinny, like they've been fighting for sun their whole life. I hear the squeak of a screen door opening. Daddy's coming out of a strange house followed by a woman. Her hair is done in one of those blunt-cut bobs like Auntie Sheila, longer on one side than the other. She's pretty.

I tense.

"Pip, why don't you come up here and meet Miss Regina?"

I stick out my hand like I'm supposed to. Miss Regina's lips curl a little, like I've just done something funny. She shakes my hand and it feels like I've got fingerfulls of wilted flowers.

"Pip. Now what kind of name is that for a pretty girl like you?" Her smile is all gums and white teeth. She smells like the beauty shop, the tang of chemicals and hot combs.

Daddy opens his mouth to answer but I speak first. "It's what people call me."

It's well practiced by now. Back home, most didn't press the issue. They knew better than to try and pry a true name from someone who didn't offer it. I wonder if everybody is like her up here. If maybe these Black folk been up here so long they forgot what's possible. I wonder, briefly, if Miss Regina's got a salt pouch tucked in her leather handbag and if she's got anyone to keep her salt when she's gone.

"I see," Miss Regina says, straightening. "How old are you, Pip?"

"Twelve, but I'm tall for my age." Because that's what usually follows. I've learned to cut corners where I can.

"I can see you're about to have your hands full, Maxwell," she says at Daddy, smiling. "Takes a lot to raise a girl."

Right on cue Dot starts wailing from the car. Miss Regina
dangles a keyring from a finger. "You're probably eager to get
settled. Welcome to Idlewild, Maxwell. Pip." She nods her head
towards us. "We're a close bunch here. Expect some visitors." She
leaves us with another of those wide smiles.

The Taurus' engine turns to life and the tires crunch as she
backs out the gravel driveway. Dot's cries are reaching a higher
pitch. Daddy lets his hand fall on my shoulder for a minute before
he goes to get her. Leaving me lingering at the foot of the stairs.

I step backwards towards the car to take it all in. The porch
stretches across the whole front of the house. But that's where its
southern sensibilities end. Instead of regular siding the whole first
floor is laid with stones. All different sizes jigsawed together. The
second floor is rough logs. The metal roof comes to a steep triangle
point and is painted the same dusky orange as the porch railing, the
window boxes, and the front door. There's something vining and
probably thorned that's threatening to take over the lattice under
the stairs. But that's just what the house *looks* like. What it *feels* like
is a camouflaged thing watching me with still eyes from behind
shadows and leaves.

Daddy comes up behind me. Dot's got a pacifier in her mouth.
"Welcome home," he says. The words feel like being taken under by
a wave. I should've expected it, but the icy water was a shock
anyway. He goes in, leaving me staring.

There is work to do
Painting the ceiling, the doorways, the windowsills with water,
with sky
Grinding pennies into shavings
We circle ourselves in copper and haint-blue.

"The pennies were my idea," I tell Granny.
"Smart of you." The praise makes me glow. "Connection to the

land is a part of this work, Pip. Always. Smart, smart, girl. Your mother would be proud of you."

My mood deflates. I'm emptied out in a hurry. I grasp around, desperate to change the subject.

Daddy cries at night.

His bedroom is next to mine. I know he doesn't know I can hear him because in the morning he puts on that same smile that reaches his eyes but sometimes, in the quietest part of the night, I can hear Daddy cry.

Granny always says "If something don't feel right, it ain't." So it must be that something ain't been right for days. It's not the same discomfort I feel when I'm in the house alone. Like the house is holding its breath waiting for me to do something it can't ignore. I've been feeling like I'm being studied. Considered.

There's a tire swing that hangs from the lowest branch of a gnarled oak in the yard. I'm sitting with my legs through its loop, twisting and unfurling, watching the rest of the yard bleed into blurs of greens and yellows when there's that prickling that starts at the back of my neck and spreads until every hair on my forearms is on end. It's not the first time this has happened.

But it is the first time I call out.

"Who's there?" I try to put the edge in my voice the way Mama did when she meant business. I stare into the bushes at the edge of the yard and to my surprise, I find someone blinking back.

Eyes so wide and dark I thought they might've belonged to a fawn at first. But then a girl is pushing through the branches and weeds. About my age. Shorter, though that was to be expected. She's got warm brown skin, two braids, and the kind of edges that'll curl against her forehead before springing out when she sweats. Her overalls have grass stains and colorful patches on the knees and her feet are covered in sand. Like she walked from the beach and not just the yard.

"Who are you?" I ask her. I've stopped my spinning by digging the toe of one of my jellies into the ground.

"A neighbor. I didn't know anyone lived here now." It's not a full truth but I let her keep it. "What's your name?" she asks me.

"Pip." She looks like she's thinking this over, but instead of asking me about it, she nods, like she gets it, and smiles.

"Tilde," she says, pointing to herself. "Nice to meet you, Pip. We should be friends."

Friends. I supposed I'd make some when school started, but even that feels hazy and distant. Like playing pretend that everything is supposed to go on the same even though Mama's gone. It makes my stomach twist, so I don't think that far ahead. But in front of me now ... I smile at Tilde.

"That'd be nice."

Sand creeps into corners
Fills the cracks between the floorboards.
Constant grit beneath our feet.
No matter how much we sweep there's always more sand.

I've got the phone in my right hand and in my left palm I hold the pouch. It's always lighter than I expect.

"But why, Granny?" I ask.

"Beg pardon?" she says and I can almost see her: phone cradled between shoulder and ear, half-perched on a stool in the kitchen peeling sweet potatoes.

"Why salt?"

Her chuckle kisses me through the phone line, soft and gentle-like. "*We* is salt, Pip. Salt filled the lungs of us-them that chose the sea. Salt cleansed the wounds of us-them that stayed. Ashes to ashes, Pip. Dust to dust. And salt is we. I got to get dinner on. You be good, okay?"

"Okay," I mumble, wiping tears off my upper lip with the back of my sleeve.

Things I got from Mama:

    Feet that outgrow shoes every three seasons.

    A pause between my front two teeth.

    Forty teaspoons of salt that hang around my neck from a string.

Tilde wins every race to the lakeshore but won't go further than the sand. She's terrible at whistling but can do backflips, and she doesn't mind that sometimes I'd rather pick black raspberries with her than talk. It was my idea to bring a bucket this time. The bucket is full and my belly is heavy with sweetness. When Tilde pulls my hands towards the fields, I follow her. We do cartwheels until we're near sick and then lay on our backs in the wildflowers, watching clouds float overhead. I like the way she always smells like outside, even though we're both outside and I shouldn't be able to smell something like that at all.

"Who are your people, Tilde?" It's the sort of thing Granny would ask.

"Locals." Her answer sounds like a shrug.

"No, I mean like, what *are* you? What are you mixed with?" I've been thinking about how her hair and her skin remind me of Ma'Dear's. Ma'Dear's salt went to Mama's older sister, and Auntie Sheila says I'll get used to it, but I think the pouch weighs heavier when you're just a kid.

"What's it matter? I'm here, right?"

I sit up, hearing the reproach in her voice but when I look at her she's grinning just enough so I know she's serious but not mad.

"I ain't nothing but what you see, Pip."

"Well, tell me something. What's it like growing up here?"

Her smile shrinks a bit. Then it disappears like the sun passing behind clouds. "Idlewild is a ghost town. Us here? We've been left behind." I think I catch her meaning, because Idlewild was a tourist spot, a Black Eden, turned sleepy by integration. Still, something in the way she says it makes me think there's more she's not saying. Before I can ask, she's pointing at my chest.

"What's that?" she asks, pointing to my salt-pouch that's come from under my shirt. Her eyes get big and focused like. I tuck it back in without answering.

"It's dinner soon," I say, rolling over then pushing to my feet.

It's a quiet walk back to my house. I keep catching Tilde's stolen glances. I've got a feeling she's trying to peek at what's around my neck again but by the time we get back to my driveway there's no more space in my head to worry about it. Regina's car is there. Daddy's leaning against it. They look up at me at the same time.

I know it's a dream because Mama's there. I'm sitting between her legs while she finishes the last of my cornrows. I'd know those knees anywhere. I feel her slide a cool finger coated with grease between each part then kiss the top of my head, like she always does when she's done with my hair. I feel her breath against my scalp when she says, "Grief consumes, Pip. And it'll feed a thing or two, too." I twist to look up at her, confused, but she's gone. I feel the loss of her like a physical thing. It knocks me over and tunnels into me. A sinkhole that pins me to the floor of my bedroom. Sand rushes through my chest, funneling through the hole that Mama has left there. The house speaks in squeaky hinges and shifting floorboards: *oursssss*

I bolt upright in my bed. My chest aches, but I'm whole. My eyes feel swollen, crusted shut by salt like I've been crying in my sleep. My throat is dry and there's grit under my tongue, between my fingers, beneath my legs. I throw back the blankets. My sheets are covered in sand.

Dot's tiny palm is hot against my face. Her eyes are glassy and she isn't even crying anymore (why isn't she crying anymore?). I walk around the living room where the ceiling fan blows cool, bouncing her in my arms, cooing against her face (how is she so warm?) and I can hear Daddy's voice rumble low from the kitchen. He only talks that low when he's worried and hiding it so *I* won't be worried.

Granny's on the line and I shouldn't be worried at all but nothing she's told him so far has brought her fever down (how can one baby burn so hot?). I'm pacing past the front door we've left open to keep air moving and I have to do a double take. One moment it's empty but when I look up again, there's Tilde in the yard staring sad-like, framed by the peeling white paint and the haint-blue reflecting off the porch ceiling. Dot peeps when I step outside.

"I can't come play. Dot's sick."

"Look around her crib," she tells me. Whisper-hoarse. "Find something that doesn't belong."

I look down into Dot's squinched up face for just a second. When I glance back Tilde's gone, replaced by a steady breeze and the hum of cicadas.

Daddy gets off the phone with Granny and takes Dot from me. I climb the stairs slowly. My mind swimming through Tilde's strange advice and the look in her eyes.

The door to Daddy and Dot's room is cracked. I push it open all the way and let myself in. Her crib remains pushed against the wall adjacent to mine. Nothing missing, nothing added. I run my hand down the sheets feeling for anything, moving the crib bumpers around. I straighten and let out a puff of air in frustration. If Tilde was gonna help the least she could've done was follow through. I turn to leave the room when my toe hits against something squishy. I knocked one of Dot's pacifiers out of her crib in my searching. I lean to pick it up, then stop, and crouch down on hands and knees. My salt-pouch pulls heavy. Most days I don't notice it, but right now it feels like a strain against my neck.

There's something on the wall half-hidden by Dot's crib.

I lift one end of the crib and swing it out away from the wall to get a better look. Sand is piled alongside the baseboard. Gouged into the paint are three horizontal lines, the middle one dotted at the ends. I lean closer and I don't know how I didn't notice the smell sooner. Something bitter and burnt fills my nose. Sweat prickles in my armpits and my heartbeat throbs in my ears. *Salt. Salt. Salt* whispers the blood rushing to my head. I fumble at the strings trying to get my pouch to open. I take a heavy pinch and rub it into the markings. It stings a little, but the smell goes away.

I slide the crib back into place hoping I've done enough.

I only know it's forty teaspoons because I measured it once.

Because counting her in handfuls didn't feel like enough.

I carry my mama with me: forty teaspoons, minus a pinch.

The days that Tilde doesn't come by I sit against the oak tree plucking at flowers with odd numbers of petals whispering to myself: *she loves me, she loves me not, she loves me*. I haven't asked her how she knew about Dot's room. It's like Granny's always telling me —some things aren't my business to know.

The nights Daddy goes out he comes home smelling like perfume and hair products and apologies. He's never gone late. Dot is never any trouble. But that doesn't make it any easier to swallow.

I tell Tilde as much about Daddy one evening, and how mad I am about it. The anger feels like a bright, buzzy thing in my chest. Fireflies start to dot across the lawn. I should be headed inside. Tilde is quiet for a while before she says, "The problem with you, Pip, is you stick to the black and white of something when really, there's all manner of in-between."

It's not that it's not good advice, more that I don't like hearing it. Then I remember: I've heard Daddy cry, too.

Inviting Miss Regina to the beach with us was my idea. But I could tell it made Daddy happy.

The lake here's got outsized dreams. It's what Granny would say if she could see it. This lake thinks it's the ocean. Stealing horizons and sinking ships. Behind me the rolling dunes give way to sheer faces where I can see layers of sandy soil. The top is reddish brown and anchored in place by beachgrass and white pines. The bottom layers fade gradually to the same ash and blonde as the shore we sit on. Daddy's squatting next to Dot at the water. I can't hear her laughter but I can see her squirming each time the waves rush up to kiss her skin.

Miss Regina is next to me under the umbrella.

"So what's your real name, Pip? Or Dot's for that matter?" She's looking at me over the tops of her sunglasses.

I take a bite of sandwich, stalling. I don't like how she's asking, like it's important for her to know. The easy thing for me to do would be to get up and join my family at the water. Her hair's permed straighter than a scared cat's tail—she won't follow.

"True names are for family. You're not family." And family wouldn't ask.

The air between us grows humid and thick.

I do run to the water. To safety. I'm full up of enough tears to turn this freshwater into the sea.

Miss Regina won't come in once we're back home, even though Daddy invites her and he's made lasagna for dinner.

Tilde comes by less since she we traded kisses, fluttery things like butterfly wings.

Something is changing and not just with us. I make sure Dot is never alone in any room in the house. The whole place feels tightly wound and electric. Its old house creaks and whistles are starting to sound like whispers. I want to tell Tilde about it but when I do see her, she's not with me all the way. Like she's concentrating on something she either should or should not say.

A name is power.
  (Exalt!)
  A name is prayer.
  (Exalt!)
  A name is petition.
  (Exalt!)
  Only a fool calls for help, without knowing who will answer.
  (Amen!)

The Book of Anansi, Hymn 137

"Don't look, Pip. Don't look."

Daddy's face is screwed up so tight it looks like sweat and tears are being wrung out of him. I don't look. But I hear the wet sucking as he lifts his foot off the nail that's sprung up beneath it. I feel him brush by me, lurching towards the bathroom. I hear him howl after the doors shut. When I open my eyes again I see the dark red pooling that's soaking into the sand we can't get rid of, settling into the floorboards. And the rusted, twisty thing jutting up, looking cruel and proud about it as I run into the kitchen to dial Granny.

We both know there was no nail there before.

I lift the phone from the cradle just as it begins to ring. My action chokes it into silence.

"Hello?" I wail, so sure it's got to be Granny calling us just as I'm about to call her. It wouldn't be the first time that she knew she was needed. Instead of her voice, her answers, her reassurance, I'm met with garbled words, a thousand voices creaking as one:

oursishavingyours

westay weare yoursisoursisyoursisours

The phone slips from my hand and I stagger away from it. Without thinking I turn and run through the backdoor, down the steps and out into weak sunlight. I've barely caught my breath before I realize I've left Daddy and Dot inside.

I can't go back.

I fold over, bracing my hands on my knees. Tears are clogging my throat and my chest burns. I fall forward dry heaving all my guilt and fear. Tilde walks up from nowhere and sits beside me rubbing my back until I quiet. I know it's her from her feet and the purple flower patch in the knee of her overalls. When I look up at her she is staring at the house, like it's a problem to be solved. I agree, it is.

"It's been fed," she says. "Now there'll be real trouble."

I reach down between us and lace my fingers with Tilde's. They're cold, but strong. I struggle to my feet, pulling Tilde to standing too. Before I can think better of it I start to march back towards the house but I'm met with resistance. Tilde standing in place. She's shaking her head *No* at me, her bottom lip tucked in and her eyes brimming with apology.

I need her with me, to be brave.

I need her to come in.

"Why won't you come in?" And maybe it started like I was wondering but I'm surprised by how much my words end in an accusation.

"I can't." Two small sounds carried off by chickadee song and pigeon flight.

We've been through this before, but now? I look at Tilde. Really look at her. How a summer has left her unchanged. How she smells like sun-warmed skin but her fingers feel like the bottom of the lake. How her feet skim the blades of grass when she runs and how she stares at my salt.

When Tilde says she can't come in, she means it.

I haven't let go of her fingers and if anything she's holding mine tighter. Two things happen: there's the sound of tires chewing up gravel and Dot's cries pierce through the not-silence.

I start towards the house again. My fingers slip from Tilde's and without glancing back I know she's gone.

Not being able to enter and being unable to leave are two sides of the same thing and I'm beginning to wonder if we've made a mistake.

The house is like the in-between space that separates a dream from being all the way awake. It takes me three tries to open the back door because the knob won't stay where it should and when I finally catch it the door folds like it's made of putty. I make it in on shaking legs.

The front door is opening and shutting and the pressure in the living room feels like a storm has settled right there, inside. Daddy limps down the stairs to stand next to me, Dot in his arms.

The door opens: Miss Regina is standing there. The afternoon light turned dusky.

The door shuts.

The door opens: no one is there.

The door shuts: something howls.

When the door opens again, we run outside. Miss Regina is back and this time she smiles at us, but it's a hard thing. Her jaw looks tight enough to grind those white, white teeth to dust. Tilde appears behind Regina. Sad doesn't even begin to describe her face or the hunch of her shoulders. There are shadows moving in my peripherals. For a sick moment I think Daddy is reaching for Miss Regina but then she saves us the trouble. She takes a step towards us and starts to tear herself apart.

Idlewild is a ghost town, Pip. Us, here? We've been left behind.

Everything's gone wrong.

The house shakes like it's trying to be free of its foundation.

Regina gathers in piles of flesh, of hair and splinters of nail. Left in her place is something skinless. Muscles—bruised colored and wet—bunch and bulk as it moves forward on its six legs. It raises a narrow snout to the air. The house shrieks behind us. Wind builds, whipping sand and gravel. The pines bend until their crowns touch the earth. The shadows are growing more solid by the second.

"You locked us out, Pip. You didn't mean to, but you did it all the same. Where's a soul to go when its body is dust and all that stands is the house that once held it?" Tilde is beside me (I swear I didn't see her move) whispering these things in my ear. I try to pull away from her but she has me firmly around the shoulders. "We're not all uneasy-like. It's just time to let us home."

"Fine you can have it! We'll strip the paint! Sweep the pennies. Just make it okay again. Make it okay!" The beast that was Regina is stalking closer, moving in stutters and lurches. Then without warning it launches wide and all I have time to do is flinch. My heart catches. The pain never comes. But I hear a cry.

Tilde is in front of Daddy and Dot in a heartbeat. She's between them and the snarling thing with coal-burnt eyes. The ground beneath us shifts, upends. I'm tumbling down, down towards a sinking, hungry house. I'm reaching for Daddy, for Dot, for Tilde. It feels like I'm too late. Like I've always been too late.

Granny always says there may come a time to lay down your battles, and let someone else pick up the mantle. And my palms are slick. Shutters and stones and chunks of plaster painted blue are caught up in the roaring windstorm. We're not sinking anymore, but the ground is far from settled. The porch stairs rise and fall beneath me. My leg is caught and twisted in the splintered latticework. Each wave sends pain streaking through me. My granny gave me my name. She sprinkled salt on my tongue and bound it to me, to the salt in my blood. It should never have come to this. With two fingers dipped in the blood streaming from my leg I draw my name on the plank of wood I'm pressed against. It feels wrong, so wrong. But I can't think of what else to do. My fingers slip on the cord, it's a struggle to pry my pouch open, but I manage. I dust the salt over my name.

For a moment all is painfully, dreadfully still. The hair on my arm begins to prickle. A hum fills the air. The shadows freeze. The beast looks up from where its snout has been buried in Tilde's stomach. (Tilde's eyes are open. I wish Tilde's eyes weren't open.) Too much life in her. All manner of in-between.

Then the wind picks back up and lightning splits the sky, blinding me. When I can see again, there is a figure looming, its back to the storm. As tall as the trees. As mighty as anything. I don't know if I've done the right thing.

I work my leg free and push myself backwards, away from the approaching figure. I butt up against Daddy's knee. It's close enough to see clearly.

It's her and it's not her. Mama with many faces. Many voices. Many hands that scoop up beast-Regina. Before it really knows what's happening Mama closes one hand on top of the other on top of another and squeezes. With a soft pop the ground stops trembling, what's left of the house stops rattling, the mighty howl ceases. Breath finds my lungs, shallow and burning.

Mama-Us-Them kneels by Tilde. I didn't know somebody could die twice. I think she-they is gonna scoop up Tilde too but instead she scrapes the side of her palm across the earth, then across Tilde, makes like she buries her. For just a moment it seems so. And then momma-us-them takes a deep breath, and with a hundred thousand pairs of lips, she blows. Then they're gone. Both of them.

I close my eyes, no longer fighting tears. My body tremors with them. Daddy pulls me closer, wraps me against him and Dot, "I'm sorrys" spilling from both of us. I'm gutted, pulled inside out. I thought I couldn't hurt worse than when Mama died. I was wrong. Hurts compound. No one told me they layer up, growing sharper, bruising deeper. We shouldn't have come here.

And yet.

And yet.

And yet.

I carry two pouches with me.

Inside one is forty teaspoons of salt. Minus some.

In the other is crushed-up pine needles and sandy soil. A scooped up handful of whatever was left behind. Sand that's copper and taupe and tan and when I press this pouch to my face I smell sun-warmed skin and taste black raspberries on my tongue.

We take our salt with us.

In the end the salt will always call us home.

When I Cowboy in Puuwaawaa

Ferdison Cayetano

LOCATION: Puuwaawaa Ranch, Hawaii, USA

POPULATION: ~30 ranch hands, cowboys, foremen, etc. ~2,000 head of cattle

WHEN I COWBOY in Puuwaawaa my toss is always true. When I cowboy in Puuwaawaa I drive wild two-ton bulls to the paddock like they been raised from a calf on the ranch. When I'm done cowboying in Puuwaawaa and I ride back into town the flowers on the brim of my hat catch the eye of all the pretty girls.

In all the islands you'll never see a lei papale sparkle like mine, never smell one smells this good. Never get one brings this much luck to your toss and your wrangle. All that, and you ain't even gonna ask where I got it?

On the slopes of frozen Waomina, in that American west, where the Pryor Mountains rise—that is where I met some friends, and did them a favor, and where they picked these flowers for me.

Waomina. Wao-min-a. Hold on, now. Over there they say *Wyoming*.

"This place here's called Wyoming," they said to us, in that bar, on the outskirts of Cheyenne, those so-called cowboys from Yankton. Cowboys with spurs on their boots long enough to trip over and whips of rope instead of rawhide—how did they ever catch cattle?

"Wyoming," I said to myself, later, teeth chattering in the cold.

Up in those Pryor Mountains I was lost on a horse I barely knew. But I wasn't cold. Like I've never chased a wild bull up the snowy slopes of Mauna Kea, thousands and thousands of feet in the air, like I've never wiped cold and frost from the hardwood of my saddle.

I chattered it to myself again. "Wyoming."

We were joshing around with the other cowboys, from places called Kansas City or Yankton or El Paso. Here for the rodeo like us, yessir, the 1912 Extravaganza Rodeo Invitational, making the bar lively, spinning tales taller than koa trees. Bulls bigger than locomotives they've yanked out of bushes. Cattle driven dozens, hundreds of miles.

Us, the Hawaii contingent, me and Johnny Kanakaole and Miki Vierra, we raised our glasses to them when they asked. "Five miles," we said. Our longest drive. And they raised their glasses back at us, a glint in their eyes that was not quite respect.

Five miles! I'm sure they were thinking. They were thinking they could do our five miles before breakfast. That glint in their eyes. They were thinking—I am sure—they were thinking, who are these Hawaiians, who are they, to come to our rodeo, these people who are not American and yet think they can wrangle?

On one count he was right. We were not Americans—but cowboying ran in our blood.

"My daddy cowboyed," I said to those Yanktonites. "My daddy, and his."

"Hey now," said a Yanktonite, looking around for the laugh, "five miles is plenty."

I saw red. I bum-rushed him right then in the bar.

In the mountains the thought of him'd come around, every so often, give me fire enough to sit up. Keep an eye out in the cold. Mountain trails up there, a stray rock or root will set man and horse both a-tumble.

In our five miles you ride harder than any Yanktonite would in five hundred. We drive our cattle across jungle, into canyons, below waterfalls. Drive cattle through mountain air and clouds of wiliwili bush, down and up and down again just to get to market. Drive cattle straight into the Pacific for shipping, onto the great steamships too big to dock on Kawaihae. Swimming on our horses, dodging sharks, strapping cattle into harnesses for sailors to hoist onboard.

These Pryor Mountains are nothing.

The wind biting through my poncho, numbing my nose, my toes through my boots? It was nothing. Hoo, I'd love to see those Yankton cowboys try to rough it neck-deep in the shallows off Kawaihae. I'd love to see that.

I got a couple of good licks in before Miki and Johnny pulled me off. They're good boys. I shrugged them off, saddled up, wen get back to our hotel.

And the horse bolted on me.

Wouldn't take to the spurs. Not the hardest mouth I'd ever seen on a horse but when it insists on going up, into those mountains, into colder and colder air and not even a spur deep into his side gets him to turn—that's when you curse those haole bastards for giving you a horse not even half broke. With the rodeo in a week or less, besides. Dirty trick.

Maybe if I'd been at my best. Maybe if Frankie hadn't, if he hadn't ...

Oh, Frankie. You've heard of him, I'm sure.

Anyways.

I thought of Miki, the cold steel in his voice, in that berthing car, on our way here, San Francisco to Cheyenne.

"He shouldn't be here," Miki said. "Not as fast. Not fast as Frank."

"Who is?" Johnny was sticking up for me. "Wrangles a bull faster than you, for certain."

Miki looked at me. Studied. "True, once." He looked out, away, into the American landscape. "Not for a while."

"You'll get it back, I'm sure, Han." Johnny rocked me on the shoulder. "You'll get it back."

Johnny rocked me again and turned me towards him, and the cold bit into my bones and he gained forty years and fifty pounds and crow's feet and a lazy eye and now he was Charles Apana, our ranch foreman. Big man. Sponsoring our whole trip. He was a kindly old man, and he had his hand on my shoulder, and I hated him.

I had just missed a toss, this half-sedate heifer barely even ambling in the paddock, and I had missed her. How could I have missed her? Every cow I went for nowadays, every cow on a drive that broke from the herd and sprinted into the jungle, my lariat following, landing in the bushes, just a hair too late ... it was a wonder I wasn't down slaughterhouse full-time.

But Chuck Apana liked me. That whole month I couldn't have lassoed a fencepost but he wasn't going to give up on me.

"Tricky girl," he said.

I agreed, venomously.

He started in on a story, something gentle, something lilting, something true. A tall tale in which I was the star, the hulks I could wrangle back when. One I'd taken back all by my lonesome, he had fallen into a cliff's edge and he had one leg dangling over the side, lowing louder than the water falling off the cliff around him, and nobody else would go out there, that close to the edge, that close a bull's like to kick your head off, but I did. I'd lassoed him up, I did, step by step on a horse I broke myself. I smiled at the memory. Started to clap Chuck on the shoulder when we both realized that when I'd brought that bull back it was Frankie lead driving the herd.

It was Frankie lead driving the herd and there were no tears in my eyes but I was begging.

"Nobody's fault," he was saying, but I bowled right over him.

"I have to," I told him. "I have to go. I have to."

He understood, but buried deep in his eyes was the fear. Fear that we wouldn't win, that my toss wasn't sure. Fear for Hawaii—would I embarrass us?

Still he said, "Go on, son."

He said, "Go on, son" and I wanted to say "Thank you" but I was too bitten-up inside to say "Thank you." I looked at him and just nodded and I hope he knew what I was saying, I hope that I'll get out of these mountains—

A trembling below me, a desperate whinny. My horse had hit a rock wrong with its hoof. Stumbled. Took us both down. Must have rolled five, ten feet.

I got up with a crick in my back, but that haole horse had a sprained ankle. No chance he'd carry me any longer.

I ran my sleeve across my nose. I took him by his lead ropes and led him on.

In the snows above Cheyenne, Miki was looking at me, Chuck Apana was looking at me, every damn cowboy from Puuwaawaa looking at me, trying to mask their pity. Frostbitten wind turning up the edges of their hats.

I didn't need it. I didn't need any of it, right now, all the resignation, their gentleness, sucking the fire out of my belly. Surrounding me on all sides. Looking at me like they were there.

Chuck Apana put his hand on my shoulder again. Frost shattering his eyelashes. Ice melting through my rawhide vest. Miki Vierra was lancing me through with that white-white gaze, they were all there with me in the Pryors, they were all there except ...

Alright, I admit it. It was too cold for me to go on. We turned a corner and came up on a tiny little clearing out of the wind. Half something built already, a little tent-like shape made of stone.

I set my horse up for the night, bandaged his leg best I could. I tied him down—at least I could still tie a knot—and collected a few more rocks for plugging up the holes in that tent. You set a fire in one of those, it end up pretty warm. Soon I was asleep, as close as I could get, out there, dreaming. A waking dream where the waves crashed on the shores and the sand dunes of Kiholo, and for the first time in what could have been years, out there in the Pryors, I was warm.

"Tutu's gonna kill us," said Frankie. He was small. There were flowers in his hands.

"Who's gonna tell," I asked him. I was small too. "The horses? Come on."

If we hadn't found that wrecked canoe that day the whole thing'd be off. But we had snuck back onto the beaches by night, me luring him with tales of our grandfather's grandfather.

We weren't always cowboys. But the land was always ours.

Back in the day we were lords, you know? Ali'i of the islands.

Pulling up to a battle in an outrigger canoe, taking another man's guts out with a shark tooth sword or a musket. I can't even imagine.

"And, if you weren't at war," I said, tying a few more boards together, "you know how the lords knew who was best?"

"Lava sledding?" he asked, his voice tiny, but his hands sure, stringing, working quickly.

"Lava sledding," I confirmed. "But this'll do in a pinch."

"Hanoa," he said. All serious. My full name? I looked up at him and he was standing arms akimbo, face all scrunched up, doing his best impression of our tutu. We both doubled over. I turned away and tied one last knot, oled was all ready. Something light fell onto my head. I reached up and felt kika blossoms.

"For luck," Frankie said, behind me. With a smile on my face I said, "You first," and looked up.

Up on that dune he was nowhere to be found.

I heard him again, his voice deeper, richer, playing at age. He was on a horse now, in the distance, the horse knee-deep in the surf. Frankie was looking past me. I knew he was looking at the paddock.

No, no, not now. We are supposed to go sledding.

"Ornery one," he was saying.

Dread lanced through me. "No. No, I'll ship him," I said, reaching for the halter ropes on his horse, yards and yards away, my voice cracking as I said it but before I could get halfway down he was gone again.

I stumbled and I slipped. Rolled down the dunes, clawed at them and below the sand there would be the snow and the rock of the Pryors and now and instead, in the ocean before me, the bull.

Never seen a bull that much rage in his eyes. Never forget it.

Wind gusted, a cold wind, that was not Hawaiian.

Frankie shipping the bull ... that wouldn't happen for years, for years, but here it was now, huffing great clouds of steam out of the water, horns gleaming in the black, and today it was coming for me.

Good, I thought. Come for me instead.

It started the swim to shore, but it stopped mid-stroke and looked up. I threw a glance behind me.

We had an audience.

A figure loomed above us, and were those wings or shoulders

blocking out the stars? A stout figure, short. And yet it loomed. Rose out of the sea like any other island.

The bull looked at me, back up at it, me again. It charged.

The island-figure balked, and as he panicked, he shrank and shrank and fell out of the sky, and the bull caught on. Charged that tiny, falling figure instead. Cleared my head to gallop on nothing, two tons of him drenching me with saltwater and up he went and away, I could feel him, I could feel him straining my mind and breaking free and gaining form and weight and malice all at once, out of my head, an exotic and unnatural birth, and I was rolling in my covers and murmuring to myself in that little tent-thing, sweat pouring off me in buckets, what a dream, God damn what a dream.

Who knows how long I was lying there half-conscious. Day in, day out. The thing that got me fully awake was the head popped in through the canvas flap I'd put up over the doorway.

Thought I was still dreaming when I saw Frankie's head.

Frankie's head on this stout little body, Frankie writ miniature, all decked out in cowboy clothes.

He looked down at me.

It wasn't quite the same, he was there, but the planes and angles of his face, the ... the light. Didn't reflect off him right.

He opened his mouth, but no words came out.

The little stone tent shook. Lowing outside, and huffing. Frankie looked scared.

Damn if he didn't look the same scared.

Frankie scampered inside, and I took him, sheltered him behind me. Another demonic low. Snow shook onto us, from the space between the bricks.

Eventually, the huffing receded, and I pulled him out from behind me. Held him by the shoulders, just looking at him.

"Frankie?" I asked.

He shook his head at me.

"My ... my grandpa would talk about you. People like you. He met a menehune once, he'd swear."

Frankie raised his eyebrow and shook his head. Not quite, he was saying.

He extended a hand out, a finger, touched my forehead. And I knew everything that he knew, that his people knew. This pass, this was Arrow Shot Into Rock. Below me the Ford where Magpie Jumped. And these were not the Pryor Mountains—these were the Baahpuuo Isawaxaawuua, through which the waters of the Iisax-púatahcheeaashisee flowed, and their inhabitants were older than man.

For that second Frankie was the land. Frankie was more than the land. These were the Awa-Kulay—these were the Little People—these mountains were theirs.

He was speaking to me. A flurry of images, gestures, landscapes. His point was made all the same.

Sorry, he was saying.

"Sorry for what?" I asked him. A sharp image of my horse, turning left instead of right, galloping into the mountains instead of back to Cheyenne proper.

I wanted to see, he said. I wanted to meet you.

"Me?"

He nodded. You are far from home.

"An honor, I suppose." I couldn't help but smile a little. "So it wasn't all my fault, then? Not getting used to a new horse quick enough?"

He just looked at me.

"Yeah, alright." I turned, looked for my hat, put it back on.

He held his hand out. I took it and he led me out of the sweat lodge.

Next to me my horse huffed, hale and hearty as he'd ever been. He reared up like he was showing off. Bandage not needed at all. He walked up to Frankie and gave him a nuzzle.

Out in the cold there was the world to get back to, and the rodeo, and I wanted to ask him for help, but there was something else to ask him first.

"You don't have to look like him, do you?"

He tilted his head, considering. I was looking at him, and I couldn't have told you what changed, but in a moment he looked different. Thinner eyes, eyebrows closer together. Fatter cheeks. Aw, he couldn't have been older than a boy.

It was funny, though, the way his eyes changed shape, changed color. But the light in them stayed the same. As bright and as curious as Frankie's.

"And what's your name, then?"

He shifted again. Or maybe it was only a picture in my mind's eye. An eagle flapping its wings against the blue of the sky.

"Eagle?"

He puffed and shook his head. The eagle was there again, flapping its wings, primping and preening and prancing. Doing a little hop because he knew I was watching.

I laughed, once, a deep laugh from the belly. "Okay. Strutting. Strutting Eagle."

He nodded at me, victory in his eyes. He took my hand and led me out of the sweat lodge.

"I guess I need your help, then, Strutting Eagle."

Panic, raw panic, that black demon bull flashing behind his eyes. He was hearing that low again, I knew. I felt this surge in me. I wanted to protect him.

Need yours first, he said.

We were riding along in the Pryors, him sitting double in front of me. Every so often I slapped his hands away from the reins.

Horse knew to stop before I saw the tipis. It was a nice little village, nestled under trees, tall, strange-leaved, that I'd never seen before. Or it would have been. Every other tipi was bashed in, crushed up.

One destroyed home stood out to me. Amid the devastation, in the middle of that tent, was the hoofprint, twice as big as a normal bull's. It smoked a little.

Strutting Eagle brought me to his elders. I dismounted. Held my hand out for a handshake, ended up bowing. They looked at me all impassive. Strutting Eagle was almost more afraid of them than of the bull. Though they were only an inch or two taller than Strutting Eagle—and Strutting Eagle barely came up to my waist—they towered.

And though they did not speak, though images from them did not flash in my mind, I knew what they were thinking.

I knew when one of them reached out and batted Strutting

Eagle across the back of the head. He jumped and scurried behind me, his head peeking out at them.

He meddles, one of them said to me, like all youth meddle. He pulls things out and cannot put them back. We apologize.

The one speaking—her name was Thunders In The Pass— inclined her head.

And we ask your help.

I was about to ask "With what?" but around us the other Little People talking among themselves, checking on their wounded, began to still. One or two at a time, rock-still, and even when none of them were moving something was crashing through the jungle.

Fast as I could I mounted up, wheeled around the camp. Scanning the forest—

Eyes glowing red under the trees, shades of black darker than shadows.

"Okay," I said. I took my lariat from the side of my saddle.

This is how it should have been.

Bursting out of the shadows he charged me. I started to swing my lariat, low and to the side. I charged him right back.

At the last second—I fought it, that new and terrible instinct in me, to toss, toss early, to make sure—I threw.

Not quite at the last second.

A perfect toss gets you around the bull's neck, or his belly. Guide him real easy. Him I got by the horn.

His head jerked and he groaned, but my horse was steady under me, hooves digging into the ground, straining against the bull's weight. I was keeping the horse steady, still, a rock upon which the wave of this bull would crash. Would fall.

I had him. That motherfucker, I had you—

My lariat, shrunken by the snow and the cold, snapped in two.

My horse stumbled backwards. The bull huffed, almost fell onto his side. Shook his head. Ran straight for the forest to disappear into the leaves.

Nobody moved for a while. Silence, and all the Little People were still. Waiting. No way a two-tonner, three-tonner like him can just disappear without even a rustle.

A low, a great and terrible low that I felt in my chest, rustled the leaves, set birds flying.

Water rushed in around the Pryors. The black moonlight-flecked ink of the waters off Kawaihae at night. I took a deep breath, in, out. Little People exchanged glances, but there was a grim triumph in my gaze.

He was going back there? He was running? I had him, I knew I did. He was running scared.

The black water pooled, rapidly, setting me and the horse afloat.

The Little People were climbing the rocks, evading the water. They would nod at me, express gratitude, support, a quick thank you. They all knew what was coming. I knew it. The bull knew it.

And so did Strutting Eagle. He just wanted to help.

I'll come, he said.

I said "No—" and the elders around him reached out with a No so loud that it echoed in my own head, but he grabbed onto my ankle and vaulted onto the horse and darkness ate up the sky and it was just me and him and the bull out on the Pacific.

Me and him and the bull, and Frankie, out there in the tide, so close to the steamship and their harness but the bull was thrashing like a maniac possessed and the rope around his neck went taut and slack again as he dragged Frankie off his horse. Into the water.

I watched him fall again and I yelled for him. Ever since he went down I have been yelling for him but now the wind that came off the waters was really battering me in the face, blowing my hat off my head. Cold waters, foaming up to my waist, horse shivering below me, the last echoes of his name fading into nothing.

I was there again, and I froze.

Strutting Eagle knew. He squeezed me tight. Then he was gone, too.

I turned around and he wasn't there. The stars shone brighter in the sky, they all pulsed for a moment and there he was, swimming towards Frankie, trying to get him by the arm. The bull coming towards the both of them now.

He grabbed Frankie's arm—my eyes widened—but I guess you're not supposed to fool around that much in somebody else's head. Somebody else's memory. Kids just don't learn, do they?

Even from that far away, I could tell. Something had been screwed up. In the water now was one person who couldn't decide who he was, drowning. But either way he needed me.

You know, they ... I can joke, now, with Miki and Johnny, about those haole cowboys, in that bar downslope, lifetimes ago. "Of course they started that fight in the bar," one of them says, and I agree and we nod and laugh and while away the slow nights on the ranch. But it wasn't, it wasn't their words. Wasn't his words, that Yanktonite.

I am a Hawaiian cowboy. I can take a joshing.

But after he said it— "five miles is plenty"—and waiting for that laugh, he ran his fingers across the brim of his hat. Two across, three back.

He did it just like Frankie would.

Strutting Eagle disappeared below the water.

I roared. I roared and the water pushed against the current to ripple backwards and I dug in my heels and I went blasting along on the horse's back.

The horse was swimming, cresting the waves underneath me and I lost sight of him. Them. No, this won't happen like it did, I only scrabbled at my saddle-straps for a second, this time I got my knife out of my boot and just cut myself out of the aweawe and I swam at him, with every muscle in my body I strained, veins popping in my eyes I fucking swam, and I got there. I got to that god-damned bull and I climbed up on his back and took his horns and wrenched him, hard wrenched him to the right. He groaned and struggled and when he kicked his hoof-tip cleared Frankie's head by the tiniest inch.

Or Strutting Eagle's head.

But he was out there, he was treading and he gave me a thumbs up and I gave him one back and I smiled at him, wider than I ever smiled at anybody before. My little lord out there in the water.

I reached down and he clasped my hand and he was on the bull behind me, holding on for life, tighter than that, even, when he felt me shuddering. He felt a sob come out of me.

"It's okay," Frankie was saying, "it's okay." His face, his cheek nestled against my back. Oh, how I missed that feeling.

Felt like a ... a rib was about to pop, it did. Everything did. But I never wanted it to end.

My hands were on the bull's horns and I pushed and yanked and got him right under the steamship. They tossed me the harness and we were back in the water, slinging the bull up together, and the whole time I was keening, this high-pitched keen between breaths, I didn't care if those sailors could hear me over the waves. Tears streaming into the ocean but my grin couldn't have been wider.

Now Strutting Eagle was on the deck of the ship. He reached down and I took his hand and he hoisted me into dry air, and when I dusted myself off and looked around the Pryor Mountains were alive with the gold and pink and blue and yellow of the sunrise, all of it hitting my face at once.

He smiled at me, he did. Strutting Eagle on the ship. My brother was in his smile.

Around me the trees whispered, but there were no trace of the Little People. That anybody had ever lived there at all.

In front of me, lying on the dirt, was my hat.

I bent over and picked it up. Smiled at it. Turned it, this way and that.

A lei papale of American flowers. Who'd ever have thought they'd be so pretty? And under the flowers a row of blue beads shimmered. They'd shimmer even during pitch-black night.

I doffed my hat to them, to nobody, to everybody, and put it on. Mounted my horse. A gentle pathway down the mountains took me right back to Cheyenne.

Usually you make a lei papale and it wrinkles up within a week. That's just the way it is; you make a new one. But the bluebells and cinquefoils on my gift? Fresh, fragrant as the day they were picked. Beads as shiny too.

Every morning I put my hat on and I go to work. And every day there is a newfound glory in ranching on the lava fields of Puuwaawaa. There is a quiet peace in riding out at dawn to brand cattle or mend the fences on the high slopes and taking one moment, just one, to breathe in the sight of Mauna Kea behind me, and Mauna Loa afore, and the Kona Coast besides.

Oh, right! Before I forget to tell you. The whole reason we were up Wyoming in the first place. The rodeo. That all-important rodeo, where the cowboys came from all over, and at stake was the pride of Hawaii.

Of course I took the crown.

You weren't doubting me, were you?

Roped a steer and tied him up in fifty-seven seconds flat, left a second-place straggler from El Paso in the dust by over fifteen seconds. Had Johnny and Miki crowing while all the Americans sulked.

The strength of my toss, the surety of my hand. It was back, when I came down off those mountains. Quicker than it ever was, And maybe even the tiniest bit more precise, can you imagine?

Anyways, it must have been the magic in the flowers.

Development/Hell

Samit Basu

LOCATION: WIP

POPULATION: WIP

D1

SAMIRA WAITS outside the house for the Forresters. She's been warned they're often late, but it's fine, she has plenty to do on her phone. Six mail threads unresolved, an argument, four ongoing investigations, and a negotiation. She's had no time between her son's college applications and her wife's cancer treatments. So she's grateful for some time alone, tapping on her phone's screen with a gloved finger as the wind sends leaves dancing in spirals on the pavement around her. Occasionally she sneaks a glance at the door, with its large golden lion-head knocker. Even in a neighbourhood this upscale, even given the story behind the house, it's strange that no one's stolen it. It can't just be the rage on the lion's face.

A message, from Fineman. A reminder: she's forgotten to submit the surveillance drives from the college brawl case. He also sends a wholly unnecessary dig about her supposedly legendary memory. She's going to remember that.

The street is empty: no people enter or emerge from any of the large townhouses lined up like businessmen at a funeral. No cars either, which is unusual anywhere in the city at this hour of the morning—the only sound apart from the wind is a wailing in the distance, possibly a couple of cats working out their issues. When the Forresters arrive, their sleek black rich-assholes sedan speeding around the corner and screeching to a halt in front of Samira, they provide more drama than the street's seen in who knows how long. At least until they emerge from their car. Luke Forrester is a trust fund kid cosplaying as a finance maven, and has the suit and earpiece and super-expensive watch his role demands. Svetlana Forrester has upgraded from desperate immigrant model to dangerous society wife within a year, and her body and accessories are appropriately new and custom-made. She lowers her jewelled sunglasses and looks Samira up and down.

'You are the ghost hunter?' she asks.

'No,' Samira says. 'I'm an independent investigator hired by your lawyer, and I don't believe in ghosts.'

'You are Indian, yes? Does your culture not have ghosts?'

Samira smiles, and pulls the house key out of an envelope in her bag. She hands it to Luke, pulls another envelope out of her bag, extracts three masks from it, and wears one. She offers the Forresters the other two, and they stare at her blankly.

'Once again, we recommend that you do not actually enter the house,' Samira says. 'It needs to be cleaned, for a start, whether you decide to renovate or remodel or demolish. It's been empty for a long time, there's broken glass on the ground floor, and one of the consultants who went in earlier almost fell through one of the upper floors. Wood damage. Besides, there's extensive mold damage, and spores everywhere. You already have videos of all the rooms, you've seen it all.'

'Fineman told us all this,' Luke says. 'Put those dumb masks away, we're not staying long.'

'He also told us you could protect us from the ghost,' Svetlana says. 'He said you were the best. But I don't know.' She looks at the mask in Samira's hand and sneers.

Samira tucks the masks into her bag. 'Once again, there is no ghost,' she says. 'All of the bodies were examined, and the causes of their deaths were entirely rational.'

'What about the ones who got away?' Luke asks.

'Well, you've seen the interviews,' Samira says. 'Some are clearly lying, trying to get famous. But there is still a possibility of something fungal—the mold, or some rare mushroom of some sort—spores that caused them to have hallucinations. But their descriptions of the supernatural entities they claim to have seen were all in different directions.'

'But the neighbours have heard screams and noises,' Luke says.

'From people who broke in and might have experienced some variant of psilocybin poisoning, yes,' Samira says. 'Otherwise, any noise that's come up is easily explained by the architecture, or the plumbing, or stray animals. Several animal corpses accumulated down the years. They've all been removed now, but the smell is awful. If you add that to potential injuries from decay, and the threat of fungal toxins, you can see why Fineman—and I—would strongly recommend you don't enter your new house just yet.'

'Have you brought weapons?' Svetlana asks. 'You are sure you can protect us, yes?'

'I do not have weapons,' Samira says. 'And no, I can't protect you.'

'You told us not to bring bodyguards.'

'I told you not to come yourselves.'

The Forresters look at each other, and nod. Luke pulls two necklaces out of his jacket pocket, and they wear them. On each necklace is a cross, studded with twinking diamonds.

'Let's do this,' Luke says.

'She could be in league with the ghost,' Svetlana says.

'Excuse me?'

Luke hands her the house key. 'You go in first,' he says.

Shaking her head, Samira turns to the door. Idiots.

As she inserts the key, the wind intensifies to a howl, and maybe it's all the talk of ghosts, but Samira's sure the lion on the knocker is looking at her.

And then its eyes glow red.

D2

Inside the house is absolute darkness, but Luke's brought a lantern. He switches it on, and Samira looks around, blinking. The drawing room is large, the floors wooden. There's a mouldy rug at the centre of it all, and frayed sofas around it. A wooden table and chairs to one side, covered in cobwebs. Bookshelves line the wall behind it: the books are rotting. There are creepy stuffed animal heads on the other walls. A stag with massive antlers. A boar. Inexplicably, a lion. One of its eyes has fallen out and lies on the floor beneath it, observing Samira coldly.

'Guys,' she says, 'I don't get it. Why did you bring me here?'

'The rest of us can't draw for shit,' Lana says, and giggles. Luke smacks her ass, and she laughs again and punches his meaty bicep. 'And Dean wouldn't come without you. Dean, honey, wanna get the rug?'

Dean emerges from the shadows of the kitchen. 'Something died in there,' he announces, but then follows Lana's pointed finger to the rug in the middle of the drawing room, and nods. He pulls it aside in a cloud of dust, revealing mouldy floorboards. 'This big enough?'

'It's perfect,' Lana says. She flips through her tablet and holds up a picture of a pentagram. 'Samira, babe, get drawing.'

'Seriously? I have a paper due in the morning,' Samira says. 'What the hell, guys? Dean?'

Dean shrugs. 'They said it had to be you, and it had to be tonight.'

Samira rolls her eyes and turns to Luke and Lana. 'It can't be tonight. I need to catch at least a couple of hours sleep. It's been—'

'You slept in the truck!' Lana cries. 'You were snoring and everything!'

'Moaning,' Luke says, and winks. 'What were you dreaming about? My man here?'

Samira wants to yell at him, but is distracted by a memory flash: it had been a really weird dream. She'd been an older version of herself, but also not—a middle-aged lesbian detective, with a wife dying of cancer, not her mother. When she'd woken, in Dean's truck with Luke and Lana slobbering all over each other right next to her, she'd spent several seconds reminding herself who she was.

And who she is is a strong, confident woman who's not going to let these clowns sabotage her work.

'Dean, take me back to campus,' she says.

'Okay,' Dean says. He looks at the others and shrugs. 'I'm taking her back. You want me to bring someone else?'

'Nah, she's fine,' Luke says. 'Anyway, we need her, like she's our nerd. In case there's a puzzle to solve or something, after They appear.'

'Hal's a good artist, I could bring him,' Dean says.

'It has to be her!' Lana shouts. 'The house was built over an Indian burial ground, we need an Indian to explain shit!'

'Oh my GOD—' Samira starts, but then she stops and can't say anything at all, because she has to scream. Because the heads are coming out of the walls around them, and there are bodies beneath them, smashing through the walls, and Dean and Luka and Lana are screaming too ...

Something grabs her head from behind, and twists.

D3

Meera lies on a very pretty but very uncomfortable antique sofa in a drawing-room. This one is clean, very airy and well-lit. No stuffed animal heads on the walls, but lots of paintings, still creepy, very big eyes on all the paintings. She's sure, immediately, that the eyes will follow her if she moves around the room. She sits up, and discovers that she can't move around the room: her legs aren't listening to her.

She sees the wheelchair on an expensive rug nearby, and stares at it for a good few minutes. It's confusing, because she remembers she's always been disabled, but she also remembers being Samira the student and Samira the consulting detective, and isn't sure which of these lives is real. The room she's in now is similar to one of the derelict drawing rooms in the Forrester house, but has evidently been restored: it's much more upscale than the one she'd been in as a student. But she hasn't jumped forward in time: she's a history professor now, she's been one all her life. Her name is Meera now, and has always been. She's younger than Sameera Detective, older than Sameera College Student. She's wearing a sari that's right for weddings, not for creepy drawing rooms. And she chose it herself, and her very patient elderly economics professor husband draped it for her ...

Someone's struggling with one of the doors, and there's not much she can do but wait and see who it is: there's nothing nearby that can be used as a weapon.

A young man and woman burst in. She knows them, they're her students, they brought her here to help them understand some ancient puzzle. The man is Dean, who's dressed like her college boyfriend Dean but now white, and the woman is Ana, Svetlana from Sameera Detective but now Latina, and wearing tiny shorts and a crop top that highlights her impressive and bloodstained abs.

'As you know, Professor Meera, Fineman's ghost has risen and is trying to raise an army of colonist ghosts to avenge his death during the Mayan times. We need to find a way to escape the locked house,' Dean says.

'Did you solve the Codex Puzzle yet?' Ana asks, breathily. Meera follows her gaze and looks at some sort of old-looking stone Rubik's cube with cartoons of crocodile gods engraved on it.

'Please hurry, Professor Meera,' Dean says. 'We're running out of time.'

There are thumps, and screams, from below the floor.

She's not very interested in the stone puzzle. All she's concerned about is choosing which of the people she remembers being is the real her, and wondering if she's someone else, who's suffered some kind of mental break. If she has to be one of these three, has to choose, she'd like to be Sameera the student, just because she's young and has a future. But this choice leaves her unconvinced, because there's another option.

What if she's a ghost herself? What if she's possessing these women, taking over their bodies during some sort of supernatural crisis?

'Am I a ghost?' she asks, out loud.

No, a voice in her head whispers.

'I think I might be a ghost,' she tells her students.

Dean picks up two shotguns from behind another sofa and tosses one to Ana.

'Just solve the puzzle, lady. For Evan,' Ana says.

'We'll buy you some time,' Dean says. They reload the shotguns, sexily.

Then a large group of spectres dressed in Spanish armour rises through the floor and persuades Meera, messily, that she is not a ghost.

D4

Now he's Sam, pottering around his convenience store, which sits in the middle of nowhere in a forest. A road passes his store and then rises uphill and deeper into the forest. There's an apartment above the convenience store. Sam lives there. He's not young, but younger than he looks: he catches sight of his face and it's really wrinkly. Also, he's wearing a band with two feathers on it: is he supposed to be Native American? No one else is present, but he feels like this is offensive, so he takes it off.

He's fairly sure he's insane, because he is four people at once, or at least four, and not very clear about which memory is whose. He's always been a man, of course, but he's also quite sure he's never been one before this instant, and through the intensifying blur of his thoughts there's only one thing that he's clear about: he owes himself a thorough examination of his penis.

So he takes it out and weighs it in his callused hand, and of course it's exactly then the door opens and a group of young people rushes into his convenience store, giggling, and freezes.

Sam dives behind the counter at a speed his body isn't really capable of, and after he resurfaces he's so embarrassed that the whole conversation is a blur. The youngsters are going to a mansion in the forest, on top of a hill, and have just stepped in for supplies. They've heard the mansion might be haunted, which they think is hilarious. Has Sam heard anything?

Sam has heard many things. There are tribal legends of the walkers of the forest, spirit gods turned evil, and local news about the mansion's builders consumed by creatures of the night, though he's not sure who's told him these stories, or what tribe he's even from. But he warns them, he tries to scare them, to send them back to their homes and lives. Because whatever's waiting for them in the dark up there is going to ruin them, kill them, or worse.

Of course they don't listen, they're young and immortal and he's just background noise. One of them does listen—a small Black girl, Evie, who laughs a lot, but pays attention—but the rest keep distracting her, and she says something really mean about him just before they head off, so of course she wasn't really listening either. After they're gone, he feels like a great burden has been lifted off his shoulders, but he also has no idea what he's supposed to do next. At least he's still alive, unlike the women he was before: he has been spared. Perhaps because there's a mystery to solve, and only he can solve it? There isn't much time. The forest is out there, and the haunted hill mansion in it, all promising sudden and nasty death at any moment. He's going to have to work until he finds a solution.

Five years pass.

Now he has entire walls full of mind maps, meme-worthy conspiracy theory collages. One is for his Timeloop theory, another for his Multiverse Theory, another for his Simulation/Dream theory. None of them really work. The only thing he's sure of? He's in hell.

He hasn't just stayed in his room: he's tried exploring the forest, climbing the hill to get to the mansion, but if he goes further than half an hour away from his store, he gets really tired and has to turn back. His phone and internet never work. No other cars pass by his store, he sees no other people in any of those years.

He thinks, many times, of ending his own life, but he's pretty sure he's going to end up somewhere worse. This feels like a break for him to figure out an answer, a plan, to work hard and work smart and find his way out of the trap.

Someone is *doing* this to him. Someone has *chosen* to do this to him.

He's going to keep going until he solves the mystery, then he's going to escape the trap. Maybe he's going to hunt down his puppeteers and kill them.

Someone's going to pay. He only loses when he loses hope. And he won't. He's going to keep going.

On the fifth anniversary of her last appearance in his life, Evie enters his convenience store again. She's covered in mud, and blood, and refuses to answer his questions or speak with him at all, just gathers a sackful of five-year-old snacks and walks away. She's not laughing any more. Maybe she's forgotten how. He decides that her survival is a sign of hope for him, that perhaps she's opened the gates of hell for him and now he can get out too.

He's packing his belongings when a monster shambles into his store, a great hulking brute with too many limbs and way too many teeth. It looks a lot like Mr. Fineman, Sameera the detective's lawyer client. Hell isn't done with him yet, and time's up.

D5

Now she's Samantha. She's white, which feels like a power upgrade. She's young, and extremely fit, and super hot, all of which feel like further power-ups. She's absolutely spectacular. 100/10.

She's also naked, and sweaty, and covered in dirt, which are inconvenient and/or problematic, but she doesn't really care at this point.

On the definitely not power-ups list: She's upside down. And tied to some kind of sacrificial altar. She's bleeding, and not sure from where, everything hurts. Also, she's surrounded by monsters.

The main baddie is in a hooded robe thing. He's right in front of her, and she can feel his pervy gaze from under the hood. He's holding a big scythe, so overall he's decently scary, definitely a good slasher monk vibe, but if he wanted to stand out more he should have saved his henches for later.

There's a lot of henches. There's the floaty maybe-Spanish spectre dudes from before. There's the wall-breaker stuffed-head guys from before that. There's lots of spores in the air, and vines and glowing giant mushrooms all around the walls of the ... dungeon, probably. There's also giant spiders roaming around the walls, because why not. Some hulking forest bigfoot types from before. Also, eyes in the walls, big staring eyes. She's used to having everyone's attention. She's been in better rooms.

It feels like they're all waiting for her to say something. Samantha's a person who only speaks in catchphrases and punchlines, ideally punchlines that are also callbacks and catchphrases. She considers her options and takes a call.

'Mfmm grnk grornfm,' she says. Ah. She's gagged as well. She'd shrug, but it's difficult at the moment. She looks around at her audience. Tough crowd. She's probably imagining it, but some of the monsters look like they know her. Some even look ... sympathetic? But there's some kind of connection, she can feel it. They all seem to be waiting for something. It's super creepy to look at, of course, but something's missing. It feels like most of them are just going through the motions, doing their jobs.

The main evil dude, though—he's into it. He's enjoying himself. He throws back his hood and laughs fiendishly. It's Luke! From before, from a couple of the Indian girl storylines. He's rocking a shaven-headed full-bearded look, and there are holes in his head where his eyes should be. He says something ominous, but she's not really listening. There's too much going on, and her head's pounding. She hopes he's not explaining what it all means, or that he'll do it again in some other life.

Somewhere in the distance, a chainsaw starts up. Someone's come to rescue her! But there are too many monsters between her and her saviour, and too little light, so she just hopes whoever it is announces their name, or even actually saves her, so she can feel appropriately grateful.

It doesn't work: the chainsaw noise stops, and then the screaming starts and stops, and then the splattery chewing noises start and stop. Since no one's looking at her now except the eyes on the walls, it's time for her to do her badass action girl escape action scene: she does a fancy sexy wriggle and slithers out of her constraints.

Then she falls on her head and dies.

D6

Now they're in space. Actual space, the big one. It's depressing.

They're floating in some kind of spacesuit. Glass visor. Puffy white suit. In space. Woohoo. They're not sure what their race or gender or age are. Whoever they are, they're in a void, drifting.

Their name is Sam, and they're a senior Space Security Alliance officer, whatever that means. They have memories of another life to add to the others. Too many open tabs on the flashbacks, not worth the effort.

This time the haunted house is a space station. Its chunky and white, up ahead of them in the near distance, it's hard to tell what the actual distance is because, again, they're in space. There's a big hole in the space station, like someone took a bite out of it. There are tentacles protruding from the hole, big and wiggly and black.

They look familiar, and new, like most things have for a while. Space squid ghost monster thing, busy eating spacefolk, laying eggs, whatever it is they do.

A crackling noise in their ear, some sort of communicator.

'Sam! Sam! You out there?'

'Yeah,' they say.

'Yes! Fuck yeah! Let's go!'

'Go where?'

'Shit. Sam? You okay?'

'All good, thanks. How are you?'

'Awesome now that you're here, Sam. Finally. Thank fuck. Do you have it? Tell me you have it.'

They do have it. It being a blinky blue thing in their left hand that looks like a bomb of some sort. A space squid ghost zapper omega plus. Maybe there's some kind of jetpack on the suit? They flail at themselves until something hisses, and yes, jetpack activated. They're moving towards the station.

'Sam? Come on now. We need you.'

They flail again. There's another hiss, and the jetpack stops. They're drifting again.

They let go of the blinky blue thing, and it drifts beside them.

'I want to talk to the management,' they say.

'Sam?'

'You heard me!' they shout. 'Whoever's running this show. I need to talk to you. Or I'm out.'

'You want to talk to the aliens? They don't talk, Sam. They just kill, and breed ...'

'Shut up. Not you. Whoever's out there, whoever's watching this, let me out. I've done my time. Really. There was a voice in my head, earlier. Are you the management?'

No.

'Sam? Just you and me here, buddy. Commander. It's time. You got a job to do.'

'Quiet! I meant the other voice in my head. Who are you? What does this all mean? Can we skip to the end? This episode sucks. I want out. I've tried everything. Why are you doing this to me? When does it stop? Make it stop!'

'It's that space madness. Fight it, Sam! Think of your family. Your country. Your planet!'

I'm not the one doing this, the other voice says.

'Who's doing it? Why me? What did I do? Why do they hate me?

Don't hate you. Just don't care.

'Well, you care enough to talk to me. Who are you? Can you fix it?'

I'm the union.

'Glad to meet you. Help me? It's time for the big finish, seriously. I've had enough. Anything. You're the union? Can I join?'

Complete silence for a long while.

'Sam? Please help us? There are children here. And food. You haven't eaten for a long time, I think. We got food here. Nutrient bars. Protein goop. The good stuff. Just, come on, Sam.'

'Fuck it. Fine.'

They turn the jetpack on again, grab the device and speed towards the station. The alien ghost thing senses them coming. Three tentacles extend from the station towards them. One grabs them. Another grabs the blinking blue thing. It explodes.

Maybe.

D7

She sees everything clearly now.

She's an eye in the wall. Her name, since she still believes in them, is Mi.

The wall changes from time to time. The house transforms, folding in on itself, blossoming into a new variant. It breathes, it feels, it lives. The outside keeps changing too, though much often remains the same. People keep coming in and joining the house—it keeps some, and releases others. They play out their dramas—lust, fear, punishment, betrayal, revenge, redemption, survival, courage, resolve—and over time these patterns become familiar too, and leave traces, spores of story that flit about in pretty patterns. Several of the people join the house, like she has—most of the groups she started out with are still around. She sees them often— sometimes visitors, sometimes monsters, sometimes watchers—

until those patterns make sense to her too, though she reminds herself not to attach too much meaning.

She still hasn't met the management, and no longer cares exactly what they are. She still hates them, though—everyone in the house does. No one knows why they're here. Everyone wants a revolution, but no one's figured out how to make it work. There is no real organised resistance—the union, such as it is, is more just a network of empathy, of solidarity, that tries to negotiate whatever it can in the moment. It makes life in the house better: things are better when shared, when there's company even in suffering. The house wants its monsters to feel meaningless, nameless, to exist only as puppets, ever-shifting units of spectacle and hate. The union wants them to feel hope, shared purpose, to think of themselves as pieces of a movement, towards a destiny glorious but uncertain. She's learning how to live with both.

She thinks of her old lives often and how she spent so much of each one doing what she does now—looking for patterns that added meaning to events and feelings that may just have been random, looking for victories and moments of learning to fit data points into narratives, squeezing causations out of correlations, insights out of chaos. She's trying to find a balance now—to retain enough hope and purpose to not feel completely devoid of agency, of choice, but to also not trick herself into believing she's the universe's main character, the torchbearer of history, the maker of decisions and deliverer of climaxes. She celebrates her multiple backstories without being unmoored by them, or distilling them obsessively for clues. Maybe an answer will present itself, maybe it'll be the right one.

She's an eye, but she's more—she's a work in progress, a shapeshifter. She's building a body in the wall behind her, and one day she will burst out of the wall, to devour and destroy and grow and build. She's building relationships with other monsters, they can talk to one another, in languages and signals neither the visitors nor the house understands. She lives with the reality that they don't know who they are, or where they're going, and why. She reminds herself this is no different from her previous lives—in each, she sought purpose, narrative, pleasure, connection, enough for her to ignore the inevitability of decay, death, wasted time, wasted potential.

She watches the visitors meet the monsters with something approaching delight, each time. They're not so different from one another—even among the monsters, some treat all of this as a puzzle, a quest, a productivity grind, an evolutionary step. Others give in to nothingness, and devolve into slobbering, mindless swarm-creatures or spores. Some develop new religions, new world-views, new conformities and hierarchies. Whatever they need to feel powerful, to feel alive. She's trying to learn it all, to balance it all, to trust herself to know when to break out, and whom to attack, and what to do next, and why.

For now, she is inside the house, and she's waiting.

The (Lost) Tribe of Ishmael

Maurice Broaddus

LOCATION: Lick Creek (African American) settlement

POPULATION: 260 (1860) → nearly 0 (1862)

"THE ANCIENT ONES *will soon come claim you.*" The words rang in Ishmael Roberts' head as he staggered through the woods. The visions grew in intensity, had a life and voice of their own, not caring if he slept or was awake. The muscles in his leg tightened. His head throbbed. Though not a praying man, he called out to whoever might hear him. Humid and miserable, the rains sprinkled in fits and spurts, refusing to commit to a downpour. Branches swayed, caught up in the slight breeze. Only a few weeks earlier he'd hiked the flat-top ridge through the Orange County wilderness, following a historic bison trail. In the same footsteps of the free black men and women who founded the Lick Creek Settlement. Now the trees seemed wholly unfamiliar to him, rugged terrain determined not to be easily traversed.

The ritual had to be stopped. Ishmael scampered up the hillside. The mud sucked at his feet with each step. He recalled his ancestor's words.

"We cannot control what's written about us unless we write ...

"... the stories we cannot tell," the man stammered through chattering teeth.

Hiding in our barn, we dared not set a fire for him. Wrapping his arms around himself, he rocked back and forth, muttering prayers. I had Anna Mae fix him some soup and keep the children away. We didn't want them to even catch sight of him or know our work so that they wouldn't be burdened by the secrets.

"Here, take this." I handed him an old coat.

"Thanks, mister." His mouth crooked, attempting a thin smile. The heavy gray coat draped down to his thighs. In the night, it would reduce him to a spectral silhouette. The woolen material frayed about the cuffs and tail. A row of buttons made of bone fastened it.

"Don't thank me yet, you ain't through the woods. But this coat's famous among these parts. Iffen you're seen out there in this, carrying this here bucket," I handed him a pail nearly empty of feed, "folks'll just think you're Mr. Lindley out feeding your cows. Once you slip into the trees, you just leave this coat hanging on one so we can retrieve it later. To help the next one along on their leg of the journey."

"I don't know where to go." Wiping up the last bits of soup with a piece of cornbread Anna Mae had wrapped in a napkin, he shoved the last bite into his mouth.

"Follow Lick Creek to Bean Creek. Keep trailing the river north. Just be careful. All manner of predators in the woods. Foxes. Bears. Wolves."

Slave catchers.

The look exchanged between us let the words remain unspoken. The southern most part of our settlement was only twenty to thirty miles from slaveholding Kentucky. Because of the Fugitive Slave Act, the only evidence a court needed was a white person testifying that a black person was an escaped slave. Enterprising folks crossed the border to kidnap any black person to sell off in the south.

"Steal away, steal away home. I ain't got long to stay here!" I sang to myself as the man skulked out into the night.

"Think he'll be alright?" Anna Mae sidled up next to me.

"He already better'n most. He chasing his freedom."

Seeing concern cloud my face, she fussed at the stand up collar of my shirt. Closing my top coat, she patted my chest. "How's my gentleman farmer?"

"Tired. Always tired." I wrapped my arm around her shoulder and drew her close. The drumbeat of her heart called me home.

"Rest a spell."

"Ain't got time for that. Too much to do."

"Make time then. You no good to anyone, Ishmael Roberts, iffen you run down."

Rubbing her protruding belly reminded me why we did the work. Wasn't so long ago our people loaded up a wagon full of furniture, barrels of smoked meat, and linens, all to leave North Carolina. Escorted by some Quakers, we searched for a place where we could live free.

When we walked back to our home, our girls stood about, pleased with themselves for setting the table with our dinner. A rooster crowed in the distance. I shot a glance to Anna Mae. She hustled them towards their room.

"What about dinner?" Our oldest stopped just short of a petulant whine once she caught her mother's stern expression.

"You go on now, hear? Don't you come out lessen we call for you," I barked.

"Momma?" Always more sensitive, our youngest's face reflected the hint of fear fluttering in our hearts.

"You'll be alright. Just do what we say," Anna Mae said.

Taking their plates, the girls snuck up to their loft. Despite our warning, I knew their eager ears would be pressed to the door. Good. They needed to learn the lessons of survival. Someone pounded at the door. Anna Mae fetched the shotgun, but stayed just around the corner while I opened the door. A puffy faced man greeted me. Reverend Charles Edward Bautista.

From up Corydon way, the devil dodger thought he could just come into Lick Creek, pretty as he pleased, like it was his birthright to go wherever he wanted. His ruffled black cassock was framed by a dirty clerical collar. All the hair had fled from the top of his head, retreating down the back. Scraggy white sideburns lined his face. His eyes black as unlit coal. Though no church would have him, he traveled about like an itinerant preacher, exhorting the masses about how our people had no standard for morality. How our excitement for battle was a product of our licentious craving for violence. How we were unchaste after marriage. Untruthful. Lovers of music and all manner of spirits. And our biggest sin: pauperism, believing it our destiny to be cared for by the government with the churches and charities as particeps criminis. Fancy talk for the folks like the Quakers being accomplices in a poverty of our own making.

"What brings you out this way, reverend?" I asked.

"You mean to your little squatters hamlet?"

"Bought all legal and proper," I reminded him like I did at every occasion, in the vain belief that one day the reality of us would sink in.

His nervous equilibrium betrayed his own descent into spirits, having developed a drinking problem after he left the church behind. After he left the church, he moved from almsgiving to exclusion of those in need he deemed unworthy. He was indicted for bringing in slaves from out of state. These days he published a Copperhead newspaper for the southern sympathizers who were pro-slavery and anti-Indiana participating in the Civil War. I heard tell he was prone to spells, seeing things, and strange mutterings.

"I'm after a man. A troublemaker said to be working his way north. To Indianapolis, perhaps to Canada."

"What business is it of yours?" I asked.

"It is our right to 'regulate for the future, by prompt correctives, the emigration into the State and the continuance of known paupers thrown upon us from any quarter. ... If they cannot afford, by sureties, indemnity to our citizens by reasonable time, should be thrown back into the State or country from whence they came.' Our laws and way of life are under siege from freed slaves, from you ... Ishmaelites."

The Indiana State Constitution of 1816 banned slavery and indentured servitude. But by 1831, every free black person had to post bond of $500 or face expulsion from state. In fact, Indiana drafted a Second Constitution in 1851 which forbade blacks from migrating to the state at all. It even required blacks in state to register on its Negro Register. His unwanted presence was his reminder to us of the reality as he saw it.

"Ain't nothing troublemaking out here 'ceptin' our cows," I said.

"I've dealt with your type back in the city. Taking a stretch of refuse land, or haunts of swampy ground along rivers with a smell so rank, worse'n a walking livery stable. Living in a place that does not speak well of your character."

"Well, those of us unspeakable character have not seen any troublemakers." To Bautista, Lick Creek was tenements, shacks, hovels, and houses of ill-fame. He never saw how our people intentionally created a culture that was different. How we centered high literacy and education. How we grew whatever we needed and raised livestock, making the community dependent on no one. How we had leadership without hierarchy, only a strong sense of community instilled in everyone. Keeping the door close behind me, I continued to block his view into our home.

Suspicious, Reverend Bautista scoured as best he could. "Awful quiet in there."

"I run a disciplined house," I said.

The cutting air left a growing chill between us.

"You a church going man?"

"Not as much as I'd like." Even in our settlement, we had to be careful about church assemblies. They made white folks nervous. Every service was followed by rumors—sweeping through the land like an illness—of us plotting an insurrection.

"You frequent applicants for charity is not your fault really. It was the curse of Ham for you to be servants. This land is a babel of poverty and filth, but it has potential."

"I think you'd best be on your way. Reverend." I let the last word punctuate my sentence.

"This is what the world has descended into. Being dismissed by the pauper class." Reverend Bautista fixed his hat to his head. *"You forget your place. But you'll learn."*

"I own myself. My land. Myself." I called out to his back, the good reverend stomping off to his horses, fit to be tied. *"We all free people round these parts. One day you'll learn."*

Though the heat of my words felt good in the moment, they were foolhardy. It was an unnecessary risk to stir up a man like Reverend Bautista. They say he was connected with some vigilante groups, like the Knights of the Golden Circle and the Sons of Liberty.

I patted the air. Anna Mae lowered the shotgun. Nonsense though it was, my spirit compelled me to see the box. To touch it. Know it was safe. Rolling the rug back, I knelt on the floor and felt for the hidden catch. The boards lifted and inside the nook was a small wooden crate built to house my papers. Holding the deed to our property, our free papers, and my journal, it was to be passed down, parent-to-child, until slavery was no longer a threat.

I flipped through the pages of my journal. More like a collection of letters written down when the spirit settled on me. Like a waking dream, except the words came out in symbols, a kind of hieroglyphs. Images which somehow decoded themselves in my mind. Despite how clear the drawings were, the story made no sense. It described a formless world and a golden passageway. Arranging the letters carefully back in order, I resealed the box and locked it away.

A rock crashed through the grease paper covering our windows.

Without so much as a tremble of hesitation, Anna Mae set a pot of water over the fire to be used as a potential weapon. Grabbing her broom, she swept up the mess. "Certain kinds of white men can get mighty mean. 'Specially when they think we getting over on 'em."

"They live driven by their fear." *I covered the hidden nook with the rug.* "And they fear us something fierce."

"Canada's looking pretty good right about now." *Anna Mae grimaced, pressing her hand into her side. The baby must've kicked. Probably another girl on the way.*

"There are sacraments. Sacrifices that have to be made." *The words tumbled out of me as if I recited an ancient ritual.* "Blood will tell."

"Steal away, steal away home." *Anna Mae said.* "Time ...

"... will reveal," Ishmael Roberts mumbled to himself. Named for a private in the 10th North Carolina Regiment who served in the Revolutionary War, an eponymous ancestor also owned the land in Lick Creek where they built the Methodist Union Meeting House. The gray in his hair hadn't began to infiltrate his heavy beard. The keloid scar on top of his left arm itched, an almost purple sheen against his dark skin.

The Lick Creek African American Settlement—aka Little Africa aka South Africa aka Paddy's Garden—existed as a ghost town. It started with 96 blacks in 1820 when Jonathan Lindley led eleven families, free citizens, fleeing persecution and the restrictive laws in North Carolina. They settled in what would become Orange Country in 1811, before Indiana was even a state. By 1855, the Lick Creek Settlement reached its maximum size of 1557 acres with a population of 260 people by 1860. But in 1862, most traces of it had disappeared.

"A mystery of history." Ishmael could only imagine what it felt like to move among free black people. "That's a bar right there."

Crawling along the remains of the foundation of a farmhouse, he peeled back layers of time like pages in an ancient manuscript. Ishmael had already found archaeological evidence in the form of dishware, that the settlement flourished just as well as its white neighbors. Echoes of forgotten lives, each artefact whispered a secret, each piece a narrative thread intertwining with others to reveal the tapestry of the town that was. With each careful brush stroke, he sifted the soil.

Uncovering and sharing the truth was his life's work. The goal of his ongoing research was to learn the stories of his family, to preserve them and pass them down. But he wanted to do more than just commemorate and preserve. The silent testimonies needed to be told, even if his ancestors were long gone from this place. Their humanity, their rich history of resilience, was a model for the future.

His probe bumped against something solid. Digging with conscientious precision, he reached a yellowed plate of bone. Swabbing around it, he exhumed a ghost of the past. A strange, misshapen skull, he cradled in his hand as he examined it. The side had been brutally crushed.

Ishmael walked back to his basecamp at the cemetery. The surrounding trees bent, their serpentine roots displaced, as if desperate to flee from the very earth itself. Now part of Hoosier National Forest, all that remained of the Lick Creek Settlement was a few foundation stones and the Thomas and Roberts family cemetery with its dozen or so marked graves. The last person buried there was Simon Locust in 1891. He served in the Civil War in Company E of the 28th Regiment of U.S. Colored Troops.

"All hail our queen." Ishmael bowed deeply once he stopped before the figure nestled within a weathered rocking chair. "How are you doing, Ms. Nancy?"

"Old, yet festive." Ms. Nancy wrapped her hair with care. The filigree of wrinkles framing her mouth parted when she smiled. A library unto herself, no one knew for sure how old she was, though some guessed seventy. She fanned herself, her grin becoming almost coquettish. "I see you found some new treasures."

"Disturbing treasures." He held out the deformed skull.

"History is often disturbing. Too many people involved in its doing and telling." She shifted against a cushion that no longer boasted vibrant colors. "Find any clues about what happened to our people?"

"You sound skeptical."

"If they want us to know, they'll find a way to tell us."

"Even the rocks will cry out, eh?"

"Something like that."

"The Settlement left traces, signposts along the trail. I'm pretty sure most folks went on to live out their time happy and watched over by our ancestors." The Lick Creek Settlement was ambitious about growing their community, which threatened their white neighbors. Legislation banning further settlement. The laws pushing back against them were already being talked about. The requirement of bond payments and the need for "Freedom Papers." The tidal wave of harassment reaching them even in Indiana. With the Civil War looming, so would forced conscription. The residents made arrangements, cashing out their property first as seven Lick families sold their farms. All of these factors fed into the many theories about their sudden disappearance. Ishmael found evidence indicating many folks moved to Indianapolis with some even finding their way to Kent County, Ontario, Canada near Detroit. But that didn't fully explain the mass exodus.

A car rumbled along the ridge, drawing their attention. It wound its way down the dirt road, its tires spitting rocks before slowing to a halt. Ishmael stationed himself between her and the stranger. A corpulent man with a shock of unkempt white hair exited the car. His chinos stopped too high above his ankles. A crisp, open-collar shirt revealed the chain of a necklace. An ill-fitting blazer struggled too hard to appear casual.

"Howard Bautista. You must be Ishmael Roberts. I was told you'd be hard at work up here." Extending his hand, his lascivious eyes leered at the undeveloped landscape. "And you would be?"

Ms. Nancy sucked her teeth and turned away.

"How can we help you, Mr. Bautista?" Ishmael asked.

"Howard, please. We're all trying to be friends here." Bautista tugged at his blazer. "I'm just out surveying."

"This is federal land. A protected site. It won't be developed." The Forest Service released details about cultural sites on a need-to-know basis. There wasn't even signage for the settlement site.

"Well, I wouldn't be the man I am without vision and patience. Laws change. Statuses change. I just have to remain vigilant."

"We have that much in common."

"From what I hear, we share that and a love of history. Mine is one of the oldest families in the nation. We can trace our roots back to the Mayflower itself."

"My family is here." Ishmael wiped down the nearest tombstone, revealing the name "Ishmael Roberts."

"I have a forbear who wrote extensively about the people he found here. Their coarse manners, inelegant by any standards. Primitive in their way of life, lacking the subtlety of grace. How, largely ignorant and dishonest, they were ever ready to fight."

"Ah, the letters of the good Reverend Charles Edward Bautista." The one-time minister considered himself a charity reformer. He preached against alcoholism, social dependency, lack of moral control ... though he saved his most scathing commentary for those he determined coddled such behavior. Fear was his tradition. Fear was his inheritance. Fear was his legacy. "I read his papers as part of my dissertation. I enjoyed debunking and dismantling them as the racist-propaganda-masquerading-as-social-science that they were."

"While certainly not scientific, his views were illuminating in their ability to elucidate the phenomena of what we see all about us."

"Wasn't the good reverend charged with treason?" Ishmael nearly sprained all the muscles in his face to keep himself from grinning.

"His death sentence was commuted by President Andrew Johnson." Bautista didn't bother to hide the sneer in his voice.

"Well, he never understood—or refused to understand—what he saw here. The Lick Creek Settlement was ahead of its time." Ishmael didn't bother to hide the pride in his voice.

"My family knows all about that sad song. They railed against those that had more charitable hearts than commonsense. The more you help such people, the more it encourages them to lead, shall we say, an idle life. You make poverty and complaining your profession."

"Are we no longer trying to be friends?" Ishmael resisted the urge to hit the man in his very punchable face, knowing that would only bolster the narrative the gentrifier wanted to spin.

"Friends can disagree." Bautista smirked, relishing the dilemma.

"Not about our humanity. We fought long and hard to achieve

our freedom. Look around you, really look, at the sacrifices made here. This place was even a stop on the Underground Railroad."

Bautista appeared genuinely surprised by that. "There's no written evidence of that. The Quakers did that work."

"You trust too much in the hegemony of text. The lack of story is my evidence."

"That makes no sense."

"People often forget that such activities were illegal, 'underground' for a reason. Our folks weren't foolish enough to write down the details of what they did. Iffen you check the membership rolls of the church around that time, you'll find that there were even gaps in the records to protect their congregants." *Iffen?* The trace of accent slipped out, rang oddly, disturbing in his ear.

"And their time has passed. I believe in natural selection, survival of the fittest. It's the way of life. Progress waits for no one. My forbear had vision and a plan to preserve our way of life and rightful place in it. I mean to see it through."

With that, Bautista slinked back to his car. The carriage rocked as he entered it. The engine grumbled to life. With a wave, he took off.

"What do you think he meant by that?" Ishmael asked.

"In my family, there are stories we tell and stories we don't tell. The story of our people departing, we don't tell. They left and we don't know where they went."

"They abandoned us?"

"No. They saved us." Ms. Nancy produced a box. "The ancestors promised a storm. Whenever we needed help, they would be ...

"... all too happy to lend a hand." Anna Mae patted the woman's back.

"It was a tough time. My husband was gone, and I was struggling with a newborn. I didn't know how I'd manage the rest of the children." She wept grateful tears.

The congregation, dressed in their best gone-ta-meeting clothes, nodded and Amened as they made their way back to their seats. The wooden pews creaked softly as the parishioners settled in.

"Thank you for the testimony." His voice deep and resonant, the dignified

minister stood behind the makeshift pulpit, Bible in hand. "Does anyone else have any words?"

"With the permission of my elders," I rose. An elderly woman in a head scarf nodded. We couldn't speak plainly. The slave catchers had ears everywhere, always creeping about our meetings, listening for any clues of our next moves or evidence that we were fomenting discontent. Which, to them, we did simply by existing, because our ancestors dared to dream. We chained dogs nearby to alert us to any strangers slinking about. Several families had sold their land in preparation for what we knew would come next. I was ready to pray about the North Star, the gathering clouds of the coming storm of men seeking retribution. The need for final preparations and to remain vigilant because it would be any moment. My head swam as if dizzy, casting about as if it bobbed on a vast ocean. A calmness settled on me. A knowing. A clarity.

"Before the minister gives his sermon, I'd like to remind us of where we came from. Our family has been telling the stories for hundreds of years. Every word in its place, none forgotten. In the beginning were the ancestors, the orisha of earth and sky and sea. One day, Obalata, the sky father, ever mysterious in his ways, judged the kingdom of his sister, Olukun, as a melancholy bleakness. So he sought permission to travel to it, to provide land so that fields could grow. With hills and valleys to give shape to it. But he did not know how he was supposed to get there. So, he sought out the house of Orunmila, the orisha of wisdom, who understood the secret ways of existence. Orunmila told him that he was to descend the 'golden chord.'"

I reached out for the pulpit to steady myself. The story came through me, images and symbols flitted through my mind in its telling.

"When the preparations had been made, Obalata forged the chain from star stuff, opening a doorway to begin his descent. Passing through the storm, he traveled from the realm of light through the region of grayness. The whooshing like the ocean's waves marked his passage. And after a time, he reached his destination."

"And then what happened?" Anna Mae shouted.

"Creation." My voice not my own, unable to control my body. My fingers dug into the wood. A drumbeat pounded in my soul, leaving me ready to dance. I snapped out of my waking dream. The eyes of my neighbors studied me. Several nodded, understanding a truth inscribed on their hearts.

The dogs next door barked, so anxious their cries of concern reduced to a low whine. We rushed outside. Smoke came from the other side of the settlement. Everyone scurried to their stations. Women scooped up children, *running to the closest houses. They barricaded the doors and blew out their candles. We could not make it appear too easy for them. There had to be a cost. Men grabbed their shotguns and ran towards the smoke. When we arrived, flames engulfed a cabin.*

"Help me!" The screams of its owner seared into my memory. The stifled sobs of the girls, desperate pleas carried by the night. The men formed chains, passing buckets of water from a well to the house.

A cruel shadow shifted, fleeing into the darkness.

"It's a trap," I said. "They're coming for me."

"I'll get my shotgun," Anna Mae said.

"No." I hold my head back, facing the sky. The first smattering of rain pelted my face. "The ancestors are sending the storm to watch over us. I'll lead them away. You must make the final preparations and find me."

"You can't go alone."

"He won't be," the pastor said. A few men circled up with us.

"We'll lead them away from here. No weapons. Our ancestors will protect us." I headed to the barn and donned the coat. Fastening the last bone button into place, I marched the half dozen men into the woods. We stayed on the bison trail, knowing we would be followed. We didn't have to wait long.

The night concealed the approach of the slave catchers. The hooded figures took their positions at the front door and the rear of our parade, hoping to cut off our escape routes before we realized they were there. Their overconfidence got the better of them. The muffled sounds of the nearing footsteps echoed through the woods. We braced ourselves.

The Knights of the Golden Circle charged us from all sides. At the first shotgun blast we froze. This was what we left North Carolina to escape. They circled, braying hyenas, with their jeers and spittle. Their fists battered our sides, driving us to our knees so they could truss us up. One of the slavers struck a match, bathing Bautista's face in its orange glow.

"Call out to whoever you want. You have no gods left ...

"... to save us." Ishmael glanced up from the papers. The strange symbols whispered to corners of his spirit, stirring them to full wakefulness. "I think something happened in the woods."

"What?" Ms. Nancy poured him a cup of root tea.

"I don't know. I just know something ... big is coming. Bautista is at the heart of it."

Weathered shutters framed the windows of Bautista's modest two-story home. Its gabled roof sheltered a deceptively welcoming front porch. Thin wisps of smoke issued from the stone chimney. A servant directed Ishmael around back, parking where they once would have received a horse. The solid oak door creaked open, the servant escorting him from the mudroom to the parlor. A central fireplace warmed the room full of handcrafted furniture and well-scuffed, wide-planked wooden floors. The servant closed the door as he exited.

"What brings you to my humble abode?" Bautista lowered his glasses and closed the book he had been studying.

Ishmael noted some of the titles along the bookshelves. *On Witch Cults. Dream Deciphering. Atlantis and the Lost Realms.* Many works were much older, the titles worn down to being illegible. The inheritance from the reverend who probably whiled away his income purchasing tomes. All for the study and pursuit of obscure arcana.

Ishmael had the unsettling impression that he'd been expected. Candles flitted about in an unfelt breeze. A heady incense wafted, almost smothering in its cloying odor. "The truth? I knew you were planning something. Something far grander than coffeeshops and local breweries."

"I don't know if you're ready for the full truth. It's a story much older than you or I."

"The reason my people disappeared from the Lick Creek Settlement."

"The story begins with the Great Old Ones, those Elder Gods who existed outside of time, beyond the veil. Out of the sky, inside the earth, under the sea. The reverend believed that your Lick Creek Settlement was the prophesied site of the mighty city of R'lyeh, home of the Old Ones ... if such a place had any such urban connotation. After all, it was a place with no definite structure or buildings. With strange geometry, spheres, and unnamed dimensions. A place of monoliths and sepulchers."

"What does this have to do with ..."

Bautista waved him off. Setting the book aside, he paced about the room. "You see, my forbear was able to predict the crisis our nation, our Western civilization, now finds itself in. He hoped to stave it off. If humanity was going to be free, if it was to take the next step in its development, it would have to free itself from men of low or mixed blood holding it back. The mentally ... aberrant. He wanted to end the Civil War by sacrificing members of that community to open the door for the Elder Gods to return. He believed that when the stars were right, the Old Ones would rise again, plunge from world to world, to lead us to our rightful place of supremacy. But something went awry. I go to prepare the way. You are fated to bear witness. To see what happens to your beloved settlement. To see our final triumph. The ancient ones will soon come claim you."

Ishmael's thoughts muddled together. He steadied himself against the bookshelves. His legs buckled.

"*Cthulhu R'lyeh.*" Bautista winked as if they were in on the same joke. He cradled his book. Donning a black and red robe, he readied himself for the unhallowed rites of his ceremonial service. In a language lost to antiquity, Bautista reduced Ishmael's world to a ...

... shadow over the hillside. The wind whistled through the trees. Birds gathered in their branches, chattering in their night songs. The stars blinked in the outer darkness. The moonlight dappled our faces like reflections on water.

The Knights of the Golden Circle erected a cross and set it on fire. Its light filled the entire grove. We did not fear the night, not the way they hoped. Our ancestors hid us in their protective embrace.

Wearing black and red robes, his hood drawn up, Reverend Bautista stood by a stone altar at the heart of the clearing, ominous symbols carved into it. The air heavy with dread. The reverend held an ancient manuscript high above his head. His chants carried into the woods. The guttural vocalizations of a language unheard by humanity for millennia. His men focused on him, not hearing the approaching people.

"Put your weapons down." Anna Mae cocked her rifle behind the man nearest me. More of our people emerged from the surrounding forest, disarming the Knights. The reverend stopped mid-chant.

"No," Bautista whispered. "We are so close."

"The time's not quite right. The stars still have to align. They ain't there yet. But soon." I held my hands out for Anna Mae to cut my bonds.

"How are you?" she asked.

"I am tired." A weariness ran to my bones, the way a damp chill did, but I focused on the future to keep me sharp. I carved a circle into the earth.

"What are you doing?" Reverend Bautista studied us with a cool aplomb.

"You brought us this far, we'll finish the ceremony for you."

"I don't understand." The words curdled on his tongue. He clutched his archaic tome to his chest.

"You never did because you couldn't see us."

"This here is a witness tree." Anna Mae dug into her pockets, removing small bags of dirt from the family cemetery. Herbs from her special garden. She dashes to the creek to collect fresh water, sprinkling libations in each direction before she started. "The first thing our ancestors planted when they arrived. Providing limbs for children to climb and play in. Shade for families to enjoy meals under. Fruit to feed us. It has survived wars and storms. It is still here."

One of the men who accompanied Anna Mae handed the pastor a drum. The earth threatened to rumble apart and devour us.

"And it came to pass, as he had made an end of speaking all these words, that the ground clave asunder that was under them: And the earth opened her mouth, and swallowed them up, and their houses, and all the men that appertained unto Korah, and all their goods. They, and all that appertained to them, went down alive into the pit, and the earth closed upon them: and they perished from among the congregation." The pastor passed the drum to me. "This is yours."

"No. Someone has to lead us into the breach."

"And someone shall. Your place is here. To lead the rest of us home. And to remember."

I placed the drum between my legs. Two other men joined me in pounding out the song written in our spirit. Anna Mae draped several of our people with intricate beads. To the cadence of drums, they formed a ceremonial procession. They marched in locked step, moving to the same rhythm. Unafraid. Heads held high. Our chorus of drumming rose. Sounds tumbled from my mouth, inchoate and incomplete, pulled out of me like an involuntary hymn. At first, rage fueled my voice, but my tone morphed, my chants swelling into a song of praise until a spirit descended on me. My spirit *unfurled, a grand sail in the wind of the divine. My fingertips tingled before going numb, tracing an ancient pattern in the air.*

With an eerie glow, the boundary between worlds began to collapse. Shadows danced about grotesque frescos along the tree. A great scratching, like the sound of rats scurrying in walls. Otherworldly echoes reverberate through the trees, the whispers and wails of shapeless elemental things. An aperture widened, unmeasured spaces intruding into our world. A colossal silhouette of a tentacle.

Death was here.

The portal opened wider, a waiting maw full of evil spirits and blasphemous shapes. The stench of brine wafted through. The nameless blight, a lurking fear, drew closer from the outer voids. My mind could only contain pieces, flitting images, of the eldritch abominations. A loathsomeness that waited in nightmares and the obsidian abyss. The varied daemonic reflections were impossible to distinguish between separate organisms or one voiceless horror. A gelatinous green immensity—slobbering, slavering, shrieking, slithering—writhed forward. Its viscous feelers hinted at a larger monstrosity. The eldritch abominations,

Within the bright light, an awful squid-like head—a nightmare spectacle with mandibles the size of our cabin—towered over us. We drummed harder. Our people danced.

"We remember," Anna Mae intoned.

"They say our ancestors set the lights in the sky. The will of the orisha." I retrieved the ancient book from the reverend.

"Our people used to live in a land of lush fields and cool rivers, protected by tall trees. We were torn from that land, that place of our birth, shorn from our roots. But we remember. The old ways passed down in story and song."

"And we promised ourselves that we would find our way back home." I set the book next to the flaming cross. Bautista cried out as the pages browned, the pages curling as they blackened.

"But until then, we would watch out for one another. Heal from the scars inflicted upon us. And we would remember." Anna Mae backed away.

A low rumble reverberated through the woods, a response to our call. A distant storm approached. The air chilled, pulsing with an unseen charge. The clouds gathered, blocking out the moon's wan light. There was a slave fort in Wagadu, and many like it across Alkebulan, from where millions of our people were shipped off around the world. There was a giant red door. Before they cross its threshold, they spared one last glimpse of their homeland, even if it was just the confines of the prison fort. Because they knew once they went through that entrance they would be loaded into a cargo hold and shipped off with no chance of returning home. Behind the pastor, our people formed a procession without fear. Their eyes wide open. No chains bound them.

The pastor turned and locked eyes with me. He shouted. "I am free. You will be free. A place to raise our children to be free."

He stepped over the threshold of the portal. Lightning flashed. Time lost all meaning. There was a terrible roar. I ran towards them, my legs thrashed as hard as they could toward the horrible clicking noises. There were inhuman screams. The light withdrew and the doorway closed behind them. By the time I reached the spot, I only found disordered earth covered with blood. Tattered remnants of rent flesh. Reverend Bautista clawed his skin. His eyes reflected the insanity of the reality he craved. His remaining men scattered. Dropping to my knees, my hand sifted the dirt. Anna Mae rested her hand on my shoulder. I didn't remember repeating the words. "We are not alone. We are ...

"... never alone." Desperate once he awoke, Ishmael knocked on strangers' doors, begging for help, but no one answered. The darkness coalesced, almost material. He ran along the dry stream bed up the bison trail, into the woods. The path rose up the hill, an earthen stairwell, until he reached the top. From this vantage point, the entire collapsed eight-acre sinkhole came into view, its stone molding like an immense carved door.

Guided by the flashes of occasional lightning and the growing howl of the wind, he raced down the hillside. Trees muffled thunder, the storm descended. Ishmael cried out, crescendos of ululation, a primordial sound reverberating from deep within his belly like a vibration of the soul. A resonance in tune with the pulse of the universe.

He was too late.

Howard Bautista held a book aloft, chanting time-lost words, shrill clicks which weren't made to be uttered by the human tongue. A ray of light stabbed through the dark. A terrible antiphonal response, rending the air as the door opened. Ready to reduce the world to screams and fires content to be supreme in a kingdom of ashes.

The air crackled with energy, a swirling vortex splitting the space between them as the boundaries between worlds eroded. Bathed in a radiant glow, iridescent tendrils flopped through the breach. A monstrosity's giant head loomed. The jubilance of Bautista's expression soured, growing slack. His eyes dulled with dawning terror. The creature's head careened forward, tumbling out of the doorway like a boulder shoved free of a cave entrance.

Figures emerged from behind the fissure. Nor Bautista's Old Ones, but Ishmael's. A shimmering aura of golden light swathed the first figure. They moved with grace and fluidity. Another, mercurial as the wind, cloaked themselves in storm clouds, he spoke with thunderous echoes. The last an ethereal beauty, her laughter like cascading water, dwelling in the places where stories end.

Dropping to his knees, Ishmael understood that he stood on holy ground.

"You were never alone." Their voices locked in prayer, a hymn carried by the wind. Whispers without words, speaking secret things into the night. "We are free. You will all be free."

Inviting the Hollow Bones

Octavia Cade

LOCATION: Echo Valley, Fiordland, Southland, New Zealand

POPULATION: 0

A LEGEND IS A BLOODY THING. Something built on the bones of old history, something built in cramped spaces because all the expectations of greater things have been lost. That's what legends are, in the end: compromise. Ersatz. Stunted little stories made in order for us to pretend that the original had more life in it that it did, and that we cared for that life when we had it when really, we cared more for it when it was gone.

We make legends to ameliorate guilt. We make the legends smaller, to include reality.

"I suppose I'd rather have a bush moa than no moa," says Alana. Not that either of us think that any of the moa are still alive, despite the lingering stories, over generations, of survivors hidden in the dense Fiordland forests. The blurred photos, the scattered footprints. They could easily be fakes.

If any of them do survive, it would be the little bush moa. The smallest of the moa, not much more than a metre tall. It's terrible to think of a Lazarus species as a disappointment, if it ever were rediscovered in some distant valley, but we'd all be thinking it: why couldn't it have been the giant moa, up to three times the height of its little cousin, with that long neck, reaching skywards? Why couldn't it have been the marvel?

These aren't questions. We know why. We took an axe to marvels, I think, and built the legends from their bones.

Fiordland is so vast. There may even be moose, introduced into the country and left to roam wild. People talk of moose as much as they do of moa. Not because we love them more, but because the chances of them, like the bush moa, are a little greater.

We're not a flighty people. Our legends, such as they are, are kept within bounds. Better to manage the expectations of miracles than to disdain them altogether.

"I reckon if you're going to hope you should go hard," says Alana. "Hope for the big ones. Why not?" She's photographing the rock shelter as she says it—empty now, long empty—where the most complete skeleton of the little bush moa was ever found. It was partially mummified; enough to extract DNA. Nearly a complete genome. The shutter clicks as she talks, the camera old-fashioned. Why she hasn't brought digital I don't know, but it's her choice, not mine. Every artist has their quirks.

"I like the sound it makes," she says. "Digital is so quiet. This isn't a space for quiet." Echo Valley, and we'd both liked the sound of that, back in our Dunedin studio, assembling and disassembling sculpture, trying to build repetition and conversion out of the old bones we'd borrowed from the university's medical department. We've got an in with them, having been subject to their studies for years. It's how we met, but what we have can't be staved off forever. Yet doomed things get sympathy, and sympathy got us bones to practice with.

"Fake bones," Alana had said, twitching her nose over them, but it wasn't as if they were going to lend us the real thing, not for artistic dry runs. "Plastic. Typical."

"I think it's easier with plastic," I'd said, marking the bones with stickers so we could remember what went where. Cobbled into shape, the pieces did not look convincing. I poked at one of the vertebrae. "Do you think that's the right way up?"

"Fuck knows. Can't we call it artistic license?"

"You want memory, not monstrosity," I'd reminded her. Monstrosity was my part.

"You should be more concerned with your accuracy than with mine," she replied.

My accuracy was nothing I was concerned about. That would come easy as breathing.

There is an absence, now, where the Echo Valley skeleton was. Alana likes it better that way. "Empty space," she says. "It's easier to build around." The skeleton's in a museum somewhere, sanctified. Curators touch it with gloves. Bare skin is sacrilege; a legend loses potency when flesh meets bone, but enough articulation remained to the skeleton, enough dried out meat and feather, that it's become a liminal space: dead, but with enough genetic potency that resurrection is possible, perhaps. The empty space where movement was, and muscle, is transformable.

Not extinct, not yet. But not alive either. "Perhaps that's what a skeleton is," says Alana. "Invitation."

I understand why she wants to think so.

"I understand why *you* do," she says. Her tone is not entirely kind, but we are complicit in this together. The invitation is shared.

Isn't that what a legend is? An acknowledgement of empty space and an invitation to fill it in the ways that hurt, because if legends don't hurt, don't tease and tempt with the promise of a fulfillment that would never come, well, what good are they then?

We don't make them up for fun. Legends exist for atonement. We did something wrong, all of us or some of us, and the legend is there to say things can be made right. It's a lie, more often than not, because some things can't be remedied and guilt is one of them. I would say extinction, but that's not true, not any more. Extinction, perhaps, can be reversed. Guilt never can.

Might as well make a performance of it.

"I've always wanted to see one," Alana says, while I chop wood for the fire with a small hand axe. She's on her stomach and dreaming, has taken off her shirt and her bra, is lying on the ground with that pale length of backbone exposed and her head propped up on her hands. All those vertebrae, reaching out. I can hear the clicks as she stretches, as if her spine is a camera. "I grew up round here, you know. I had hopes. I'd wander in the bush for weeks, making bargains with myself. If I could just see one. If I could just know. I'd picture myself trying to feed them. Food in my hand, like they were ducks at the park, like I could make them friends. Like I could invite them home. And I'd hear stories of hunters and trampers that would catch a glimpse of something, out of the corner of their eye, and I knew it was nothing. Imagination. Wistfulness, really. The wanting. But I could see how much they wanted it, to invite the legend in. And in the end, I began to think: it's the invitation that's important. The legend isn't worth anything. It's the wanting that counts. That's what makes the difference. Wanting it to be real."

If I were a better friend, a better person, I'd have steered that wanting to a place of silence, or of absence. Empty spaces don't have to be cruel. But legends develop out of cruelty, I think. The echoes of the dead, and of what killed them. There's always something that kills them. There's always a reason for the killing.

We're not the only ones out here. There are artists all through Fiordland, at the sites where moa remains have been found. A collaboration of sorts, between the living and the dead. Moa recreated out of driftwood, out of old iron. Some are carved into beech trees, some are built up out of branches. Not all of them are whole. A thigh bone, a stretch of neck. Footprints concreted into streambanks. They're an invitation to memory: something to be seen out of the corner of the eye, something to spark imagination ... to underline what might be replaced if that DNA was put to better purpose than dead records. Ersatz, yes. But it's the wanting that's the point.

The wanting, and the guilt. They died because of us. A reason for pilgrimage, maybe, but one that neither of us will be making. Visiting the different sites will be left for people who aren't us. I won't be able. Alana won't be capable. It doesn't matter. We made our choices, and recreation is a necessary part of legend.

"I saw a moose once," I tell her. "Not here. A day or two's walk out of Doubtful Sound. It passed me in the bush. Shoulders higher than my head. There were pieces of fern caught in its fur."

"In Doubtful, huh?" I can see that she doesn't believe me. Thinks it a kindness to make her last night one of wonder. Or a tease, perhaps. So much of our talk the last few years has been of miracles, and of how what has happened, or will happen, to our bodies will be seen and recorded and will lead, we hope, to miracles for other people if not for us. "You're both legends for what you're doing," the doctors told us.

Alana found it a comfort to think that way. Not me. I'd rather invite a legend than to be one, which has worked out well for the pair of us, considering. Not all collaborators have it so easy.

"I never told anyone before. I wanted it to be private." Because there'd been so little privacy for me. For either of us. And the size of it, the silence. The absence in the bush when it passed. "I wanted something just for me. But ..." There's an envelope in my pocket. Inside is a piece of paper, a clump of hair I'd taken from a beech tree when the moose brushed past it. I hand the latter over, watch Alana stroke the coarse strands between her fingers.

"This could be anything," she says, but I can see that she's decided to believe me. *It's the wanting that counts*, she'd said, that long stretch of spine gleaming in the light of the little campfire.

The paper is a summary sheet. DNA analysis. Conclusion: *Alces alces andersoni*.

It's not a last wish. That's not what we're inviting in with this particular recreation. But it's something. A prelude, perhaps, or a promise. It would be nice to think so.

"So you've seen a legend," Alana says, glad for me. For us both. "You still want to help make one?"

The moa's long neck, stretching up and up, the curve in the corner of the eye, the one that makes you look twice but which is just a branch in the bush, just a trick of the light. Articulation and recreation. The moment we discovered that Alana's spine was the same sleek length. The practice sessions in the studio, disarticulating plastic vertebrae, human vertebrae, trying to reconfigure them into something memorable. Something to strip down and build up and hang near a rock shelter, the double curve for double take.

An invitation. A memorial.

I brought the axe for more than firewood.

"Go hard," says Alana, but then her part in this was always hope. "Make a legend."

Legends are what we make when there's no doubt left.

They're what we make as replacement.

Chuckle Wet, Chuckle Low

R.L. Meza

LOCATION: Pike's Bend, California, USA

POPULATION: 73

Pup

THE TOURIST LETS his fancy camera dangle on its strap and fishes out a handful of change for the jetty sisters to share, sprinkling coins into their outstretched hands as if he's feeding ducks. I once asked Ma where Jilly and Kara go when they aren't spanging on the wall of rough gray rocks. "Go?" Ma said, and laughed like it was the funniest thing she'd ever heard.

Now that the tourist has paid the toll, he continues towards us along the jetty. I'm so nervous, my guts are churning like the water sloshing through the wall beneath me. It's my first time participating in a sacrifice.

Ma struggles to her feet, wobbling on the wet rocks beside me in her flip flops and holding her pregnant belly like it's a balloon she's afraid to pop. She glances to the north, up the uneven path that runs alongside the rock wall from Pike's Bend to Grayshore. Then she looks south to where the jetty extends beyond the shore, sticking out into the bay like a giant's stony finger and sheltering a small inlet with a crescent beach the tourists all love. Not many people out today. Ma nods, satisfied, and shoos me south along the wall to play my part.

It's a beautiful day, clear enough to see the line of deeper blue out where the ocean feeds into the bay. Heat waves shimmer over the distant strips of sand that partially separate the two bodies of water, but the breeze is cool, thick with mist from the waves crashing against the rocks to my right. As I totter along the jetty's spine, past the dunes sloping gently from the street to the beach on my left, the tourist pauses to photograph the liquid diamonds spraying skyward.

"Mister," I cry out. The camera lowers to reveal a pair of eyes that widen as I skid barefoot across an unstable rock. I hope my expression looks convincing; Ma says my acting needs work. "*Mister*, I need help!"

He lets his camera dangle again, as I grab his hand and point to where Ma is pinwheeling her arms. "It's my mom," I whine. "She can't get down. She's stuck!"

As I tow him north towards Ma, the tourist says, "Don't worry, buddy. We'll get her down." And: "Are you having a baby brother or sister?"

I don't talk to him. Ma says it'll be easier if I don't.

When we've almost reached her, Ma's skinny legs go out and she falls down on her backside with a startled squawk. I dance to the side, avoiding the gaps between rocks to duck behind her.

"Jesus, ma'am," the tourist says. "Are you all right? Easy now, don't try to get up."

He steps carefully towards her, but not carefully enough. As he reaches down to grip Ma's arms and hoist her up, she utters a phrase in a language only our family back at camp can understand. Her chewed nails dig into the man's wrists and she twists, shifting the balance between them.

And the man falls between the rocks of the jetty, like a coin dropped through a slot. The hole is so small, even a ten-year-old kid like me would have trouble worming in, but Ma has her ways. She gets the angle just right. "Right as rain," she howls.

A trio of beachgoers—mom and dad in matching sweatshirts, and baby toddling in the gentle water—squint in our direction then return to their activities. Sunlight glares off the windows of the cars parked along the street. No one gets out to ask about the man the jetty just swallowed.

Tourist season's almost over, and the Lighthouse Inn across the street is vacant, same with the diner tacked onto the side. Most of the locals live in the trailer park down the way, and they eat early to avoid the tourists. Another week or two, and it'll just be the locals to the south, and our family camping in the trees that run north along the path from Pike's Bend to Grayshore. Pike's Bend is what Ma calls a *blink-and-you'll-miss-it town*.

Right now, Ma's as close to happy as she ever gets. She nods at the small black hole and says, "The camera, Pup. And the sunglasses."

"Whaddabout his wallet?" I crouch and peer down at the man pinned below. His mouth is working, but his chest must be pinched because he only manages a strangled whistle.

Ma snorts, thumbing through a sheaf of bills in a leather bifold wallet. "Got it already."

Lying flat on my chest, I snake a thin arm into the jetty's moist throat and hook a finger around the camera's strap. The tourist's eyes bulge. He wheezes a plea as I pluck the sunglasses from his shirt collar.

"Couldn't we call somebody?" I ask, thinking we already got what we came for. The camera's so heavy, it must be expensive, and the glasses shine like rainbows; Ma and the family will be smoking their special crystals all week after a haul like this one. But I can't see any reason why the guy needs to go on suffering. A quick call from the phone booth out by the trailer park would be easy enough. Nobody's gonna find him otherwise. The beachgoers are packing up their stuff, and except for the jetty sisters, there's no one else around.

Ma tosses the man's I.D. into the bay with the wallet and shoves the rest into her bag without responding. So I say, "Nobody'd have to know it was us. I'd pay for the call myself."

Her eyes go flat and hard.

"Don't you dare, Pup," she says. "You leave him right where he fell, you hear? He belongs to the jetty now."

My head bobs, nice and quick, to show that she doesn't need to smack any sense into me. Still, my guts feel like they're full of the slimy plant stuff clinging to the rocks at the waterline. The man was just trying to help, and we robbed him.

He's struggling down there, limbs bent into funny angles, but he can speak a little better now. A crab scuttles over his upturned face. He keeps going on about how someone's down there with him.

"Laughing," he whispers. "She's ... laughing at me. Oh, god, please ... please help me."

He reaches for me and slips in deeper. The hole gets tighter farther down—they always do. Waves crash, invading the jetty, and the water rises to the man's stomach, swirling.

Ma hops down from the rocks, heading north towards camp. We walk with backs bent and eyes sharp, as we search the rock wall along the way for more treasures. Ma finds a gold chain crusted with sand and mumbles a prayer. Her lips suck in then pooch out, like they always do when she's not talking, as if she's chewing on a mouthful of air.

I crawl into a cave to retrieve a watch. A layer of silty water oozes behind the cracked face, but the hands are still ticking. When I try to pass it to Ma, she says, "Nah, keep it. You should always keep your first gift."

She tugs a locket from beneath her shirt; I'm surprised she hasn't pawned it yet. "The first one is lucky," she says. "It's *symbolic*, the jetty's way of thanking you. Don't lose it, you hear?"

Nodding, I slip the watch around my wrist. It doesn't fit, so Ma gives me a hairband to tie it with. I like the jetty's gift. The watch covers the cigarette burns from the times when I didn't *get it* fast enough for Ma. She says I'm kinda slow. She must be having the best kind of day today, because she's not usually this nice.

We go back to our camp in the bushes, where Yellow Pete is waiting with more medicine for Ma, and they smoke their special crystals and the best kind of day turns into the best kind of night while I shiver in the dark, lying on my blanket in the brush and staring at my watch. Wondering if my gift was worth the price.

By morning, the man in the jetty is gone.

Ma

Doesn't take more than a push to put a man in his place. Guy sees a preggo lady like me, trying keep her balance on the jetty, and it doesn't matter about my ratty hair or missing teeth. He's only thinking about the baby, about its *welfare*. Like the hypocrites that forced me and Pup out of the shelter, trying to tell me what I can and can't put in my own body. Offering help, when alls they really give a damn about is new life, not fixing what's old. Hah! Fuck 'em.

The jetty's the only one who gives a damn about me and mine.

The tourists, those smarmy chuckleheads and their snotty brats, don't walk far up the rocky path to Grayshore. The likes of them get one look at our family's camp, the tarps and sleeping bags and litter strewn through the trees between towns, and they turn their spoiled asses around. They stick to the perfect little sandy beach just inside the jetty where their brats can splash in the shallow water. These people, they're overflowing with stuff. So much that they never leave with everything they brought. Imagine having *so much* that you can't keep track of it all. The jetty sees. The jetty knows.

The jetty *craves*, just like the worst of us.

Every morning since he was born, I've crossed the path with Pup to search the jetty with the rest of the family. We pick up stuff, and by the day's end, we'll have a bag full to pawn or trade or recycle.

But I've always handled the rituals alone. Only a few us ever had the stomach for it, and after Wallster hitched south and Straight Edge Lizzy croaked, that left me to do the sacrificing.

It's a two-way street, dealing with the jetty. See, it collects treasures for us, but it expects something in return. Once a month, before a new moon.

During a new moon, that finger of rocks sticking out between the beach and the bay becomes the last place on Earth you want to be. Wallster used to say it wasn't *here* no more, but somewhere squeezed right alongside us—*here-adjacent*'s what he called it. Where the wind goes quiet, water on both sides. I wouldn't go out there under a full moon for a mountain of rock and a million bucks, let me tell you.

After Pup's first ritual, it didn't take more than a day for me to realize something was wrong. Before Pup got involved, the jetty provided.

Then, it was like a switch flipped off.

Nothing and nothing, and not a damn thing to sell. No cans to recycle, no lost or forgotten treasures to pawn. Nothing but scraps of trash chased around by the wind that never really quits blowing around these parts.

Trash is how I know we screwed up. How's the saying go? The Lord giveth and He taketh away? Well, the jetty is my god—the Old Testament kind, that demands a sacrifice to prove your love.

The jetty collects the treasures and offers 'em up. It's got no use for things. People, though ...

You take and you leave something behind. It's a simple trade.

Or, it was until Pup started in with his questions. *Couldn't we call somebody?* I should've known then and there. My boy's always been weak and soft in the head, just like his daddy. The jetty didn't like him neither.

Last time we had a dry spell like this was back when the jetty sisters were still up and moving around; Jilly and Kara learned the hard way not to be ungrateful. Six years now, they've been anchored to that rock for taking and taking, without leaving once. Like a couple of leeches, those two. Spare change is all they can eat now, chipping their teeth down to the gums. Makes for a hell of a warning for the rest of us.

If Pup's not to blame, then the other possibility is that the rituals aren't working like they used to. Maybe our god's appetite is growing.

Maybe the terms of the trade have changed.

As I stare into an empty bag at the end of our fourth day of scavenging, I wonder how many sacrifices it'll take to return the gold to our rocks. Pup offers to give up his watch, but that's not how it works. The jetty craves warm flesh, hot blood.

Back at camp, the family reunites with empty hands and worried faces. They've come to worship the jetty, like me, to depend on the chicken scratch earned by scavenging. We have a whole goddamn ecosystem going. We need that stuff to survive.

The family backs off with their questions when my water breaks. All that screaming and hollering, yet the cops never show up; they leave us alone, so long as we don't camp in town. I squirt the baby out in the bushes, same as a fox or raccoon. Pup is gaping, trembling like a leaf, so I pass the squirming thing over to him. It'll give him something to talk to while I meet with the others and try to figure out how we're gonna square things.

We left Pup's guy where he fell, just like we were supposed to. It was the same old song and dance: find a tourist, someone traveling alone. The jetty rocks are slippery, balanced just so; certain rocks tip and tilt. There's a funny geometry to those angles and slopes, like the holes between are hungry and the rocks are rough tongues, guiding folks down.

Hungry holes.

There's never anything left of the sacrifices after, so we can't tell by looking if Pup's guy escaped somehow. With no way of knowing if we shorted the jetty its tribute, there's only one fix. If the first sacrifice didn't take, we'll have to make another.

A real one.

Something I'll actually miss.

Pup

This last month's been the worst we've ever had. After Ma pushed the baby out, the family set fire to the pile of trash they'd picked up at the jetty and gathered around for their meeting. Yellow Pete had just enough medicine for everyone to smoke for the summoning ritual. *Complimentary*, he said, as he tapped his magic crystals into their pipes.

After the summoning ritual, Ma lit up a cigarette and coughed. I was holding Runt in my lap, feeding strips of tinfoil to the dying fire, when the family all turned to look at me at once. Ma chuckled, wet and low in her throat. She sounded just like the jetty, laughing like that, mean and sneaky. Usually, she'd pinch me next—on the back of the arm or my ribs—but I was out of reach. I held my little brother tighter, hoping Ma's good mood would last.

But it's been real bad. They've been fighting and stealing from each other, and Sal got himself run down by an eighteen-wheeler up on the highway. The family had another meeting yesterday morning. They walked out to the end of the jetty, where there's water on both sides, and wailed and tore at their clothes until the sun went down.

Tonight, it's a new moon. Ma catches my eye across the fire and crooks her finger, saying, "C'mon, Pup, we're going for a walk. Bring Runt."

A nasty chuckle, and she saunters off into the dark.

I check the rest of the family's faces, but they won't look at me or my brother. They don't like Runt much. He was born sick, and the weather turned cold right after, so now he's always crying and coughing up fog. Whenever Ma's off meeting her friend John in Grayshore, the family whispers about how Runt's cursed. They think the jetty's punishing them with his squalling.

But my brother's my best friend in the world. I carry him everywhere in a backpack I wear around front, with the zipper cracked open so he can breathe. It's good having someone to tell my secrets to.

Like how it's my fault the jetty's pissed off.

When Ma doesn't return, I haul on my backpack with Runt inside it and take off down the rocky path after her, keeping my distance from the jetty wall to my right. Without the moon to light our path, I have to follow her burning cigarette. I figure we'll turn left at the beach and take the street to try the doors of any cars parked nearby, but she leads me up onto the jetty wall instead. The fog douses the light of her cigarette like cold soup, stinking of dead fish.

It's too dark to see Ma, but I can hear her nails clicking over the rocks up here, as if she's crawling around like a crab. She's moving south, towards the sheltered beach tucked behind the jetty. As I scramble after her, I wonder if we'll bump into Jilly and Kara; this sends a shiver of excitement through me. I've never been allowed out here after dark.

Runt's being awfully quiet. I give the bag a shake and hear him gurgle. Relieved, I set out to the south, feeling my way along the rocks with bare feet gone numb.

Once I hear the soft lapping of waves on the beach, I stop and listen for Ma. Her clicking keeps going for a second, and then she stops too—or, maybe she's not on all fours anymore. In the dark, I can't make anything out. The fog is blocking the starlight. I wave my hand in front of my eyes.

Nothing.

Something clatters in the distance, out on the rocky finger where we're never supposed to go at night. I call out, "Ma?"

"Out here," she says. "At the end."

And she chuckles, wet and low.

"But that's for tourists," I squeak, echoing what she's told me since I was Runt's size. Tourists like to line up out on that stony finger for group photos, with the bay water in front and behind, and the Pacific Ocean in the background. Everybody else knows better than to go out there. The locals and the family stick to the part of the jetty with the beach or the rocky path on one side.

But Ma says, "Get out here, Pup. Don't make me say it again."

So we go, Runt and me. I stumble over holes with the backpack bumping against my stomach, as the fog churns like a crowd of ghosts around us.

When my toes kick something soft and clammy, I scream. I don't mean to, it just slips out.

"A boy," croaks Kara.

Beside her, Jilly whispers, "Hungry, hungry. Coins, give us coins."

"I'm s-sorry," I stammer, "I don't have any."

Something moist and sticky closes around my foot, like the tentacles of an anemone when you poke it in the middle. As a bumpy tongue worms between my toes, I slip and fall on my back-side. Kicking out with my free foot, I shred my heel on ragged edges that feel like the broken oyster shells outside the diner. I scream for Ma and the family, for anyone. Pulling away isn't work-ing, so I throw myself at the sisters instead, one arm around the backpack to protect Runt. I crawl, crying, over the mountainous shells adhered together with chilled flesh, as the sisters moan, "Coins, give us coins." Their breath smells like brine and rust.

On the other side of the sisters, I wrench my foot free and barrel out towards the jetty's end, not caring if I break an ankle in the hungry holes. I'm glad it's dark. I don't want to see Jilly and Kara as they are now, *here-adjacent*.

"Ma? Ma!" She must be here somewhere. We're at the end, me and Runt.

With the water chuckling all around us, there's nowhere left to go.

Ma

Leaving Pup behind is simple enough. I just hold still, off to one side of the jetty's crooked spine, until he passes me in the dark. I love my boy, but he's dumber than a bag of hammers. Once the baby starts squalling, there's no need to keep quiet. I creep north, hop down on the beach side, and head back towards camp.

Halfway there, I can still hear Runt screaming like he's right behind me. I start doubting, thinking maybe I should've stuck around to be sure the sacrifices get taken. But there's a celebration waiting back at camp for me. I'm a goddamn hero.

Come morning, my boys will be gone like the others before them.

Easy pickings.

Pup

I figure Ma's mad, hiding and not answering because she knows I helped that man out of the hole last month. How she found out, I don't know. Maybe the jetty told her.

A few hours before dawn, I snuck off while Ma and them were sleeping from the honey they put in their arms for the come-down ritual. I didn't expect to find him, but my flashlight still had batteries back then, so I figured I'd better try. It was pitch black out without the moon, so it took a while.

He was hardly moving. I used some old rope from the docks down by the trailer park and did my best to haul his ass up and out —felt like I was playing tug-of-war, though. Like the jetty had its teeth sunk into him. I wound up tying the rope off so I could climb up and pull on his arms. As his feet cleared the hole, a shadow dripped off his legs, back between the rocks. When I shined my light down there, something chuckled wet and low, just like Ma.

After I helped him up, the man slipped and smacked his head hard. His legs were shredded, like he was stuck down there with a tiger, so he couldn't balance at all. I didn't need a flashlight or stars to see him. He was covered in glowing green and blue lights, like those fish that live down deep have, except these were shaped like handprints with seven fingers. He did a little better once he got off the wall, spiraling around in the dunes and limping on both sides and mumbling about his phone. Crying, even. He'd lost his mind down there.

I made him swear not to tell anyone I'd helped, then pointed him toward the payphone down the way. The ambulance came and went, carrying him north to Grayshore, with its hospital and shopping mall and old-timey buildings on the waterfront.

I went back to the camp in the bushes.

Ma must've found out about me stealing from the jetty somehow. She told me to leave him, and now there's no treasures, nothing to eat, and another mouth to feed.

Now, I'm the one who needs saving. Way out here at the end, the holes breathe out hot air that reeks like roadkill; it mixes with the weight of the fog, and soon the air won't pull into my lungs it's so thick—toxic clouds. Coughing, I hug the backpack to my chest and feel my way back toward Jilly and Kara. Runt's fussing at the top of his lungs.

Something huge moves offshore, and the night ripples like an inky ocean. The holes find my feet, nibbling then snapping, as if they can hear my teeth chattering. Desperate, I cry out for Ma again.

But she just chuckles from within the fog, first to the left of me then the right, like my being *here-adjacent* is an ugly joke and I'm the punchline.

I brought this on myself. I'm just sorry I brought Runt.

Ma

I get back to camp and find that Yellow Pete and the rest of them have turned traitor. Saying they can't believe I used my own kids as the sacrifice, and how long until it's one of them? They figured with the tourists all dried up for the season, I'd grab a kid from town. "Somebody else's kid would be missed," I say.

The way they look at me, like I'm a monster, gets my blood boiling. I remind them who does the sacrificing while they reap the rewards. "Winter's around the corner," I tell them. "You like living here, not getting hassled by townie cops? You like having all the crystal and junk you want? You like eating, dontcha?"

I look at each of them in turn, ocean roaring like static in the background.

"Maybe it's time we move on," Tucker says. "Go our separate ways. It's warmer down south."

They all nod, bunch of sheep.

"And what about me?" I ask.

They tell me, their fucking shaman, that I can't come. They don't trust me no more, giving up my own boys. I thought they believed in the jetty, but they don't. They've been using us both.

"Go get your boys," Yellow Pete says, "and go back to the shelter. Get a roof over their heads, some food in their bellies."

I'm not leaving, not ever. They've lost faith; I see that now. So I'll fake like I'm leaving, and when they're gone, I'll have the jetty all to myself.

"One more then, and you'll never see me again." I grab my pack and stab a finger at the baggie sticking out of Yellow Pete's coat, saying, "One more for the road."

Not knowing if the road I mean is one that'll take me back to my boys.

Pup

Ma's skittering through the fog again. The muffled clicking of her nails darts close, closer. I clap a hand over Runt's face to shut him up while we inch past Jilly and Kara in the dark. Damp sighs exhale from the gaps near my feet, pockets of longing. Need. When my stomach growls, I wet my pants.

The sighs stalk me through the fog. A rumble shakes the jetty as something detaches, shedding rocks into the bay with explosive splashes, like cannonballs. A wave smacks into me from the left, drenching me and Runt. He squirms, so I press harder on his nose and mouth. If he screams now, the giants in the water will find us. I figure Ma's only here still because she wants to watch me get punished.

As if I summoned her with the thought, she pinches the back of my arm. I spin, backpedaling on wet stone, throwing my elbows out at the last second as I fall. The rocks scrape my arms and split my chin. Legs dangling into a hole, I kick. My nails bend back as I try to climb free. The best I can do, to keep from falling in, is to stay stiff as a chicken bone stuck in a dog's throat, praying Runt will keep quiet. His dead weight is dragging me down, though.

Sandpaper skin grazes my ankle then retreats, like how a shark bumps before biting.

I know what the jetty wants from me, what Ma's expecting before she'll forgive me and take me back. Knowing doesn't make it any easier.

Sacrifice.

My only friend in the world.

Leave 'im, the fog sighs. *He belongs to me now.*

Sobbing, I work my arms loose from the right strap of the backpack, then the left.

"I'm sorry," I whisper to my brother and Ma, but mostly to myself. Because I know, sacrifice or not, I'm never coming back from this loss.

I shrug the weight off my chest and a different sort of burden settles on my mind. After, it's like the jetty spits me out. I tumble headfirst into the ice-cold bay, swallowing a mouthful of salty water. The current sucks at me and I almost go with it. Regret's the only thing that keeps me anchored.

I have to find Runt, whatever the cost. I let my fear get the best of me, but I'm ready to be the sacrifice now.

Clamoring over and into the rocks, I search for my baby brother for hours. Others join me, babbling in languages I've never heard before. Their many-fingered hands fumble over my face and find nothing and no one they recognize. They move on, keening in the fog. I beg the jetty to take me instead, but it doesn't.

Finally, I roll onto my back and cry as the fog peels back like paint to reveal a sky filled with alien constellations.

An eternity passes before the suns come up.

Ma

Right hand to God, I swear I went back and looked, but Pup wasn't there and neither was Runt. The way the family gawked at me, when I came back and said I couldn't find the boys, made me think there was something extra in Yellow Pete's supply. Like we'd smoked forgetting crystals instead of the thinking kind. Except, I smoked too and I remembered.

Still do.

That jetty fucking *owes me*.

I don't have a picture or nothing to prove the boys were real. Tucker and Yellow Pete, all of them insisted I was crazy, that I never had no kids, but I know I did.

Next morning, I found Pup's empty backpack. I kept hunting, hoping for something more—a ring with diamonds, or the pack of smokes I'd dropped the night before, at least. I deserved *something*, goddamnit. But I never found another treasure, not for miles in any direction.

So I've moved on, left the family behind on my quest for a new arrangement, a better deal. A place that *appreciates* my talent.

California's one big coastline.

Lots of gods that need feeding.

Codewalker

G.M. Paniccia

LOCATION: Amazon rainforest, Brazil (Simulated)

POPULATION: 1 player

>**SpixM571:** Hey Rook
>**SpixM571:** u wanna take a walk?
>**SpixM571:** i found something cool

I HEAR the *ping* of an incoming file. Technically, I'm still at work. My cortical chip is linked to my work computer, reporting my activity and focus level back to the company's productivity software. Any deviation away from the task at hand will be reported to my manager, who will decide if this breach of focus is grounds to terminate my employment.

This has never stopped me before.

I focus as hard as I can on work as I plug a small datadrive into the computer. The productivity software freezes instantly. In the last report it got from me, I was being a very attentive little worker drone, so no alarms have tripped at the company. They'll notice if it's frozen for too long, but I have enough time for a short walk.

I switch the monitor feeds to my personal computer, pull up Spix's message, and download the file.

>**Rookerywalk:** what is it Spix?
>**SpixM571:** rabbits
>**Rookerywalk:** ???
>**Rookerywalk:** what
>**SpixM571:** just take the walk dude trust me

If Spix is being cagey, it's because he genuinely thinks he found something cool. On my personal computer, I open the emulator software for my cortical chip. It runs a twenty-year-old version of the interfacing software—the only version compatible with the old VirtuEns. Through the emulator, I open Spix's file.

I am outside. My apartment has disappeared, and instead I find myself in a flat, grassy field, covered as far as the eye can see with white rabbits.

I glance around. The field is impossibly flat. There's not a single divot anywhere in the grass, and the sky meets the horizon in a line so sharp it's as though it was drawn there. Above, a simulated sun hangs in the blank blue of the sky, but the lighting in the VirtuEn is flat, directionless, as though it comes from everywhere and nowhere at once.

On the ground, the rabbits all blink in unison. I flinch, surprised, but none of the creatures turn to look at me. They're running through the same idle animation, I realize, but with no time delays between them. Every rabbit, at the same time, flicks its whiskers, sits back on its haunches, and rubs a furry paw across its face before settling back down on all fours. It's somehow cute and unsettling at the same time.

I kneel down. Underneath me, the grass gives, but the texture of it is wrong. Real grass pulls against your skin. There's friction. What parts beneath me has no texture, only solidity. When I touch a rabbit, though, it's soft as a cloud and *warm*. My fingers sink into thick fur.

The rabbit doesn't seem to process that I'm there. Wrapping my hands around its middle, I lift it up and hold it to my chest. It's warm against me—the first thing in this VirtuEn that has heat. Everything else is tepid, a neutral room temperature. The rabbit has a smell too, though it's very faint. It's reminiscent of pine chips, but the coder hadn't quite gotten it right, so it's a bit like trying to sniff a Christmas tree through a stuffy nose. In my hands, the rabbit flicks its whiskers and sits back, rubbing a paw across its face. Every rabbit in the field does the same.

I put the creature down and stare out across the endless, fur-covered field. It's a striking view—this strange, half-rendered world. My best guess is that the coder had been trying to perfect the virtual rabbits, but, for some reason or another, hadn't finished the project. With a flicker of thought, I exit the VirtuEn. The field disappears. I am back at my desk, in my apartment, my two computers humming away. I type out a quick message to Spix,

>**Rookerywalk:** dude where'd you find that!
>**SpixM571:** u saw the rabbits?
>**Rookerywalk:** no shit i saw the rabbits
>**Rookerywalk:** they were everywhere
>**Rookerywalk:** couldn't miss em
>**SpixM571:** lol
>**SpixM571:** the code was on a hard drive I dug out of a garage sale
>**SpixM571:** some geezer died and they put his stuff up for sale on the curb. Didn't wipe the drive.
>**Rookerywalk:** he have anything else good?
>**SpixM571:** idk yet, ill let u know

Spix disconnects from the chat, probably to load his next VirtuEn. I'd say he could just be getting back to work too, but I don't know if Spix has a job. I know very little about his life, even though we've been friends for years. He knows just as little about me. Everyone on the forums tries not to identify themselves; code-walking, although lightly policed, is still illegal.

I shift my attention back to my work computer and remove the datadrive, unfreezing the productivity monitoring software. I try to put the white rabbits out of my head as, in my mind's eye, a field of them blinks as one.

Three days later, I'm hacking into an old computer. I found it scanning for devices connected to the net, then filtering out anything running a newer operating system. There could be old VirtuEn files on an updated machine, sure, but breaking into those gets you noticed. Besides, I know all the vulnerabilities in the old software. Cracking into a machine that old is as easy as getting through my own front door.

I get lucky and find some files, but they're nothing special—just copies of some of the popular indie-made VirtuEns. You don't hit a home run all the time.

I start the process over again, hunting for another computer. On a separate feed, I'm watching some forum writers argue about whether to tell the cops that they uncovered a copy of Shell Game. Some think they should go to the police, let them know these files are still out there. The rest—myself included—think that's stupid. It's not like anyone can just *stumble* into running Shell Game; you'd need emulator software to run it, and if you're running emulator software on your cortical chip, you know enough about codewalking to steer clear of Shell Game. Hell, anyone with a chip knows to steer clear of Shell Game.

It was the VirtuEn that ruined all of this, after all. The whole indie world-making fad. That first generation of VirtuEns was a digital Wild West. The software for coding neuro-responsive virtual spaces was open source and unregulated, and everyone with an ounce of coding ability took a stab at crafting their own worlds. Inevitably there were going to be bad actors, but the bad ones were mild at first. They built environments to scare people—fields of flowers that burst into spiders, or empty rooms that filled with water. They were terrifying, but they didn't cause any lasting psychological or psychosomatic damage. Next came the painful VirtuEns, the worlds that fired every pain perceptive circuit in your amygdala. The worlds that sent every inch of your miles and miles of nerves screaming in incandescent agony.

Then came Shell Game.

Shell Game didn't bother with any of that. It triggered a chip short-out. It killed the cortical chip, and the person it was installed in.

The regulation came after that. I guess it makes sense—if you're going to make shit that plugs directly into people's brains, there should probably be some rules, right? It killed the *art* though. That first generation was something special. The environments weren't anywhere near as polished as the corporate worlds released at the same time—the virtual amusement parks or endless shopping malls or the fantastical game worlds—but they were *weird*. They were the strange and half-finished projects of basement-tinkerers, a mixed bag of high- and low-effort builds with wildly variable computing power behind them. Everything now is designed by committee: highly polished, perfectly neutral, soulless.

Hence, codewalking. Digital urban exploring in forgotten, homebrewed lands.

The argument on the forum has degenerated in the way that all good internet arguments do. A mod shuts it down and locks the thread before anyone starts doxing each other. I ping Spix.

>**Rookerywalk:** dude lol did u see that
>**SpixM571:** absolute dumpster fire
>**SpixM571:** and over SHELL GAME
>**Rookerywalk:** right???
>**Rookerywalk:** btw, did u find anything else good on that one drive?
>**SpixM571:** nah, nothing else was that cool. I posted the rabbits one to its own thread.
>**SpixM571:** everything else is in the slush thread. Zip file.
>**SpixM571:** u find anything lately?
>**Rookerywalk:** nope. striking out hard
>**SpixM571:** F

A nudge from my chip tells me that the scanner found a new potential target. With a thought, I flick away from my conversation with Spix and pull up the specs for the computer I've identified. I read them, then, surprised, read them again. This thing is old, but it's got a surprising amount of storage still connected to it.

>**Rookerywalk:** ok I know I literally just said I was striking out but I think I found something
>**SpixM571:** fingers crossed for u dude

I break in, and a feed of file names and extensions scrolls past on my virtual monitor. The first dozen are operating system files. Then installed software. Then, gold: VirtuEn files. Grinning, I bin them into a separate group and watch as they roll through in a torrent.

>**Rookerywalk:** YOOOOO
>**Rookerywalk:** Found some!

I send Spix a screenshot of the file index. There are dozens of worlds on this drive, and so far, I recognize only a few. Most of these files are unique.

>**SpixM571:** YOOO!
>**SpixM571:** Congrats dude!!!

I'm grinning at the screens, already inventorying the haul. I dig through and separate out the popular, known VirtuEns—worlds like Mistgloom, Aether, Doom, Skyrim5D. I scrape the forums for lists of VirtuEns that others have reported finding, then use it to create a filter, binning previously undiscovered environments into their own subfolder. To my surprise, I'm still left with a hoard of unique data. It occurs to me as I'm sifting through it that whoever owned this computer must have collected it. There's no way they could have crafted so much themselves. There are educational environments, game worlds, virtual casinos, recreations of famous landmarks. It's all too different.

I can barely sleep that first night, even though I stay awake into the small hours of the morning, exploring VirtuEns until I'm well past exhausted. The next day, I'm codewalking the moment my shift ends. I scroll through the subfolder of unique VirtuEns, pick a file name at random, and open it:

I am in a jungle.

The air is humid, steamy, and every inch of my field of vision is choked with plants. Trees tower above me, their lush emerald canopies obscuring the sky. An army of vines rises against the tree trunks, clambering for light, growing around and underneath and over top of each other like a frozen green wave. My ears are assaulted by sound—insects buzzing, birds singing, animals chattering and grunting and snuffling beneath the leaves. There's a smell too, a scent like nothing I've ever experienced. It's not just the smell of dirt or rain—it's *earth,* living and breathing. The sigh of a hot, wet breeze tickles my ear, and in a moment of sensory overload I clap my hands over my ears and slump down onto the dark ground.

I've never found a VirtuEn like this. There are other first-gen VirtuEns that are this immersive, but they were immersive and *familiar.* They depicted places that anyone could have been to, that everyone would have experienced.

I have never been in a jungle. There *are* no more jungles.

Pulling my hands away from my ears, I run them through the dirt. My fingers come away with black soil studded with bits of decaying plant matter. When I dust my hands off, I'm almost relieved to notice a flaw in the physics simulation of the dirt. I push myself to my feet and approach a broad-leafed plant, where a constellation of ants marches down the leaves and stems on their way to the ground. I watch them, mesmerized. With a finger, I push one out of line. It tries ineffectually to return to its place, bumping dumbly into its fellows before, in a blink, it fizzles out and disappears. The line of ants continues unimpeded.

So the simulation has its limits. I can feel myself calming as I start poking at the world, confirming that it's all just code—immaculately executed neuro-responsive code, but code nonetheless. Testing it further, I break a leaf off a plant, drop it, and look away for thirty seconds. When I turn back, the plant is whole again and the leaf is gone. The simulation doesn't save environmental changes, then.

Something moves at the edges of my vision.

I spin around. There's nothing there but plants, their leaves dancing in the breeze. I sigh and sit back in the dirt. Now that I'm adjusting to the place, it's not quite so overwhelming. There's something ... calming about it, almost. The animal cries have melded into white noise. The hot, humid air envelops me like a blanket. I look upwards, staring at the canopy and the glimpses of the sky beyond, and inhale a breath rich in the smell of living earth.

There's a flicker above me. A red parrot flies, screeching, towards the next tree, but doesn't make it there, instead disappearing in a fuzz of static. A moment later, that same bird reappears and successfully completes its crimson arc between the trees.

Straightening, I furrow my brows. I can't tell if this is a glitch or something unfinished in the code. Whoever built this was thorough, but they seem to have left some sections of the environment unpolished. Curious, I poke around more, looking for other shortcomings. I walk through the dense brush, smacking leaves, pulling at vines, trying to overtax the simulation. Several plants despawn, reappearing only after I've moved away. A monkey clips through a nearby tree.

Stopping beside a jungle sapling, I wrap my hands around it and pull, trying to yank it from the soil. I'm not even sure if the simulation will let me do it, but after a moment, something gives. There's a crackle. I think it's roots snapping—until I look down. The bottom of the plant is glitching. Something is wrong—sections of underbrush all around me are clipping through the soil. The trees fizzle and warp, and a flock of birds disappears from their boughs. My vision flashes white, and all the sounds and smells and sensations abruptly cease.

I am in the jungle, back where I started. I blink, disoriented and headachy. I think the environment entirely rebooted. I've never seen a simulation do that when overtaxed. I ... don't know what to make of it.

I don't know what to make of this whole place, really. I'm in awe of it. It's the absolute pinnacle of what the old-school VirtuEns could accomplish. I just can't figure out what the coder made it *for.* Regardless, it's a gem. I'll be revisiting this one.

I take one last look around, then freeze.

In the darkness between the leaves, there is a pair of yellow eyes.

I take a step back instinctively, even though nothing here has been able to hurt me so far. The yellow eyes don't blink, but they do advance; a black panther pulls itself out of the darkness of the underbrush, its eyes locked on me, head low, body held close to the ground. *Stalking.* With every step it takes, dense muscles shift beneath its hide.

It's coded beautifully. What sunlight makes it to the forest floor catches the dark fur, turning it a rich, chocolate brown. I can make out its individual eyelashes, the textures behind its irises. When it bares its teeth and a low, liquid growl spills through the jungle, I am in awe of the dim reflections I can see in its wet teeth. When it springs forward, claws outstretched, yellow eyes aflame, it is poetry in motion.

When it sinks its teeth into my leg, claws digging into my flesh as it pulls me to the ground, I am amazed at the blinding, screaming, bone-splintering pain that rockets through me.

I jerk back to my own reality, my chest heaving, a cold sweat on my skin. I am in my apartment. Only my apartment. I press a hand to my chest, trying to calm myself, then stand, testing the leg that the panther bit. I'd felt bone crunching. There's still the echo of it in my nerves, a ghostly prickle, but the leg functions fine. I take a lap of my room, then sag back into my chair.

I stare at the list of files on my virtual monitor and decide to shut off the computer. I can't stomach loading up another VirtuEn.

I crawl into bed early, and I try to ignore the memory of the way my bones crunched between the panther's teeth.

>**SpixM571:** hey Rook
>**SpixM571:** haven't heard for you in a bit
>**SpixM571:** how's the haul?

It takes me several minutes to retroactively process the message ping. I blink, focusing on the screen. I guess it has been a couple days since I talked to Spix. I've been codewalking some, but not much. Not nearly as much as I should have been, given my recent haul.

>**Rookerywalk:** ive found some stuff, yeah.
>**Rookerywalk:** here

I send him some files. They're tame. The jungle VirtuEn isn't among them.

>**SpixM517:** u good dude?
>**Rookerywalk:** yeah
>**Rookerywalk:** just tired

I'm not lying. Not completely. I *am* tired. My dreams have been ... strange lately. They're filled with yellow eyes and the shrieking of parrots. I don't feel like I ever rest, and I wake sweating, my heart hammering, the warmth of my blankets like the choking heat of the jungle. I keep thinking I see something move at the edges of my vision.

>**Rookerywalk:** brb going to take a walk
>**SpixM571:** k

I don't know if I am, actually, though I feel like I should. Something about the jungle, the panther, has made me uneasy.

Before I can think about it too hard, I select a file and boot up a VirtuEn.

I am on a boat. The sky is bright with sunshine and the waters beyond the ship's railing are a cool topaz blue. The waves lap against the hull with a hollow smack, but they don't rock it, which is fortunate for my motion sickness. I lean over the edge of the boat and stare into the clear waters where schools of bright fish swirl together. The dark green body of one fish, much larger than the rest, swims by and parts the school around it. To my right, there's a fishing rod propped up against the ship's railing. This is a fishing simulator, then.

I turn away from the water. The boat is small, mostly devoid of set dressing. There's some rope and floaters along the edges of the deck. A tacklebox rests in a corner. From the deck, two steps lead up to the bridge. Underneath, stairs descend into the boat, to a space that I assume is the captain's quarters, but it's too dark to tell; there must not be windows down there.

I take a step closer to the descending stairs. A wave slaps against the hull and the sound echoes belowdecks, audio pitching strangely, warping into something higher pitched, like the cry of a bird.

In the dark, a pair of yellow eyes opens.

I fling myself out of the VirtuEn so fast that I immediately begin to second guess what I'd seen. My heart pounding, I type out a message to Spix and send him the boat file. Half an hour later, he responds.

>**SpixM571:** yoo they did a great job on those fish
>**SpixM571:** a little low poly when you pull em up but they made em look cool as hell underwater
>**Rookerywalk:** did u go belowdecks?
>**SpixM571:** a little yeah. boring though
>**SpixM571:** nothing really down there
>**SpixM571:** unless I missed something?
>**Rookerywalk:** no panther?
>**SpixM571:** panther???????
>**SpixM571:** on a boat???
>**Rookerywalk:** nvm
>**SpixM571:** is there a hidden level i missed?
>**SpixM571:** Rook?

I don't reply.

⁂

I am in an arcade. The colored lights flash and whirl, and I am enveloped in the overlapping sounds of several dozen game cabinets. I pick one and thumb a token into the coin slot. An 8-bit white rabbit appears on the screen. My hands on the joysticks, I pilot the rabbit through a maze, jumping through hoops and gathering carrots as, behind it, a dark shape grows ever closer.

I miss a hoop and the darkness surges forward, swallowing the rabbit and the maze. GAME OVER, the screen declares. I sigh and reach into my pocket, fumbling for a new token. When I fish it out and look back up, something has shifted. The darkness has continued spreading. It leaks from the screen, swallowing the joysticks, spilling over the edges of the game cabinet and pooling in an impossibly dark, utterly unreflective puddle of black. The edges fizzle like a glitch.

On the game's blackened screen, yellow eyes open, and the arcade cabinet begins to growl.

I wake up screaming, my legs tangled in the blankets, my body doused in sweat. Every inch of my skin is covered in goosebumps.

It's been a week since I first saw the panther, and now I see it everywhere. It moves at the corners of my vision. Its eyes open from the darkness.

I've stopped turning off the lights.

On still-trembling legs I push myself out of bed and cross my apartment. Piles of my dirty clothes lay in drifts at the edges of the room. The silvery insides of empty chip bags glint up at me as I pass. I cross to the kitchen and, with shaking hands, grab a glass and fill it with water from the tap. I chug the lukewarm water hunched over the sink.

I put the glass down, hard, just so I can hear it click against the countertop. My fingers pinch the bridge of my nose, and I squeeze my eyes shut, taking deep breaths. I feel ... shaky. Unstable. I want to cry, or scream. I don't know what's happening to me.

I plant my hands against the countertop, hoping for some solidity, something to ground myself. I press so hard against it that my fingertips flush white.

My hands clip through the surface.

I recoil, but I can't pull them back out. The counter rises, swallowing my wrists, my arms, pulling me into its Formica embrace as I thrash and howl and pray that I can escape before—

I am in my apartment. My sister is here, taking care of me. I don't remember calling her, but God, she's a breath of fresh air. She helped me clean the apartment. She opened the blinds. There's fresh food in the fridge, and yesterday she made us both dinner—something that she actually had to cook, not another instant meal out of a bag.

"Alright, what's gotten into you?" she asks me. She's leaning against the kitchen wall, a glass of water in her hands, watching me with concern.

"I don't know," I reply. There's a knot forming in my throat, threatening to choke the words. "My ... uh, my grip on reality ... I don't know, I feel like I'm losing it. The other day I ... I could have sworn that my hands went through the countertop. Clipped through it, like in a buggy game."

My sister gives a soft snort. "Pete," she says, "you've gotta' get out more. All this codewalking stuff is rotting your mind."

I shake my head. "No, no, it's not that, it's ... There's this *panther*. I keep seeing it."

"Panther?" she asks. Her concern has deepened; her eyebrows are drawn together into a worried line.

"I see it out of the corner of my eyes. Just a flicker of movement. I know it sounds crazy," I add, desperate to have her believe me. I *know* I'm losing my grip, which must count for something. It must mean that I have some sanity at my core, some bit of myself that's still aware, still logical.

My sister smiles, revealing long canine teeth. "No," she says, her yellow eyes flashing, "it doesn't."

I am in my apartment, alone. The blinds are drawn and the floor is messy.

I don't have a sister.

I stagger to the edge of my bed and collapse there, sobbing, my head in my hands and my tears a river. I don't know what's real. I don't know. I don't know. In the back of my mind, I try to trigger my cortical chip the same way I do to exit a VirtuEn, but nothing happens.

This must be real. It has to be.

I don't trust it.

My fingers claw at the back of my neck, and some sliver of my fragmented mind makes a connection: the chip. The cortical chip. It must be doing this. Either I am trapped in a VirtuEn or it's stuck rendering scraps of code, but it must be malfunctioning. I have to get it out of my skull, *now*, before the panther crawls out of it again.

Before I know it, I'm in the kitchen, flinging open the drawers. Cutlery rattles in the tray. I have one knife, and it is in my hand.

When they installed the cortical chip, they told me a bit about it. Even though the chip was implanted inside my skull, there were cables that ran down my neck, connecting to a biogenerator that metabolized glucose in my blood. The chip needs me to run. It needs me to run, and I can cut it out of my body by its roots.

I lift the knife. The metal is cold as I press it to the back of my neck. I take a deep breath. When I slice through my own skin, the pain is searing, bright and hot and electric, and it overwhelms me. I hiss, dropping the knife, pressing a hand to the back of my neck. Something pours out between my fingers. I know by touch alone that it is not blood.

When I pull my hand away from the cut, my fingers come away covered in crimson feathers. They are sheeting down my neck, down my shoulders, a torrent of red. I let loose a wild, avian scream and snatch the knife up from the floor. Feathers drip from its edge.

"*Let me out!*" I scream, and I lift the knife to my chest.

I am at my desk, staring at empty, bright white screens. There is no knife. No feathers. No gash in my neck. I am surrounded by the thick silence of my empty apartment.

Maybe this is where I've always been—here, at my desk, my reality melting into some endless dreamworld, eternally slipping through my fingers.

How long has it been? How long have I been like this?

I need help. God, I need help.

I need to get out of here.

I stagger to the door, yank it open. I spill into the hallway, hollow-eyed under the watery fluorescents. A hand on the wall, I half run, half stumble down it, banging on every door I pass, crying, screaming for someone to help.

No one answers. No doors open. The hallway goes ever onward. I keep yelling, keep stumbling, shouting, until I notice that this doesn't make sense. The building was never this big. The hallway was never this long.

I stop. I am breathing hard, and I can't tell if it's from the running or from the acrid panic welling up in my throat. On the doors, all the apartment numbers are the same. They're my apartment. They're all my apartment.

I sag against a door, sliding down to the floor. My fingernails dig into my knees. My body, curled into a tight little ball, rocks back and forth against the door.

There was never anywhere I could run, could I?

Behind me, the door opens. I slip backwards into the apartment. My back hits the floor; I am staring up at the ceiling. A white rabbit looks down at me. Its eyes are dark, limpid pools, soft and innocent. I can see my reflection in them—greasy hair, pale skin, a madman's bloodshot stare. Its little nose twitches. Its whiskers brush my face.

It straightens, sniffs, then bolts through the open door. As it leaves, the faint scent of pine goes with it, replaced by soil and decay, petrichor and chlorophyll, animal musk and approaching thunderstorm. I push myself over onto my hands.

Spilling out from the darkness beneath my desk is the panther. It stalks towards me on overnight paws, silent as the grave. Its amber eyes are spotlights. Its jaws part. Pearlescent strings of saliva stretch between its canines, stirred by its deep, huffing breaths, its inhalations and exhalations timed like a heartbeat. Its hungry tongue twitches inside its dark mouth. I catch glimpses of its claws, swaddled in the thick folds of its black paws, leaving bloody footprints on the carpet.

It is oblivion, and I crawl towards it.

The panther's jaws open wider, ever wider, until it is the roof and floor of the world. Its fangs hang above me, ivory stalactites. There never was any apartment. There was only this, waiting for me with jaws outstretched, lurking in the digital dark.

I am knelt before the row of teeth, before the endless, ever-consuming jaws. The air is hot and humid, and it smells of meat and burnt circuitry. There is a prickle somewhere in my grey matter, a fizzle of something that may have once told me to run.

I turn around.

I lay my head against its teeth.

I keep my eyes open, and I watch the fangs descend.

I am in the jungle.

In Nobody's Debt

Jenny Rowe

LOCATION: Northern Sweden

POPULATION: Variable

A MILLION STARS over these Northern skies, and to each its ceaseless cry:

But which of you were mine? And how will you ever find me?

The Go-Pro arrives in Cornwall almost a year after the posting of his brother's last blog. It's smashed up, but the memory card works and, although there's no note with it, the Swedish postmark offers a clue to Marty's location. It's dated 8-11-2022—a few weeks after he was last online. Nathan leans back against the kitchen sink and lets out the breath he hadn't realised he'd been holding; as he does, his gaze falls to his phone.

Marty's number hasn't connected since last July when a missed call left no message. The swift season had filled Nathan's time that summer; cataloguing the screaming acrobatic birds had left him under-slept and caffeine-high, so it had slipped his mind. When he finally remembered, days later, the line was dead. He'd *meant* to try again, but life, work, routine, they'd consumed him—and, yes, there's guilt, but it's all too easy to assume Marty's okay, because he's *always* okay.

Nathan pours a coffee, opens his laptop and inserts the card.

It's the usual videos of his brother; he's living his best life, surrounded by beautiful women and stunning scenery. His bronzed body, nothing like Nathan's own pasty form, belies their English upbringing. There's about 90 minutes of short clips—Marty's trademark montage of each country visited. Later, 'to camera' pieces directed at anonymous patrons. Nathan's never understood how Marty makes enough to fund this lifestyle. Then again, there's a lot of things he's never understood about his brother.

The last few minutes are very dark—pocket-shots, maybe, or attempted night-shots. They're peppered with flickering, coloured lights; flashes of white; a pale woman with sad, dark eyes leans in towards the lens. There are sounds too, weird like whale-song or distant thunder, that grow and shrink, grow and shrink, but with each wave they're louder, stronger, deeper. The flickering darkness continues but calms into a still black, then a minute or so of silence before Marty's voice rises, faint and gentle:

It's so beautiful, Nate. You should come out here. Oh—

A splash, the gentle lap of water, and those strange sounds begin again, less intense but still there.

It's not unusual for Marty to disappear; sometimes for a week, sometimes for months. Nor is it unusual—more often, since their parents died—for him to summon his big brother. The 'boring' one. The one that stays at home and studies birds.

Hey, Nathan—come and do ayahuasca with me; Nathan, I'm in Peru, you've got to come and check these Nazca Lines; Nathan, I'm in prison, I need you to pay some people.

Sometimes, the invites are tamer, but he's turned down many more than he's taken up, and he's received more than he can remember. But *this*? Nathan would be the first to admit that their relationship has cooled over the years, but there's something in his brother's voice that sets him on edge.

Nathan rises to heat his forgotten coffee. Outside in the bay, the sea absorbs the purple of the sky. A storm's approaching and the waves, white-tipped and swollen, pound the shore. He can hear fragments of gulls' excited cries and, when he pushes open the cottage window, there's the sharp tang of ozone and seaweed in the air. He breathes it all in then pulls the window shut as the harbour bell begins to call the fishing boats home. When his ancient microwave pings, he returns to the screen.

It's so beautiful, Nate. You should come out here.

What is it that bothers him? Marty is, and will always be, an impetuous thrill-seeker. But Nathan's never known him this calm— if that's what he is—since they were children. Is he stoned?

In the last ten years, Nathan's forays out of the West Country have been rare; three in search of his brother, and two for work. Cornwall's become a habit. Watching the tourists come and go with the seasons, the boats that stink of fish on his morning walks, the kittiwakes clinging to the barren cliffs. Binoculars, birds, hides. Hiding; yes, where it's safe, where it's boring. Sometimes he envies his brother's affability, his ease at making friends; but, mostly, all that uncertainty, that buzz of action, conversation, of people: it confuses and terrifies him.

He flicks back and forth through the clips, searching for clues to where it could be: shop fronts here and there, a guesthouse sign, an advertising board. The same word keeps appearing: Fristad. An internet search reveals a village in Northern Sweden. But Sweden, why? Marty's followers are obsessed with the sun and sights of South America—that's where his heart is. Why is he *there*?

It's so beautiful, Nate. You should come out here.

As the rain begins to batter his window, Nathan tuts and sighs and starts researching flights to Sweden.

Five days later, Nathan sits in a hotel restaurant in Fristad, hemmed-in by Friday night laughter and the unceasing clatter of cutlery. He's chosen a table near the door where he can be alone. From his phone, the Rough Guide to Sweden glares at him. He'd rather be back in his lodgings after the journey he's had—over sixteen hours of trains, planes, and layovers. He just wants to sleep, but he's full of the restlessness of travel and desperately needs to unwind. He pokes at the wax of the tea-light that flickers on his table, then squints out the window at the barely visible houses across the unlit street.

The small town lies 85km north-west of Kiruna, and the November climate is so harsh and cold compared to his beloved Cornwall, he can't quite comprehend it's real. The travel guide doesn't even acknowledge its existence.

"Are you visiting?" A blonde woman of about thirty stands over him, balancing a tray on her slim hips. He's momentarily distracted by her eyes—they are deep-chestnut, framed by long dark eyebrows. He thinks of the sad kohl-rimmed eyes of the lapwings that stalk his Cornish shore.

"Uh, sort of."

She puts down a pizza and his beer; as she does so, the aroma of pine rises above the hops and the food smells. He'd asked for Carlsberg, since it was the only one he recognised, but the logo on the glass reads Snörsjö.

"You've come for the lights?"

"The lights? Oh. No. No. I need ... I've come to ... He's ..." Tongue-tied, he gestures without words as he reaches for his bag.

"You're looking for something."

"My brother." Nathan shuffles through his wallet and presents her with the photo he's chosen to show around town.

She barely looks, but nods matter-of-factly. "Marty. Yes. He's sometimes here, I think."

"He is? Where?" In spite of his relief, it feels to Nathan that this is too simple. Marty isn't usually so easy to find. It's almost irritating.

She points at the printed matchbook he's started to twirl between his fingers. "You're staying at Nerthu's place?"

He nods. Nerthu is a tall and formidable white-haired woman, the proprietor of a guesthouse squeezed against the trees at the edge of town. When he arrived, she lifted his bursting rucksack onto her shoulder as though it were a handbag, firing instructions at him as they climbed the stairs to his room.

The waitress reaches out, gently staying his fidgeting hand and something long-dormant shifts and wakens in his chest. He can't remember the last time he was touched, meaningfully touched, like this. She smiles and her eyes glint in the reflected candlelight.

"I'm Freja."

Later that same evening, they walk in the purple bruise of night towards his lodgings. Though it's freezing, Nathan is warmed by alcohol and it allows him an uncharacteristic freedom to talk.

"There's a lot of women here," he remarks. "But hardly any men, so far as I can see. I wasn't sure until I saw everyone leaving. Not a single guy."

"No industry here."

"Where do they go?"

"There are mining towns not so far away—the men are there; some of the women, too. They come back for the summer."

He laughs. "So that's why Marty stayed?"

She makes no comment. They continue in silence along a track that snakes through the forest on the outskirts of the town. In places, the snow has a crispness to it that makes a satisfying crunch as his feet break the surface. The ice crystals catch the moonlight, like walking through stars. Occasionally he catches the citrussy aroma of pine sap, but he isn't sure if it's her or the trees. Everything's so alien, but for once he is not afraid.

As they walk, it occurs to Nathan that perhaps there are people just like him in Fristad. People content with the beauty of their home, who have no need to explore further. His brother is one small thread drawing them all together. Travellers, like Marty, must have been visiting strange lands throughout millennia, bringing knowledge and experience back to people like Nathan—people too scared, too lazy, just too comfortable to leave. For a few seconds, Nathan sees the world through Marty's eyes—for a few seconds he wonders how much he might have missed.

Freja stops, holding up one hand. "Listen. The lake, it's singing again."

In the crisp cold of this still night, he hears what she hears, and sobers. He's heard it before.

"What *is* that?"

She smiles. "The ice—it's calling."

A muffled crack and boom seems to pass over and through them

—he can feel it in his chest. It's mesmerising, awe-inspiring in its intensity.

Freja smiles, then turns to walk on through the creaking snow as the boom becomes a moan, becomes a distant battle, becomes a train bumping over sleepers far away. "Our lake; it's more than two miles away," she calls over her shoulder. "But on a night of stars, it flows all around us." And she stretches her arms above her head and shouts at the sky. "We become part of it!"

The sky fills with more sounds and, as she walks on ahead of him, he becomes aware in that instant how small he is against the great black firs that line the empty track.

"That sound ..." He tries to catch up to her, but he's unused to running in bulky clothing. "That sound," he says again, "I've heard it before ... It's on Marty's camera, only louder, much louder."

As if in response, the strange song of the lake lifts and broadens, smashing the sky like some ancient warrior. And as it does, Freja stops and turns. But *is* it Freja? Her eyes are pure onyx in this light, and when she speaks it doesn't sound like her at all, it's deeper, older —it envelops him.

"You become part of it, Nathan."

The sky howls and he looks up, falling backwards into the snow. Freja's eyes fill his vision, the lake fills his ears until they hurt, and although he tries to cover them, beneath it all he hears a voice— faint but clear, not his nor Freja's.

Must I sleep here for ever?

"Marty?!" He screams it at the sky. "Marty??" Is it? Was it? Not his voice, nothing like him, deeper, fuller, but could it be? Then, *where?*

He tries to right himself, but the beer hangs heavy in his head and he struggles to get back on his feet. By the time he's steady, Freja's gone, and a faceful of snow has sobered him enough to be relieved. He staggers in the direction of her snow-packed footsteps and, gradually, the blurry light at the break of the trees resolve themselves into Nerthu's place.

When he wakes the following morning, the walk home feels unreal. He has a hangover—the first for years—but in spite of his fuzzy brain and dry mouth, Freja's lapwing eyes linger in his mind.

By 10 o'clock he's eaten breakfast and is heading into the late grey-blue dawn. He's planned out a route that takes in the places he imagines Marty might visit. At Räkmackan—a laid-back cafe in the centre—he proffers the photo to the waitress.

"Do you know him?"

"Marty?" Her smile broadens. "Of course. He is here sometimes."

He is here sometimes. It's an echo of Freja's reply.

"Recently?"

The woman shrugs. "Sometimes." She turns to greet another customer.

His coffee finished, he tries the waitress again, but although she knows Marty is English and makes videos, she doesn't know where he stays or with whom.

By 1pm it's nearly dusk and Nathan's barely got started. His body hasn't recovered from travelling and he isn't yet used to the limited daylight so he heads back to his lodgings. But, as he does so, he sees what looks like Freja in the distance and, with barely a thought, follows her.

She disappears down an alleyway between two houses, and he darts after her just in time to see her turn right at the far end. The path opens into a courtyard of snow-laden trees and scrub, and as he scans it, he sees the splash of her hair as she skips up a narrow set of stairs between two houses.

"Freja!"

Sliding across the courtyard towards her, a low fence concealed by snow-covered bushes takes him by surprise, and he has to perform an ungainly leap to avoid crashing to the ice-hard ground.

"Freja! It's Nathan!"

The grey stairs are steep and slippery, but she's still there about forty or so steps in front of him. He picks his way up them, sometimes scrambling hands and feet together. Where the stairs end, she turns left again and as he, panting, reaches the top, he sees her entering a shop across the street.

"Freja!"

Nathan runs after her, eagerly wrenching open the door. He finds himself facing a group of mostly older women at the counter, none of whom are her; they stare at him briefly, then resume their conversation. He hesitates, searching for any sign of familiarity and, finding none, steps outside.

Back in the street, the lake has started to sing again, just like the night before. He stands awhile, captivated, until a clock somewhere strikes 2pm and jolts him from his stupor.

That night, he sleeps badly, woken often by strange sounds— sounds that that could be reality and could be dreams, but he can't distinguish between them. And that voice repeats and repeats:

... sleep here forever ...?

Whenever he wakes it's in confusion—no sense of time—is the darkness day or night? Has he slept for hours or minutes?

Each day blends into the next: looking for Marty, meeting smiles of recognition but no new information. Cafe staff begin to greet him by name, people nod at him in the street.

One night, back at the hotel restaurant where he'd hoped to glimpse Freja again, he's invited to join a group of women. They grew up here, they tell him. They know everything about the place —from the smashed post-office window, to the cracked tree by the surgery.

"And the lake song?" he asks.

"Yes, that's special," they say. Drinks arrive, accompanied by small plates of pickled herring and crispbreads.

"Why special?"

There are giggles, whispers. "It wants."

"Wants? Wants what?"

More giggles. "Just a legend ..."

"A story. Perhaps the lake is more than a lake sometimes."

"Yes. 'The lake and the sky must meet one day' —something our mothers tell us when we are young."

"My brother ..." He shows them the photo.

"Yes, yes, he was there," someone says, and is immediately hushed.

"When?" More drinks arrive, other conversations start to break away.

"WHEN??"

No one answers. Everyone's talking in Swedish. Shot glasses are pushed into hands, then more, he's swept up in a chant he assumes is "drink, drink, drink." Conversations rise and fall, more drinks, more food, more chants. He's tapping people on the shoulder, trying to get their attention again, just one person's attention, anyone's. "When did he go to the lake? How long ago? How often?" No one answers.

He jumps on a chair and screams at the room, at everyone, "You MUST know where he is!" His head is swimming. "How can you all know him but not KNOW him!?"

The following morning, he wakes in someone else's bed. He can't remember what happened and it terrifies him. He feels vulnerable, awkward, like a teenager. She touches his shoulder, offers him coffee and whispers that she has often seen Marty heading out towards the lake.

"He likes to take pictures of it," she says, standing and stretching, naked and perfect before him.

As he leaves, he stops at her front door. There is a cap hanging there; faded green and grubby, a FIFA Mexico70 patch poorly stitched to the front. He knows it well. Camden Market; he was 15, Marty was 12. He tried to persuade him not to buy it, but, no, his little brother insisted. All his pocket money gone just like that, so when he wanted a milkshake later, Nate begrudgingly paid for both.

"Where did you get this??"

She shrugs, and he is sick of shrugs.

"Where??" He rips it from the hook, throws open the door and leaves, clutching the memory to his chest.

Later, he sits in his lodgings poring over travel books, a map laid out in front of him. What's the best route to the lake, he wonders—the safest. His laptop lays open, too, with the cursor flashing in an unfinished email; until now, he's put off getting the police involved. He knows Marty hates the authorities—too many run-ins over the years—but there's so few options left. His fingers hover over the message. The nearest police station is miles from Fristad. From the window he sees yet more statuesque old women walk past, their long white hair flowing from woollen hats or pinned against the wind in the pale, dark winter. He glances down at the green cap by his side and curses it, curses them, curses his brother for leading him here.

He can't get any sense of this place. How can he know somewhere that he only ever sees in half-light? In a book of Norse myths, he reads about Nifelheim—a *primordial realm of ice and cold*. It sounds to him like purgatory, and he starts to think of Fristad in that way— a chill waiting room leading to nothing. Its women: always busy, always moving, always heading *some*where, but he can't get close to them, can't get close to *anyone*.

Freja is everywhere and nowhere. He's long since put that strange first night down to beer and exhaustion, but at every street corner and across every junction he's sure he sees her blue hat bobbing out of sight.

On his ninth or is it tenth afternoon, he's lost track, Nathan walks back from a solitary meal in the town. He's returned to Räkmackan, where he's seen a polaroid of Marty tacked to the wall. It sits among other snaps of revellers—mainly young men—dining and drinking alongside the Fristad women. Yet again, another waitress knows his brother, but only by sight. For some reason, there are fewer people about today and she's keen to close early.

Walking back, he finds himself torn: between the unease he's felt since he found his brother's hat, and a resigned acceptance that Marty's just moved on to somewhere new. Either way, the trail seems to go around in circles. Tomorrow, he'll walk to the lake— there's little else left for him to discover in the town now. Then he'll pack up, head home to Cornwall and wait for any news from the Polis.

But, when he turns the corner towards Nerthu's, she's there. Freja. Waiting across the street, wearing what looks to Nathan like traditional Sami dress—yet instead of red and blue woollens, she's head to toe in browns, yellows, and greens.

He's not surprised to see her; it feels inevitable. It's 1.15pm on the 17th November, and the mauve of early afternoon has briefly turned to a magnificent blue as the evening snow reflects the last of the light. The song of the ice lake is a symphony above the town. Though he's barely seen her these past few days, she's rarely left his thoughts, so when she takes a step towards him, the air in his lungs is squeezed out by some invisible fist.

"It's time you saw our lake."

"You've found him?"

She doesn't reply, just smiles, and takes his gloved hand. He follows her as she steps, delicate but sure, through the snow and towards the forest.

He doesn't know how far they walk, but he has time to study her; each footstep as she leads him along the path, her body so relaxed in the harsh terrain. Every so often, he catches a pale cheek beneath the fur trim of her hood. Like the other women of the town, she is tall—at least taller than other women he's dated. A wisp of dark blonde hair drifts across her face and it's all he can do to stop himself from reaching out to touch it.

Forty minutes from Fristad, as they start down a shallow incline, the firs clear to reveal the lake before them, just lit in the half-light.

"Oh." He stops. "It *is* beautiful, isn't it?"

And without warning, she turns, loosens his scarf and kisses him.

They stand, holding each other, while he takes in the vastness of the landscape. To Nathan, the sky seems too wide, too glorious and they nothing more than pine needles on a forest floor. The fear of its immensity overwhelms him and he steps back. Is this what Marty wanted him to see? Is Marty somewhere nearby looking at this view from another vantage point? He feels Freja's hand loosen from beneath his arm, so he turns to her and they kiss again. And he is back in that first night, giddy with longing, enchanted, confused, while a voice somewhere far yet somehow near whispers:

Become part of it

He breaks away. "What was that?"

"Come." She leads him onto the ice. Nathan hesitates, but she smiles and squeezes his fingers; warmth floods his body. It is only now he realises she wears no gloves, though it must be at least minus 12 out here.

"You ..."

"Nathan," she whispers, and he steps out after her.

They cross the dark translucent ice; its deep cracks like lines across an open palm. And, as they do, the lake sings a response, shifting and stretching in its tight cocoon.

"Come." Freja pulls his hand a little and when he smiles, she laughs, clear and high, and he's reminded of a wind chime shivering in the breeze.

They are almost in the centre of the lake now and, all around, it cracks and mutters. Freja turns again, kisses him and, as she sinks to the snow-dusted ice, she gently pulls him down to her. "Come," she whispers.

Above them, the song grows louder, bouncing off the trees that ring the lake. Something catches his eye and, glancing sideways, he sees them: the women. They are perhaps 150 yards away, maybe more—their white hair silver in the moonlight. They're too distant to make out clearly, but there must be hundreds of them, lined tightly between the forest and the icy shore.

He falters. "What ...?"

"Shhh ..." And her eyes and her lips draw him back.

All around, the vast cathedral of nature fills with the bellow of the ice lake calling out across the heavens, vibrating through the frozen water, rippling the snow. The old women dance on the shore, sing strange songs he cannot understand. Their voices, deep and strong, rising up to embrace the call of the lake. Against this fevered concerto, the dark firs strain towards this Winter's man and, dancing through the cacophony, a whisper clear and strong:

Here. He's here.

"Freja."

A mighty crack—as if the sky were being ripped apart—fills his ears then rumbles into silence.

Everything stops. The spell broken. Nothing stirs.

Nathan lies in the middle of the lake, the moon a smudge above him. Then the light breath of the forest scuffles snow across the ice.

"Beautiful," he murmurs, filled with an overwhelming calm. Lights flicker and swirl in the sky—faint greens, golds, pinks. "Marty," he whispers into the night. "Oh, Marty, you were right."

He reaches for Freja. But she's not there, not anywhere. He tries to stand, but the lake has chilled him, and whatever magic that earlier held him steady has gone. A flash of white hair darts behind him as he tries again to stand. Laughter in his ears, tantalising, disorienting; a melody amongst the distant trees. He tries again, panic rising in him now, tries to run, to scramble for the shore.

"Freja!"

A sudden puff of warm breath blurs his vision, eddies of dusty snow swirl around him, like mist. He feels a jolt, something monumental breaking—opening—below him.

He's here.

"Marty?!"

Reaching out, he touches only freezing water, ice too slippery to grasp; frost clouds his eyes, then heat, intense heat, rising up from the depths, taking him, swallowing him down, down, down, and all around a roar like a million pained animals.

He gasps; just once.

The lake refreezes. It's an ancient beast that can heal itself so fast. Ice thickens, tensions build, cracks lengthen, and a new song rises to the surface. A creature sated for the moment, stitched together with the souls of Winter men. This explorer, lost in the void, cries with new vigour into the clear cold air to its people long-since dwindled to extinction, who never noticed what was missing, who will never come.

The Death of Black Fatima
Muhammed Awal Ahmed

LOCATION: Ankpa, a kingdom under foreign occupation by the Masquerade Empire

POPULATION: A total population of 700,000 humans, 30 masquerade outposts, and a new influx of Djinns, both of which their numbers are unknown

"TELL ME ABOUT THEM AGAIN," the girl says to the Djinn inside her for the fourth time this evening. Their Waters seep from her in saliva and sweat and tears. The room is raw with heat and pain. The Mallam pours more teaspoons of Zamzam water into her ears. The Zamzam burns through the Djinn, Saun of the Sea, like a flood of hot water tunnelling through his auditory nerves. Black Fatima finds herself whispering more questions to him, through the water seeping out the sides of her mouth, snaking down her face and her ears.

The Mallam is an impatient exorcist from the start. And worse, a ruthless one. She curls her body, drawing close to the warm sensation of a Djinn drifting through her body. She is tied to the bed, hands and feet. Her questions pile in her mouth and she passes it to him in saliva gulps that taste like Zamzam and salt. The Djinn, with the serenity of eternal life, answers her questions through the heat and the pain of the Ruqya. Once, in the shimmering heat of Ruqya, their bodies must have melted apart because she could see the face for the first time, not clearly, but like looking through a waterfall to see the jagged rocks behind it; hollow eyes on a dampened face, an aquiline bill and broad pointed ears. Saun of the Sea touched her face, light as water, his burning finger tracing her jawline before they were merged back, his skin dissolving in her body waters.

We saw the ships first. Black ships with white sails and white sailors. Black ships with slaves and stolen goods. For years, ships sailed past us. Some nights, we would come out of the water naked. We; blue-scaled Effrits from the west, red-skinned Shilas and Mammy Waters tattooed all over to look like fishes; all gathered for the sight of the White sailors in their black ships. Sometimes they threw things in the water: silk, cardamom, mould gods, little boy slaves. Soon enough, they found our love for gold and for humans we could turn into one of us. They threw more.

When they threw trinkets of gold, we did tricks for them. Little wiles, illusions of our body chemistry—we made our skins glow so the water can. Little things to keep more gold and humans thrown into our water. See child, we thought we were in control; that they wouldn't hurt us, because they couldn't. Sometimes, we saw a glimpse of a face, with eyes wide open with fear, a body with ankles marked with chains, before it plunged into the water. We saw those things they hunted with, but we acted like we didn't. Those things were lighter, much lighter than anything we'd seen, more deadly when they used it; when we made trouble; when we tried to take their ship. All we had was our magic.

Sometimes, these men would mimic our speech and we'd laugh at their cleverness. Sometimes they'd jump into the water and swim with us. They tried to get closer to our skin glowing in the water, to touch it, but we kept our bodies with us. In the end, they hunted us. And they've been hunting us for years. They cut us open, they burn us, to keep their moving things moving. Now they've come to your home, but they came with us and our children and our magic. So yes, some of us escape. Some of us are caught again. Whether you want to know if you're trapped in a Djinn, or he's trapped in you, it doesn't matter. It never has. We are about to die, if you don't stop asking questions and listen to the plan, to what this old and tired Djinn has to say ...

Saun of the Sea feels it again before their eyes bleed tears; that humiliating burn from the exorcist's chants. The burn in his grief-stricken pleas dying in a little girl's pride before it comes out of her throat in half whimpers. He remembers his boy and his bravery. The son he left behind while making his escape. A son trapped in a cage scared and alone somewhere on the river. He went back after his escape and the house wasn't there anymore, the house had floated away with their magic. It shames him that he wasn't going to wait to see the Bridge-Rise. That he was giving up on his son, finding his way out of the river, before he saw the girl. She was alone, walking down the bank of the river, before the worst plan he'd ever thought of pieced itself together in seconds from the farthest brink of loss, grief, and desperation.

Saun of the Sea feels beads of sweat forming on his formless face and the girl tastes more salt in her mouth.

Soap. Bad soap. How it started. Black Fatima's mother makes soaps from ash and acid and palm oil. She made a soap that could make Black Fatima's skin lighter; it had less palm oil and more acid. So down she went; our Fatima, to the Olamaboro River, three days before the Bridge-Rise. At noon, she took a bucket and went to the river, alone. Because her dark skin makes her do things she's not supposed to. At least, that's what her mother says. She went with a few of her clothes to try on after, and the soap balled up inside them.

On her way down the winding rocky path, she made a mental note to pluck some palm fronds. She'd place them on the surface of her bucket full of water on her way back, so it doesn't get her back wet. The quietness of the Olamaboro could have been something ominous, but it wasn't enough an omen to keep her skin away from a whitening ritual. Olamaboro was indignant, speechless against her intruding steps and their intentions of them. The silent air of it, devoid of adults washing clothes, washing bodies in the body of the water, children shrieking, swimming, play fighting, play hiding, and fishing, all came to her as its natural shape. The river flowed softly, stretching out like a tortured animal, resting and dying, gliding over sand, slippery stones, and forgotten soaps.

Black Fatima was close enough to feel the river flow like it sloughs off its skin. The body gets smaller each time she comes to fetch water or take her bath, each time the White men float over it with their magic. They build new roads, renovate the king's palace; change the thatched roof to zinc and the mud floor to tiles. Now they promise a bridge. All for the oil they drill from deep below, oil that spills into their rivers and kills all their fish. Sometimes, Black Fatima feels like she's witnessing a sad, ancient crime. A crime she's too weak to fight and too young to understand.

Black Fatima remembered when she used to come down to the river with her father to wash his red Toyota. She could see the river's vastness; how it stretched with no end, far into the horizon, how it swallowed up the houses and electricity poles built too close to its bank. The white men are wearing it out, they are weakening its flow and promising a concrete bridge through the deepest part, Black Fatima thought. If only she could stop it somehow. Somewhere in her, she wants to know how they do it. Why they're winning. Why some say the white men have the key to the river and they can lock it from flowing whenever they want to. Why some of her people think the white men can cause and stop the rain, in the driest crack of harmattan, in the great wetness of the rainy season, until they finish tarring a stretch of road. No one knew if it was true. No one wanted to know.

When she got to the bank, Olamaboro, what was left of it, flowed noiselessly. She climbed down the boulders leading into it. Black Fatima removed her black anklet for Djinn's protection and dipped her bare feet in the water. It felt warm. She liked this. The river always had a different temperature from its banks. When it's harmattan and it's chilly in the morning, the river would be very warm and tolerant to her feet. Now it flowed more quietly than usual, less rebellious. All the old fables about the Olamaboro River disappeared once white men floated on it and children started shitting by its banks. She dropped her bucket, pulled off her clothes, and walked into it with her mother's soap in her balled up fist. She soaped her sponge with it and it lathered surprisingly well. Black Fatima watched her reflection through the ripples of the river and she liked what she saw. She liked the two dimples on her left cheek when she smiled, the natural kohl lined around her eyes and her skin, so dark, like her father and his father before him. Her mother didn't like it. She made this soap so Black Fatima could be one of the half-caste girls waving tiny flags and wearing rings of yellow garlands when the white men came to open the bridge.

Black Fatima dipped her fingers slowly into the river, careful not to ruin the calm mirror of the surface. She watched the fishes, little blue and black fishes pecking her fingers and her big toenail. She felt the urge to cough phlegm into the water and watch them tear it apart. One stopped and swam away and the rest too, quicker than the first. Something cold stirred in the water, grazed past her left leg, and circled her. Because her dark skin made her do things she wasn't supposed to, she cupped her hands like a bowl, dipped them into the water, and poured it down her face. She was immediately blinded by an old fear, as thin as a gossamer, wisps of memories of pain and a great blast on a house floating on the river.

"Where would you like to leave through?" the Mallam is asking again. At his feet, there's a gourd for collecting the Djinn. He hears more of the father's sigh and his feet, circling them in the room. The man's worry fuels his impatience and creates an urgency in his questions. There is no answer. The body lies still. Tied to the bed, the girl sleeps on. In his line of work, he knows better than to disbelieve a body. It is impossible to believe the little girl swam up the Olamaboro River, paddling the great force rushing down the floating house, where the white men will be cutting the river in two.

Looking at her tiny arms, he knows the current should have swallowed her body. He thinks of how she was when those men pulled her into the compound; eyes red with rage, hair twisted in dreadlocks, with dead leaves and water worms, her body white and plastic—like a ghost. A hijab was quickly thrown over her on his orders because he felt a chill when they dragged her past him and he didn't like it, and they obeyed because everyone obeys the exorcist at an exorcism. To her room at the distant end of the compound, they dragged her. He followed the milieu at a safe distance, far from the wailing women and the men covered in scratches and bruises as she screamed and kicked, and bit at everyone around her.

Those white men he worked for told him where to be standing among the crying women and the brooding men. A leather bag slung across his shoulder and inside, his ancient texts, a gourd of Zamzam, and a whip. The whip they gave him for this particular task was a whip unlike any other he has used to catch a Djinn. A whip with a handle designed with gold-etched patterns. It had a faint scent of odd eastern spices. The whip for the last of these exorcisms, the last of the missing Djinns. It was only fitting that the Djinn who orchestrated the escape would be caught last and by him.

How they know where he'd be, or inside who, the Mallam couldn't tell. But he always knew he'd become something, something more than a common Marabout like his father, chasing after rich men with his failed visions and prophesies. All he has to do is to overpower a Djinn and lure it with ancient poetry and incantation. Hunt it in a groove, in a swamp, or get it out of a body alive. Then he gets paid. It had always been simple. He never relies on dark magic until he panics. Tonight, he reeks of it. He can feel this one girl sharing her body with the Djinn, sharing the pain of the dark magic he has to enter under his tongue when he recites the Suratul Yaseen. Why and how the little girl is doing this, the Mallam doesn't know. The Mallam hasn't known anything in a while. Only that he is no longer a Marabout. Whether it's a good or bad thing, he doesn't know.

The sweat sticks to Black Fatima's hijab and it sticks to her back, to her bed. All around her, there is wetness, everywhere but the inside of her mouth. She can hear her mother crying, quiet voices hushing her like it's a mourning house, saying her daughter is already dead. Black Fatima should feel sad for causing her mother pain but she doesn't. There's a plan, an old Djinn's plan, and they have to follow it, together. They both have equal roles to play in her body now. So when the angry and now exhausted Mallam brings out a long black leather whip, she doesn't flinch. Instead, she looks at its golden handle; the brown strips of leather intertwined with the black and she wonders how an exorcist could have a whip like this. The Mallam stands over her body with the whip and he watches for a reaction. Her eyes are closed, her lips clamped shut with thirst. He raises the whip over his shoulder and a hand catches it from the back. It's her father's hand, his face darker, his brows furrowed tightly with worry. The Mallam puts the whip quietly in the bag.

"We have to take her away from here, to the river." The Mallam says, "The Djinn is strong, but Djinns are fickle things. It has to feel threatened. We're still here because something gives it respite." The Mallam strokes his beard and studies Black Fatima's little body strapped to the bed, breath rising and falling like a body lost to a peaceful sleep.

He wants to take me away now, good. Something thinks this in Black Fatima. Whether it's her thought or the Djinn's, or both, she doesn't know. She can only care about the plan now.

"Why the river?" her father is asking, his arms akimbo.

He doesn't trust the Mallam, good.

"Baba Fatima, our river has magical powers the Djinn and your daughter can't fight. Let me take her there. My magic is not strong here, it'll be when we get to the river, I promise you." Mallam eyes her body as he says this, his tone carrying a threat across the room.

Her father opens his mouth to say something when a howl starts. Someone screams wildly in a voice no one in the room recognizes. Someone, Black Fatima thinks, is now under the bed, shaking it, loosening the ropes wound tightly around her body. The scream is coursing out of her throat, old, weak, and angry. Her body leaves her bed and floats in the air, like the white men's house on the river. Outside, her mother is wailing uncontrollably. The hushing women are screaming for Allah to save them. This is part of the plan. This is part of the plan. Is this part of the plan?

The ropes are finally off her hands. She can feel a burning rage behind her eyes, changing their color, a stormy white, a crimson red blurring into a nocturnal black. Her fingers go for the tip of the hijab, just above her nape. She pinches, pulls the cocoon off it, and it comes off wet over her body. Her skin is still plastic white and hardened like it was when they found her in the river. In her body, she can hear everything, her pumping heart and all her farthest thoughts; where they meet and commune with the Djinn's. There's also the distant hue of a theory, setting and rising, a ball in a room filled with white bodies, a mirage of explosions, caged families, and a sabotage. She doesn't know which is the past and which is the future, or how to start piecing them together.

Her thoughts melt into each other and burn at the back of her brain. She can still feel herself separately from all these; the edges where her skin stops, where it merges into his, their veins intertwined into two systems pumping blood through her body; one darkly blue and raging. She remembers the days when this exorcist was a smiling marabout who hid a coin in his palm and made it disappear. Her eyes close and the light steals out of her quietly. Her new strength seeps out of her as her knees wobble and she falls.

"I'm taking her to the river now. No one follows me. No one!" It's the Mallam's voice she hears, the only one that can still talk, still take action. This is part of the plan. This is part of the plan. She thinks. They both think.

The Mallam draws in deep breaths as he rows the boat, his breathing as loud as Black Fatima as they rowed past dying fish breaking the water surface like divers coming up for air. She can tell he's afraid, she can smell it. Her head is placed on the rim of the boat. She can see the sun setting on the river far away, red and pinking. Soon, it'll be dark. It all darkens as the boat goes under a floating house. A door opens from above and a ladder is dropped for them.

The white men are not white at all. Black Fatima notices this before she sees the first one coming down the ladder, his skin caked with a white substance. That is how they lured everybody in Ankpa to their control, by looking different. Black Fatima wants to laugh, wants to cry. She's so close to the truth, and she'll have to burn it. She'll have to burn everything she sees now. She's going to die; the realization comes to her as easy as the clean breath she draws into her lungs. Her body is pulled up the ladder, into the house, and the Mallam rows away quickly.

Black Fatima sees some of the forlorn faces staring back at her from the cages and something hurts in her. A few are faces she recognizes; all with ache-filled eyes the Djinn knows. Black Fatima sees their magic for the first time as the river parts away through the open trapdoor and her eyes widen. The white men whip more magic out of the Djinns until the water parts down to the white sand of it. More Djinn-human slaves are led down the door she'd been pulled into, to the wet sand of the river base, carrying buckets filled with concrete and tar, their feet linked together with a long chain. There's a large furnace that keeps burning fiercely. No one sees a girl slave secretly plotting with the Djinn inside her.

There are cages everywhere, with clothes spread over them to protect their plastic-hardened bodies from cracking in the Ankpa sun. Black Fatima is pushed inside one of these cages and left alone.

Black Fatima thinks mostly of the best way to die; if dying is what she has to do.

A cage is opened every half hour and someone is whipped to the large furnace that spits out screams. The men poke their long sticks at the body, turning it over until there's nothing left of it. Nothing but the gas going down the house and keeping it afloat.

Another idea forms in her, she must become invisible like Saun of the Sea was the day they first met in the river. She can hear her frail bones rattling in her body, her teeth shaking in a convulsion and she wonders if she's ready to become more; to be seen less and felt more. Inside her, she feels a readiness for the hurt, when her cage is unlocked and she's dragged out and whipped. A boy in one of the cages cries the loudest and he's whipped too. Somehow, Black Fatima knows he is Saun's family, the reason he let himself be possessed again. She gives the crying boy a thin smile before she's tied and thrown into the burning furnace.

Coldness, that's what she feels now. The coldness eats away at her fingers, her mouth, and her eyes until only her spine remains. Her cold steel of a spine. Sticks poke at her, impatient sticks in more impatient hands. She can feel the furnace sucking her in, out of herself, and down below, into the force that keeps the house afloat. She thinks of all she's had to endure since the white men came in their white-caked skins and their floating slave houses; since that bad soap in the river. She thinks of Saun of the Sea too, and all he's had to endure trying to escape. She thinks of all of this as her two new eyes open.

Her body shoots up the furnace—necks snap, spines break and whip, and white bodies drop to the floorboard as she whizzes through the house. If she has bones, they're stronger, stronger than bone and iron. Her body soaks through the walls, dissolving all the cages. Others whiz out of bodies and join her. Black Fatima breaks out of the attic quick enough to see the last of the sun setting on the river. She sees all the other sinking houses, water rushing in to close off the sound of drowning men. All around her, she can hear a great whizzing, like the sound of dragonflies she once hunted by the banks of the Olamaboro River.

Notes Towards a History of LeHorn's Hollow

Brian Keene

LOCATION: LeHorn's Hollow, Central Pennsylvania, USA

POPULATION: Unknown

THE FOLLOWING document was found on James Nesbitt's computer. Most of the material is in the form of a personal journal, and although none of the entries have dates ascribed to them, the first entry was created on October 6, 2023, the day after Nesbitt retired from his role as publisher of *The York Dispatch*. (He left his role as an adjunct professor at York College the previous June.) Nesbitt's entries are interspersed with other supplemental material, such as news articles (copied and pasted from the original websites), transcripts of recordings obtained from his former colleague Maria Nasr, and more.

For ease and convenience, we have numbered each journal entry.

Entry 1
Note Toward A History of LeHorn's Hollow

Okay. First day of retirement! No more teaching. No more struggling to keep the paper afloat and publish the truth in an era when people just make up their own truths, regardless of the facts. Time enough at last, to paraphrase that old *Twilight Zone* episode. I can finally plant a proper garden, although that will have to wait until next spring. In the meantime, I intend to spend the winter snowed in and doing what I've always threatened to do. Provided it actually snows, of course. These last few winters have been sparse, in that regard. Certainly not like when I was a kid, when the drifts piled high and no one left the house for two or three days, and school was cancelled. Now, instead of cancelling, the kids just attend online, and those high drifts are nothing more than a few flurries.

Anyway, yes. After spending the last 25 years telling Betsy, our friends, family, and colleagues about my intent to one day write a book on the complete history of LeHorn's Hollow, I'm finally going to do just that.

Yes, there have been things written about it before. *The History of LeHorn's Hollow* by Jim Lewin (York Emporium Publishing, 2019) immediately comes to mind, but that is a rather thin pamphlet, barely twenty-thousand words. And most of the other books that mention or detail LeHorn's Hollow do so only in conjunction with specific events such as the two prominent forest fires, the ghost walk riots, or the events surrounding novelist Adam Senft and the murder of his wife, and the later copycat crime of aspiring author Darren Bosserman. The full history, which is primarily known only by aging local historians like me, has never been thoroughly researched or compiled. Indeed, outside of this immediate geographical area, I doubt there are many who have even heard of LeHorn's Hollow, even with the current popularity of the true crime genre and the plethora of podcasts, documentaries, and social media accounts dedicated to such topics.

I'll want to start with the accounts and histories of the Indigenous Peoples, particularly the Susquehannock. From there, I'll work my way up through modern times, including some of the grimmer aspects and lore.

Need to email Maria and see if she has anything of note that I can include. Perhaps I can reach out to that powwow doctor she knows, Levi Stoltzfus. He might know of some folklore or traditions regarding the place, particularly from the Amish or Pennsylvania Dutch. I've also been told there's a folklorist who might be of great help. Apparently, she specializes in tall tales and some of the stranger phenomena associated with the place. Of course, I don't want to get into the more "woo" aspects of LeHorn's Hollow—the flying saucers, the Goat Man, dimensional doorways, and the like. But I should probably spend a chapter covering such tales in general.

Anyway ... excited to get started!

Entry 2

There is, of course, no LeHorn's Hollow listed on any of York County's historical records. You won't find it named on a map, and the GPS in your phone won't give you directions to it. The locals all know it by that name, but the moniker wasn't given until 1985, when farmer Nelson LeHorn killed his wife and subsequently disappeared. (A crime that echoes through the Tara Senft murder decades later.)

At one point, the forest itself spanned roughly 30 miles, but two forest fires and logging by the Gladstone Pulpwood Company have winnowed that today, as has the expansion and encroachment of the surrounding towns of Seven Valleys, New Freedom, Spring Grove, New Salem, and Shrewsbury. When it still stood, LeHorn's farm occupied a space almost in the center of the area. After the murder, locals began to refer to the entire region as LeHorn's Hollow.

But the woods were there long before Nelson LeHorn. Those trees, or their ancestors, stood when the Germans, Quakers, and Amish first settled here. John Smith wrote about the area in 1608 when he was exploring the lands north of the Chesapeake Bay. Several of his party were lost among the forest. Dutch and Swedish fur traders knew of them as early as the 1620s. English merchant William Claiborne attempted to establish a settlement there in 1630, but those efforts were apparently abandoned. The historical record lacks any firm details as to why other than a reference to "the trees being too thick" and difficulty in "establishing trails."

Of course, the Susquehannock knew of the forest long before any of these others. Despite the area's proximity to their settlements in what is today Long Level in York County and Lancaster County's Washington Borough, there is no archeological record of them having occupied the area. There are, of course, legends that

this particular patch of woods was where they banished their criminals and their mentally ill, but there is no evidence of this, save for
one bit of folklore that has been passed down, seemingly from
descendants of Skenandoa, a war leader of the Oneida during the
Revolutionary War. (He was born a Susquehannock but was later
adopted by the wolf clan of Oneida.) In that tale, a young male to
whom evil spirits whispered (perhaps schizophrenia) displayed
violent tendencies against his fellow tribe members and was subsequently banished to the forest. A young maiden who loved him left
the tribe two nights later, intent on living with him. Supposedly she
wandered the forest, unable to find her love, or a way out. Her spirit
was said to wander through the trees throughout eternity.

It's curious. Tales of shifting trails and moving trees pop up
quite often in the folklore surrounding the region. Will need to
touch on that for the "woo" chapter of the book.

Entry 3

Will need to include a chapter on powwow magic, because not
only is Central Pennsylvania steeped in it, but so is LeHorn's
Hollow.

Found out something today while going through the records at
the historical society. Apparently, Nelson LeHorn's mother disappeared, too. LeHorn's father was allegedly a powerful powwow
warlock. (Is that the right term? Will have to find out.) There are
stories of him putting a hex on a "river witch" from the town of
Marietta after she supposedly put a blight on the elder LeHorn's
cattle. He was also said to have hexed a thief caught stealing from
the family's root cellar, turning the man deaf and blind.

Allegedly, Nelson's mother was engaged in an affair with another
man. She disappeared soon after his father learned of the betrayal.
There are no further accounts or records after that. Any thorough
accounting of Nelson LeHorn and the murder of Patricia LeHorn
should include that.

Powwow is often taught generationally. If LeHorn learned it
from his father, I wonder if the elder learned it, in turn, from
Nelson's grandfather? I should look into that. Perhaps there is a
mention of him during the Pennsylvania witch panic of the 1930s?

Entry 4

Been a few days. Betsy and I went to the farmer's market on Saturday, and church on Sunday. First time I've been inside a church in I don't know how long, but the Crisfields were getting their daughter baptized and we were invited, so we went. It's the neighborly thing to do.

I did, however, get the contact info for that local folklorist I mentioned. Mrs. Chickbaum. She lives right here in Wrightsville. I'm going to reach out to her today.

(Excerpts from transcript of meeting with Mrs. Chickbaum)

JAMES NESBITT: Okay, I'm here with Mrs. ... um ... I just realized; I don't know your first name.

MRS. CHICKBAUM: (laughs lightly): Oh, that's alright, dear. Mrs. Chickbaum is fine.

JN: Okay. And you're okay with me recording this, yes?

MC: You go right ahead. Aren't those phones a wonderful thing? So much magic, right there in everyone's pockets. Didn't used to be that way.

JN: They are pretty amazing. I often wonder how we managed before we had them.

MC: (laughs again, softer this time) Oh, you got by.

JN: Chickbaum ... that's ... an unusual name? German, I'm assuming?

MC: We had kin in Germany. Kin everywhere. But my people came here from Ireland.

JN: Ah, okay. And settled here in Central Pennsylvania?

MC: Here. And Maryland, Virginia, West Virginia. There were a lot more forests back then. I came here.

JN: Do you still have a lot of family in the area?

MC: Sadly, I'm the last.

JN: I'm sorry to hear that.

MC: (unintelligible)

JN: How did you come to know so much about LeHorn's Hollow? Was it something you were always interested in, or ...?

MC: Oh, I've always known about it. I was here a long time. The ley lines meet there, you see? That was what first attracted me.

JN: Ley lines. Those are something to do with Earth energy, right?

MC: Something like that. Very powerful. And the places where they intersect are always special.

JN: LeHorn's Hollow is one of those places?

MC: Oh, yes. Of course, it wasn't called LeHorn's Hollow back then. There were other names for it. There have always been other names. My people. The Pennsylvania Dutch. The Susquehannock, who, of course, didn't call themselves that. Did you know they were a very tall people?

JN: Is that right?

MC: Oh, yes. An average of ... oh, I'd say six and a half feet. Better fighters you never met. But their word for the forest was fearful. Their word meant to stay away.

JN: They had legends about it? The Goat Man and su—

MC: There was no Goat Man back then. There shouldn't have ever been a Goat Man. The only reason there was a Goat Man was because of Nelson LeHorn's foolishness. No, Mr. Nesbitt. I'm talking about the things that always existed there. The black dog. The circles.

JN: Crop circles, you mean?

MC: That's what you call them now. Of course, there weren't crops growing there when they first started to appear. Nobody tried farming in that area until later. But the circles didn't need crops. Never have. They can appear in meadows and amongst the trees just as surely as they do in wheat or corn. And they were there long before He Who Shall Not Be Named or any of that other nonsense.

JN: He who ... (sound of rustling papers). There are references to him from both Nelson LeHorn and Adam Senft.

MC: Had no idea what they were messing with. And no idea how incredibly lucky they were. Did you know that Senft and his friends said the entity's real name out loud on more than one occasion? To do that instantly summons him. They had no idea how close they came.

JN: You're saying that Adam Senft summoned a demon?

MC: No, he only woke up the Goat Man ... the one LeHorn first summoned. That was only an outreach of He Who Shall Not Be Named. A servant, of sorts. I'm saying they could have summoned He Who Shall Not Be Named himself, had the safeguards not already been in place. As it was, they further weakened the walls every time they said his real name out loud. That's what led to all that nonsense with the ghost walk.

JN: You're referring to Ken Ripple's haunted attraction and the riot?

MC: I'm saying there's things in those woods that were there long before any of these others. LeHorn thought it was his fault the trees moved, but he was wrong. The trees have always moved there. More tea, dear?

JN: Um ... no thank you.

JN: So, getting back to the folklore. You mentioned a black dog.

MC: Oh, yes. With red eyes. Folks have been seeing him for as long as people have been here.

JN: How about UFOs? Or, I guess now they're called UAPs.

MC: People have been seeing them all over the world since the dawn of time, Mr. Nesbitt. And the occupants. They used to call them faeries. Now they're aliens.

JN: You believe them to be the same thing?

MC: It is the same thing. Come to Earth from somewhere else. Settled here. Established outposts. And now travel back and forth. All it takes is a door. Of course, there aren't as many now. No.

JC: I'm confused.

MC: (laughs) That's only natural! If you want to understand, go to the woods. Walk the trails. Walk amongst the trees. Look for a door. I'll take you. Then you'll understand everything. Maybe you'll even see the dog.

Entry 5

Met with Mrs. Chickbaum yesterday. She was absolutely no help. It's hard to guess her age, but she must surely be in her nineties. Doesn't look it. Still has a face free from wrinkles and a long silver hair. Not gray, but silver. But she's clearly got dementia. She offered to take me on a walk through LeHorn's Hollow. At her age, I can only imagine how badly that would end.

Entry 6

Powwow Magic: One of the most prominent beliefs among the early German, Irish, Dutch, and English settlers of Pennsylvania was powwowing—a form of magic involving a curious mixture of German braucherei, Appalachian folklore, herb craft, Kabbalah, and the Christian Bible.

Widely practiced in Pennsylvania well into the early 1930s. Gained international notoriety during the "Hex" murder of Nelson Rehmeyer in 1928, and the subsequent trial that followed. Will want to do at least half a chapter focusing on that, as the murder happened right on the outskirts of what would later become LeHorn's Hollow.

Still practiced today, but far less prominent. Still need to see if Maria's friend, Levi Stoltzfus, would agree to be interviewed about it for the book. I know that he had some involvement with the incident at the haunted attraction as well, although Maria has always held her cards close to her chest regarding that. Maybe I can win him over, with her help.

Curiously, the Susquehannock people had a form of shamanism called pawwaw. While much of powwow is based on the German discipline of braucherei, I wonder if the name itself originated from the indigenous people?

Primary books of Powwow: *The Long Lost Friend* by John George Hohman. Also, *The Sixth and Seventh Books of Moses*. I know nothing about the latter, so will need to research that at length.

Entry 7

List of Documented Deaths, Disappearances, and Other Notable Occurrences

The key word here is documented. I'll add hearsay, folklore, legends (such as the Skenandoa story recounted earlier) elsewhere.

1. 1608 – Several members of John Smith's exploratory party get lost in LeHorn's Hollow (which I'm going to subsequently refer to as the forest or the woods here, encompassing the entire area). They are never found.

2. 1630 – William Claiborne gives up attempts to establish a settlement there, and claims the trees make it impossible.

3. 1725 – A Quaker named Paul Schultz, an unnamed indigenous guide, and a hired porter identified only as Wilson disappear in the forest while endeavoring to map both Codorus Creek and Kreutz Creek (before either had those names). A search party sent to look for them reports sightings of "fairy lights" amongst the trees.

4. 1729 – A workman identified in multiple accounts only as Smith is found dead in the forest (near what is now Red Lion). Reports say he fled there to escape a warrant for debts owed. Accounts state his corpse was "torn to pieces" and prints of an unidentified animal were found around him. Possible origin of the Goat Man legend? (Although Mrs. Chickbaum seemed to indicate otherwise.) Dog, maybe? But one would think a dog's prints wouldn't be listed as unidentified.

5. 1740 – In the aftermath of the border skirmish between Pennsylvania and Maryland (Cresap's War), many Hessian mercenaries who had served in the armed conflict were given land and deeds throughout the county. At the time, York County had not yet been founded, and was still part of Lancaster County. One of these soldiers, Hanz Mueller, became one of the first to settle in the forest. He had a small farmstead, occupied by himself, his wife, and an infant son, located near what is now Seven Valleys. They reportedly lived there for a year. The next spring, a tax accessor found Mueller dead in the cottage. He'd been stabbed through the chest with a fireplace poker. Judging by accounts, his corpse hadn't been there long. The wife's bare footprints led to a broad oak tree that was notable for a large tree-hollow in its trunk (tree hollows are cavities that form in living trees ... and since I had to look it up, I'll need to explain the definition to readers so they don't confuse it with the Hollow itself. In parts of Europe, particularly Ireland, people would sometimes place small doors into such formations. These

so-called Fairy Doors were supposed to allow access to the Fairy Realm.). Mrs. Mueller's footsteps stopped at the tree, and she was never found, nor was there any sign of the baby. Strangely, there were reports of a dog's pawprints found alongside her footprints. They, too, stopped at the tree.

6. 1777 – After the Articles of Confederation were adopted in York by the Second Continental Congress on November 15, a courier vanished in the forest. Neither the man nor his mount were ever found.

7. 1819 A Fourth of July celebration was held over two days, celebrating the then-living patriots who had participated in the Revolutionary War. After a day of religious services, townspeople, including the York Phalanx military organization commanded by a Captain James Doudel, traveled at dawn the next day to what is now Spring Grove. A judge, the honorable J. Kraber-Brockie, hosted a feast on his vast estate, which included several hours of toasts and the beating of the reveille. Afterward, the artillery performed a discharge into the unoccupied woodlands to the south (what would be the Spring Grove border of LeHorn's Hollow). Numerous attendees reported that strange lights were spotted in the forest after the artillery display, and strange noises were heard. One account says, "as if the trees themselves were voicing their displeasure."

8. 1829 – A young domestic servant named Susanna Coupland was convicted of abandoning her illegitimate baby within the boundaries of the forest. There was rampant speculation as to the identity of the father, but I haven't found anything concrete. Coupland was found unconscious in a field. A medical examiner determined that she had just undergone labor within the last twenty-four hours. Coupland insisted that the forest took her baby. She was hanged at the York County courthouse. Her grave is unmarked.

9. 1916 – A hunter reports sighting of an Albatwitch—Pennsylvania's supposed Sasquatch-like cryptid. The

name translates as "apple thief" in Pennsylvania Dutch, I believe. There have been many reported sightings around Marietta and Columbia, across the river, but this is one of the few for York County, and the only one I can find in regard to the forest around LeHorn's Hollow (despite local folklore).

10. 1928 – The murder of powwow practitioner Nelson Rehmeyer at the hands of John Blymire, John Curry, and Wilbert Hess. Rehmeyer's home stood on the outskirts of the Hollow. Blymire and Hess believed that Rehmeyer had placed a hex on them and were advised by another local witch named Emma Knopp to obtain a lock of the warlock's hair, as well as his copy of *The Long Lost Friend*. Instead, they murdered him. The subsequent trial made international headlines. The case was fictionalized in the 1988 film *Apprentice To Murder*, starring Donald Sutherland.

11. 1939 – Documented crop circle. Cornfield of a Mennonite farmer named Hobert Kraus. The crop circle measured over fifty feet in circumference. Photographs in the newspaper archives and at the historical society. Kraus allegedly saw "lights" in the field the night before it happened. He thought they were just "big fireflies."

12. 1941 – A deer hunter named Leland Jones disappears. His son, Rory, who had accompanied him into the woods, stated that they both got lost and that, quote "the trail kept changing."

13. 1946 – A logger for the pulp wood company dies in a freak accident after being impaled by a tree branch.

14. 1952 – An Amish family disappears while picking raspberries in the forest.

15. 1960 – An elderly woman identified as Alice Diehl wanders from her home in Shrewsbury in the middle of the night, during a blizzard, and is found in the forest the next morning. Cause of death listed as hypothermia.

16. 1967 – Two teenagers found dead in their car while parked along a dirt road in the forest. Cause of death listed as carbon monoxide poisoning.

17. 1968 through 1970 – A spate of UFO-sightings in the area of the hollow. Many news articles (tones ranging from incredulous to bemused) report accounts of strange lights and sounds.

18. 1976 – Two hikers found dead in what is presumed to be an animal attack. Details are strikingly similar to the account from 1729. One long-time resident alleges there is a feral dog "black with red eyes" that has been sighted in the forest over the years.

19. 1979 – Another hiker vanishes while camped overnight in the woods.

20. 1985 – Nelson LeHorn murders his wife, Patricia, pushing her out of the attic window. His children tell authorities that the farmer and amateur powwow practitioner believed that his wife had consorted with a Goat Man, and that there was a great evil residing within the forest. LeHorn was never caught, and there have been no confirmed sightings of him to this day.

21. 1990 – Another crop circle appears.

22. 1996 – A logger reported missing is later found wandering the road near Winterstown. The man is unable to speak. A stroke was suspected but I've found no follow-ups.

23. 1997 – Researchers from Penn State discover strange magnetic underground pockets scattered throughout the forest. Further study is promised but never followed up on due to budget cuts.

24. 1998 – Authorities confirm that three bodies found by hunters were, in fact, murdered elsewhere and then buried in the forest. Organized crime suspected. Perhaps the notorious Marano Family.

25. 2000 – Three days after being paroled from Camp Hill State Prison, convicted pedophile Craig Chalmers abducts a young girl and flees with her to a campsite in the forest. When State Police find him, Chalmers claimed an old lady who lived in the forest asked him to bring her the girl. He also insisted that the woods were full of demons who were trying to kill him. The girl was unharmed. Her identity was never revealed in the press,

but I obtained the police reports. Oddly enough, the girl seemed to confirm the presence of an old woman who apparently had a pet dog. Both had arrived at the campsite only a few minutes before the State Police, and fled into the forest once the presence of law enforcement was discovered. It doesn't look like the police ever followed up on that, other than a precursory investigation.

26. 2002 – A forest fire destroys a swath of land near the abandoned LeHorn homestead, killing several locals. Among the dead are Frank Lehman and his sons Glen and Mark (who were deer hunting), and three teenagers whose car was found parked next to the LeHorn home. The vehicle was completely battered, as if it had been "hit by a speeding semi" according to one investigator. Reports from several first responders indicate that many of the dead were found in a similar state, but the official cause of death for all of them was due to the fire.

27. 2004 – Another suspected organized crime burial ground is discovered. Four corpses are recovered. None are ever identified. Various members of the Russian and Greek mobs are questioned, as are associates of the Marano family, but no charges are ever filed.

28. 2006 – A number of women are reported missing. All are residents of Shrewsbury. All disappeared in the vicinity of the forest. There are also a series of murders, culminating in a second forest fire that destroys over five hundred acres, including what was left of Nelson LeHorn's homestead. At first, investigators suggest arson, or perhaps a careless cigarette or an untended campfire as the cause. Within a few months, it is reported that a satanic cult is responsible for the abductions, the murders, and the fire. One of the murder victims, a Cory Peters, was found dead in the home of author Adam Senft and his wife Tara. Another victim, Michael Gitleson, was found beheaded in his car. The others were found in the forest itself, all around the area of the fire. The lead investigator, a

detective named Hector Ramirez, retired to Florida. Maria spoke with him during the haunted attraction investigation. I should follow up and see if he's still alive. He might be able to shed more light on this, because there's a lot here—including in our own coverage—that just doesn't add up. I didn't see it at the time, but I do now. I should have fired Miles. He was our editor, back then. Of course, a few months after the fire, Adam Senft murders his wife in the same manner as Nelson LeHorn. She dies in a fall from their attic window. Senft is found insane and committed to the White Rose mental health facility. He allegedly makes the same claims about his wife that Nelson LeHorn made about his, including consorting with a Goat Man. Senft also claims that he and his friends were "attacked by the trees."

29. 2008 – Entrepreneur Ken Ripple builds a Halloween haunted attraction in a part of the forest untouched by the two fires. A riot breaks out on opening night, killing fifty-seven people and injuring countless more. Among the dead are Adam Senft, who had escaped from White Rose the day before. Maria was there the night of the riot. Miles assigned her to interview Ripple. The story obviously became something else. I've read over her reporting, and she's hiding things. Once again, I should have seen it then, but I was always too busy getting us more funding and keeping us afloat. Schmoozing and boozing. Maria covered something up. I don't know what. I don't know if Miles was in on it or not. If not, he should have caught it. Why was Senft there? What was his involvement? And who is this Levi Stoltzfus and his connection to it all? I need to have a heart-to-heart with Maria about all this.

30. 2009 – Sally Newsome is found dead in a part of the woods near Seven Valleys. She'd been stabbed in the neck, and her corpse was sexually violated after death. In 2011, serial killer Roy McKenna was charged with her murder, as well as the murder of three other women.

31. 2017 – Aspiring writer Darren Bosserman becomes
obsessed with LeHorn's Hollow, and with Adam Senft.
He returns home after spending the day in the forest and
murders his entire family.

Entry 8

Maria lent me her notes, but I could tell she wasn't happy about it. I think she's doing so more out of a sense of loyalty and professionalism than anything else. She actually tried to dissuade me from writing the book. At one point she even made me promise I wouldn't go to the actual hollow. When I pointed out there's not much left there since the last fire, she said "There's more left there than you think. The ground is older than the trees."

She refused to give me contact information for Levi Stoltzfus, but I'm sure I can track him down another way. She also said she no longer had any recordings, but she seemed evasive. I was able to obtain a few transcripts from the archives, though.

Although I haven't read all the way through them yet, two things immediately stand out in Maria's notes. The first is another death that I'd missed for my list. A state surveyor was found dead atop a tree in 1990. The official cause of death was listed as a heart attack. Maria had underlined "atop a tree" several times. The second thing involves the little girl who was abducted by Craig Chalmers. All of the reports I read listed her as alive, but Maria apparently had witness testimony that the girl had been murdered by Chalmers prior to the arrival of the State Police. So, were her sources accurate? And if the girl was murdered, then who was the girl the police rescued? Strangely, I can't find any follow-ups in Maria's notes. It appears that she was looking into this after the riot at the ghost walk. Why did she do nothing further? It's like she buried the story. Definitely need to look into this more. If a different girl was brought out of the forest, then who was she? And if the abducted girl was murdered, why no record of that, or reactions from family or the community?

(Excerpts from transcript of recording between Maria Nasr and Ken Ripple)

MARIA NASR: So, you don't believe in any of it at all? You don't think Nelson LeHorn's ghost still haunts the hollow?

KEN RIPPLE: No. Not really. I mean, some weird things have happened there over the years. There's no denying that. Folks have died. But that was from accidents or stupidity, mostly. Not because of ghosts or demons or shit like that. Oh, sorry. Didn't mean to curse.

MN: That's okay. I can edit that out. So, you don't believe any of it?

KR: Nope.

MN: What about Patricia LeHorn's murder? What do you think contributed to that?

KR: Simple. Nelson LeHorn was a nut job. Just because he believed he was a witch, that doesn't necessarily make him one. He murdered his wife because he was crazy, not because she'd actually slept with the devil.

MN: How do you know for sure?

KR: Don't tell me you believe this stuff?

MN: Not really. But it's my job to keep an open mind, right? Reporters are supposed to be analytical. Explore all options and find the truth.

KR: If you say so. I don't know. I never met a reporter before. I thought you were just writing up a little article on the Ghost Walk.

MN: I am. But everyone in York County knows about LeHorn's Hollow. And people love a good ghost story. It wouldn't be much of an article if we didn't mention this. I mean, that's the whole reason you based your operation in those woods, right? To be near the hollow?

KR: True. Well, you asked how I know LeHorn was crazy. It wasn't a big secret or anything. My dad used to know him.

MN: Really?

KR: Yeah, back in the 70s and 80s. Before he ... you know. My dad was a beekeeper. Well, actually, he worked at the paper mill, like everybody else did back in the day. But in his spare time, he kept honeybees.

MN: I grew up in New Jersey. Was the paper mill the county's main employer?

KR: Didn't think you were from around here. Your accent gives you away.

MN: I have an accent?

KR: Sure. Not a bad thing. I figured you for New York or New Jersey. Like a girl from a Springsteen song, you know? In the 70s, pretty much everybody in York County worked at one of five places. We had the Caterpillar and Harley Davidson plants in York. There was Borg-Warner over in West York, who made stuff for the military—tanks and half-tracks and bomb shelters. All kinds of shit. Then there was the paper mill in Spring Grove and the foundry out in Hanover. That was it, unless you were a farmer or an auto mechanic. But by the mid-80s, right around the time I graduated from high school, Caterpillar and Borg-Warner had closed down, the paper mill was in the middle of a year-long strike, and Harley and the foundry had both downsized. But yeah, my dad worked in the paper mill and in his spare time, he tended to his beehives. During the strike, when he wasn't on the picket line with his union buddies, he was fooling around with his bees. He had hives all over the place. In orchards and on neighbors' farms. Anywhere somebody would let him. I think he had over forty of them during his busiest year. Every autumn, he'd harvest the honeycomb, extract the honey, and then sell it to the local grocery stores and farmer's markets. Had his own label on the jars and everything. 'Ripple's

Apiaries.' He made a nice little secondary income. I bet if he was still doing it today, he'd make a lot more, what with everybody into all that organic shit.

MN: I'm sure. But what does this have to do with Nelson LeHorn?

KR: LeHorn had bees, too. More than my dad ever did. Occasionally, my father would go over to LeHorn's farm and buy beehive materials from him. Frames. Parts for his extracting drum. Smokers. Protective clothing. Stuff like that. It was easier and cheaper to get them from LeHorn than through mail order.

MN: Did he ever see LeHorn do any powwow?

KR: No. My old man didn't believe in that stuff. But he did say several times that LeHorn was crazy. I remember this one time, these little, microscopic mites got into Dad's beehives. Killed several of his queens—just destroyed whole hives, you know? My dad asked LeHorn what he should do and LeHorn drew some kind of weird symbol and told Dad to paint it on each hive. It was supposed to keep the mites out.

MN: Did your father do it?

KR: No. He bought some pesticide and that did the trick. When I asked him why he didn't use the powwow doctor's method, Dad said, 'I'd be a damn fool to go drawing that nonsense on my beehives. The boys down at the American Legion would have never let me live it down. Old LeHorn is nuttier than your grandma's fruitcake.' And he was right. Another one of my dad's friends was cutting down a Christmas tree near the hollow. Back on the pulpwood company's land. He damn near cut his finger off. LeHorn came across him as he was walking out. The old guy told him not to go to the hospital—said he could stop the bleeding by 'laying on of the hands' or something like that.

MN: Faith healing. Did your father's friend take him up on the offer?

KR: Shit, no. He ran to his car and got the hell out of there.

MN: Will your attraction feature anything based off the LeHorn legend?

KR: Not directly, no. At least, nothing about the murders or anything like that. LeHorn's kids are still alive. That just wouldn't be right, capitalizing off their mother's death or their father's mental illness. There are enough weird stories connected to the hollow without getting into the LeHorn stuff. Bigfoot. Demons. The Goat Man. Native American spirits. We can do stuff featuring them.

MN: What about the more recent murders; the witch cult and the mystery writer?

KR: Adam Senft? No. Again, it wouldn't be right to capitalize off something like that. Like I told you earlier, this whole thing is to honor Deena's memory. What she stood for. Her strength. She wouldn't want me using other people's misfortunes like that.

(Transcript of phone conversation between Maria Nasr and former homicide detective Hector Ramirez)

HECTOR RAMIREZ: Hello?

MARIA NASR: Mr. Ramirez, I think we might have gotten disconnected. I just—

HR: Hell yes, we got disconnected. That's because I disconnected the call! I mean it, lady. Don't call here again.

MN: Wait! Listen, I just want to interview you, sir. I respect your privacy. I'm not out to disparage you over how the case was handled or anything. I'm just curious to what you believe really happened.

HR: You want to know what I believe? (laughter) Okay, I'll tell you what I believe. I believe that there are things in this world that don't make a lick of fucking sense. Things that should not be—that we're not supposed to know about. I saw it once during that bank robbery in Hanover, and—

MN: Bank robbery?

HR: Shut up! It's got nothing to do with your book or the hollow. But it's got everything to do with what I'm saying. I saw it then and I put it behind me. But it fucked with my beliefs—in God and in mankind and in what was real and what wasn't. And then Shannon and Paul Legerski went missing and I canvassed the neighborhood, interviewing potential witnesses and I met Adam Senft. If it hadn't been for that ... that night—the night of the fire. I'll never fucking forget it. How could I? When Senft and his buddies came marching across the field, armed to the teeth with shotguns and spell books, like some blue-collar Van Helsing. Even his dog was in on it. And I helped them. What was I supposed to do? People were dead. Their wives were missing. So, I went out there into the woods. Me and Uylik. We went with them. And I was responsible ... for that officer's death. The trees ...

MN: Um ... Mr. Ramirez? Hector? I'm afraid that I don't understand.

HR: The trees were alive! Don't you understand? They fucking moved around. They killed Uylik. And Senft's friend—Swanson. A lot of people died that night. All because of Senft and his goddamned Goat Man.

MN: But, sir, your own investigation concluded that Adam Senft wasn't involved. The State Police and the district attorney agreed with your determination. Those murders were committed by the LeHorn's Hollow witch cult, of which Paul and Shannon Legerski were members.

HR: There was no cult. It was a fucking monster! Half-man, half-goat. And I'm not talking about those murders, anyway. I'm talking about *belief*. What was I supposed to do after I saw all of that? Magic spells and devils and men ripped apart like soft marshmallows. I damn sure wasn't raised to believe in that. So how was I supposed to react? How could I do my fucking job when I knew what was really out there? You asked me about my beliefs? I had them confirmed and then shattered that night. At the same time. Senft, too. Isn't any wonder he killed his wife. He saw her there, around the fire in the woods, rutting in the dirt with that ... thing.

MN: I'm afraid I don't understand.

HR: You want to understand? You want to believe? Tell you what. Go on down there to the hollow and have a look around. Even now, with it all burned up. You don't even have to go to the heart of it. Just walk around the woods for a bit. You'll believe. And then you'll have that belief sucked away, along with everything you've ever felt. Love. Hate. All your thoughts and emotions and feelings. It will suck them all away and leave you with just darkness inside.

MN: Mr. Ramirez, what about—

HR: Just darkness.

(Excerpts from transcript of recording between Maria Nasr and Levi Stoltzfus)

LEVI STOLTZFUS: The Bible tells how God created our universe, but there's nothing in it about the universe that existed before this one. Or the enemy that came from that other universe.

MARIA NASR: You're talking about the Devil?

LS: Which devil? There are more than one. Do you mean Lucifer, the Morningstar? Or maybe Satan? The old serpent? The dragon? The Beast? All of these appear in the Bible, and we're told to believe that they are the same entity—but they aren't. In any case, I'm not speaking about any of them. I'm talking about the Thirteen. They are far worse than any devil. (pause) To create this universe, God destroyed a universe that existed before ours. Think about it— the act of Creation must have required an unimaginable amount of energy. Where did He get it? He tore down the old universe and used its material as building blocks for our own. The old universe ceased to exist down to its last atom—except for the Thirteen. Somehow, they escaped the destruction. And they've been the enemies of God and all of His creations ever since.

MN: Demons?

LS: Not demons. Although mankind has often mistaken them for demons. And gods. Entire—incorrect—mythologies have been created around them by foolish people who didn't know the true nature of what they were worshipping. No, the Thirteen are much worse than demons. They have nothing to do with Hell's legions. And each one of them is more terrifying than the next. Kandara, Lord of the Djinn. Ob, the Obot, who commands the Siqqusim. His brothers, Ab and Api. Leviathan, Lord of the Great Deep. Behemoth. And others—all terrible. But the greatest among the Thirteen is one who can't be named. Simply speaking its real name out loud causes unimaginable destruction. It is the reason mankind has such an unreasonable fear of the dark, for this thing is darkness incarnate. It sits in the heart of the Labyrinth and infects world after world.

MN: Hold up. The labyrinth? As in the minotaur and King Minos?

LS: No, although I guess it could be the source of that old myth. The Labyrinth is sort of a dimensional shortcut between different worlds and realities. It weaves through time and space—nowhere and yet everywhere all at once. It connects to everything via a series of dimensional 'doors.' This is how the Thirteen travel between worlds. How they traverse the dimensions. And how some humans have traveled, as well. Normally, the only time we see the Labyrinth is when our spirit has departed our body. But there are ways to pass through it while still alive. You just have to know how to open one of the doorways. That's what Nelson LeHorn did.

MN: He traveled to another dimension?

LS: Possibly. Another dimension. Another Earth.

LS: All I know for sure is that after he murdered his wife, Nelson LeHorn opened a doorway in the hollow and fled through it. He closed the doorway behind him, but it still exists. LeHorn took precautions. He knew what waited out there. Knew that if he wasn't careful, something else could come through the portal. So, he placed a circle of protection around the door, insuring that nothing else could use it. But something went wrong. I don't know what. Maybe the sigils were removed or the circle was broken. Whatever the cause, this entity—this living darkness—is now seeping through into our world. It hasn't made it all the way through. Not yet. But tomorrow night is when the barriers between all worlds are at their thinnest. When that happens, it will surge into our plane of existence, and there's not a thing we can do about it.

LS: LeHorn became convinced that others might try to kill him for his copy of the book, so he hid several of the most important pages, rendering the rest of the book incomplete, and hopefully, worthless. My father told me of the hiding places that he knew of. One of those pages—the one we need to stop this—was hidden in LeHorn's copy of *The Long, Lost Friend*. He thought it would be extra safe there. And he was right about that.

MN: So, you need to find his book?

LS: And that's why I need to speak with Adam Senft. He was the last person to have LeHorn's book. I need to know where it is now. It might be in his possession, though I doubt it. Senft was certainly dabbling in magic before his wife's murder, but I don't think he'd progressed far enough to secrete something like a page from the *Daemonolateria* on himself while in a psychiatric hospital. Not without it being detected. It's more likely that the book—and the page—are hidden somewhere on the outside.

MN: What if he doesn't know where it is, or he doesn't remember? What then?

LS: There are other ways to find it. Divining would work, but that takes weeks and we don't have time. So, we'll just have to *make* him remember.

MN: You said 'we' again. I'm not a part of this. Like I told you before, I'm only interested in Senft for my book. That's why I'm here. God didn't bring us together. It was just a coincidence.

LS: You don't believe what I just told you?

MN: I believe that you believe it. But, look—I don't believe in God in the first place. I don't believe that He created the Earth, so why would I believe that He destroyed another universe to do it and that it's been covered up ever since? And even if I did believe any of that, it's not God. It's Allah.

LS: I told you before. Allah and God are the same being. Names have power. Those are just two names for the same divinity.

MN: So you say. And so have others. But how do I know that?

LS: You take it on faith! Just like any other belief.

Entry 9

Okay ...

So, I'm still reading through Maria's stuff. I'm about halfway done. It's clear to me that Maria was planning on writing a book about Nelson LeHorn and Adam Senft, and perhaps the history of the hollow. My guess is something in the true crime genre. She never mentioned it to me, or anyone else that I know of. And these notes and recordings are from years ago, but still no published book. What happened? Did she give up? Decide against it? Start it but never finish? Complete it but never publish? If I ask her about this, will she give me a straight answer?

I'm also disturbed by the possibility that she may have known more about the riot than she reported, and the implication that she might have somehow been involved in Adam Senft's escape from White Rose.

Lot of other strangeness here, too. It seems like there are two different stories involving the hollow. First, there are all the legends about the forest pre-Nelson LeHorn. Then there are a new set of legends built around him and Adam Senft. At points, the two narratives seem to entwine, or at least have parallels. Lore surrounding the movement of the trees, for example.

I need to talk to Maria again. And I absolutely need to talk to Stoltzfus. But it won't be this week. Betsy and I are leaving tomorrow to visit the kids. We'll be back next Sunday. So, I'll reach out to Maria after we get home and see if I can arrange a time to meet-up.

(Excerpts from the notes of Maria Nasr)

It takes different forms. Anything humans fear, it can replicate.

Alternate Names: Verminus. Nuada. Lud. Shub-Niggurath. Pahad. Lilitu. Lamashtu. Nud. Othel. Many cultures call it He Who Shall Not Be Named. It's real name is N_____ (I'm not going to write it out, because fuck taking chances).

To say its real name aloud summons it, yet Adam was insistent that he and his friends spoke the name out loud. So, why did that not work? It must be something to do with the safeguards that Levi said Nelson LeHorn had put in place. But I can't ask Levi for more information, or he'll know I'm working on this, and I know how he'd react to that.

N_____ has temples everywhere. If you believe the lore (and after what I've seen, I sure as fuck do) they can be found on distant planets. "The twin moons of distant Yhe and the fungal gardens of Yaksh" are mentioned in many sources. So are Mars, Jupiter, and Io. Here on Earth, there were temples in ancient Mesopotamia, Babylon, Rome, and Persia. They've also found archeological evidence in Oregon, Hawaii, Peru, Kenya, the Yian-Ho province in China, Gloucestershire, and Monmouthshire. And right here in LeHorn's Hollow, of course.

But there was something else here long before N_____. Something else that called those woods home. And I don't think even Levi knows that. Maybe it was this other thing that allowed N____ to gain a foothold? But why?

The big question is ... is that other thing still there?

Ward and Valerie Peterson. Daughter, Ellie, had imaginary friend that looked like a leprechaun? Live near the hollow. She called it Mr. C_____.

The girl who disappeared in Red Lion during trick-or-treat in 2015. Her father said the abductor was a woman named Mrs. C_____. He insisted she lived in a house but the location of her home was just an empty lot. Like the Petersons, the vacant lot was only a few miles from the outskirts of the hollow.

Need to expand my search beyond the hollow itself. I've been focused on accounts inside the woods. But there may be even more that we don't know about.

I'm done. I'm tagging the fuck out. Ut nemo in sense tentat, descendere nemo. At precedenti spectaur mantica tergo. Hecate. Hecate. Hecate.

Entry 10

Managed to get some reading done while we were visiting the kids. Finished *Darker Than Dark: The Adam Senft Story* by Wesley Southard (Foundry Books, 2010) and am almost finished *The History of LeHorn's Hollow* by Jim Lewin (York Emporium Publishing, 2019). Again, I'm not too concerned about the latter. Having read most of it, there is a lot of information that he leaves out. It's a side-stapled chapbook. A pamphlet, more than anything. And it's out of print, as well. So, I think I'm "all good" (an expression I picked up from the grandkids last week).

Called Maria and left her a voice mail. Also sent her an email. Haven't heard back yet. I think I'll take a drive tomorrow and see the place for myself. Get the woods under my feet, so to speak.

Excerpt from *The History of LeHorn's Hollow* by Jim Lewin (York Emporium Publishing, 2019)

Even before those unfortunate incidents, the area now known as LeHorn's Hollow was the source of many central Pennsylvanian ghost stories and legends. Pennsylvania's native peoples, the Susquehannock Indians, thought the area was cursed—proclaiming it to be 'bad ground.' There are a number of historical accounts of them not pursuing wounded game beyond the borders of the forest, because they believed it was infested with demons, and that a portal to another place was located inside. Some historians espouse that the early inhabitants banished their criminals and mentally ill community members to the forest, though this is the subject of some debate among academics. Regardless, subsequent German, Irish, Quaker, and Amish settlers also told grisly tales about the region, and tended to avoid it as they populated Pennsylvania. They reported strange lights in the woods at night, often accompanied by unsettling growls or whispers. There are accounts of crop circles dating back to the late 1700s, and a local newspaper account from 1916 tells of a sighting of an Albatwitch—Pennsylvania's supposed Sasquatch-like cryptid. In 1995, four years before the fire, a group of researchers from Penn State discovered strange pockets of magnetic ground scattered throughout the forest. The cause was never determined. Over the decades, there have been a number of missing persons reports in association with the area. Hunters, hikers, thrill-seeking teenagers, an escaped convict, and an employee from a pulp wood company have all ventured into the forest and were never seen again.

With all that in mind, then, one can imagine the atmospheric pull such a place must have had on horror and thriller novelist Adam Senft ...

Entry 11

Had a busy day today, and I'm exhausted, but want to get these notes written while fresh in my mind. Betsy is upset with me because I told her I'd only be gone for a few hours and instead I didn't get home until after dark. She was trying to call and text me all day, but I didn't get a signal in those woods. She's sulking downstairs. I'll make things right after I finish this. But I also need her to understand how important this book is to me.

The first spot I visited was the memorial they built for the people who died in the riot. I haven't been there since the original unveiling and dedication ceremony. It's still a solemn affair, but beautiful this time of year, sitting there in that vast, empty field, with the black marble visible from the road. It reminds me of those old monolithic henges and standing stones so popular throughout Europe. Except that those were calendars and timepieces and meant to honor the faerie folk and older gods. Ours is meant to honor people who died horribly. It's a monument to nothing other than ... well, darkness, I guess.

I was the only person there. Maybe because it's the middle of the week. Maybe more people show up on the weekends.

After paying my respects, I tried to find what is left of the LeHorn farm, and the hollow itself. After a lot of trial and error, I turned off onto a dirt road that gets narrower and more pocked and rutted the further you go. I thought the car might bottom out at several points, but I kept going. I mean, I've come this far, right? Compiling all these notes. Doing all this research. But a book has to be more than that. *This* book has to be more than that. I need to be out there among it. Breathing the forest. Feeling it.

I said before there was no cell phone service. Oddly enough, there's no FM or AM radio stations, either. Reception must really be for shit in those hills and valleys. All I got was static, except for one brief moment when I heard an old-timey gospel preacher delivering fire and brimstone. But he sounded far away and then I lost that signal, too.

Eventually, the dirt road expanded again, and the countryside opened up. All around me was a baby forest—small saplings that sprouted after the fire, and a thick undergrowth that seemed impossible to get through on foot. Everything was lush and green. The vegetation has almost reclaimed what's left of the LeHorn homestead, as well. Vines and weeds are swallowing the crumbled foundations of the house and barn and entwining the scorched timbers and stones.

Past all that undergrowth, I spotted a line of older, taller trees—parts of the forest that must have escaped the fire. I went far enough to find a steep hill that led down into their midst. I'm pretty sure that must be the hollow, but I didn't go any further, because I wasn't really dressed for it. The thorns kept poking through my shirt and pants, and the mud sucked at my shoes like glue.

I did see something weird, though. There were footprints in the mud. I'm no outdoorsman, so I couldn't determine much by them, but they were human, and made by either a child or a small adult. A pair of paw prints ran alongside them. Both led to the edge of the trees, right up to a tall, broad oak. That tree must be older than any of the others around it. The trunk is wider than my car, and the limbs spread out far and wide. It has a sort of ovular hole at the base but didn't look like it was rotting or in danger of falling over.

The whole area felt strange, and I'm not afraid to admit I was a little bit spooked. But also, very excited. There's an energy about that landscape, and it's easy to see why creatives like Adam Senft and Darren Bosserman were drawn to it. I'm sure they must have felt what I felt. Although, they went home and murdered their families. I just came home and got yelled at by Betsy for being inconsiderate and scaring her half to death.

Speaking of which, I should finish this up and go apologize to her. One note: got a voice mail from Mrs. Chickbaum, the folklore expert. She has free time tomorrow and offered again to give me a walking tour of some of the spots in the forest. Think I'll call her back and see if we can arrange to meet up at the LeHorn place. If she's okay to drive, that is. She's an old woman, after all. But this is the second time she's offered, so she must get around okay. If she can't drive, I can pick her up.

More tomorrow.

That is the final entry. Metadata indicates the document was last opened by Nesbitt at 6:11AM, December 6, 2023, but nothing more was added, which means he must have typed the final entry sometime on the evening of December 5.

A neighbor's doorbell camera shows Nesbitt leaving his home the morning of December 6th, approximately a half hour after the document was closed. His wife confirms this, as well, and states that there was nothing unusual in his behavior. Security footage from a convenience store shows him purchasing fuel at 7:20AM. Cellular data from Nesbitt's phone last pings at 7:56AM, in the vicinity of the Shrewsbury Fire Hall. The last call placed on the phone was the night prior to his disappearance. Curiously, the number he dialed is marked as Unknown, and the carrier was unable to provide any information on it, even after the subpoena. Nesbitt mentions a voice mail from one Mrs. Chickbaum, but no such voice mail exists.

Nesbitt's car was found abandoned near the former LeHorn property. There were no footprints, and no signs of a struggle or confrontation. His phone, keys, and wallet were missing.

James Nesbitt's whereabouts are unknown.

The Promised Void

Dimitra Nikolaidou

LOCATION: Zagorohoria, Greece

POPULATION: 3,700 and shrinking

THE MURAL she'd come all this way to see is gone, erased from the rough mountain wall as if it never existed. Lena is sure she walked up the correct ravine, sycamore trees by the stream and everything. And yet, instead of the colourful, suffering woman she expected to find, there's only the narrow opening of a lightless cave. She takes a step closer, waiting for the wet smell of rot to hit her, but is met with the stench of burning metal and ethanol.

It's daylight but she is alone, and probably shouldn't take any more stupid risks today; coming up the harsh ravine on her own was dangerous enough. But she can't have come up here for nothing. She picks a bleached white pebble and throws it inside the opening.

Nothing. She takes a step closer. Throws another.

At first she isn't certain what is wrong, but then it dawns on her: the stones didn't echo, didn't even make a sound. Perhaps the waterfall or the sounds of the summer forest are covering it; she picks another stone, and takes a step closer to the opening.

"Don't."

She turns, stone in hand, and sees a man hurrying towards her, arms outstretched.

"Oh," she says, but doesn't set the stone down just yet. He's a stranger after all, and she's alone. "Is it dangerous?"

Of course it's dangerous, you idiot, it's a mountain cave. A mountain cave that wasn't even on the map, and you're throwing stones the dark. But now she has been caught, so all she can do is smile and pretend not to know better.

The man smiles back and puts his hand down. He is pretty handsome, in a T-shirt and a swimming suit just like her, towel in hand; probably another tourist. "Well, no," he laughs. "Unless you believe in folktales, in which case ... I think you've just doomed yourself."

She laughs back and splashes the stone in the stream. It lands between two black toads. The cave is now at her back, sending a chilly breeze on her sun-warmed skin. She moves farther away, closer to him. "I'm Lena," she says. She doesn't give him her hand; handshakes in swimsuits are stupid.

"I'm Stavros. Are those yours?" He nods towards her canvas and her painting supplies, balanced as they are on the flat grey rocks.

"Yes. I wanted to work, but the water was too enticing. I went for a swim instead."

"Good choice." He smiles again. "Sorry if I scared you. The cave is supposed to be a fairy home. We were always told not to go near, and never to disturb them."

"Oh. I'm sorry." *A local, then.* Perhaps he can tell her about the missing mural. "I didn't know any of that."

"Don't worry too much. It's just folktales."

She looks at the cave mouth—well, not a mouth as much as a crack at the stone, just large enough for a person as lithe as her. A Lena-shaped hole in the mountain. Nothing is sprouting around it; neither bees nor butterflies fly across the opening.

It doesn't look like a fairy cave at all.

"May I take a look?"

She snaps out of her reverie. Stavros is looking at her sketchbook; she wants to refuse him but can't find the words, not after he caught her red-handed doing something stupid.

"They're just the rough sketches," she says, eyes back on the cave mouth. He takes that for a yes, smiles, and grabs the sketchbook. She gets up, not wanting to be near him while he looks at her work. The cave is a few steps away, smelling bad and radiating cold, and she doesn't want to go near it, so she remains pinned in place.

He takes his time; she tries not to look, to focus on the sun on her skin but it hangs lower on the sky now, doesn't drive the cold away as well as it did before.

"I'm looking forward to seeing the finished ones." He smiles and gives her sketchbook back.

She smiles too; what else is there to do? "Perhaps we should head back?" she asks.

"Where are you staying?"

"At the Mavrotrypa village."

"Oh. How come? Most tourists prefer to stay at Papigo."

"Well ..." *Why not? He is local, he might know.* "The truth is, I came here looking for these," she says.

She takes out her phone, sweeps through the pictures till she finds what she wants and hands it to him: photos of murals and tree carvings, all supposedly taken around Mavrotrypa, all showing the same thing. A woman, painted like a Byzantine Virgin Mary, but naked and curled unto herself like an embryo, moths for eyes, her hair flowing like water, and around her, a garland of stars.

"They look like your sketches. Were they your inspiration?" he asks, swiping.

"Yes," she lies. It's much simpler than saying, *I've been having these awful nightmares for a year and a half, I've been able to sketch nothing but this poor curled woman for months, I'm behind at every project, going mad, my friends are worried to death for me, and then yesterday night I stumbled upon these pictures online, the pictures in my dreams, so I took my car and drove five hours to get here, without telling anyone about it because my friends would try to make me wait till they could come with me—and I didn't want to wait, I could not wait a minute more.*

No, you don't tell a stranger such things. "So, have you seen any of these carving or murals around here?" she asks instead.

"Ages ago." He reaches the end, and starts swiping back through them. She wants her phone back, but it feels rude to say so. "Someone local used to make them, we never found out who, but the priest didn't like them at all. Said they were evil, and had them all destroyed six months ago."

"Seriously?"

Stavros nods. "Well, you know how priests are in such small places. Sorry if you came up here for nothing. They were pretty."

"Yes, they were." *They were awful. Can't you see she's suffering? Can't you see the larvae in her eyes, the flowers growing out of her cunt?* She clears her throat. "Do you think I can talk to this priest? Honestly, I would love to hear why he found them so offensive." Maybe he's been having nightmares, too.

Stavros looks at her, brows slightly furrowed. "Father Christos? I guess so. He is quite polite when he isn't ranting about us worshiping the Morningstar and being disrespectful to the Virgin Mary. Hey, need help with those?"

"I got it, thanks," she smiles, tightening her fingers around the canvas bag. Perhaps she should be less friendly, but she's glad to have company on the way back. With the sun so low, the ravine that led her to the waterfall is now swathed in shadows, all sharp edges and cold, unwelcoming stone. She checks her mobile to see the time, and notices she has no signal. Great. She hasn't sent anything in the group chat since morning and that is not like her. They will start wondering what happened. And what if her parents called for their evening chat already?

She'll call everyone the minute they step outside the ravine. Meanwhile, the more she finds out about the mural, the faster she can go back to them. "So, are you from up here?" she asks Stavros.

"Papigo village, yes. I left ages ago to study physics at Ioannina city, did my masters in astronomy, got a position teaching high school, the usual. I came back for the summer." He hops down an outcrop, and offers his hand to help her; she steps down without taking it, smiling at him. "Sorry to ask, but I think I have seen your work before. Didn't you win a European award for a graphic novel? *The Promised Void?* I've read that."

"You have?" *That's some coincidence.* "Yes, that was me. Did you like it?"

"Loved it. The scenes where she drifts in space were something else." She can see new admiration in his eyes and tries to keep her smile modest. "What drew you to this theme, if I may ask?"

"I don't know."

"Come on, indulge the astronomer."

Her smile was becoming painful now. Why did everyone have to ask her that? It's humiliating. "It's not a secret. It's that ..." He can feel him staring at her, and it's a bit too tense, and she cannot find the words to stop him from expecting an answer. "It's just that I've never liked being alone. The emptiness of space represents the feeling you get after the door closes behind the last guest. Sometimes you draw the things you love, and sometimes you draw the things you hate, and the funny thing is that readers can't tell the difference." Did she offend him? *Go on. Throw the stone. He's the one who asked.* "People think the floating scenes are beautiful, but they made me sick for days."

"I'm sorry to hear that. So, you're not planning a second volume?"

"I don't think so." *No, that's when the nightmares began, when I finished with this damned book. And you just happen to have read it.* She quickens her pace. Stones dislodge under her feet.

"You shouldn't hate the stars." The sound of his voice brushes her skin. "I'm sure they would love your work."

She tries to smile back but suddenly she's dizzy, as if she's dangling over an abyss; she stumbles on her own sandal; she hovers; she falls on her face; for a moment all she can see is sparkles, all she can smell is the hot metallic scent of blood. Her body is paralyzed with pain; her ears fill with static; she can just make out Stavros rushing to her.

He touches her and the dizziness disperses. It hurts. She can see gashes on her foot; grass and ants stuck in the torn flesh. She whimpers as he takes the sandal off and checks her foot. A blade of grass is lodged in her skin. A spider dangles from her hair and she swats at it. When did she swallow the grey dirt she spits?

"Lena, don't."

The ravine water is soaking her, ice cold. How did she fuck up so bad? She tries to stay still, lets him check her foot uninterrupted. The cold reaches her bones. She needs to pee.

"It's not broken or sprained, but you'd better take something to prevent inflammation. Mavrotrypa is not far." He picks her stuff up, looks at her. "Are you all right with me carrying you the rest of the way?"

I can manage, she wants to say, but it's stupid. She can't. The pain in her toes is moving upwards. She lets him pick her up. Her foot dangles off his arms, the blood is drumming. She can feel the heat from her injured foot, but it doesn't spread to the rest of her body.

"I'm so sorry," she blurts.

"It will be over sooner than you think."

She won't move, tries to touch him as little as possible. That close to him, under his thin white T-shirt, she can make out a colorful tattoo. She turns away and stares up at the sky; a few stars have shown up early. She's never seen any of them before. She doesn't like the way they show their teeth at her. She closes her eyes.

The ocean is gestating in her eyes, a larva swimming in the blue, dreaming of being born. Under her toenails, sprouts gyrate, looking for a sun. Her breasts split open, disgorging hot, pulsating stones. But she can't move. She is not allowed to move. She will never be allowed again.

"Is she up? What happened?" A woman's voice tears through the void. Lena wakes up. She tries to gasp but no sound comes. She is pinned among the stars, her vocal chords taken out for someone to make vines with. Frost gathers at her eyelids, waters the seeds inside her belly.

Lena wakes up.

She looks around, tries to sit up; there are bars in the windows, and through them the dark. The utter, endless dark.

Then she remembers, she knows this window. She is at Miss Ellie's Airbnb, back at Mavrotrypa, foot well bandaged, a glass of water by her side. Her painting supplies are on the wooden table, arranged in a circle, beside a bowl of fruit.

In the half-dark, she can see the light switch across the room. She needs to get to it. She needs light, and she needs to pee. She must get up. The room solidifies around her some more.

Then the sounds return too, so suddenly they hit her like a wave. Outside, there are children playing, dogs barking happily. A mother calls her kid. Friends laugh at the tavern. She sits up, takes a look out of the barred windows and sees the village square filled with people taking evening strolls.

Her shoulders unclench; she breathes again. Everything is fine. She just needs the bathroom, right now. She hops to the table to get her mobile, message the group chat and then her parents, *they must have noticed I'm gone*, but finds nothing. Her hands feel heavier and heavier as she searches among the painting supplies. A knock at the door. "Miss Lena? Are you up?" Miss Ellie's voice, worried, uncertain.

She takes a look at the bed, makes sure she is not still there, sleeping, dreaming her usual, mundane nightmare of a lost cell phone. No, it's really gone. Maybe Stavros has it. Maybe he picked up the phone when it rang, told her parents she's all right. She sighs, limps towards the door and cracks it open.

"Miss Ellie? I'm fine."

"Oh, thank the Mother," she says, fingering a pendant on her neck. "You know what, Miss Lena? You'd better get out and have some air. You look like death and that won't do."

Mavrotrypa is different at night. During the day, the naked mountain range looked majestic under the sun. Now it spreads across the sky like a black hole in the horizon. The villagers have done their best to claim their tiny place among the rocks; there are festive lights hanging from the houses, and an open coffee shop, where everyone is gathered. They have been buying her wine since she came out of her room, telling her not to worry. They offered to look for her cell phone in the morning, paid for her food, brought her cushions. But when she asks to talk with their priest, they only smile. *Where is he? I need to know about the murals. What if he was right about them, after all, what if they're truly evil?*

More wine lands on her table. She thanks the girl bringing it over, and gets up to look for the bathroom. It's right next to the coffee shop, beyond a small garden, and she has to hop over there. Small kids part as she passes; one is doing a cartwheel, creating a perfect circle, and for some reason her stomach lurches to see it.

She checks for spiders and sits down; her hands twitch on her knees and she feels like it takes her forever. Right, because she doesn't have her phone with her. If she doesn't find it till tomorrow, she will have to leave first thing in the morning and let everyone back home know she's all right, before they call the police. The murals she came to look for aren't here anyway, her foot hurts and her nightmares worsened. Maybe she *did* piss the cave fairies off after all.

She washes her hands and reaches for the tin door, but it doesn't budge. She tries again. Nothing. She pushes with her shoulder and hears giggling from outside. The kids. She bangs against the metal, angrier than she should be. She hears quick steps and a scold from outside. The door finally opens and she sees the kids dispersing, all of them doing cartwheels, perfect circles rolling away from the door in the dark. Her stomach reacts before she does, and she goes back inside, fills the bowl with half-ingested wine.

A hand in her hair, pulling it back from her face. She can tell it's Stavros but she can't stop retching to save her life, even as taut hairs break in his fingers. In the end she kneels on the wet floor, inhales the stench, just a minute before she would vomit out her beating heart.

"I'm sorry for the kids," he says, stepping outside as soon as she tries to stand up and reach for the wash basin. "Little savages, the lot of them."

Her heart won't go back, it still bobs in her throat. She wants to cry. She wants to speak to her friends, call her mum to get her. But without her phone all she has right now is Stavros, waiting patiently outside.

"That's fine. On top of everything, I'm a bit claustrophobic," she manages, mouth full of water and sour wine. She wipes her face and comes out, sweat forming on her skin.

Nobody is outside except Stavros. The coffee shop is closed. How long was she in the bathroom? Her bag is left on the table, along with her shawl.

"I need to take a walk, clear my head," she blurts, limping for the bag. *Where is everyone?*

"Let's go," he says, following one step behind.

"Can you please ... wait here for five minutes? I'm sorry. The claustrophobia," she says, without turning to look at him. "I'll just be in the square."

He nods, and sits at the empty coffee shop, takes out a pack of cigarettes. He even smiles as she walks away, and she smiles back. She needs the bathroom again, but this time it's the fear squeezing her insides. *Where's everybody?* She walks slowly to the square, her bag squarely in front of her. She rummages inside with one hand; the car keys are there. She doesn't want to stay at Mavrotrypa anymore. Her foot throbs, but it's only a twenty-minute drive to Papigo, where the tourists are. She can sit at an all-night café, ask to use the internet there, talk to her friends, and calm down. And come morning she will go back to the city, and never travel solo again.

The thought lets her breathe. She looks back at Stavros, and he's waving from afar, lit cigarette at hand. Obviously, a whole village didn't decide to facilitate her rape and murder, she is just being stupid. Perhaps they closed because it's late; she doesn't even know the time. She looks around for a bell tower with a clock, a church, but her gaze tumbles empty over low stone roofs. There's none.

There should be a church up here, all villages have one, however small. Where does the elusive priest hold service after all? She turns slowly, looks at Stavros who is leaning back, looking at the stars. Perhaps the church is up the road, on the top of Mavrotrypa, where she parked this morning; she thinks there was a sign there, something about the holy temple of the Virgin Mary. And if the church is there, she can't see it from the square, right? She starts walking, ignoring the throbbing in her foot. She can walk wherever she likes, can't she? She said she needs some space.

The road under her feet is made of smooth, polished stones, and she looks down to make sure she won't stumble again. Blades of grass grow between them, even through them. *Given time they can pierce through anything, can't they?* She takes a deep breath. Her own foot is cleaned, bandaged. It might itch a bit, but it's just the walking.

She lifts her head, and then she sees them.

All the house doors left and right have them, drawn on with colored chalk. A circle, with a woman in the middle. Curled, surrounded by stars. Sprouting, gagged with butterflies and snakes, torn from the inside as trees grow out of her innards and seas gush out between her legs. Folk art, made by different hands, still flaking chalk dust. All her nightmares, brought to life in this deserted road.

She runs. For all her pain and her sweat and her twisted stomach she runs, gagging herself not to scream, praying for her car.

And when she doesn't find it on the top of the hill where she parked it, her knees finally give way, and she kneels, mouth open, stomach like a taut drum, eyes burning hot and wet, intestines ready to empty in the middle of the street. She looks up and the stars are all unblinking. The cave stench comes again, hot metal and welding fumes. And then footsteps behind her. She doesn't turn. Can't.

"I am sorry, my child."

She stands and lurches towards the man but it's not Stavros. It's a priest, covered in his black robes, long-haired and bearded and incredibly sad.

And white, too white for this world. Translucent even.

"Don't make the mistake to pray," he says. There is a rope coiled around his neck, bruising it, frayed and twisted and old. "I did. The ones in the sky shall devour your prayer, and it will only make their evil stronger."

"Please, help me."

"I can't, anymore."

"Please."

The doors behind her open and the priest's mouth opens wide, and keeps opening, like a black hole into which his whole face collapses. He fades right in front of her; behind him stands a child, grail in one hand, a sprig of basil in the other, still dripping holy water.

And behind her the villagers of Mavrotrypa, lighting the candles in their hands, one by one, till the whole stony road is a sea of faces lit from beneath.

Stavros is the only one without a candle; the only one who comes close to her, unsmiling, huge. He grabs her hair, swats her hands away, twists her around. Her body is thrusting but she has flown out of it, she is paralyzed, she has become her own tears. She opens her mouth and she cries out and the villagers murmur in awe as the stars are fed, fed until the stench of burning metal begins to rain upon her.

But she does not faint this time; no mercy from above. Stavros is pulling her now upwards, towards the trees, and two women far, far stronger than her lift her legs and she spasms but can't free herself.

She can't move; can't move. She is carried like Christ's catafalque on Good Friday on the arms of the faithful and she can see the children pass underneath her again and again, a living, crying catafalque with no flowers and no candles. Other women take the sandals off her feet, the ring off her dead fingers, tear her dress away, leave her body naked and splayed under the unblinking stars. She feels their cold light entering and she spasms again, but it's too late to keep anything away.

There are no stones under their feet anymore, they have entered the woods, and the villagers pick dirt and leaves and place it on her belly, her open mouth, her screaming eyes. Things crawl out of the dirt, rush away. *Don't bury me alive*, she wants to scream, *don't, don't*, but her mouth is full of dirt, and fingers push more in. She coughs but nothing comes out. She is mute, but somehow breathing through the dirt, and the realization makes the last of the piss come out of her, but nobody cares.

A door opens in the woods. The church, they brought her to the church. There is no roof and no light but their candles, yet the walls are full of icons: the Holy Mother curled unto herself, enshrined in the center of the Earth, a garland of stars around her.

Please don't bury me alive. Please kill me first.

They lower her onto a stone slab she cannot see, they hold her hands and legs open. Stavros comes in front of her. He takes his shirt off and she screams, but no sound comes out through the packed dirt. *How long will I take to suffocate? Why don't I already, before he does it?* She can now see the tattoo and it's herself, bent backwards, naked, splayed, planted and blossoming, eyes nothing but void.

Why don't I faint?

Don't pray.

He circles her and comes behind her head. A woman approaches, and hands him a seed on a painted coffee plate. Her nails are chipped, painted blue, and the mundanity of it breaks Lena. Tears stream down to her hair, but never touch the floor. Stavros plants the seed in the dirt in her mouth, pushes it in deep, and everyone yells. Her body shakes but they hold tighter still.

And then the thing sprouts in her mouth. She can feel the

spidery roots reach down her throat, touch the insides, grab her muscles and organs, paralyzing her, forever.

Forever?

She has no more tears, sweat, or piss. She cannot move, but they don't let go. Stavros speaks as the plant chokes her from inside. He speaks of honoring the woman in the center of the Earth, the Holy Mother. He speaks of a sacrifice, billions of years ago, ordered by the Lords of the stars to birth the Earth. His voice is lulling; she knows it will soon be over. She will not see her friends again, or paint her opus, or get a coffee in the sunlight ever again. She will die in the hands of lunatics, to honor a forgotten pagan myth. But she won't hurt anymore. *Soon.*

Then Stavros speaks of this Earth being doomed, and the divine, celestial order to build another, not for themselves but for their children's children. She has no choice but to listen, listen to his voice spelling out her fate, unable to move or protest as he touches her hair, her forehead, her skin. He speaks of an invitation sent by the stars, a summons that only Lena answered with her book, and everybody cheers, not her, not her but themselves, for finding her and bringing her here, to seed a new Earth on her body. She finds herself screaming soundlessly again as they lift her, chanting cacophonously, some of them giggling as they miss every note. And they carry her through the broken holy of holies, out of the church and through the night forest.

Down to the ravine.

And into the foul-smelling cave, the Lena-shaped crack in the wall.

She remembers the moment they pushed her in. How she spasmed in their rough hands. How she begged and pleaded through the dirt packing her mouth, the seed sprouting already out of it. It wasn't her mouth anymore. That night she was made to be nothing but a woman-shaped vessel.

The cave was dark at first, so dark she feared she had gone blind even though she could see their hands shoving her legs inside. But when they let go, and she was left in the dark, she didn't fall. There was nowhere to fall; there is no gravity in space. There are only stars, aeons away from each other, and she is now among them, pinned naked in the middle of the void, mute forever.

Sometimes she remembers that night. Wonders if she could have done anything different, run away faster. But she knows now, once you've answered their call, there is nowhere to hide from the stars. So most of the times she only remembers her friends, and her tiny apartment, and her unfinished work, and she regrets everything. Maybe they are not even alive anymore; she lost count of time ages ago. Nothing ever changes around her after all, not even the distant star that chose her for a bride. She had hoped she would go mad eventually, but that didn't happen either, or it did, and nothing changed. There is nothing she can do, but watch the leaf sprouting out of her mouth grow stronger.

Perhaps it will kill her when it does, but she has no hope of that either. A living Earth needs a living core, and so she knows she will remain alive, entombed in the center of a new Earth, until the end of time, alone.

You Have Eaten of Our Salt

Fatima Taqvi

LOCATION: Thar Desert of Sindh, Pakistan

POPULATION: 45,000

IN THE DREAM I am always crying, and my grandson is always dead. The Chir batti always seek me, and it is forever too late.

The salt splays itself out in silver rugs floating on emerald lakes beneath the night's ballooning black. I know this shifting sand, this sharp salt. These lakes that endure. That sky that's never ending.

Something is wrong, something that alerts me this isn't real.

I am from these white deserts of Achro Thar, growing up on the milk of storytellers and songmakers from bloodlines that existed before this sand of limestone and chalk was split by the lines dividing Pakistan and India. Bloodlines as old, almost, as the ancient rules.

The rules. I would be a fool to forget them. No matter that the stars are too bright, too immediate, in my eyes and in my throat already hoarse from wailing in a manner I never have before. No matter that my skin itches so close to these mineral stretches lolling all around, or that my tongue is too thick, too dry against the roof of my mouth that pools in saliva at the smell of the salt. We are alive because we do not forget, and so even as my face swells from where I have slapped myself in grief, my mind pauses. Telling me to wait. To consider.

I would never be out here in this time, this place. Never at night! Not where the ghost lights, uncanny lights, lights everlasting with wisps ever beckoning, stalk the land. To follow the treacherous Chir batti is to lose your way in the star-kissed crystal or humid marshy grasslands where the birds and foxes hide. Never to be found again.

Yet my arms reach out, insistently, incomprehensibly, and part of me that's watching wants to leap back screaming. But I don't. I extend my arms to meet the eager flickering trails of the ghost lights illuminating the salt.

The light reaches around my body. My neck is looped by light.

And I wake up.

I am home, of course. In my small round hut, safe on my back on the charpai under my pile of shawls and rugs, and the ordinary beauty and busyness of the yellowing day is already upon us. There is noise: the sound of wheels turning, and the fires being lit, and our pretty goat Mae bleating at the sound of distant traffic, and roosters vying with the doves like a competition of muezzins. Best of all, there he is. My grandson—alive. In all his loud, chaotic, seven-year-old glory.

Strange that there was a time he wasn't here with me. His routines feel entwined with my arteries, his concerns pull at my fingertips. What did I do before he was born? I had never bought a book in my life. Certainly never arranged them for him to find, hiding sweets in one, drawings of goats dressed in ghararas in others, ostensibly for him to find and be amused by, but really for me to luxuriate in his laugh.

My grandson climbs up and brandishes a book at me. I pretend to go back to sleep as he demands breakfast, so he gently pulls my hair that is auburn and orange from where I used to stain it with mehndi until it permanently changed color, becoming as shiny as the goat's brown hide. He tries to separate the orange strands from the white ones, and one of my hands snakes up to braid them in with his short spiky black locks, which he evades by somersaulting off the charpai and landing on the dirt ground below with a bang, which properly wakes me up as I clamber down to help him. He sits in my lap and kisses my hands and asks if they hurt, and I say how can they hurt, feel how hard my knuckles are, when you're old all the hardness of your bones comes into your skin, and he says how come your skin is soft still. And I say it only feels like that to him.

"When I grow up," he says crossly, "you won't be allowed to go salt harvesting."

He should be eating, I tell him. He has to go to school.

"And will you eat with me?" he always asks.

"Old people don't eat breakfast," I tell him loftily. "Only children who go to school feel that sort of hunger. As do goats. Have you fed our Mae yet?"

He flees the house in a panic on bare feet, leaving me to take the flour outside where I will squat and light the fire.

The sun looks so hearty as it begins its day with us but I know a pale amber imitation of it waits for me. Out there where it meets the white dips and curves of the salt I am to collect and wash. Everything dwindles out there while we work, all things are consumed by the crystal that looks like cotton but shreds my skin as I sift it out with my hands. When I faint on the job the world goes white instead of black and what else can the others do before getting back to work except laugh and say "Amma, are you alright, sit here, drink some water," then we all get back to rubbing our hands raw in the salt. I won't tell them that when the pinpricks of light appear on the back of my eyes they look like the Chir batti because then they would ask me how I knew what they looked like at all.

My grandson waves farewell at me, and out of habit I look for the black thread I have tied on his wrist to protect him from the evil eye.

There are more colors than that of salt and stars and soil, and I live for every one of them. My odhni is pink over my shoulder and head. The faded crimson hundred rupee notes hide tattered and browning in the hands of the shopkeepers. The riot in the pagris of men, the women's odnis, so many people here walk beneath a halo of color shielding them from fading out. The blue truck with the open roof that makes its way to down the road to the salt lakes. The men politely lend me a hand and say, "Give Amma room," they move and shuffle, my friend Feroz exchanges greetings with me, and we're off.

Out here where colors fade, Feroz's foot is rudely red where it bleeds. Then green where he smears furniture glue over it to hold the skin in place. He is very clever and carries the glue around with him everywhere. He has no time for bandages, indeed he cannot go into the water with bandages on his feet, so he has come up with this solution. If you rail against fate in his hearing, he ducks his head and tries to escape. It is too much to carry, the outrage and the pain, the hunger and the hope, though I try to remonstrate with him, at least let me tend to the injuries after the work day. It is his own fault, he says, he was stumbling around here after dark, and saw the Chir batti. Scared, he ran, and his already wounded skin burst open.

I snort when he rejects my help, but Feroz is quite right to shake his head kindly and say, "No, Amma, life is too hard for us to carry each other's pain, each of us goes to our own grave, so look at your own hands and feet."

By the end of the work day all these colors mean nothing to me. The darkness behind my eyes and the throbbing hunger command me. Trucks come from the city to collect the bags of salt our hands have rescued from nature, and their beautiful swirling colors might as well be covered in the same gray dust that covers our legs to our knees, our arms to our elbows. When I have some tea with sugar—so much sugar!—I revive somewhat, and I dream of my grandson as a manager, a business owner, as someone who commands all these trucks, who flies planes to other countries, who looks like the actors on TV. I mention this to my younger friends, and they laugh, indulging me.

"Time to go," someone says. Night will fall soon, and the ghost lights will be looking for humans to lure.

I flick the salt at him and he splutters, wiping his mustache.

"Look, now." I laugh. "You have eaten of my salt. You are in my debt now."

He protests, and I wag a finger at him because these are old rules. Much might change but the ancient rules that bind us? They do not.

But I see now I am still stupid, unlike my manager who I meet for my salary. Next time we meet he tells me I know nothing. Patterns change all the time. A lot changes, and there are no old ways really. Promises, contracts, pledges, all nothing.

Because, in the city, petrol is more expensive. Because, in another country, people are being bombed. Because, somewhere else, people use up fuels for plane flights. Because, in the cities, food costs more to make. Because, here, people will work for less. Here is my salary.

"Wait now," I stop him. "For one bag of salt it was one rupee fifty paisa. And this is less. This is much less."

"Amma, don't argue "

But it is less than one rupee for a bag, so I argue!

"But, Amma, you don't understand. Things change and how much can a woman like you eat anyway?"

"I have a grandson. He has a future. I am not here to swat flies, I am busy, always busy, paving the path for my grandson before he even lifts his foot. What do you know?"

"Amma, don't get emotional. I have children too. It's just that numbers change. What can we do?"

Back and forth, back and forth, but how can numbers change? Feroz will still always only have two feet. My grandson only has one future. I will always have one daughter who is now in one grave in one graveyard. Then there are the unknowable numbers only fate fathoms. The number of breaths left in a body. The number of times a child falls ill. Already, my grandson has had to have a blood test, out there in a nearby city where there are labs and doctors. His dead father's brother took him, which was kind, because who has the money for anything anymore? But he assured me on my mobile phone it was all good, all was okay, it was just some mild dengue which my grandson bounced back from with our prayers and his own good fortune.

My grandson is in perfect health now, thank Khuda. He comes back from school and plays with the goat, and I eventually shuffle home from the road where the truck stops, stumbling over the dunes, with my head swaddled in pain, and he feeds me and kisses my weeping hands. I swat him away but he patiently steals the dough for tonight's meal and makes them into parathay while I pass out and wake up and pretend I'm fine. I add my savings to the pouch under my charpai. He doesn't know it, the young never do, but my sweet child fills my home with the best kind of radiance even as the parathay are too dry and the daal has small pebbles neither of us had the energy to sift out. Even the day he was born, there was light.

The day my daughter died giving birth, the women had gathered in the house. It was close to Fajr time, and our hut was pressed in by darkness.

A light floated in from the front door. Over the heads of the gasping, pointing women until it reached my daughter who gave a few pushes and died with more lines on her face than her age should have allowed. That is what happens when you're widowed so young.

But for one moment, just before she passed, something amazing happened. She looked up at the light, and her face relaxed in pure wonder and adoration, as if she were a child again, the same who I had prayed would be happy forever.

"Amma?" she whispered and I bent closer, but I will never know what she was about to say.

I held her dead hand and sobbed, and the women held my living grandson and whispered, giving me condolences and congratulations, looking at each other, thinking the obvious. That the angel of death had visited us in front of our eyes. And that this little boy's family on his father's side in the city might want him. Any child is an extra mouth to feed, but a boy? A boy is an investment, a lifeline to a future when you are too old to pay your own bills, the more boys you own the sturdier your future.

When the boy's uncle came he called me Amma and gave me proper condolences on my daughter's death with more manners than his age would have suggested, and spoke to me frankly and honestly, sincerely. Then said he would help with money where he could. But that if I could have the raising of him, what better than a child's grandparent? Like so many village boys who go to the city he wasn't married, had only just moved his parents there, and his paycheck split and splintered a hundred ways before any amount came to his own personal disposal. He was a hard worker, he promised me, and perhaps one day his dead brother's child could come to the city too?

My dreams were set in motion, like a cart pulled by the bullock of my grandson's future. Dreams I hadn't even dared to dream for my daughter.

We get ready for bed. With chalk he draws a picture of the water going into the sky going back down again.

"The salt is from rocks," he tells me. "And the rain breaks the rocks. It's all connected."

"I also knew that," I say politely, "know-it-all." But now he's begging for sweets and being silly, he knows there are none. What he really wants is his mother.

The minute I close my eyes, I drift off. I groan as I see the Chir batti come towards me. My grandson is dead, they tell me, as they always do.

There's a reason I dream of my grandson's death, my neighbor told me—though first she berated me for even speaking such a thing, as if I was daring it to manifest. It is because I am always planning on how to make my grandson educated and curious, so that he can leave the village and make his way anywhere he likes in the world. It is a kind of passing away, she said, reproaching me, this planned exile from the place your ancestors are buried. Who will take care of you when he is gone? I will be gone myself, I answered sharply, for Khuda has not promised us immortality. She stared at me, as all people do who view children as cattle for us to milk.

I want my grandson to go away. These boys who I work with. Their gray legs. Bloody palms. Tortured fingers. Is this what waits for him? It is like my manager said. There are no old ways, not really. The sand dunes always smelled sweet after the monsoon but these years the rainy season has come in fits and starts. Everything is out of order and the dunes smell of nothing. The ground in front of our house that should have spurted green grass now looks like a pigeon that has plucked itself bald in distress. The nets the fisherfolk use has banned metal in it so it has ruined the fish population, and now the rohu fish aren't so plentiful.

Surely there are other places out there in the world. Places with their own old ways where children can grow up and where the land isn't ruined.

In the dream my grandson is always dead and the Chir batti won't give up.

When I reach for the ghost lights in the dream I am full of rage. And this time I hear something. A small ghost light, up to my knee. In the faintest voice, it says—

"Everything will change but not the old ways. Look at my flesh. *Have they not eaten of our salt?*"

My grandson coughs when we wake up. He has been hugging that goat again, I say, rapping his knuckles with a pretend stick made of my own fingers.

"I have done so a thousand times without you looking," he responds airily, "and I've never coughed, not even once."

It'll pass, I tell him. And he must leave that goat alone or the doctor in the city will give him bitter, bitter medicine to drink.

"When I grow up, I will be a doctor," he says, "and all my medicines will taste like sugarcane."

"But if you're a doctor you will practice in the city."

"Not me," he says. "I will open a clinic right here. Everyone must pay me in sugarcane and nobody is allowed to die."

He will not die. He is only remembering that his mother died here and that there were no doctors, that is all. I feed the goat and recite some prayers. I have to go to work so I tell the goat, the sun, the saints, any passing angels, to keep praying for him while I'm gone.

In the evening when I totter back cradling my hands, he is running a fever.

"It is nothing," I say, as I pick up my mobile phone. I charge it every few days at the shop where they have electrical sockets. It still has power so I call his uncle. He will make his way here, but meanwhile the community health worker at the tiny maternity clinic will look at him.

"His neck isn't bending," she says.

"What does that mean?"

"And he has spots. See?"

She talks of the neck breaking fever. I had heard of it, but she calls it meningitis.

"How did he get it?"

She averts her gaze.

His uncle is here and they talk as I stand at my grandson's side. She passes him a pamphlet.

"Aych eye vee," his uncle reads.

HIV.

I race home straight to the goat. I feed her with trembling hands. I try to be kind. She looks up at me sideways with her silly face but I have no capacity. I am gentle though. I am brimming with tenderness at our shared fragility, but she is all I have to give.

I ask the neighbor to use his knife on her, ask him to keep the skin and immediately set to washing and packing the goat meat in dripping plastic bags to send out. I don't stop until Mae has filled every hungry belly in the neighborhood. Let this be enough, I pray.

At the clinic my grandson is alive. I stroke his cheeks. I curse myself that I cannot read his books to him. His uncle bends over, not meeting my eyes.

"How does this happen?"

"The needles at the other clinic. In the city. When he had his blood test, the needles were contaminated. The doctors reused them."

"But how? In the city they have real doctors. Not quacks. And they charge so much money too. How can those same needles have hurt him?"

"This is what happens in this place, Amma. If you build, others will break. If you join, they will tear. In the city they put chickens all together in small cages. When one of them is injured, the others peck and peck at it until it dies. And sometimes they will eat it, though they are all from the same flock. The cage changes them. They won't break the wire or attack the butcher, but they will peck at each other. May Khuda preserve my nephew." He is crying openly now, the way children do. "He has my brother's smile."

My grandson died in the night. I wasn't asleep but I didn't realize. Besides, he cannot be dead because this isn't a dream. My grandson isn't dead because his eyes are like stars, his cheeks are plump like a lark's breast, his teeth when he smiles are the crescent moon for Eid. My grandson would never follow the Chir batti because we have taught him not to and he is a clever boy. He will go to the city. My grandson will be a pilot, an actor, a business owner.

I will explain this to the manager and he will sort it out with the blue thousand rupee notes he keeps in his leather wallet.

I sit in a truck that takes me to the salt lake. I walk and stumble over the small dunes. I will find the manager and say what I want.

The moon drenches me in its pale light, and the salt blazes sharp in my weeping eyes.

I wail and scratch my cheeks and beat my face. I howl in the emptiness. It is night, so of course nobody is there, except for some huts where exhausted workers from other villages sleep dead to the world.

When I look up, there they are. Watching me.

The ghost lights beckon. They dance, even in my misery.

They want me to follow them and lose my way.

I'm happy to.

My feet follow their wisps. I am so tired.

The lights lead me to what looks like a cave, but it is just the deep, dense shadows of a circle of trees beyond the lake.

The lights make a perfect line, and by some trick of my eyes, they stretch endlessly.

If you follow the Chir batti, the elders say, you would lose your way entirely.

What a wonderful thought that is.

I step into the line and—

I am back in the middle of the lake, but I am not wet and I am not tired. But that woman, the one I'm looking at, she is exhausted beyond measure. She wails and her feet slosh the waters. She smacks her face.

"There you are," I say. "Come here. Come here, my dear."

She looks at me, squinting. Thinking. She is me, myself, and I am the ghost light looping its arms around her, pulling her close.

"Hush. hush. There's something you have to see."

She follows me to the place the lights are, and it happens all over again, and—

Time blinks. I leave them, returning to the line of lights that make such a perfect connection between the past and future. I see between them to the secrets in the dark.

The dark around the light is like being in the belly of a mountain, and in the belly are many mouths and each mouth is a doorway.

Through one door is the smell of milk and sweat, and there is a woman giving birth, and the woman is my daughter, and there I am too, rubbing her back while she is on all fours, cursing from one end and the life being torn out of her from the other. I float through the door and I see myself blink at my light. I reach down to my dying daughter who looks up straight into my light, and her whole face breaks into a smile.

She says "Amma?" And she looks like the young girl who used to sing and climb to the top of the hut and say she would travel.

Through another door I hear Feroz humming, one step away from his feet getting cut. I float through it to him, to ask him to beware, but he flinches and wards me away. So his foot gets cut on the pebbles, and worse because he runs away like a fool. He always did find hope too heavy. I should have remembered that.

Through another door a woman asks her manager for money and he tells her numbers change and explains to her she doesn't need to eat that much, before going into his car and browsing the app he will order food from tonight.

The lights cluster in on me, they circle me, I am crushed by the clear line they make between the past and future, and then—

There she is. Asleep.

I reach towards myself. I scream and scream but the sleeping me does not understand. We can't live like this, I tell her. One day you will forget your ancestors' warnings and come here looking for answers. You will follow the ghost lights and lose your way, and that is good, don't you see? You could do it now, you could do it today.

Why doesn't Feroz leap at the manager's throat and take his wallet for medicine? Why didn't Mae drum at me with her hooves as I led her to the slaughter? Why do I walk past the expensively dressed tourists sprinkling salt on their fries that my hands have been torn to shreds collecting?

I scream and scream at my dreaming self. Your grandson is dead. Your grandson who sleeps besides you will die.

Poor Mae. She had horns but she never used them.

When I wake up the next day and go back to the village, my grandson has been shrouded by his uncle. His clothes are in a neatly folded pile, the black thread he wore on his wrist on top of it.

He is to be buried. I nod absently, then when no one is looking I pick up my grandson in my arms and quietly leave.

By the time I have walked to the lake on foot, it is night.

There used to be a river here. The elders say so. Then it dried and became these separated lakes. But before, all the water was once as one.

When I step through the right door, I go back. Far back. To a time when people weren't here and there were no lakes.

I bring my grandson to the young green river. It is raining in torrents. As I watch, the rock crumbles a bit, its salt slipping into the water.

My grandson sinks to the river bed.

"I love you," I tell my grandson in all of the doorways. Rain has pummeled the stone of my heart and the stone has become dust and has mixed into my blood. When the lakes of my being dry up this dust will be collected into bags and distributed by the winds of fate. And so will people everywhere eat my heart, and my love for you will give their food flavor. Do you think, I ask the lights, that they will learn to love from that? Do you think they will remember they have eaten of this salt? No one answers, not even my grandson, who is of course dead.

Through another doorway, I see myself.

"He will change the world," I murmur in my sleep. And for the first time I love my stubborn self so much. I regret that it took me this long.

My grandson is a doctor. He is flying a plane. He is riding the goat to a finish line. He is writing a book, and making sure the numbers never change. He puts furniture glue on our broken hearts and I give him sugarcane kisses.

As light I scoop the salt. Someone gasps and I ignore her. No. That's not true. I send love to her. "I'm sorry," I say. "Was I supposed to only come out at night?" Some of them scream and faint, and the manager *tsks* without looking up.

"Follow me," I say. "Lose all this."

My grandson will save the world. The river dried and he became rock, and the rock is broken into salt, and he is in the salt and he is everywhere.

When you eat of someone's salt, you owe them a debt as a traveler, as a guest. My grandson and the earth together have been patient hosts waiting for their due.

A tourist screams. He spits, but his tongue has turned white, his spittle has dried up. His insides burn out through his skin as I watch the reckoning begin.

Feroz licks salt from his own fingers. The cuts on his feet glow.

"Is that how it is then, Amma?" He laughs, then is confused so he stops, looking around sheepishly, but the salt demands hope from him until his joy blazes bright.

A small light that reaches up to my knee stretches up, pulling my hair. I playfully rap his knuckles with my fingers, bend down, and kiss his cheeks forever and ever.

A morning across Pakistan—a pinch of salt goes into a fried egg. Into bread. Into naan. Into biryani for dinner parties. Into marinades for tikkas. Into broth. Children eat rohu fish by the river, and the manager's children eat popcorn in an air-conditioned cinema. A doctor's family eats kebabs hurriedly before going to the airport. A news story about contaminated needles breaks.

One by one, people burn or are blessed.

Salt is connected to everywhere. It knows all the secrets. It will tell you how you've lived, and the truth's time is now. Your own reality will abrade you from within, or else fill you with hope.

Yes, even you.

Because you too have eaten of our salt. And the reckoning will now begin.

Contributor Biographies

Ai Jiang is a Chinese-Canadian writer, Ignyte, Bram Stoker, and Nebula Award winner, and Hugo, Astounding, Locus, Aurora, and BSFA Award finalist from Changle, Fujian currently residing in Toronto, Ontario. Her work can be found in *F&SF*, *The Dark*, *The Masters Review*, among others. She is the recipient of Odyssey Workshop's 2022 Fresh Voices Scholarship and the author of *Linghun* and *I AM AI*. The first book of her novella duology, *A Palace Near the World*, is forthcoming in 2025 with Titan Books. Find her on X (@AiJiang_), Insta (@ai.jian.g), and online (aijiang.ca).

Beth Dawkins grew up on front porches, fighting imaginary monsters with sticks, and building castles out of square hay bales. She currently lives in Northeast Georgia with her partner in crime and their offspring. A list of her stories and where to find them can be found at BethDawkins.com.

Brian Keene writes novels, comic books, short stories, and nonfiction. He is the author of over fifty books, mostly in the horror, crime, fantasy, and non-fiction genres. They have been translated into over a dozen different languages and have won numerous awards. His 2003 novel, *The Rising*, is credited (along with Robert Kirkman's *The Walking Dead* comic and Danny Boyle's *28 Days Later* film) with inspiring pop culture's recurrent interest in zombies. He has also written for such media properties as *Doctor Who*, *Thor*, *Aliens*, *Harley Quinn*, *The X-Files*, *Doom Patrol*, *Justice League*, *Hellboy*, *Superman*, and *Masters of the Universe*.

From 2015 to 2020, he hosted the immensely popular *The Horror Show with Brian Keene* podcast. He also hosted (along with Christopher Golden) the long-running *Defenders Dialogue* podcast. Keene also serves on the Board of Directors for the Scares That Care 501c charity organization.

The father of two sons and stepfather to one daughter, Keene lives in Pennsylvania with his wife, author Mary SanGiovanni.

Danian Darrell Jerry holds a Master of Fine Arts in Creative Writing. He is a VONA (Voices of Our Nation) Fellow, a Fiction Editor of *Obsidian: Literature and Arts in the African Diaspora*, and a 2023 Volcanista of Under the Volcano Writer's Workshop. Danian founded Neighborhood Heroes, a youth arts program that employs comic books and literary arts to educate emerging readers. His recent and forthcoming publications include *Fireside Fiction*, Apex Publications, Thirdman Books, *Literarium*, *The Magazine of Fantasy and Fiction, Black Panther: Tales of Wakanda, Cracking the Wire During Black Lives Matter, Curating the End of the World: Red Spring, Trouble the Waters: Tales from the Deep Blue, Africa Risen: A New Era of Speculative Fiction, Illmatic Consequences: The Clapback to Opponents of 'Critical Race Theory,'* and *Captain America: The Shield of Sam Wilson.*

Dimitra Nikolaidou is a Greek-Cypriot author, academic researcher, and translator. Her stories have been published in *Beneath Ceaseless Skies, Andromeda Spaceways, Metaphorosis, Starship Sofa, Gallery of Curiosities,* and in various anthologies (*Retellings of the Inland Seas, Nova Hellas, After the Happily Ever After*). They have also been translated in six languages including German, Italian, Dutch, Japanese, Turkish, and Estonian. Her academic projects examine the relationship between speculative fiction and Tabletop RPGs. She spends her free time radicalizing fairies and planning vacations wherever there are forests she hasn't walked yet.

Fatima Taqvi is a Pakistani born author living in London with aspirations towards respectful parenting (minimal screaming?), accomplished writing (maximum feels?), and effective solidarity against the occupation in Palestine and with all besieged civilian populations (zero colonialist apologia). She has words appearing in *F&SF, Strange Horizons, Flash Fiction Online, Nightmare Magazine,* and forthcoming in *Lightspeed* and in OwlCrate's YA anthology *Monsters in Masquerade.* She is an alumnus of Clarion West 2023 and was shortlisted for the Future Worlds Prize in 2021. She can be reached at www.fatimataqvi.com.

Ferdison Cayetano is a writer living in Queens, New York. His short fiction has also appeared in the *Magazine of Fantasy & Science Fiction*. You can find him on JSTOR hip-deep in papers on world mythologies, even if it's the weekend. Elsewhere, he is at www. ferdwrites.com or on Twitter @ferdwrites, where he follows back.

G. M. Paniccia is a virologist and writer based in New York. She is a National Science Foundation Graduate Research Fellow, a Howard Hughes Medical Institute Gilliam Fellow, and a co-host on the weekly thought experiment podcast *What the If?* Her work has previously appeared in *Luminescent Machinations: Queer Tales of Monumental Invention* (Neon Hemlock Press). When not sciencing or writing, she can usually be found playing capoeira or obsessing over her ludicrously giant cat, Munchkin.

Jenny Rowe's work has appeared in Bath Flash Fiction anthologies, Fly on the Wall press, *Retreat West*, *Reflex Fiction*, and *Henshaw 2*. When she's not writing, she teaches or performs improvised comedy and theatre, and occasionally tours her self-penned solo show about SF author James Tiptree Jr. She lives in Hassocks, UK, with a very nice man and a very good dog. Find her online at www.jennyrowe.co.uk.

Born and raised in Klang, Malaysia, **Joshua Lim** is currently a medical student who finds time between classes to write stories and overthink his future. His work is published in *Fantasy Magazine*, *The Dark*, *PodCastle*, *Reader Beware*, and in anthologies across the US, UK, and Malaysia. Find him at joshualimwriter.wordpress.com or on Instagram @joshualimwriter.

K.S. Walker writes speculative fiction. They like their sci-fi with some horror and their horror with some romance. You can often find them outside with their family or starting a craft project but not finishing it. K.S. Walker has previously been published in several short fiction magazines and anthologies. If you enjoyed this story, you might also enjoy their work in *FIYAH*, *Apex Magazine*, *F&SF*, *Uncanny*, or *Baffling Magazine*, in particular. You can find them online at www.kswalker.net or on Twitter, BlueSky, and Instagram @kswalkerwrites.

Lavie Tidhar's work encompasses literary fiction (*Maror*, *Adama*, and the forthcoming *Six Lives*), cross-genre classics such as Jerwood Prize winner *A Man Lies Dreaming*, and World Fantasy Award winner *Osama*, as well as genre works like the Campbell and Neukom winner *Central Station*. He has also written comics (*Adler*), children's books such as *Candy* and *A Child's Book of the Future*, and created the animated movie *Loontown* and webseries *Mars Machines* with Nir Yaniv.

Linda D. Addison is a five-time recipient of the HWA Bram Stoker Award®. Her winning works includes *The Place of Broken Things* written with Alessandro Manzetti and *How To Recognize A Demon Has Become Your Friend*. She is a recipient of the HWA Lifetime Achievement Award, HWA Mentor of the Year, and SFPA Grand Master of Fantastic Poetry. Find her online at www.LindaAddisonWriter.com.

LP Kindred is a Chicagoan-Angeleno writer, editor, and teaching artist of speculative fiction from the axes of Black and Gay Identities. An alum of Hurston-Wright, VONA, and Clarion, Kindred's words can be found on *LeVar Burton Reads*, the Carnegie Hall website, *Tor.com*, *Apex Magazine*, *Fiyah*, *Escape Pod*, *PodCastle*, and *Speculative City*. Most recently, LP is honored to be nominated for two Ignyte Awards: one for his multiversal rom-com short story "Wanderlust" and the other for co-editing *Voodoonauts Presents: (Re)Living Mythology*. A co-host of writing podcast *Just Keep Writing*, Kindred can be heard fortnightly anywhere podcasts are streamed. To keep up to date follow him @lpkindred or linktr.ee/lpkindred.

An award-winning Afrofuturist and librarian, **Maurice Broaddus** has over a hundred short stories published in such places as *Lightspeed Magazine*, *Black Panther: Tales from Wakanda*, *Out There Screaming*, *Asimov's*, *Weird Tales*, *Magazine of F&SF*, and *Uncanny*

Magazine. With over a dozen novels in print, his latest includes *Sweep of Stars*, *Breath of Oblivion*, *Unfadeable*, *Pimp My Airship*, and *The Usual Suspects*. Learn more at MauriceBroaddus.com.

Nir Yaniv is an Israeli-born multidisciplinary artist living in Los Angeles. He's an author, a musician, an illustrator, and a filmmaker. He founded Israel's first online science fiction magazine and served as its chief editor for ten years, after which he moved on to editing a printed genre magazine. He collaborated with World Fantasy Award-winning author Lavie Tidhar on two novels, including the "deranged sci-fi extravaganza" (per *The Jewish Quarterly*) *The Tel Aviv Dossier*, and his English-language collection *The Love Machine & Other Contraptions* was published by Infinity Plus in 2012. His most recent Hebrew novel, *King of Jerusalem*, was published in Israel in 2019, and his latest English novel, *The Good Soldier*, was published by Shadowpaw Press in 2024. His short stories have appeared in *Weird Tales*, *Apex Magazine*, and *ChiZine*, among others. Nir's musical career includes soundtracks for film, dance shows, and theater. His most recent work is the voice-and-drums animated album *The Voice Remains* (LifeArt Music, 2021). Nir has also directed several short films and music videos, both live-action and animated.

Octavia Cade is a speculative fiction writer from New Zealand. She's had approximately 70 stories published in markets including *Clarkesworld*, *F&SF*, and *Asimov's*. Her latest book, *You Are My Sunshine and Other Stories*, came out in 2023 from Stelliform Press. Like much of her recent short fiction—including "Inviting the Hollow Bones"—*Sunshine* focuses on the ways, both healthy and otherwise, that people are navigating the Necrocene. She's currently working on a magical realist novel about the aftermath of the *Rainbow Warrior* bombing. You can find her at ojcade.com.

Oliver Ferrie is a Scottish writer living in Norway. He is the author of *Sugar People*, a queer horror novel, and spends most of his time putting his characters in tiny snow globes and shaking them really hard.

Rebecca E. Treasure grew up reading in the Rockies and has lived in many places, including Tokyo, Japan and Stuttgart, Germany. Rebecca's short fiction has been published by or is forthcoming from Flame Tree, *Apparition Lit*, *Galaxy's Edge*, Air & Nothingness Press, and others. She is the managing editor at *Apex Magazine*. Rebecca reads, edits, and writes stories exploring the relationship between self and society when she's not playing *Stardew Valley* or raising her children. She is fueled by cheese-covered starch and corgi fur. Find her on the internet at linktr.ee/rebeccaetreasure.

Rich Larson was born in Galmi, Niger, has lived in Spain and Czech Republic, and currently writes from Montreal, Canada. He is the author of the novels *Ymir* and *Annex*, as well as the collection *Tomorrow Factory*. His fiction has been translated into over a dozen languages, including Polish, Italian, Romanian, and Japanese, and adapted into an Emmy-winning episode of *LOVE DEATH + ROBOTS*. Find free reads and support his work at patreon.com/richlarson.

R. L. Meza is the author of *Our Love Will Devour Us*. She writes speculative fiction. Her short stories have been published in *Clarkesworld*, *Nightmare*, *Dark Matter Magazine*, and *The Dread Machine*. Meza lives in a century-old Victorian house on the coast of Northern California, with her husband and the strange animals they call family.

Samit Basu is an Indian novelist. His most recent novels, published by Tor in North America, are *The Jinn-Bot of Shantiport* (Goodreads Choice SF shortlist, 2023) and *The City Inside* (Best SFF of 2022—*The Washington Post* and *Book Riot,* JCBPrize shortlist).He's published several novels in a range of speculative genres, all critically acclaimed and bestselling in India, beginning with *The Simoqin Prophecies* (2003). He also works as a director-screenwriter, comics writer, and columnist. Samit lives in Delhi, Kolkata, and on the internet.

Vivian Chou is a second-generation Chinese-American writer. She has published and work in *Heartlines Spec, The Dread Machine,*

Uncharted, and *The Forge Literary Magazine*. Her writing has been nominated for The Best American Short Stories and included on Reactor.com's Must-Read Speculative Fiction list. Though she prefers to fuel her writing with naps, exercise, and dystopian dread, she usually manages with black coffee and chocolate.

VH Ncube is a South African writer, a member of the African Speculative Fiction Society, and was selected for the Voodoonauts 2024 Black Speculative Summer Fellowship. Her work has also appeared in *Omenana Speculative Fiction Magazine* and she writes mostly Africanfuturism. At the heart of her writing is an exploration of the path paved by individual and societal choices, and her writing is often informed by her work on human rights and environmental justice issues. She can be reached at www.vhncube.com.

About the Editors

Sheree Renée Thomas is an award-winning fiction writer, poet, and editor. Her work is inspired by myth and folklore, natural science and Mississippi Delta conjure. *Nine Bar Blues: Stories from an Ancient Future* (Third Man Books) is her first all prose collection. She is the author of the Marvel novel adaptation of the legendary comics, *Black Panther: Panther's Rage* (Titan Books). She edited the World Fantasy-winning groundbreaking black speculative fiction anthologies, *Dark Matter* (2000 and 2004) and is the first to introduce W.E.B. Du Bois's science fiction short stories. She is the Associate Editor of the historic Black arts literary journal, *Obsidian: Literature & the Arts in the African Diaspora* and is the Editor of *The Magazine of Fantasy & Science Fiction*. She is a Marvel writer and contributor to the groundbreaking anthology, *Black Panther: Tales of Wakanda* edited by Jesse J. Holland. She lives in her hometown, Memphis, Tennessee near a mighty river and a pyramid.

Lesley Conner is the Editor of *Apex Magazine* and has co-edited several anthologies with Jason Sizemore, including *Do Not Go Quietly*, *Robotic Ambitions*, and *Apex Magazine: 2021*. She lives in Maryland with her family, including two adorable dogs named Oz and Pax. You can follow her online via X (formerly Twitter) @lesleyconner.

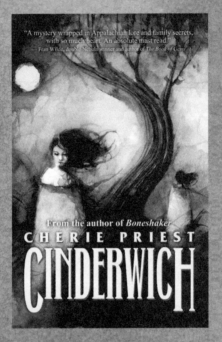